BOOKS BY ANNE BISHOP

THE OTHERS SERIES

Written in Red
Murder of Crows
Vision in Silver
Marked in Flesh
Etched in Bone

THE WORLD OF THE OTHERS

Lake Silence
Wild Country
Crowbones

THE BLACK JEWELS SERIES

Daughter of the Blood
Heir to the Shadows
Queen of the Darkness
The Invisible Ring
Dreams Made Flesh
Tangled Webs
The Shadow Queen
Shalador's Lady
Twilight's Dawn
The Queen's Bargain
The Queen's Weapons
The Queen's Price

THE EPHEMERA SERIES

Sebastian
Belladonna
Bridge of Dreams

THE TIR ALAINN TRILOGY

The Pillars of the World
Shadows and Light
The House of Gaian

The Lady in Glass and Other Stories

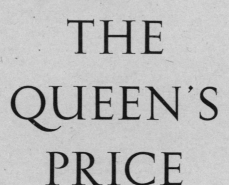

THE QUEEN'S PRICE

A BLACK JEWELS NOVEL

Anne Bishop

ACE
New York

ACE
Published by Berkley
An imprint of Penguin Random House LLC
penguinrandomhouse.com

Copyright © 2023 by Anne Bishop
Penguin Random House supports copyright. Copyright fuels creativity, encourages
diverse voices, promotes free speech, and creates a vibrant culture. Thank you for buying
an authorized edition of this book and for complying with copyright laws by not
reproducing, scanning, or distributing any part of it in any form without permission.
You are supporting writers and allowing Penguin Random House to continue to
publish books for every reader.

ACE is a registered trademark and the A colophon
is a trademark of Penguin Random House LLC.

ISBN: 978-0-593-33737-0

Ace hardcover edition / March 2023
Ace mass-market edition / February 2024

Printed in the United States of America
3 5 7 9 10 8 6 4 2

Book design by Alison Cnockaert

For Patricia Briggs and Ann Peters

JEWELS

WHITE
YELLOW
TIGER EYE
ROSE
SUMMER-SKY
PURPLE DUSK
OPAL*
GREEN
SAPPHIRE
RED
GRAY
EBON-GRAY
BLACK

*Opal is the dividing line between lighter and darker
Jewels because it can be either.

When making the Offering to the Darkness,
a person can descend a maximum of three ranks
from his/her Birthright Jewel.

Example: Birthright White could descend to Rose.

Note: The "Sc" in the terms "Scelt" and
"Sceltie" is pronounced "Sh."

BLOOD HIERARCHY / CASTES

MALES

landen—non-Blood of any race

Blood male—a general term for all males of the Blood; also refers to any Blood male who doesn't wear Jewels

Warlord—a Jeweled male equal in status to a witch

Prince—a Jeweled male equal in status to a Priestess or a Healer

Warlord Prince—a dangerous, extremely aggressive Jeweled male; in status, slightly lower than a Queen

FEMALES

landen—non-Blood of any race

Blood female—a general term for all females of the Blood; refers mostly to any Blood female who doesn't wear Jewels

witch—a Blood female who wears Jewels but isn't on one of the other hierarchical levels; also refers to any Jeweled female

Healer—a witch who heals physical wounds and illnesses; equal in status to a Priestess or a Prince

Priestess—a witch who cares for altars, Sanctuaries, and Dark Altars; witnesses handfasts and marriages; performs offerings; equal in status to a Healer or a Prince

Black Widow—a witch who heals the mind; weaves the tangled webs of dreams and visions; is trained in illusions and poisons

Queen—a witch who rules the Blood; is considered to be the land's heart and the Blood's moral center; as such, she is the focal point of their society

Note: A list of characters in this story is provided at the back of the book.

ONE

Daemonar Yaslana spread his dark membranous wings to their full span before letting them settle into a relaxed position—or as relaxed as he could manage, all things considered. Then he blew out a breath and raised a hand to knock on his uncle's study door.

The school that wasn't officially a school had been in operation at SaDiablo Hall for a month. The instructors were still adjusting to teaching a very select group of thirty-six students as well as adjusting to being under the scrutiny of the Black-Jeweled Warlord Prince of Dhemlan, who was not only their employer but also the patriarch of the SaDiablo family—the wealthiest and most powerful family in the entire Realm of Kaeleer. The students were still adjusting to living in a massive gray stone building that, with all its wings and interior courtyards, could be mistaken for a small enclosed village, as well as dealing with that same Black-Jeweled Warlord Prince as an administrator and benefactor who was benign—most of the time—but could swing to cold, lethal rage in a heartbeat if provoked . . . and was their instructor in Craft and Protocol.

All that adjusting meant *someone* had to act as leader or liaison or some other nonsense word that basically meant being the one who explained things to the adults when stuff happened. And who better to do the explaining than the Warlord Prince who wore a Green Birthright Jewel *and* was the nephew of that Black-Jeweled Warlord Prince?

He *never* looked forward to explaining *stuff*. If his sister hadn't been involved in this mess, he might have refused, but he couldn't let Titian fly into a potential storm on her own. *Cherish and protect.* Those commitments were bred into the bones of Warlord Princes, so he had to get some answers without getting Titian into trouble.

Daemonar gave the door a quick knock before he stepped into the room, leaving himself partially shielded by the door. He didn't *need* the protection, not from his uncle—at least not right now—but it made him feel less . . . exposed.

The man behind the large blackwood desk looked up from the papers he'd been reading and smiled a welcome.

Daemon Sadi was still a breathtakingly beautiful man, with a well-toned body, golden-brown skin, and thick black hair that was now silvered at the temples. That he was also the most lethal man in the Realm was something people often forgot when they looked at his face and felt the seductive pull of his potent sexual heat.

Having seen all the sides of Sadi's temper, Daemonar never forgot the man's lethal nature, but it was something he could dismiss—most of the time.

Giving Daemon what he hoped looked like an easy smile, he said, "Hypothetical question."

Did he detect a hint of panic in his uncle's gold eyes?

Daemon capped his pen and said in that deep, cultured voice that always held a sensual edge, "All right."

"If someone tried a bit of Craft inside the Hall instead of going outside because it's cold and rainy today, and the spell went a wee bit wrong and punched a hole in a wall, how much trouble would that person be in? Hypothetically."

He watched Daemon swallow. Started counting the seconds before getting a reply. Not so different from counting between seeing lightning and hearing thunder to determine the distance of a storm.

"How big is this hypothetical hole?" Daemon finally asked.

"More decorative window than door," Daemonar replied.

"No risk of any part of the Hall collapsing because of this hole?"

"Not at all. Easily repaired." He hoped.

"Well then. If no one was injured and there is no structural damage that might cause future injuries, I think the person or persons involved in the spell that went a wee bit wrong could make their own arrangements to have the repairs done without requiring me to get involved. Hypothetically."

"That's what I thought."

"However." Daemon uncapped his pen and made a mark on the paper in front of him.

Hell's fire, here it comes, Daemonar thought.

"I would expect to find a copy of this bit of Craft on my desk when I return to the study after the midday meal so that I can review it and use it as part of the next Craft lesson, since it *had* gone a wee bit wrong."

Daemon looked up and gave Daemonar a smile that made the boy's knees turn weak.

"That's a sensible idea," Daemonar said.

"I'm delighted you think so." The words were purred, and that, in itself, was a warning.

Daemonar closed the study door, smiled at Beale, the Red-Jeweled Warlord who was the Hall's butler, and Holt, the Opal-Jeweled Warlord who was Daemon's secretary, and strode across the great hall, heading for the staircase in the informal receiving room. Once out of sight, he bounded up the stairs and ran to the part of the Hall where the other youngsters waited.

Seven of the twenty-two girls who were now living at the Hall had been involved in whatever had gone awry. The rest of the girls and the fourteen boys who also lived at the Hall had come running at the sound of something going *boom*. Everyone had looked at the remains of the table that had held the items used for that spell, then looked at the hole in the wall—and then the other thirty-five youngsters had looked at him.

When he walked back into the room, they stared at him, their expressions all some variation of "Oh, shit, how much trouble are we in?"

Granted, they had good reason to be concerned. It was the first time any of them had blown up a piece of Uncle Daemon's home.

"Well?" Titian asked, catching her lower lip between her teeth. "Are we in trouble?"

"What did Prince Sadi say?" Zoey asked.

"We'll all chip in to pay for the repairs and get them done *quietly*." He was pretty sure there wouldn't be anything quiet about sawing and hammering and whatever else was needed, but this was a remote part of the Hall, so the noise shouldn't be *too* obvious. "Zoey, write out what you and the other girls were trying to do, what you used in the spell, and the steps you took before things went . . ."

"Out the wall?" Titian suggested.

"Yeah. That. Don't leave anything out. I'll slip it on Prince Sadi's desk when he's away from his study."

Everyone sucked in a breath. It was Jhett, one of the young Black Widows, who finally said, "Why tell him what we used for the spell?"

"Because that was his price for allowing us to take care of this ourselves," Daemonar replied.

When Beale and Holt walked into his study, Daemon kept his eyes on the paper and continued to write random words—as if this conversation were casual enough not to require his full attention.

"There is a hole in a wall?" he asked mildly.

"There is, Prince," Beale replied.

"A big hole?"

A hesitation. "Big enough to require repairs, but small enough that it shouldn't require reconstruction of the entire wall."

"I see." Daemon noticed his mind had given up on the challenge of forming words and he was simply writing the same three letters over and over. "No one is at risk from falling debris?"

"I checked," Holt said. When Daemon looked up, he shrugged. "One of the Scelties told Mikal there was a *boom*. Since Mikal was working with me today, we went to take a look. Discreetly."

"But you didn't think to inform me?" Daemon asked, his voice still mild.

Another shrug. "Daemonar was heading toward the study as Mikal and I headed toward the room, so I didn't think it was my place to report the incident—unless Daemonar failed to tell you."

Unfortunately, that made sense—or as much sense as anything currently made in the Hall.

"It's raining," Beale said. "And it's cold out."

Daemon capped his pen, abandoning the attempt to look unconcerned. "Yes, it is."

"I believe the young Ladies would have tried this bit of Craft outdoors if it hadn't been raining."

"That it is cold and rainy has been pointed out to me." He had to give the youngsters a chance to figure things out for themselves and work together to correct mistakes, just like they would have to do in the future when they were part of a Queen's court. Wouldn't his father have done that when Saetan had had the job of teaching and protecting Witch's coven and the boyos? "Along with correcting whatever Craft has gone wrong, I think a review of creating shields will be in order for this week's lessons, don't you?"

"Absolutely," Holt said.

"It would be prudent," Beale agreed. "Experience indicates this will not be a singular event."

Daemon sighed. "Very well." He waited, but Beale and Holt didn't leave. "Something else?"

Beale looked at Holt. Holt looked at Beale.

"It's time," Beale said. "Will you show him, or shall I?"

Holt hesitated, then said, "I'll show him."

Daemon studied the two men. "Show me what?"

His study was in the shape of a reversed L, the short end holding floor-to-ceiling bookcases behind his large black-wood desk. The sides of that part of the study were covered in dark red curtains. Behind one set of curtains was a door that opened into a storage room. Large shelves—some open, some with doors—started above Daemon's head and went to the ceiling. Beneath the shelves were two rows of wooden filing cabinets that held paperwork and records for the family's various estates and business interests.

Holt walked into the storage room. Daemon pushed away from his desk and followed his secretary to the last filing cabinet on the left-hand side. Holt called in a gold key and unlocked the cabinet. Then he handed Daemon the key.

"Beale has one key. I've held the other," Holt said. "Per our instructions."

"Instructions from . . . ?" He knew. He just wanted someone to say it.

"Your father. About a year before he went to the final death, he gave us the keys and told us to make the contents of this cabinet available to you when it would be helpful."

"And that's now?"

"Prince, you have a hole in a wall, so it's time."

Hell's fire.

He'd been aware of this locked cabinet for centuries, but he'd never tried to find out what it held. Saetan had written *Private* on the label that had been slipped into the brass holder on the cabinet's top drawer. These locked drawers had been his father's business—and apparently, that business was now his.

Holt opened the top drawer, scanned the neatly labeled files, pulled one out, and handed it to Daemon.

He opened the file, read what amounted to a report, read it again—and looked at Holt. "I'll double your wages this month if you can look me in the eyes and tell me this is fiction."

Holt said nothing.

"I'll triple your wages."

Holt looked regretful but said nothing.

Mother Night. "Tell me what you remember."

"Their intentions were good," Holt began. "Well, their intentions were always good, but this time it started because a child in the village was playing with some friends and through some foolishness put his arms through the glass in a window. Serious injuries, lots of bleeding, panicked adults, hysterical friends—and the possibility that the boy would lose the use of both arms. Halaway's Healer requested assistance, which is how Jaenelle, Karla, and Gabrielle got involved."

"The healing was successful?" Daemon asked. Not that he had any doubt it would have been. Besides being Queens and Black Widows, those three witches had been the most powerful and talented Healers of their generation—and were still considered to have no equals.

"Yes. The child recovered completely and suffered no loss of movement or strength in his arms. He had one scar on each arm to show to his friends, but those faded after a year. However, the concern about a window breaking and someone being badly hurt had the coven working on the idea of adding some Craft to window glass so that it would break into pieces with no sharp edges, like glass worn down by sand and the sea."

"That explains the notation here about a visit to Lady Perzha and the beaches around Little Weeble," Daemon murmured.

"There's probably another file about *that* visit," Holt muttered. Then he continued. "Once the coven thought they had a working spell, they had to test it. So Jaenelle and Karla purchased a couple of pieces of window glass that they inserted into freestanding frames so that they could do the test in one of the Hall's outside courtyards."

"And it worked."

"Pretty much. The glass broke into small, smooth-edged pieces just the way they wanted it to. But the High

Lord pointed out that glass that obligingly broke in a way that wouldn't cause a would-be thief any harm and also didn't have the *sound* of glass shattering was a potential invitation for mischief." Holt breathed in, breathed out. "So the girls added another bit of Craft for the second test. When the glass broke that time, it started shouting, 'Intruder! Intruder! I'm hit! I'm hit! I'm hit!'"

Daemon reminded himself that breathing wasn't optional.

"Well, if the warning wasn't loud enough to be heard, it wouldn't be any good, would it?" Holt continued. "But the sound in the test window had been punched up with Jaenelle's Birthright Black and Karla's Birthright Green, so . . ."

"Everyone in the Hall heard it, didn't they?"

"In the Hall *and* in Halaway. Caused quite a commotion, especially because some of the windows in the rooms surrounding that particular courtyard in the Hall must have absorbed some of the spell, so when that booming sound rattled the frames, the affected windows began to yip in higher voices, 'I'm hit! I'm hit! I'm hit!'" Holt blew out a breath. "Since those higher voices sounded like young Scelties, that got all the kindred excited, and *they* were racing around the Hall looking for the intruders."

Daemon leaned against one of the other filing cabinets and closed his eyes. *Nothing to do with me,* he thought. *Nothing, nothing, nothing.* "And . . . ?"

"After Jaenelle and Karla managed to quiet all the windows and the Scelties, and the High Lord sent his apologies to Lady Sylvia for the unplanned excitement, he firmly suggested that that particular bit of Craft be retired." Holt offered a weak smile. "A few months later, a Warlord and his brothers, who were builders by trade, showed up at the Hall. They'd heard a story about this bit of Craft and thought it would be a fine addition to a school they were building and offered to buy the proprietary rights to the spell if the Ladies could show them how to do it—without the verbal alarm. So the High Lord negotiated with the Warlords for exclusive rights to the spell for . . . I don't remember how many years . . . for a modest annual fee."

Daemon eyed the files in the open drawer, then looked at the other drawers in that cabinet. "That's what is in those drawers? Reports of unusual Craft the coven performed when they lived at the Hall?" *May the Darkness have mercy on me if that's what I'll have to deal with.*

"Records of one sort or another," Holt replied. "Beale and I were told that the top drawer held the most . . . memorable."

As Daemon replaced that file and brushed a finger over others, a red folder appeared, sealed with black wax and labeled with Saetan's elaborate script. He pinched the top of the folder with his thumb and forefinger—and vanished it before he closed the drawer and locked the cabinet.

"Is there a reason for this story?" Daemon asked, turning to face his secretary.

"No matter what Zoey, Titian, and the rest of those youngsters throw at you, you don't have to deal with the power Jaenelle and the coven brought to the table when they were the equivalent age and learning Craft," Holt said. "That should be some comfort."

Late that night, Daemon called in the red folder with the black wax seal and studied the words written in the Old Tongue.

"For my sons," he whispered, brushing a finger against the words.

When he pressed his thumb to the wax, the seal broke in a jagged pattern that seemed designed to act like a lock.

Daemon pulled out two dozen sheets of paper. His father's writing.

He skimmed through the pages, not sure what he was seeing at first. Then he poured a large brandy and sipped it while he read all the pages again—especially the ones that had penciled notations added at the bottom.

One page in particular caught his attention because the completion of the spell it contained was still pending, even after all these years.

Laughing softly, Daemon said, "Oh, you wicked bastard."

Tucking the papers back into the folder for safekeeping, he swallowed the brandy, vanished the folder—and went hunting for a special window.

TWO

Regretting the impulse to invite Saetien SaDiablo to dinner in order to give the girl a break from some hard truths about the sanctuary where Jillian worked and Saetien resided, Jillian continued to cut up the vegetables for the salad. The beef and mushrooms were heating in their gravy; the egg noodles were almost cooked. When the food was on the table, this whining would end—one way or another.

"So, you've been telling the instructors at the sanctuary that the reason you fell in with Delora was because you felt neglected, that you never had enough of your father's time and attention, that you didn't learn things like Protocol that would have helped you." Jillian added a light dressing to the salad and mixed it. When she set the bowl on the table, she looked Saetien in the eyes. "That is so much crap, I'm surprised you're not choking on it. And just so you know? The instructors don't believe a word of it."

She turned away to drain the noodles and put them in a serving dish while Saetien sputtered. She ladled the beef-and-mushroom mixture over the noodles, then set the dish on the table. Bread from the bakery and freshly churned butter from the SaDiablo estate on the other side of the village completed the meal.

"If I'd been a Queen—" Saetien began.

"You would have been thumped so hard for being a

bitch, you'd have had to walk backward to see where you were going," Jillian said sharply. "Tell me this, oh poor, neglected child—and remember I'm part of this family. Who taught you how to ride a horse? Who taught you how to swim? Who taught you the simple country dances so that you could participate at harvest parties in Dhemlan and in Scelt? Who taught you to air walk? Who taught you to read before you went to school and read you bedtime stories? Who taught you—or tried to teach you—basic Craft and Protocol? Who wouldn't let you fudge the rules and be a brat? Who took you riding when you were in Amdarh, and took you to the theater and to art exhibits? Who was that, hmm?"

Saetien stared at the table, one tear rolling down her cheek.

"Your father. You received more time and attention than most children who come from aristo families, but you probably heard someone whisper that you must have been neglected and that's why you became Delora's pet, and you seized on that as the excuse for ignoring what you knew to be right because that puts the blame on someone else and you're just a victim."

"He never—"

"Went with you to the country houses and the parties there?" Jillian nodded. "He couldn't. With his sexual heat being as potent as it is, if he showed up at one of those parties, every female past puberty would have been on him like starving cats that had found a bowl of cream, and if he couldn't get away from them fast enough, his temper would have slipped the leash and your happy little party would have turned into blood-soaked ground and corpses who would have had the unpleasant experience of meeting him again when they made the transition to demon-dead and learned why you shouldn't piss off the High Lord of Hell."

Jillian filled small bowls with the salad before dishing out beef and noodles for both of them.

"If I'd been a Queen—"

"Your education wouldn't have been any different.

Well, as I understand it, you would have been required to learn more and would have been required to practice your lessons in Protocol every time you were in public—which, come to think of it, your father did insist on except during playtime with your friends. And that's no different than any other child after the Birthright Ceremony. The real training begins after that ceremony, and the rules become a lot stricter."

"If I'd known about that war and Dorothea—"

"What?" Jillian snapped, losing patience. "Kaeleer's history, which includes that war, is supposed to be taught in the schools. If the school in Halaway is neglecting that part of the children's education, Prince Sadi should be informed."

"He didn't tell me he'd been . . ." Saetien grabbed a piece of bread and scooped up enough butter to generously cover three slices. "And *she* didn't tell me that she'd been . . ."

"Maybe Daemon and Surreal thought you weren't mature enough to understand their pasts, and they were waiting until you were older," Jillian countered. "Or maybe because so much of the family's history circles around a Queen you don't want to know about, you always dragged Titian away when Daemon, Lucivar, Marian, and Surreal told stories about their lives before they came to Kaeleer. No one forced you to come back and listen, because the adults figured you weren't ready to listen. And those stories were told in steps, depending on the age of the listeners. How many times have you heard Lucivar say, 'You're not old enough to hear that story. Someday, but not now'? Plenty of times."

"My father should have stopped the party!"

"As I understand it, he intended to return all of you to the school in Amdarh when he had to leave to investigate a reported attack, but *you* whined about being allowed to stay and have the party. And when Beale, who stood in your father's stead and is strong enough and ruthless enough to turf out the intruders, told those boys to leave because they were not supposed to be there, you undermined his authority and set up half of the girls at the party to be attacked, including your cousin and a young Queen. So if you're feeling sorry about what this has cost you and want to point the finger and say 'It's your fault'? Well, it is *your* fault, Saetien. Your father carries some of the blame, and he knows it. Lucivar would have hauled all of you into the Coach and taken you back to the school, regardless of what you wanted, instead of *hoping* you had a glimmer of honor left."

Jillian set her fork down, too churned up to eat. But she'd had a few weeks to think about this and realized something that felt like truth. "In a way, I understand why you did it. You were born into the SaDiablo family, but you don't really belong to that family because Saetan and his sons have been committed to serving and protecting the Black-Jeweled Queen of Ebon Askavi from the moment Saetan made a promise to stay connected to the living for as long as it took for her to appear in the Realms. You think a promise that held for over fifty thousand years is going to fade away now?" She shook her head. "And it's all there in the Hall—the history, the promise, the choice to serve. Some people fit into the family, and it has nothing to do with being related by blood. They *feel* the connection, feel the echo of a promise in the very marrow of their bones. Daemonar feels it. Marian. Lucivar. Mikal and Beron. So do I. So did all the Territory Queens who served in the Dark Court. But my sister, Nurian, doesn't fit into what would have been the First Circle or even the Second Circle. Because of connections, she is welcome and included in gatherings when she wants to be, but she remains distant enough that she doesn't have to face the raw power in the family on a daily basis, not alone. She wouldn't be able to cope with the Black in a cold rage. And that's all right. Not everyone can."

"You didn't mention . . ." Saetien hesitated. "Surreal."

"I think Surreal is like Nurian, needing enough distance from what drove—and still drives—Lucivar and

Daemon. It just took her some years to remember that."
Now Jillian hesitated, then decided to say the rest. "You
love your father—I know you do—but you're never going
to be comfortable being around him, never going to be
able to accept him, when he's anything but the courteous
and controlled Warlord Prince of Dhemlan. There was a
time when you might have. I don't know. But that's not the
case anymore. And maybe something in you recognized
that you couldn't survive a tight connection to the SaDiablo family. So you did something that broke the bonds, that
set you on the outside and has allowed you to get away
from your father—and get away from the memories of the
Queen who still rules the family. I think if you'd told Daemon that you were having trouble living at the Hall and
had been honest about *why* you were struggling, he might
have found another way for you to be independent."

Jillian reached across the table and patted Saetien's
hand. "You're not the first who needed to leave in order to
survive. I doubt you'll be the last. Just stop pretending that
you weren't the one who made the choice, even if you
didn't understand the truth of it at the time."

Saetien sat on the side of her bed, willing the tears not to
fall. She didn't know who she was anymore, didn't know
what she wanted—except to be free of this *burden* of
blame.

"I made a mistake," she said quietly. "I wanted something so much, I didn't listen to anyone who tried to tell me
I was wrong about Delora, about the other girls. About the
boys who were close to those girls."

Shelby, the Warlord Sceltie puppy who was her special
friend, sat at her feet watching her closely. *But we are
learning now, and we will listen to our teachers. Then we
will know when humans tell us to do a wrong thing.* He
paused. *And we will bite them.*

The puppy sounded a bit too pleased with that idea. "I
don't think biting would be acceptable."

Sometimes we need to bite. He sounded so sure of that.

Maybe she should talk to the adult Scelties who lived at the sanctuary to find out if—or when—biting was considered an acceptable response to some human behavior.

When her bedroom door opened, Saetien wished she'd locked it after returning from Jillian's house. Most of the girls locked their doors before trying to sleep, which wasn't surprising. This place housed girls who had been raped in order to break their power. Many of them struggled with an aversion to being in a bed for any reason, and sleep was precious when it came at all—and it was a rare night when everyone wasn't awakened by a girl screaming herself out of a nightmare.

Teresa walked in. She had been a natural Black Widow before a male had . . . done what he'd done. She was still a Black Widow, but her power was broken now, leaving her with nothing but basic Craft. And her mind had shattered under the attack, leaving her walking the paths of the Twisted Kingdom, her thoughts and memories fragmented.

So much like Tersa, Saetien's paternal grandmother. But Tersa had chosen madness in order to regain some of the Hourglass's Craft, and she was strange in ways that had always made Saetien uneasy. Most days Tersa seemed absentminded, dithery, unable to alter even the simplest routine without becoming flustered. On other days, when the clarity of madness filled her gold eyes, she was . . . terrifying.

Not something Saetien could say out loud about her father's mother. Daemon Sadi loved Tersa and respected her skills as a Black Widow. So did Lucivar Yaslana. In fact, no one else in the family felt uncomfortable around Tersa, which was another way in which Saetien had felt like an outsider among her own kin.

Teresa sat next to Saetien and held out a sheet of paper. "This is you."

The drawing looked like the top of a box with rounded corners. The design was made up of strong lines and

curves, bold but not hard. Two-thirds of the design resonated with something inside her, appealed to her in ways
she couldn't put into words. But the right-hand side turned
into a mash of chaotic lines—bloated dissonance that
spilled over the edge of the box, filaments reaching and
reaching as if to ensnare the unwary.

"This is how you see me?" Saetien asked, still feeling
raw from the things Jillian had said.

"Yes." No condemnation in Teresa's voice. Nothing unusual in the voice as she pointed to the strong lines and
curves. "This is who you were." Her finger moved over the
chaotic lines. "This is who you are. You don't fit in the
SaDiablo box anymore. You did once, but not anymore.
You need to find a new box."

A new box. A new family was what Teresa meant.
"Where am I supposed to find it?"

Teresa pointed to the paper. "She can tell you. She
tastes of sadness—and truth."

Saetien looked at the name under the chaotic lines.
"Who is she?"

Teresa blinked. "Who?"

"This girl. Is she here at the sanctuary?" Doubtful, unless the girl had just come in.

"What girl?" Teresa looked down. "The puppy!" She
slid off the bed and sat on the floor. "Hello, puppy!"

Shelby gave the girl kisses and received pats and hugs
before Teresa got up and wandered off, hopefully to her
own room.

Saetien sat for a long time, staring at the drawing. Staring at a name.

*"This is who you were. This is who you are. . . . She can
tell you. She tastes of sadness—and truth."*

"That's all well and good," Saetien told Shelby. "But
who *is* Wilhelmina Benedict?"

THREE

Restless and unable to sleep, Daemonar wandered some of the corridors in the uninhabited areas of the Hall. He would have gone outside to do sparring warm-ups or fly to the estate's lake and back, but another storm had kicked up early in the evening—driving rain and winds strong enough to rattle the windows in their frames. Even if he was well shielded, it wasn't the kind of weather for flying unless there wasn't a choice. So he walked while he wrestled with his conscience.

Posing the incident as a hypothetical question when he'd told Uncle Daemon about the spell going awry and breaking a wall scratched at him, even though he'd done it to protect the girls. If *he'd* made the mistake, he would have told Sadi straight out and offered to pay for the repairs. Daemon might vigorously voice his opinion about the careless use of Craft, but he wouldn't boot his nephew out the door.

Everyone had known he wasn't reporting anything hypothetical—you didn't hire carpenters and stone masons to repair a hypothetical hole—so he hadn't told a *lie*.

It still felt like a lie. It still felt like the kind of pissing around with words that would have had his father backing him up against a wall and *insisting* on straight truth.

But Zoey, Titian, Jhett, Arlene, and the other girls who had been trying . . . whatever . . . were still adjusting to life at SaDiablo Hall—and living under the hand of a man who was the Warlord Prince of Dhemlan, as well as the High Lord of Hell. The lines for what Daemon would and wouldn't tolerate were still being drawn—daily, it seemed. It wasn't like those lines were hard to figure out most of the time, since each of the students had been given a printed list of the Hall's basic rules—and what behaviors would earn immediate expulsion from the Hall. But the hurt of Saetien's involvement in the coven of malice was still too fresh. That Witch, the living myth, had intervened to spare Daemon from having to execute his own daughter wasn't forgotten either. That was one reason why there was sometimes a sharp chill in Daemon Sadi's gold eyes when anyone's behavior leaned a little toward being the bitch.

It wasn't Daemonar's job to ride herd on the other thirty-five youngsters. He was here to study too. And yet he stood apart from the rest of the boys. He was older, for one thing. He was an Eyrien Warlord Prince who wore Birthright Green, for another. He'd stood on his first killing field when Zoey and Titian had been under attack. Because of that, he wasn't like the other boys anymore—even the other boys who were Warlord Princes.

He had friends here. There was Mikal, who was Daemon's legal ward and was doing a revolving apprenticeship with Beale, Holt, and Lord Marcus, who was Daemon's man of business. There was Prince Raine, who had been an instructor at the school in Amdarh and now was an instructor here at the Hall.

There was Beron, who was Mikal's older brother. Beron had reached his majority and was no longer Daemon's legal ward but was still under Sadi's protection. Daemonar didn't see the Opal-Jeweled Warlord often, because Beron was an actor living in Amdarh, Dhemlan's capital city, but the man understood and fit in with the power and temper that were part of the SaDiablo and Yaslana families.

There were men like Holt and Lord Weston, who was Zoey's sword and shield—adults who didn't forget they were adults but weren't *that* much older and took working at the Hall in their stride.

And there was Uncle Daemon. Patriarch of the family, yes. Merciless and lethal when his temper turned cold and he slipped into an aspect of himself that the rest of the Blood called the Sadist. Oh, yes. Only a fool didn't fear the Sadist. But Daemon was also a loving uncle and a friend who would listen. Someone who would teach, who could be counted on to have your back when you needed help. Someone who would defend and protect.

A fierce gust of wind hit the Hall. Rain lashed the windows. No curtains or shutters over the windows here. Maybe all the students could help Uncle Daemon put shields over the windows in this part of the Hall to keep out the damp and chill? They were coming into warmer weather, sure, but they were still looking at plenty of cold nights and rainy days.

Daemonar reached a corner and was about to turn back when he heard . . . something. A muttering? He stood quietly, listening. Then he released some of his Green power in a careful probe of the corridor. Nothing. No one. But . . . there was that muttering again.

Putting a tight Green shield around himself and calling in his Eyrien club, Daemonar stepped around the corner.

No one there. If someone was hiding in shadows or trying to sight shield, he would feel them, pick up the psychic scent. Unless the person wore a darker Jewel, but neither Beale nor Uncle Daemon would be standing in a corridor in this part of the Hall at this time of night on the off chance that someone would come along.

Daemonar blew out a breath and vanished the club. Time to go back to his own room and . . .

Another gust of wind—and the nearest window began a snarling roar of sound, savage and . . . Eyrien. The window was *swearing* in Eyrien. One voice? Two?

What in the name of Hell?

An Eyrien war cry sounded as the wind rattled the window.

It made no sense. There was no reason to be afraid of a *window*. And yet the sound made his skin crawl. It was too strange and unnerving for him to face alone at this time of night. So Daemonar Yaslana did the only sensible thing to do—he ran to the suite of rooms where Uncle Daemon now resided and pounded on the bedroom door.

The door swung open. Daemonar wasn't sure if he was looking at the High Lord of Hell or the Sadist—or if this was Uncle Daemon, just sleepy and pissed off at being jolted awake. No matter which aspect of Sadi had opened the door, at least the man was wearing silk pajama bottoms and wouldn't go charging through the Hall showing off his male pride the way Lucivar would have done.

"Something weird is happening in one of the corridors," Daemonar said. "*Seriously* weird."

Those glazed gold eyes studied him before Sadi said, "Show me."

Daemonar didn't worry about going too fast. Daemon might not look like he moved quickly most of the time, but he had a gliding stride that covered a lot of ground when he wanted to get somewhere.

When they reached the corner and would turn into the corridor with that window, Daemonar held up a hand—and didn't appreciate until Sadi stopped that he'd just given a command to a Black-Jeweled Warlord Prince.

"It's a window in this corridor," Daemonar whispered. Lowering his hand, he called in his Eyrien club for the second time. Then he took a breath, wrapped a Green shield around himself, and turned into that corridor, aware of Daemon, wrapped in a Red shield, moving a step behind him and a long step to the side. Fighting room.

He nodded at the window. "This one. I heard muttering at first; then when a gust of wind rattled the frame . . ."

Daemon called in one of his gold and ruby cuff links and held it out.

"Uncle Daemon, I don't think—"

A gust of wind shook the windows and that savage voice—voices?—rumbled and roared out language that might have made Daemonar blush if he hadn't felt so *threatened.*

The wind faded. The voices muttered for a few moments longer before they, too, faded.

Daemonar glanced at Uncle Daemon, who stared at the window and looked like someone had dropped him into a mountain lake in the middle of winter.

"Sir?"

No response.

"Uncle Daemon?"

He felt a flutter of Red power before Daemon vanished the cuff link.

"There's a chip of my Birthright Red Jewel under the ruby," Daemon said. "It holds an auditory spell that retains conversations. I've found it very useful over the years when I didn't want to rely on my memory for what was said at an official meeting."

"So you can replay . . . that?" Daemonar tipped his head toward the window.

Daemon nodded. "I want Lucivar to hear this, and there's no guarantee we'll have gusts of wind when we need them."

"You'd just need to rattle the window frame. Wouldn't you?"

"Maybe. Depends on if specific conditions have to be present for this bit of Craft to manifest."

Daemonar stared at the window. "*Is* it just Craft?"

Instead of answering, Daemon raised his right hand and created a Black shield at one end of the corridor. "Let's go." When they reached the corner, he created a second Black shield. Then he nodded. "That will keep anyone else from stumbling across whatever this is."

They headed back to their suites.

"Just out of curiosity, what were you doing in that part of the Hall at this time of night?" Daemon asked.

"Walking. Couldn't sleep."

Daemon said nothing for a minute. "Troubled by hypothetical questions?"

Daemonar winced. "I didn't want the girls to get into trouble, but I wasn't going to let them hide it from you."

"Would they have tried to hide it?"

Spoken mildly, but not an idle question.

"I think some of the girls were afraid of being expelled. They would have stood up eventually, but it would have taken a while for them to work up the courage. Zoey and Titian would have dithered a bit, but they would have strapped steel to their spines and told you what they had done before the evening meal." He knew from experience that sitting at a table for a meal with his uncle or father—or worse, both of them—when you'd done something wrong or stupid and hadn't told anyone was a lesson in how excruciating silence could be when you were certain they knew what you'd done and were waiting with a predator's patience for you to tell them.

Zoey and Titian would never have gotten through a meal with Uncle Daemon if they'd tried to hide that a spell had gone wrong. And Uncle Daemon would not have been happy about sitting at a table with weeping girls once they felt the weight of his cold displeasure. Oh, he would have sat there, but he wouldn't have been happy about it.

"But you were the one who entered my study to tell me that something happened," Daemon said.

"I'm the oldest, and I have the most experience with getting into trouble." He stared at the wall. "But saying it was hypothetical felt like a lie."

Daemon laughed softly. "Having grown up with Lucivar, I can see how it could feel that way, but I'd bet even your father posed a few hypothetical questions when Jaenelle and the coven lived here. That's not a lie, boyo. That's love." He paused, then added, "Cherish and protect, but don't be too much of a shield. Learn from my mistake. Have their backs, yes, but also insist that the girls strap on that steel and be the ones to face me—and accept the consequences of their own actions."

"Yes, sir."

Daemon wrapped a hand around the back of Daemonar's neck, then kissed his forehead. "Get some sleep, boyo."

"Good night, Uncle Daemon."

Daemon walked into his bedroom—and locked the door.

The High Lord's square of rooms. Saetan had occupied that suite for centuries. Andulvar and Prothvar Yaslana had occupied suites that looked out over that courtyard. So had Saetan's eldest son, Mephis SaDiablo. Now it was off-limits to everyone because Daemon used that courtyard as a place to drain some of his Black power, as well as the overwhelming sexual heat that was part of the price he paid for being a Warlord Prince who wore the Black.

Across from the High Lord's square was the Queen's square. The rooms Jaenelle Angelline and Daemon Sadi had occupied when Jaenelle had been alive were also off-limits, as was the suite that Lady Karla had occupied since the summer that Witch's coven had first come to the Hall. Other suites in that courtyard were now assigned to some of the girls who had been at the Hall when the coven of malice had attacked, including Zoey, Titian, Jhett, and Arlene. They were still skittish, and being so close to the Black was the only reason any of them could sleep.

The next square of suites was reserved for the most trusted of those who served, a group that included Lord Holt, Lord Weston, Prince Raine, Prince Chaosti when he visited the Hall—and Daemonar. Another difference between him and the other boys.

The rest of the youngsters were in squares that were within easy reach of the protectors but not as close to Uncle Daemon.

Feeling easier about the hypothetical hole in the wall—which was going to take more work to fix than he'd realized—and a little easier generally now that he wasn't the only one who had heard that damn swearing window, Daemonar went to his suite, stretched out on his bed, and was asleep in minutes.

"Shit!"

Daemon prowled his sitting room, trying to sort out the implications of what he'd just heard—and felt.

He'd spent three nights hunting through the Hall, look-

ing for the spelled window Saetan had created as a lesson
and a bit of payback for the shouting windows Jaenelle and
the coven had made. Tonight he'd retired to his suite to
sleep because he was giving Craft lessons tomorrow, and
with thirty-six youngsters with varying ability in basic
Craft, let alone things that required more skill, he did not
need his mind clouded by fatigue.

The first night he'd chosen to sleep, and this was the
night that the boy, trying to walk off a guilty conscience,
stumbled upon the damn window!

Daemon called in the cuff link, stared at it a moment,
then vanished it. He didn't need to hear those voices again
to know that something was very wrong. The spell Saetan
had created as a lesson for the coven would not have had
the feel of threat and violence, would not have felt . . .
bloated . . . with intent. Saetan would not have aimed a
spell filled with violence toward his daughter or the young
Queens who considered him an honorary uncle.

Which meant something had gone wrong or the spell
had been tampered with. Or . . .

Traps. Snares. *Could* there be demon-dead trapped in
that window, looking for a way out in order to attack the
living? He hadn't *sensed* that kind of danger, but something about the feel of the spell reminded him of that damn
spooky house a writer named Jarvis Jenkell had created to
trap—and kill—members of the SaDiablo family. Except
Jenkell hadn't taken into account the one member of the
family who wouldn't play by the rules even *before* entering
the house.

The one member of the family who might recognize
whatever was in that window. If Lucivar's solution was to
blow out the whole damn wall, then so be it. They would
deal with the structural challenges afterward.

Daemon looked at the tall freestanding clock. Considering the time, it would be courteous to wait a couple more
hours.

Since Daemonar and Titian were in residence and that
window posed a potential threat, Lucivar would thump

him against a wall if he waited—and he would deserve the thumping.

Standing in the middle of his sitting room, Daemon closed his eyes and sent out a call on an Ebon-gray spear thread. *Prick?* He waited a moment. *Prick?*

Bastard? What . . . ?

He could picture Lucivar Yaslana slipping out of bed and out of the bedroom as the Eyrien's temper rose hot toward the killing edge. *I need your help with a bit of Craft I found at the Hall.*

Craft? Oh, Hell's fire, what did they do?

The children? They blew a hole in a wall, but that's not important. It's a bit of Craft that Father created. Sweet Darkness, Prick, I hope this wasn't what he'd intended, but . . . Well, you walked into that spooky house; I didn't. If this is something similar . . .

Are you going to get any more sleep? Lucivar asked.

No.

All right. I'll tell Marian where I'm going and give Rothvar his orders for the next couple of days. Then I'll head out. I'll be at the Hall in time to meet you for an early breakfast.

Good. Daemon ended the link between them. Shivering, he called in a robe and added a warming spell. Then he rubbed his hands over his face and through his thick black hair.

Hell's fire, he needed some sleep. Maybe that's why he wasn't seeing something obvious.

Then again, Saetan had created that bit of Craft, so maybe obviousness hadn't been the point.

FOUR

Wake up, boyo.

That mental shove from Uncle Daemon had Daemonar lifting his head off the pillow. "Wha . . . ?"

Your father's here. I want you with us when we check out that window. If you want any breakfast, meet us in my sitting room.

"Wha . . . ?" Daemonar kicked the covers out of his way and stood beside the bed, shivering. He'd forgotten to add power to the warming spells that kept his suite of rooms comfortable. Then again, getting up in the cold here wasn't any different from waking up outside during an early spring or late autumn hunting trip.

At least he wasn't responsible for maintaining the hot water tanks for this square of rooms. And no one else in this square would be up this early.

Hell's fire. Who *wanted* to get up this early? Then again, his father had traveled here from Ebon Rih. He didn't want to think about when *Lucivar* had gotten out of bed in order to arrive in time for breakfast. And which members of Mrs. Beale's kitchen staff had been roused to make breakfast at this hour?

As long as it wasn't Mrs. Beale herself, there was nothing to fear. Maybe.

The quick shower and hot water helped trick his brain into believing it was time to function.

The smell of coffee when he opened Daemon's sitting room door a few minutes later convinced his stomach that it was time to eat, even if the windows barely showed a gray smudge of daylight trying to shoulder out deep night.

"Good morning," he said, nodding to his father and uncle. Then he dropped into the empty chair that had been pulled up to a small rectangular dining table and lifted the lid that covered the dish. Bacon, a vegetable omelet, and a couple of pastries. There were also a basket of muffins and a bowl of soft butter on the table. Not much of a meal by the Hall's standards, but it *was* early. "Who did you wake up to cook the food?"

Lucivar picked up the coffeepot and filled Daemonar's mug before topping off Daemon's mug and his own. "We didn't wake up anyone. There is now a full auxiliary kitchen just across the corridor from this square, and your uncle and I both know how to cook."

It might have been a full kitchen, but it had a limited menu that was prepared by the apprentice cooks on duty. Still, you could usually get a bowl of soup and a sandwich there throughout the day, as well as fresh fruit and cheese.

"You made pastries?" Daemonar took a big bite out of an apple and cinnamon pastry and decided not to mention that the pastry wasn't light and flaky—and the flavor of the filling was a little off. Just enough that he doubted it would have been presented in the breakfast room for the Warlord Prince of Dhemlan's official first meal. Which would be funny if Uncle Daemon had made the pastries. Or it would be funny as long as no one told Mrs. Beale that the Prince was eating substandard fare.

"Those pastries and the muffins were left over from yesterday's baking lessons," Daemon replied as he sipped his coffee.

Well, that explained why the pastries didn't taste quite right. Since they weren't inedible and he was hungry, Daemonar took another bite.

Daemon lifted the basket and held it out to Lucivar. "Muffin?"

"Thanks." Lucivar took one.

Looking at their plates, Daemonar realized that Daemon and Lucivar had already finished their meals and were waiting for him. He probably had another five minutes before his father hauled him out the door, so he applied himself to eating while he could.

They gave him seven minutes. Daemonar figured Uncle Daemon was the reason he got the extra two minutes. But as soon as Daemon set his mug on the table, Lucivar was on his feet, and seeing the look in their eyes, Daemonar thought it was fortunate for everyone that those two men weren't hunting for anything except a weird piece of window glass.

Daemon and Lucivar walked through the corridors side by side, the dominant Warlord Princes in the Realm of Kaeleer. The predators who had no rivals.

He didn't usually think of them that way, didn't usually see them that way. They were his father and uncle, and usually when they were together it was for family, and there was an easiness to being around them. As he followed a couple of steps behind them, he saw them as the rest of the Blood must see them. Ruthless. Merciless. Power and temper controlled by a Queen who was no longer flesh but was still the will that commanded their lives.

As she commanded his.

Witch's public return had shaken the entire Realm. The High Lord of Hell and the Demon Prince might be her weapons, but her power eclipsed theirs in ways no one could measure—except in remembering the purge that had destroyed all the Blood who had been tainted by Dorothea and Hekatah SaDiablo. And he'd heard a few whispers of warnings issued by Black Widows who had looked for answers in dreams and visions. No matter what she had been when she'd walked among the living, Witch, the living myth, was more ruthless, less merciful, and far more feral than her weapons, and it was in everyone's best interest not to give the Lady who resided in the Keep a reason to look too closely at the living.

She was feared now in ways she hadn't been feared before, but she was still his Queen and, more important, she was still his beloved Auntie J.

They slowed when they reached the Black shield that closed off one side of the corridor with the weird window.

Lucivar looked over his shoulder at Daemonar and said, "Shield."

As soon as Daemonar wrapped himself in a Green defensive shield, Lucivar shielded in Ebon-gray and Daemon shielded in Black. Then Daemon dropped the shield blocking that side of the corridor, and the two men slowly walked to the window, with Daemonar still a couple of steps behind them.

"This one?" Lucivar asked quietly.

Daemon nodded. "Storm passed, so it might not respond."

"Did you hear what the window said?" Daemonar asked.

"I heard," Lucivar replied. He curled his right hand into a fist and raised it so that the Ebon-gray Jewel in his ring pointed at the window. Then he drew in a breath and let out an Eyrien battle cry enhanced by enough Craft to rattle *all* the windows in that part of the Hall.

The sensation of dark power, sluggish yet slithery, before the voices in the window roared in answer to Lucivar's battle cry. Then . . .

Nothing.

Daemonar breathed out a sigh of relief. "Is it gone?"

"No," Lucivar said darkly. "It isn't gone. It *moved*." He turned and looked at his son.

Daemon looked at Daemonar.

Daemonar took a step back and raised his hands. "I didn't do it. Any of it."

Lucivar stared at him a little too long before looking at Daemon. "The pup doesn't have that kind of skill, and there's nothing in that spell that felt like the Green."

"But it definitely moved from this window to . . . where?" Daemon asked.

"Good question, old son. And a question you need answered in a hurry."

"Mother Night," Daemon said quietly.

"Yeah. You need more help than I can give you, so you know what you have to do."

Daemon sighed.

"My advice? Start with piss and vinegar. Let Jaenelle and Karla work to calm you down."

Daemon looked at Lucivar. "You don't know that this has anything to do with them."

"With *those* voices?" Lucivar laughed. "Hell's fire, Bastard, are you that naive?"

As they went back to Daemon's suite, Daemonar wondered what Sadi would have said to Lucivar if he hadn't remembered there was a youngster with them.

He was pretty sure he would have learned some interesting new words.

As soon as Daemon caught the Black Winds and headed for Ebon Askavi, Lucivar headed for the butler's pantry, which was Beale's domain. Maids and footmen were stirring now. So were the youngsters who were apprenticing under Mrs. Beale, may the Darkness have mercy on them.

Barely a month into this arrangement of the Hall becoming a training ground for promising witches, Warlords, and Warlord Princes of all kinds of professions—including Queens, Black Widows, and Healers who might be targets for Blood with malevolent ambitions—and he and Daemon were looking at challenges. Well, Daemon was looking at challenges. He was there to watch his brother's back—and to make sure that this arrangement didn't undermine Daemon's sanity.

He found Beale and Mrs. Beale in the butler's pantry, along with Helene, the Hall's head housekeeper, reviewing the tasks and assignments for the day.

"Good morning," Lucivar said, staying in the doorway. No space to maneuver with three people already in that room.

"Prince Yaslana," Beale said. "I wasn't aware you were here."

"Arrived very early." Bracing himself, Lucivar looked Mrs. Beale in the eyes and tipped his head in greeting.

Mrs. Beale had already had a fearsome reputation despite wearing a Yellow Jewel. Her wearing one of the lighter Jewels didn't mean much, because she was a large, strong woman who brought her well-honed meat cleaver to any and every meeting she had with members of the Sa-Diablo family. After the coven of malice's attack on guests at the Hall, she had become a terrifying fascination for the youngsters who had applied to work in her kitchens because her meat cleaver, which she'd used to kill one of the evil girls, had a kiss engraved on one side—a kiss made by Daemon Sadi's lips as a thank-you for her part in defending the Hall and the girls who had been under attack.

She stared at him too long for comfort before saying, "You and the Prince made something to eat?"

It sounded more like an accusation than a question. "We did," he replied. "A token meal, since I arrived so early."

Her eyes narrowed—and Lucivar had to resist the urge to call in his war blade.

"You sampled the pastries and muffins that were made yesterday?" she asked.

"We did."

"And?"

Oh, Hell's fire. "They were acceptable but not up to *your* standards."

"The *Prince* ate something I wouldn't approve for his table?"

Would you rather he went hungry? Certain there wasn't an answer that wouldn't get him—and Daemon—into trouble, he said nothing.

"Well, I suppose an empty belly makes do," Mrs. Beale

grumbled. "I'll get started on a proper breakfast for the two of you."

She couldn't flank him. He could hold his ground. "Prince Sadi has already left. There are things he needs to discuss with the Ladies at the Keep. But I would appreciate a meal of whatever you would like to serve." He would have suggested eating with the instructors to avoid extra work for the Hall's staff, but right now he would eat the meal in whatever room Mrs. Beale deemed appropriate.

Lucivar glanced at Beale. "I need a few minutes of your time before the youngsters start their day." Pulling his dark membranous wings tight against his back, he stepped aside to let Mrs. Beale and Helene leave the pantry, then stepped in and closed the door. "So. Hole in the wall. How is that being handled?"

"As it was handled in the past," Beale replied. "The young Ladies who were attempting whatever they were attempting decided they should be responsible for paying for the repairs rather than have all the youngsters put a few marks in the pot."

"That's fair."

Beale nodded. "I contacted the workmen in Halaway who usually take care of such things at the Hall. The bill that will be presented for the cost of the repairs will be steep enough to pinch everyone's pocket."

"But it won't cover the full cost."

"Prince Sadi agreed to continue his father's arrangement for such adventures and will cover the rest of the cost of the repairs." Beale offered Lucivar a tiny smile.

Lucivar hesitated. "My brother is doing all right?"

Now Beale hesitated, reluctant to discuss the man who ruled Dhemlan and so much more, but Lucivar and Beale had an agreement when it came to Daemon Sadi. "He is heartsore, and he misses his daughter. That is to be expected. However, seeing the young Ladies who were saved from the coven of malice's intentions is a daily reminder of why he made the choices he made. I think that helps him. Being here certainly helps *them*." Another hesitation. "If I may make an observation, the Hall as it is now, with so many young people, feels more like it did when the Prince's Lady lived here. I think those were happy years for him."

Lucivar nodded. "The happiest." He blew out a breath. "But we have a problem here. Daemon has gone to the Keep for help in fixing it. Until then, this is what the senior staff needs to know."

FIVE

A few days of discreet inquiries provided no answers. There wasn't a girl at the sanctuary named Wilhelmina Benedict. There was no Benedict family in the village. Jillian had the vaguest recollection of hearing the name but couldn't remember where.

That left Saetien with two other choices for information. Her father's letters held warmth but were written with almost painful care. Daemon Sadi didn't mention any of the youngsters who were currently in residence at SaDiablo Hall, including her cousins Titian and Daemonar. He wrote about Mikal, who was his legal ward. He wrote about the gardens and bits and pieces of gossip about the people in Halaway, the village adjoining the family seat. But he didn't say much about himself beyond what books he was currently reading. She didn't know if that was because something was wrong and he wasn't going to tell her or if he believed she wouldn't care.

Of course, her letters to him were just as carefully written, because anything that sounded like whining was met with a chilly response, and some days it was hard not to feel sorry for herself and blame everyone else for her Birthright Jewel being stripped down to Purple Dusk instead of being in the range of power that had been in Twilight's Dawn, and for her being banned from Amdarh and Askavi for two years, and for her ending up living here.

And she wanted to blame Witch most of all, for condemning her to nightly visits to Briarwood during which she had to walk through the place and listen to the screaming and crying and pleading, and see things that shouldn't be seen by anyone, even in the worst nightmares.

She saw the pattern. She wasn't stupid. She noticed on the days when she was petulant or bitchy about having to do chores around the sanctuary beyond keeping her room tidy, when she complained about the quarterly allowance her father gave her being a portion of what it used to be, when she pushed at Jillian because the Eyrien woman was part of the family that didn't want *her* anymore, that she saw more of Briarwood, saw things too awful to bear. And somewhere there would be words painted in blood on a wall: *You dream about this. We lived this.*

A harsh reminder that usually had Shelby nudging her awake because she was crying in her sleep.

No, she couldn't ask her father about someone who might not even exist, since Teresa was the one who gave her the name and then had no recollection of who it was or what the name meant. That left her with one other choice.

Saetien waited until Surreal SaDiablo arrived for her weekly appointment with the sanctuary's administrator and instructors. Before Surreal completed her business and left for her next appointment, Saetien sent a request to see the Warlord Prince of Dhemlan's second-in-command.

Her mother but no longer a mother. Saetien had obliterated that bond between them with deliberate, well-aimed words. She could say now that she hadn't meant what she'd said, but that was like someone saying, *The knife slipped; I didn't mean to kill my friend, just hurt her a little*. She'd killed something inside Surreal, something that may have been vulnerable all along, and they both lived with the scars and the consequences.

She met Surreal outside, having hurried because it had taken her longer than she'd expected to get Shelby to agree that he shouldn't come with her.

"Problem?" Surreal asked, her voice suggesting she would be helpful but impersonal.

"I need help finding someone," Saetien said.

"You could write to the historian/librarian at the Keep and request information. Geoffrey would know if anyone does," Surreal replied.

"I'm not sure the person is real." She called in the paper with the drawing and name and handed it to Surreal.

Surreal stared at it for a long time. "Where did you get this?"

"Teresa drew it for me. It's sort of a portrait of who I was and who I am now." Saetien shifted her weight from one foot to the other. "She says this person tastes of sadness and truth and can tell me some things I need to know."

"I don't know if she can," Surreal said quietly. "Not anymore. And I don't know that you really want to find out about her."

"Why?" Something in Surreal's reluctance made Saetien uneasy. "Who is Wilhelmina Benedict?"

Surreal sighed. "She was Jaenelle Angelline's sister."

SIX

As soon as Witch and Karla entered the sitting room across from the Queen's suite, Daemon glided around them and shut the door—and stood between them and a way out of the room. At least he blocked an easy exit for Karla. Witch's body was a shadow made out of power and Craft, so she could disappear anytime she pleased. But when dealing with him, she usually observed whatever rules would have applied if she still had a physical body.

Piss and vinegar, Lucivar had said. Well, he was primed to deliver.

He held out the cuff link and engaged the auditory spell in the Red chip beneath the ruby.

Grumbles and deep mutters before those voices roared out with language foul enough to make Lucivar blush when he'd heard it.

Karla looked taken aback before she frowned at the cuff link. "That's Eyrien, isn't it?"

Witch, wide-eyed and mouth open in shock, finally said, "Mother Night, it certainly is."

Karla had picked up enough Eyrien over the years to be able to converse in that language, but Witch was fluent and probably knew *all* the words that had been said.

"Lucivar and I think this is somehow connected to the two of you, so you are going to help me fix this," Daemon said. He shook the cuff link at them. Voices muttered and grumbled.

They all stared at the cuff link, waiting.

"Why would this have anything to do with us?" Witch asked.

"Because Lucivar identified those voices as belonging to Andulvar and Prothvar Yaslana, so this was done before they became a whisper in the Darkness. I'm sure Saetan created the original bit of Craft as some kind of lesson for the coven, but something happened and this spell is still working. It was placed in a window, probably in response to the tests you made on window glass."

"Tests?" Witch said warily.

"'Intruder! Intruder! I'm hit! I'm hit! I'm hit!'" Daemon raised an eyebrow. "Remember that?"

"Hell's fire," Karla muttered. "How would *you* know about that?"

"Saetan kept notes about your more memorable adventures." No need to tell them—yet—that there was a whole filing cabinet filled with those notes.

The look on their faces. His daughter used to call that puffed-up, huffy attitude "going all hissy cat." In fact, the Scelties *still* used that phrase when human females got overly exercised about something.

"If the spell is in a window, can't you remove the window?" Witch asked.

"That was our intention, once we'd confirmed that it was only sound and not something more malevolent—like someone trapped in that window—*but the damn spell moved!*" Daemon shook the cuff link again, then stopped when it began to mutter.

"Moved where?" Karla asked.

"That is the question," he replied. "But I'm telling you both now, if that spell shows up in a bedroom window and I end up with twenty-two adolescent girls piling on top of me in the middle of the night, scared out of their wits, I am going to be pissed."

"You think the boys will hold out?" Witch asked.

Didn't even take a moment's thought. "Considering that Daemonar found this and it spooked *him* enough to have him pounding on my bedroom door, the other pups will be piling in with the girls." He gave them a sharp smile. "And if that spell shows up in the Beales' apartment, I am bringing Mrs. Beale *and* her meat cleaver here so that *you* can explain this to her."

They stared at him.

"That's a threat," Karla finally said.

"Uh-huh," Witch agreed.

She tried to look contrite. They both did. Contrition coming from the two of them made him nervous, but he held his ground.

"Can you leave the cuff link here so that we can study the sound?" Witch asked.

Daemon held out the cuff link.

A small crystal bowl appeared in front of him, floating on air. He dropped the cuff link into the bowl. The bowl vanished.

"Something must have activated the spell, if it's been dormant all these years," Witch said. "Did something unusual happen at the Hall?"

"Apparently nothing that would be considered unusual when you have a pack of adolescent girls," Daemon replied. "A bit of Craft went a wee bit wrong, and they punched a hole in a wall."

"A hole the size of a decorative window or the size of a door?"

He stared at his Queen, the love of his life and his reason for living—because she had asked him to stay among the living for as long as he could. "Does it matter?" he asked too calmly.

"It could," Karla said.

"Decorative window," he replied. "Or so I was told."

"Well," Karla said. "The sun is up, so it's past time for me to retire for the day."

The silence in the room held a hum of anticipation as

the three of them acknowledged that a witch who was demon-dead needed to be careful around the High Lord of Hell, even if she was a Gray-Jeweled Black Widow Queen and a friend.

Daemon stepped aside and used Craft to open the door. Karla walked past him without another word.

"You're looking a little peaky, Prince," Witch said. That was as close as he allowed her to come to acknowledging the damage he'd done to his heart and lungs when he had tried to suppress his sexual heat.

"Lack of sleep; that's all." That was as close as he came to admitting what they both knew—that the sand that marked his time among the living was falling in the glass day by day.

"Then you should take a couple of hours to sleep and have a quiet meal before you throw yourself into the chaos at the Hall."

He hesitated, then asked for what he really needed. "Stay with me?"

Witch smiled. "I'll stay."

She gave him time to go to the Consort's suite, strip out of his clothes, and get into bed before she walked in from her adjoining bedroom.

A shadow he couldn't touch—not while he still walked among the living—but a shape that could touch him. When her hand rested on his chest, his body relaxed in ways it never did when he wasn't with her.

"How are you, Daemon?" Jaenelle asked softly.

"I'm all right." He chuckled. "Most days, dealing with the girls is like being run over by a pack of happy puppies. The novelty of living at the Hall hasn't worn off yet."

"And the boys?"

"Let's just say I haven't had to prove—yet—that I have the biggest cock."

Jaenelle's silvery, velvet-coated laugh filled the room. "You left a kiss on Mrs. Beale's meat cleaver. I think it will be a while before any of the boyos start a pissing contest with *you*." Her laughter and amusement faded. "Your daughter?"

Daemon sighed. "She's . . . adjusting . . . to life at the sanctuary. She's sent me a couple of letters. She hasn't said much, but she has written. And I've written back. Not much else I can do for her right now."

"No," Jaenelle said gently. "Not right now. But the core of who she is, the core you and Surreal helped shape, is still there. She just has to find it again in her own way."

"Have you seen something in a tangled web?"

"No. I just know you." She leaned over and gave him a soft kiss on the cheek. "Sleep, Daemon."

"Yeah. I will." He closed his eyes. "I left Lucivar at the Hall. He'll be giving the Craft lessons today."

"Mother Night," she breathed.

"And may the Darkness be merciful."

He drifted to sleep thinking about how thirty-four of those youngsters at the Hall would get their first full experience of dealing with Lucivar Yaslana.

After Sadi headed back to SaDiablo Hall, Karla sat on the sofa in the sitting room across from the Queen's suite and listened to the roaring voices coming from the audio chip in Sadi's cuff link. "Do you remember what we did that pissed them off so much?"

Jaenelle Angelline, the Queen who was Witch, stared at the cuff link and shook her head. "No, but it had to be more than the window we'd made—although that window did cause a fair amount of excitement."

"Are you sure this is Andulvar and Prothvar?"

"The voices are . . . bloated . . . or multiplied, but definitely Andulvar and Prothvar."

"Which means that spell was made . . ."

"Before the purge."

"That was centuries ago. Even a spell created by Uncle Saetan should have run out of power."

"Depends on the conditions that were woven into the spell. It could have been dormant until it was found—or until someone else blew a hole in a wall." Jaenelle jammed her fingers into her short golden hair—hair that looked more like fur—until it was standing on end.

"Besides," Jaenelle continued, "there's been another Black-Jeweled Warlord Prince living at the Hall all of these years, feeding his power into the defensive shields. It's possible Daemon fed this spell, too, without realizing it."

"And also fed it some of his rage when his control had been slipping?" Karla suggested. "That could account for the way the voices sound."

"Possible." Jaenelle looked at Karla. "If Saetan created this spell and set it in a window, he meant for us to find it—and fix it. A lesson in undoing something that had been done."

"Except we didn't find it," Karla pointed out. "So either Uncle Saetan forgot about it . . ."

Jaenelle huffed. "Not likely, since he left notes."

". . . or it had originally been in a place where we should have found it. Except something else twined with his work and the spell scampered off to windows unknown."

"Which means Daemon is right. That spell was originally designed to respond to us and should have been dealt with a long time ago."

Jaenelle looked at Karla. Karla looked at Jaenelle.

"Well," Karla finally said. "This will be exciting."

SEVEN

Since he had no intention of teaching Craft to a pack of adolescents or following Daemon's precise schedule for the day's lessons, Lucivar summoned *all* the youngsters to the large room usually used for sparring and weapons training. He hadn't seen all of them together since the day they'd arrived at the Hall, and today he wanted to get a feel for who they were. *What* they were. And how they were with one another.

This review would have come sooner or later. Daemon's absence today meant neither man had to come up with an excuse for the youngsters having to deal with him instead of the Warlord Prince they were accustomed to seeing.

The girls walked into the room, speculating about why they'd *all* been summoned here for their Craft lesson—as if a simple psychic probe couldn't have told them they were facing Ebon-gray instead of Black, and *that* should have told them the Craft lesson wasn't going to be what they expected.

It also raised the question of why they hadn't done something as basic as a psychic probe before entering the room.

Titian hurried into the room and gave Lucivar a bright smile, quickly followed by a look of wariness.

Yes, witchling, he thought, amused by his daughter's reaction to his presence. *I know about the wall.*

Equally wary, Zoey offered him a proper bow—young Queen to a Warlord Prince of his rank.

Jhett, a Black Widow, and Arlene, a Healer—both good friends of Zoey's—also bowed.

The other four Queens who were now residing at the Hall looked confused by Zoey's formality, then hesitated a few moments too long before they, too, bowed to acknowledge who, and what, he was.

The lack of understanding about who determined when a meeting could shift from formal to informal was something Daemon would have to correct—and fast. Of course, at this age, they could have a brilliant understanding of Protocol one moment and be completely brainless the next.

Altogether, there were five Queens, three natural Black Widows, three natural Healers, and eleven witches. They had come from different Provinces in Dhemlan. They had been selected by the Province Queens after being recommended by the District Queens, chosen to be trained at the Hall because they were deemed young witches of considerable potential who could be the next generation of leaders in one way or another—and targets for someone who saw them as rivals the way Delora and her coven of malice had done.

Yes, he saw that potential in the way they carried themselves and in their psychic scents.

What he also saw, in the way the girls clustered on one side of the room, were the seeds of five courts instead of one. Trouble? Possibly.

And in more ways than one, he thought grimly as Daemonar led the other thirteen boys into the room, followed by Lord Weston, who was Zoey's sword and shield, and Prince Raine, an instructor from Dharo.

He watched the way one of the girls stared at the boys—specifically the five Warlord Princes. Daemonar was the only one old enough to be in the first phase of his sexual heat. The other four wouldn't have to deal with it for a few more years, but they would have to deal with it—and so would any witch who served in a court that held a Warlord Prince.

He watched the girl. Watched the way she swished her skirt to draw the eye to her hips. Watched the way her attention fixed on his son but also flicked to the other four Warlord Princes as if she were sizing up the best piece of meat in the market.

A man didn't need much experience to guess what he wouldn't find under that skirt. And he had plenty of experience.

Well, no one had ever accused him of being subtle. Or tactful.

His sharp whistle had all of them looking his way. He focused on the young witch and said, "Leave the room and finish dressing."

She looked at the other girls, looked at one of the Queens in particular, her feigned bafflement fraying the leash on his temper. Then she lifted her chin. "I don't know what you mean."

Lucivar nodded. "All right. *Put some underpants on.*" The words thundered through the room. "If I start showing off what you've got between your legs, I will take a strap to your bare ass. Do you understand me?"

"I—I—"

"Do. You. Understand?"

She burst into tears and ran out of the room.

Lucivar scanned the faces of the other children. Some looked stunned. Some looked shocked.

And five boys, including his son, looked relieved.

Something else he needed to mention to Daemon.

Before he could say anything else, Mikal opened the door and stuck his head into the room.

"Oh. Hey," Mikal said. "I guess this explains it. Alvita crossed a line?"

"She did," Lucivar replied. "Someone should escort her back to her room and make sure she doesn't do something stupid for the sake of drama."

"The Scelties are taking care of that."

Lucivar almost felt sorry for her, since one of the Scelties now living at the Hall was a Green-Jeweled Warlord Prince who didn't see any reason why he had to put up with nonsense from puppies, regardless of their species. "Tell them she should stay in her room until the midday meal."

Mikal gave him an assessing look. From someone else, it might be seen as a challenge. But Mikal was not only family; he understood the give-and-take required to work in a court—or to work for the Warlord Prince of Dhemlan.

"I'll tell them." Mikal shut the door.

Lucivar scanned the children's faces again. "Listen up. Sexual heat is a wicked bitch to deal with, and it's just as hard on Warlord Princes as it is on the rest of you. But it's part of what makes a Warlord Prince who and what he is, and if you are going to rule a court one day or serve in a court or even reside in a village where one of us lives, you'd damn well better learn how to accept that part of our nature and let it flow past you, because sexual heat isn't an indication of interest in you. If a Warlord Prince is interested in you specifically, you will know and so will everyone else. Believe me. You will know because all that heat and fire and strength will be focused on you. But until that day comes, you will show him the courtesy of not forcing him to defend his body and his honor, because if he has to do that, he will hurt you."

"Perhaps a review of the Protocol specific to living around and working with Warlord Princes would be appropriate," Raine suggested. "Unless Prince Sadi wants to handle that personally, I could make that the lesson this afternoon."

Lucivar nodded. "You do that." He looked at the young Warlord Princes. "You five. You stay with me. The rest of you . . ." He looked at the girls. "You have until Sadi returns to decide if you have the self-control to stay here and deal with the Warlord Princes who are in residence. If you can't—or won't—you don't belong here, and I'll make sure you get home safely."

"Prince?" Jhett raised a hand just enough to catch his attention. "Are you allowed to decide that?"

It was a valid question, since this wasn't his Territory. "You're all here because you have been potential victims of Delora and her coven of malice, and the Province Queens were concerned that there might be someone else out there with similar ambitions that we haven't found yet." He gave that a moment to sink in. "Am I one of the people who decides who stays or who goes? Yeah, I am, because who you are and what you do here will decide if I'm willing to step onto a killing field to protect you. Children, I watched another group of youngsters live here and train here and learn what it meant to rule the Realm of Kaeleer, and they were magnificent. Prove that you are worthy of being protected by the Demon Prince and the High Lord of Hell. Sadi and I know you'll make mistakes. At your age, it's expected. But we will not tolerate some lines being crossed."

Lucivar took another look at each of them. "That's enough for today. At least from me. Prince Raine?"

"Some time to reflect would be valuable," Raine said. "Then I'll meet with the Ladies for the Protocol lesson after the midday meal, and the gentlemen later in the afternoon."

"Very well. You're all dismissed—except you five."

Lucivar walked to the end of the room and looked out the windows. Then he waited for the young Warlord Princes to join him. Still looking outside, he said, "Have any of you had a problem with her? Any questionable or inappropriate behavior that Prince Sadi should have known about?"

No response.

He turned and looked at Daemonar.

The boy sighed. "Alvita came into my bedroom recently and displayed her breasts."

Four boys sucked in a breath. Lucivar couldn't tell if they were envious or appalled. But *his* boy . . .

"And when you mentioned that to Prince Sadi?" Lucivar asked mildly.

"Well, I haven't had a chance to talk to him, have I?" Daemonar protested.

Lucivar stared at him.

"I handled it," Daemonar said, an edge in his voice. "I told her to leave. When she didn't, I put a Green shield around her and shoved her out the door. And *locked* the door."

"But didn't mention it to the man who has made the commitment to protect all of you who live here?" It was a struggle not to snarl at the boy. If they'd been alone, this discussion would have been a lot louder.

"It wasn't an *immediate* concern, so I asked Holt to give me a slot in the Prince's audience times. Hell's fire, Father. If Uncle Daemon didn't draw a line about when we could talk to him about . . . whatever . . . the man would spend all day every day listening to people complain about something or about each other or whine about something else until Breen got annoyed and started nipping people to get them out of his study. I didn't think it was important enough to interfere with his other duties. He's got plenty of those."

Protective of the man. He couldn't argue with that.

The other four boys looked ready to bolt—or lose their breakfast out of fear of being so close when Green squared off against Ebon-gray. Good. Let them learn when to yield and when to stand.

"Do you still think it isn't important?" Lucivar asked.

"Considering what Uncle Daemon is dealing with right now, it can wait," Daemonar replied.

"What's he dealing with?" one of the boys asked.

"Some old trouble."

A dismissive response, and an interesting way to put it. The question in his son's eyes was also interesting.

"Tell them," Lucivar said. "Better to have all the Warlord Princes on guard for possible trouble."

"Yes, sir."

Lucivar walked out of the room and headed for the part of the Hall where he would most likely find Holt and Beale.

"Ah, Prince Yaslana," Beale said when Lucivar located

the butler. "If you wouldn't mind waiting in Prince Sadi's study, Holt and I will be with you in a few minutes."

"Sure."

He prowled Daemon's study, turning when the door opened. But it wasn't Holt or Beale who'd opened it; it was the Dharo Boy, who was now Mrs. Beale's primary assistant cook. Lucivar still didn't know what the young Warlord's actual name was, since nobody called him anything but Dharo Boy.

"Compliments of Mrs. Beale," the Dharo Boy said, setting a mug of coffee and a plate of food on the table in front of the long sofa. "She thought you could use some sustenance."

"I guess she heard about my way of giving instructions."

The Dharo Boy grinned. "Prince, we've *all* heard about it."

Well, wasn't that just fine?

The Warlord left.

Lucivar had time to enjoy the food and the rich coffee before Holt and Beale returned to hear whatever he wanted to say officially.

Daemon stepped off the landing web in front of the Hall and let his Black power gently wash through the place to get a feel for what he'd be walking into.

No hot fury, so nobody had pissed off Lucivar too much. But . . .

Breen, along with several more Scelties, rushed out to greet him and give him the news.

One human female went hissy-cat boo-hoo and had to be penned in her room. Yas said so. The other females had special lessons instead of going where they were supposed to. Teachers were confused but no one wanted to ask Yas about that. Except the Scelties. They asked so they would know where to herd the females. Lord Weston and Prince Raine and Daemonar were herding the young males.

Daemon walked into the great hall and saw Beale waiting for him.

"High drama?" he asked.

"High drama," Beale agreed. "Your brother is staying over for a day or two."

"He's in his usual suite?"

Beale hesitated. "Not the suite he occupies when Lady Marian is with him. He's in the suite he used to occupy when he lived here with your father."

Which meant Lucivar was in the High Lord's square of rooms, which was now *his* square of rooms.

Daemon felt a moment's light-headedness before his temper iced and he strode to the staircase in the informal receiving room.

Daemon? Breen called, running after him. *Daemon!*

He was halfway up the stairs before her unhappy whine penetrated his fury. He hurried down the stairs, scooped up the puppy, then went back up the stairs and headed for his suite. The cold that crackled around him had everyone scrambling to get out of his way.

When he reached his sitting room, he set Breen in her basket, gave her a quick pat, and said, "Stay here while I talk to Yas." Then he went out the glass doors that opened to the large balcony and spotted Lucivar in the garden below.

Almost blinded by rage, Daemon rushed down the stairs to the courtyard. "What in the name of Hell are you doing here?"

Lucivar rose slowly and dropped a weed in the basket next to him. "Weeding. This garden needs work. I guess you don't let Tarl in here very often."

"Don't play with me, Prick," Daemon snarled. "What are you doing *here*?"

No one came to this square of rooms. This was where he stayed when his control was slipping, when he needed isolation. At least, that was how he'd used this square in the past. When Surreal was at the Hall and wanted his company, he stayed in the bedroom adjoining hers. Otherwise, he was here now, close to Titian and Zoey and the other girls who needed to feel protected—even if that protection came from the Sadist.

But having Lucivar here . . .

"I asked Beale and Helene for my old suite." Lucivar tipped his head to indicate the open glass doors on the second floor. "Those rooms were mine when I lived here."

"Lucivar . . ."

Lucivar looked him in the eyes. "You and I both know that you could have me on my knees begging if that's what you wanted to do. But the Ebon-gray I wear is as dark as that Jewel can be without being Black, and frankly, Bastard, when it's leashed your sexual heat rolls off me like it always did. I'm in the same position you are, have been for years, but I saw it happen to you and did what I could to minimize the problems the last phase of the sexual heat causes for men who wear Jewels as dark as ours."

Daemon took a step back. Felt the cold of his temper break against concern. "You and Marian?"

"Like I said, we learned from your hard lessons. And a particular kind of cleansing spell was sent from the Keep—the same spell you were given to use here. That helps Marian. And it helps me, because I don't have to live apart from her as much." Lucivar gave him a tired smile. "You've already got shields on shields around this square, so I don't have to be as careful—or as vigilant against unwanted attention." He shook his head. "I shouldn't have made the decision to use the suite without talking to you first."

Daemon stepped forward and rested his hands on Lucivar's shoulders. "It's all right. I didn't think about . . . Hell's fire, Prick. You never said anything."

Lucivar gave him that lazy, arrogant smile that always meant trouble. "And you didn't notice. That's been a comfort." He hesitated. "I also had another reason for wanting to stay in this square."

"What's that?"

"Discretion. I need the Sadist's help."

Daemon eased back and studied his brother. "Why?"

"Because the Sadist knows how to inflict pain—and how to find pain."

"Your back is bothering you?"

"Yeah. Not as bad as other times, but since I'm here . . ."

"After dinner?"

Lucivar nodded. "Once all the pups are in bed."

"Speaking of pups . . ." Daemon looked up at his balcony. Breen looked down at him and wagged her tail.

"You going to let your darling come down and help me dig out weeds?"

He winced, remembering another darling who used to kneel beside him as he and she weeded one of the gardens and planted the annuals she wanted in her little patch of earth. "I'll change out of these clothes, and we'll both give you a hand."

"Doesn't Holt have a list of things to review with you?"

"Probably. But if he scolds me for not reporting to my study, I'll just blame you."

Lucivar laughed. "Fair enough. You can help me weed, and I'll tell you about the trouble I caused."

EIGHT

H ere," Titian said. "Let me do that."

Zoey stopped struggling to close her dress and turned around so that Titian could do up the buttons in the back. "I'm so nervous. Are you nervous? This has to be about the spell that went wrong, although I still don't know *what* went wrong. What if we're expelled? Grandmother always made sure I had good teachers—except she didn't know about some things that were going on at the school in Amdarh because *I* didn't appreciate that it was more than not getting along with Delora and her friends, so I didn't say anything to her—but I'm learning so much here. Has Daemonar found out anything? Would he tell you?"

"All Daemonar knows is that the seven of us who tried that spell and the five Warlord Princes are to report right after sunset," Titian replied. "Uncle Daemon didn't say anything else."

Zoey didn't want to leave the Hall. She really didn't. She had the same small group of friends that she'd had at the school in Amdarh, but everything felt different here. *She* felt different here. Maybe trying some of the spells in that Craft notebook she'd found tucked behind some books in one of the Hall's libraries hadn't been her best idea—not without checking with Prince Sadi first—but something about seeing that handwritten page had made her feel bold.

Feel daring. But not reckless. They'd obviously made a mistake, but they hadn't been reckless.

Still, she should have been the one who told Prince Sadi that they'd broken a wall instead of letting Daemonar go in her place. She was a Queen after all. How could she stand up for her people if she wouldn't stand up for herself and accept the consequences of her own actions?

"There," Titian said, doing up the last button, and pressed a kiss against Zoey's cheek. "We'll get a scolding, but it will be all right. Uncle Daemon won't tell you to leave. He won't."

Taking Titian's hand, she really hoped her friend was right.

They all followed Daemonar since he seemed to know where they were supposed to go. An out-of-the-way section of the Hall, not so different from the section where they had set up the table and tools for that bit of Craft. When they reached an odd archway leading to an open area, Daemonar and the other four boys stepped aside, letting the girls enter first.

Nothing threatening, then, not if Warlord Princes were allowing a Queen to enter first, but . . . Hell's fire, Mother Night, and may the Darkness be merciful!

Zoey had expected Prince Sadi to be there for this . . . discipline. She'd kind of expected that Prince Yaslana would be there as well. But she *hadn't* expected the Gray-Jeweled Black Widow Queen with the ice-blue eyes and spiky white hair who was also waiting for them.

"Kiss kiss," Lady Karla said.

Do you know her? Titian asked on a distaff thread.

I've seen her. Once. Was she here to take back the gift she'd delivered before Zoey had come to the Hall? Please, no. Not before she had a chance to ask even one question.

"We'll talk about your adventure in a few minutes," Karla said. "Right now, you're all standing witness to the unraveling of a different spell."

"You found an answer?" Prince Sadi asked.

"We think so," Karla replied.

"First we have to find the damn thing," Prince Yaslana growled.

"Unless it will come when it's called," Karla said brightly.

Prince Yaslana swore.

Daemonar sucked in a breath and whispered, "Hell's fire."

Karla held up a small wooden frame that contained a crystal chip woven into the center of a simple web. The chip began to shine and . . .

That voice! Soaring, summoning. A single phrase, sung over and over in a language Zoey didn't recognize.

The Scelties howled. The wolves who lived in the estate's north woods howled. The stallions who were in paddocks near the Hall bugled a challenge.

The singing stopped.

"Lucivar, darling, would you tell the kindred that the Lady wasn't calling them?" Karla asked.

"Yeah." Lucivar sighed. "I'll do that."

But there was another sound. A muttering that had Prince Sadi focusing on one of the windows that overlooked this open area.

Karla vanished the wooden frame and called in another frame that held another crystal chip woven into a web. When that chip began to shine, Karla said loudly, "Our apologies, Uncle Saetan."

A second voice, the same voice that had sung that summoning, said at the same time, "Our apologies, Papa."

"We should have paid more attention to the spell we were working on," Karla and the other voice continued, "and we should have considered how to undo that bit of Craft *before* we tried it. And we're very sorry that the explosion knocked down that wall, but we did get the hole shielded before the second floor collapsed." Karla waited a moment before her voice, and only her voice, added, "Kiss kiss."

Nothing. Nothing. Nothing. Then . . .

Weird streaks of black appeared in one window. A moment later, a corner of the pane changed to white sand and spilled out of the window frame. More glass changed and spilled to the ground until there was a small mound beneath the empty frame where the pane had been.

"Well," Karla said. "That was unexpected." She turned to Sadi and gave him a bright smile. "But it did solve your problem."

"I'm delighted," he replied dryly.

Zoey didn't think Sadi was delighted, but Daemonar breathed a sigh of relief, so hopefully he would explain this later.

"Now," Karla said, turning to Zoey. "Where did you get the spell that went awry?"

Zoey wished Prince Sadi had asked instead of Lady Karla, but she called in the notebook and held it out.

Karla raised her hand, and the notebook obligingly floated on air and crossed the space between them. She opened it to the page that still had a strip of paper marking it. "Why did you ignore the notes on the back of the page?"

"Notes?" Zoey shook her head. "No, there was just . . ."

Karla turned the page and held up the notebook.

Notes. And the words *Needs work!* in large letters.

"We thought that was for something else," Titian said, pulling her wings in tight.

"Uh-huh." Karla gave them another bright smile. "My darlings, *never* ignore the notes that follow one of these bits of Craft."

"May I see that?" Prince Sadi reached for the notebook. He looked at the page and swore softly.

"We just found it behind some books," Zoey said hurriedly. "There's no name on it, so . . ."

"I was married to the woman for seventy years," Daemon growled. "I recognize the Queen's handwriting."

Mother Night! This was a book of *Witch's* spells and Craft?

Zoey took a step toward Sadi. "We'll take very good care of the notebook. And we'll be careful. We promise."

Sadi made a sound that might have been a laugh. "Yes, you will, because you're not getting this back." He vanished the notebook.

"However," Karla said, "Daemon will review the Craft—and the notes—and select some of these spells for you to learn under his supervision."

Sadi stared at Karla. "Did I agree to this?"

"You did."

"When?"

Prince Yaslana made a strange sound. Zoey wasn't sure if he was laughing or swearing. Or both.

Karla linked her arm with Sadi's and just smiled.

As he escorted Karla to the occupied part of the Hall, Daemon wondered if any of the children had noticed that the Glacian Queen floated on air just above the floor and he was doing the walking for both of them.

"Will you join us for dinner?" he asked. "All the children will be at the table for this meal, and I'd like your opinion."

"Any particular reason?"

"I'd like to know what you think of them."

"I'm rather curious about them myself, so I accept your invitation," she replied. "Besides, I doubt any of them have sat at a table with someone who drinks yarbarah."

That was just one of the reasons he wanted her to join him and the children tonight.

"You're going to have to find the other notebooks. You do know that?"

He almost missed a step. "I beg your pardon?"

"We all jotted down notes from lessons, as well as how this bit of Craft reacted when mixed with that level of power, and the coven used to tuck the notebooks on the shelves with the Craft books," Karla explained. "If Zoela found one of Jaenelle's notebooks on the shelves, it stands to reason that there are still more tucked away, since each of us filled quite a few of them. And the boyos used to keep notes too. You'll want to find those notebooks and look through them. They might contain useful hints for the young wiggle-waggles."

He could have sworn his brain spun a couple of times in his skull. "Do you know how many rooms qualify as a library here at the Hall? Not to mention that every social room and sitting room connected to a square of bedrooms has shelves of books. It will take weeks to check every shelf in every possible room."

"Hardly. I'll show you how to construct the summoning spell. All you have to do is hold Jaenelle's notebook in one hand and the summoning web in the other. Have Beale station a footman or maid in every room that has books and watch for something trying to escape from the shelves in answer to your call."

"You could do the summoning."

Karla laughed. "Oh, no, boyo. Lucivar is taking me back to the Keep, and we're leaving before dawn."

Coward, Daemon said on an Ebon-gray spear thread.

Fool, Lucivar countered. *Ask her why she chose that particular spot for the summoning. Assuming you have balls enough to ask.*

Ah, Hell's fire. Thinking about the apology that had ended Saetan's spell, he had a bad feeling he wouldn't like the answer. "Why did you choose that part of the Hall for the summoning?" Daemon asked.

Karla didn't reply for a long moment. "Did you notice the archway?"

"I did. It's an unusual feature." The archway connected an interior corridor with an open area exposed to weather without the benefit of a door to keep the interior and exterior separate. It also didn't have a perfect construction that would accommodate a door—or provide any confidence that it would stay up if you were under it.

Karla gave him a sharp smile. "When that particular spell went wrong for Jaenelle and me, the hole we punched in the wall was a bit bigger than a decorative window. But you'll notice that the wall above the archway hasn't fallen down, even after all these years."

"Sweet Darkness," he whispered.

She patted his arm. "You survived your initiation, Sadi. You'll be fine. Just make sure you collect all those notebooks."

NINE

Wilhelmina Benedict, Surreal thought as the estate
carriage took her to Jillian's cottage. *Why in the
name of Hell would Saetien want to know about Wilhelmina? And why now?*

More to the point, why did a young broken Black Widow
who walked the roads of the Twisted Kingdom give Saetien
Wilhelmina's name? That wasn't something she could ignore. But how to get the information without drawing the
attention of one of the Keep's residents? Because the one
thing she didn't want to do was open any heart wounds for
Jaenelle Angelline. Witch carried the weight of plenty of
wounds, and Surreal didn't want to add any new ones.

She could slip into the Keep and ask Geoffrey, the histo-
rian/librarian. Unless someone asked him what she had been
doing there, he would be discreet about her inquiries. Hell's
fire, even after all this time, he could probably recite the basics
of Wilhelmina's life after she came to Kaeleer without needing to look up anything. Those who guarded the Keep—and
the Queen—would have kept an eye on Wilhelmina Benedict.

She just needed to decide if providing help with this
quest was something she wanted to do.

Jillian's cottage was charming and slightly eccentric in a
way that reflected the years the girl had spent with Lady

Perzha in Little Weeble. The exterior fit into the village, but some rooms—like the bathrooms—had been torn apart and rebuilt to accommodate a woman of the Eyrien race. The kitchen had also been redone—and had been inspected by Mrs. Beale and her meat cleaver before the workmen had been permitted to declare the job complete. The carpets in all the rooms were from Dharo—a gift from Daemon that might be overlooked except by a person who understood that Dharo carpets of that quality were considered art, not a floor covering. Lucivar had purchased the furniture for the sitting room and the room Jillian used as her office and library. Marian had fitted out the kitchen with everything a young woman in her first home would need. And Surreal had purchased the bedroom furniture and all the linens.

Jillian still had to purchase a dining table and chairs, and the family had deliberately left out some things that the girl would buy for herself—like a bed for the guest room.

The two Scelties who lived with Jillian greeted Surreal and then disappeared, an indication that there might be an agenda behind this invitation to dinner.

She and Jillian ate and talked about books and the theater, and how Beron was rehearsing for a new play. The two women made plans for Jillian to join Surreal and Daemon on opening night.

When they were down to coffee and delicately made pieces of chocolate, Surreal said, "Want to tell me what's on your mind?" Since she was staying at the SaDiablo estate located near the sanctuary and had received hints that a certain young vintner was showing special interest in Jillian—and Jillian was showing interest in him—she had a pretty good idea what was on Jillian's mind.

"I'd like your help." Jillian selected a chocolate, then dropped it onto her dessert plate.

Surreal smiled. "You're finally ready to have your Virgin Night. And the Offering to the Darkness after that?"

Jillian sucked in a breath and stared at her, wide-eyed.

"Was there some reason you didn't do this before now?"

Surreal asked gently. Jillian was past the age when most young women would have gone through those ceremonies. Had something happened that the family didn't know about that had made the girl reluctant to participate in the sexual act that would protect her Jewels and power?

"I did make arrangements for my Virgin Night a couple of years ago. More than once, actually."

"And . . . ?" Surreal said when Jillian hesitated.

"The men who had the training and were interested in providing the service . . . When they found out I was the Demon Prince's daughter, their enthusiasm withered on the vine." Jillian held up a forefinger, then slowly curled it.

Surreal choked on her coffee, trying not to laugh. Then she thought about it. "Hell's fire." She couldn't imagine any man being able to perform with Lucivar Yaslana and his war blade standing on the other side of the bedroom door. "You didn't tell Lucivar you're ready for your Virgin Night?"

"Are you mad?" Jillian squeaked. "He'd want to be in the room to make sure nothing went wrong!"

Just proved the girl knew the man. Considering that *everyone* in Askavi knew how Lucivar had responded to Jillian's first romantic encounter, negotiating distance away from the bedroom might be tricky.

"Why now?" Surreal asked.

Color rose in Jillian's cheeks. "Stefan."

That confirmed what she'd suspected. "The young Prince who works as a vintner on the estate here?"

Jillian nodded. "He made the wine we had for dinner. His own blend that he's been developing over the past few years. He's intelligent and kind and funny and enthusiastic about his work—and enthusiastic about mine. And now we'd like . . ."

"To be lovers?" Which meant Jillian had ignored the permission-before-action rule up to the part that could get Stefan killed if Lucivar found out after the fact. But the girl *had* reached her majority, so that rule shouldn't apply anymore.

Except they were talking about Lucivar. And Daemon.

"Yes," Jillian said.

Surreal selected a chocolate and nibbled on it. "You wear Birthright Purple Dusk. That means you have the potential to come away from the Offering wearing Sapphire. It's better to have your Virgin Night first. The darker your Jewel, the more difficult it is to find a partner who is strong enough to see you through your first sexual experience." She huffed out a breath. "I appreciate how difficult this will be, but, sugar, you can't do this without Lucivar and Daemon being present. Not after everything we learned about the coven of malice."

Jillian looked ready to faint. "But you see . . ."

"No. It will be impossible for them to allow a girl they care about to go through the Virgin Night without them being present. So we'll do some negotiating and compromising to get you through it—and keep the man who has agreed to perform the service alive. What you will not do, as tempting as it may be, is throw caution to the wind and let Stefan see you through that first time. The Virgin Night isn't about making love. It's not even about sex. It's about the preservation of the girl's power. *Your* power and potential. Stefan should be your first lover, not your first time."

"You don't understand," Jillian whispered, bracing her head in her hands.

"I understand that Lucivar and Daemon want this for you. They do. You just need to give them time to accept that you're ready for this." Surreal poured more coffee for both of them. "As for the other, I would be honored to be with you when you make the Offering to the Darkness."

"I was going to ask Nurian to be there too. And Marian."

"Well then. I'll talk to everyone and we'll work out the details."

After Surreal returned to the SaDiablo estate, Jillian washed the dinner dishes and kept reassuring the Scelties that she was fine. Having picked up her emotional turmoil, they ignored her words and watched her until she sent them into the garden for a last piddle before she locked up for the night.

She'd had the conversation planned so carefully, had lined up her reasons in a way she was sure Surreal would understand. But she hadn't anticipated Surreal making the wrong assumption and running with it. Not wrong, exactly. The attraction between her and Stefan had grown to the point where she wanted to invite him to be her lover, which was why she'd wanted this conversation with Surreal, thinking Surreal would be the most levelheaded adult in the family who was also strong enough to handle Lucivar.

Levelheaded and practical Surreal might be, but she was also Daemon Sadi's second-in-command—and an assassin who wore Gray Jewels. And once she told Daemon and Lucivar that Jillian was ready for the Virgin Night, they were going to expect to have some say in who performed that service.

Now that she'd kicked this pebble and started the avalanche, Jillian wondered how she was supposed to tell *any* of them that she'd already gone through that female rite of passage and had kept it a secret.

TEN

SaDiablo Hall

The next morning Daemon made his way to the Hall's private library—the library his father had created to preserve books and journals about the history of Kaeleer's Territories as well as books about Craft that required intense skill. Unlike borrowing a book from the fiction libraries available to guests and staff, or the library that held nonfiction about a variety of subjects, borrowing a book from this room required his permission—or Beale's if he wasn't in residence.

It was a good bet that some of the notebooks Jaenelle and the coven filled with their various work would be tucked in here for safekeeping.

Except for Mrs. Beale and her staff, every single person at the Hall—including the Scelties—was assigned to watch a room or assist in this hunt in some way. Beale was watching his study. Holt was acting as a runner and collector of notebooks and was currently positioned within shouting distance of the private library.

He'd read through some of Jaenelle's notebook last night. She'd been an adolescent when she'd worked on the Craft written in that book. Some things were staggering in their simple brilliance—simple for a person who could draw from an unfathomable well of power. Other bits of Craft were simply staggering, and he had no idea, none at all, how she had combined the various items she had used in order to do what she had done.

He did know that so much of what Jaenelle had created was beyond his skill, let alone what Zoey and the other youngsters currently living at the Hall could safely and successfully achieve. Which made him appreciate the need for getting those notebooks away from everyone who didn't have the strength or training to deal with what could come out of those spells.

Are we ready? Daemon asked Holt.

We're ready.

Holding Jaenelle's notebook in one hand and the summoning web in the other, Daemon engaged the spell, staying tightly focused on summoning the notebooks that had belonged to Jaenelle, the coven, and the boyos who had lived at the Hall.

Books on several shelves started to move, as if something was trying to push them out of the way while the spell in the summoning web rolled through the Hall.

The summoning went on for a minute, maybe two, because he'd guessed that it would take a while to reach the farthest ends of the Hall. During that time, he kept watch on the books being pushed closer to the ends of the shelves.

Then . . .

"Prince!" Holt shouted. "Stop! *Stop!*"

Daemon disengaged the summoning web and heard the flutter of paper before everything quieted.

Holt burst into the room.

"What's wrong?" Daemon demanded.

"Beale said the overhead shelves in the storage room connected to your study must contain a lot of those notebooks. He heard some banging and crashing behind the door, as if something was trying to escape. And there must have been some loose papers in with the rest, because *those* managed to slip under the door and tried to get out of the study. Beale put a shield on the study door before any of the papers bolted."

Daemon tried to clear the tickle out of his throat. Damn tickle. "Anyone else find any notebooks?"

"The men residing in the protectors' square of rooms captured a few," Holt said. "Stands to reason, since that square of rooms was used by the boyos when they lived at the Hall. I gather the Scelties wrestled a few notebooks into submission, so those might be a bit chewed."

"Lovely," Daemon murmured.

Holt hesitated. "One of the girls tried to vanish one of the notebooks, but Helene was also watching that room and put a shield on the notebook and prevented that."

He could guess which girl had tried to take what wasn't hers.

"That one is going to be trouble, Sadi," Karla had said. *"Watch her—and be glad she's not a Queen."*

Alvita wasn't a natural Black Widow, or a natural Healer either. He hadn't decided yet if she truly wasn't skilled in Craft—Hell's fire, Breen was still a puppy and was better at air walking and creating witchlight than this girl—or if it was a ruse so that he would spend more time working with her than with the other girls.

She already had two marks against her for inappropriate displays of her body. Since she wasn't close to being old enough to have her Virgin Night, he wondered if she simply couldn't handle being around males—especially him and Daemonar.

"I'll gather the notebooks in this room," Daemon said. "You, Helene, and some of the senior staff should confiscate the rest and bring them to my study."

"Yes, sir."

When he returned to his study, he found Beale listening for whatever was behind the storage room door.

"Haven't heard anything since the summoning stopped," Beale said.

Daemon released a slow breath. "Then open the door."

Beale had to lean against the door to shove the notebooks out of the way in order to look into the room. "Mother Night."

"And may the Darkness be merciful," Daemon said, looking over Beale's shoulder. He stepped back and Beale closed the door before Holt and other members of the Hall's staff brought in what the summoning spell had revealed.

Considering the number of notebooks Saetan had found over the years and had already stored out of reach, the number that had still been stuffed in various bookshelves was impressive, in an unnerving sort of way.

"Is that it?" Daemon asked Holt and Beale after they'd made an effort to sort the notebooks by the handwriting on the first pages. At least the boyos had written their names on the first pages—most of the time—but the coven had used just an initial when they identified a notebook at all, and he couldn't tell if a notebook had belonged to Karla or Kalush, Grizande or Gabrielle. Since Karla and Gabrielle were Black Widows and Healers as well as Queens, knowing who had worked on those spells was important.

"Yes, Prince, I believe . . . ," Beale began.

Daemonar walked into the study, holding one of the young Scelties, who had a notebook between his teeth.

"It was the only way to bring it to you intact," Daemonar said.

Daemon smiled at the Sceltie, who gave Daemonar's hip an enthusiastic thumping with his tail. "Thank you for bringing this to me."

For a moment Daemon wondered if the young Warlord was going to relinquish his prize, but the dog was happy to be praised and, with only a little reluctance, released the notebook when Daemon took hold of the other end.

"Mikal says the Scelties should have some playtime and a treat for doing a good job of helping round up the notebooks," Daemonar said.

More enthusiastic tail thumping.

"Excellent suggestion," Daemon agreed. "Why don't you, Mikal, and any other youngsters who are interested take care of that?"

"Yes, sir." Daemonar gave him an assessing look before leaving the room.

"Are you thinking that more than one youngster tried to hold on to a notebook?" Holt asked.

"I'm thinking that someone who hasn't been around them for very long doesn't appreciate how keen a Sceltie's hearing is or how much a dog understands when humans are revealing secrets."

"Well," Holt said after a moment. "The kindred always were a good way of sorting who belonged at the Hall and who didn't."

Once Beale and Holt left to resume their normal duties, Daemon put Black shields around each stack of notebooks and took them into the storage room. Mindful of Karla's comment that the notes the boyos had made might be useful to the boys currently in residence, he would look at those first. For now, he had the business of holding the leash on the Hall's residents as well as ruling a Territory and reviewing reports about some of the family's other estates.

But he wondered if the Scelties had already decided that someone didn't belong.

ELEVEN

Since she had to talk to him anyway, Surreal contacted Lucivar on a Gray psychic thread and arranged to meet him at his eyrie the following day.

She had ridden the Winds without the encumbrance of a Coach, so she didn't bother with the landing web that was on flat ground below the eyrie. Instead, she dropped from the Winds and landed on the flagstone courtyard right outside Lucivar and Marian's home.

"Surreal!"

She turned and saw Marian walking toward her, carrying a few flowers that bloomed in early spring. She felt a stab of guilt that she hadn't replied to the last couple of letters Marian had sent. She just wasn't sure what to say. That the relief of having renegotiated her marriage with Daemon was almost painful some days? That she had no desire to herd the group of adolescents now occupying the Hall and she used her position as Sadi's second-in-command as an excuse to stay away from the family seat? That every time she had to deal with Saetien it felt like someone scraping a dull knife along the edges of a still-bleeding wound?

She didn't want to say any of those things. Sometimes you just had to fill the days with duty until you were ready to give sorrow a place to exist for a while.

Marian opened the wooden gate that separated her garden from the flagstone courtyard and hurried toward Surreal.

"Lucivar said you were coming to visit today. He's gone down to The Tavern to pick up a couple of steak and ale pies for the midday meal and should be back soon. Come in. You're looking well." Marian hooked her arm through Surreal's and led her into the eyrie. "Hang up your coat while I put these in water. I usually leave the flowers where they grow, but today I wanted a few blooms for the table."

"They're lovely." Surreal hung up her coat on the coattree near the door and followed Marian to the big kitchen. "But they came from your garden, so that's not a surprise. I heard you're displaying some of your loom art in an exhibition in Dharo."

Marian blushed. "Yes. It's an honor for someone who isn't Dharo born to be invited, but I *do* use wool from Dharo—and from Scelt."

"Considering the family connection to the Sceltie school in Maghre—and its little farm—how could you *not* use wool that came from Sceltie-raised sheep?"

"Those poor sheep," Marian said as she arranged the flowers.

"Better to let Scelties herd the woolly sheep than have them herding us."

Marian laughed.

Surreal went to the cupboards above the kitchen counters and reached for the plates. "How many?"

"Just the three of us. Andulvar is having his meal with Nurian and Rothvar's children." Marian stepped up beside Surreal and opened the silverware drawer. "We weren't sure what you wanted to talk about—or how private you wanted it to be."

She set the plates on the table. "There are things I want to discuss with both of you."

"Are you all right?" Marian asked quietly.

She laughed. "Me? Yes. But you might want to pour your husband a large mug of ale to go with his meal. He'll need it."

"Oh, dear."

Marian didn't have a chance to say anything else before the front door opened and Lucivar's presence—and sexual heat—filled the eyrie.

Surreal grabbed the back of a kitchen chair, over-whelmed by the heat. Then it was gone—or so diminished that it was almost unnoticeable.

"Surreal?" Marian helped her into the chair.

"I'm all right." She looked toward the archway that connected the kitchen with the big front room and saw Lucivar standing there, watching her. "Just took a funny turn for a moment."

"There is a kind of cleansing spell that absorbs the heat, but it takes a few moments to start working," Marian said.

"I'm fine now. Truly."

Lucivar set the steak and ale pies on the table, then backed away. "It's like a poison for you now, isn't it? The trouble you and Daemon had burned out your tolerance for the heat. Is that true of every Warlord Prince you cross paths with, or just the ones who wear Jewels darker than the Red?"

Why the Red? Surreal thought. Then she knew what he was saying. Did she also have trouble with the sexual heat of Warlord Princes who wore the Gray? "I don't know. I haven't thought about it that way." But she would now that he had raised the question.

A cleansing spell that could absorb a Warlord Prince's sexual heat. If she'd had access to something like that when Sadi's heat had gone into its last phase and become intolerable . . .

Except a spell like that hadn't existed because it had taken all the mistakes she and Sadi had made to bring back the one person who had the knowledge and power to create such a spell. Without Witch's skill in Craft, would Marian be able to continue living with Lucivar? Had she unwittingly spared these two people from a heartbreaking choice?

"Are you okay with me being here?" Lucivar asked.

"Yes. The heat is quiet now," Surreal replied.

"You sit," Marian said when Surreal pushed up to help finish setting the table. "You still look a bit peaky. Maybe some ale would do you good."

Lucivar went into the pantry and returned with three glass mugs filled with ale.

She liked Lucivar and Marian, had been easy around them for a lot of years. Now? She thought Marian still considered her a friend, but she wasn't sure about Lucivar. Was she an outsider or still considered a member of the family who needed breathing room?

"Does Helton share any of the gossip about the Hall with you?" Lucivar asked as they settled into their meal.

"Helton is the butler at the town house, not at the Hall," Surreal said primly. "He never gossips."

"Uh-huh."

"He does inform me of any developments that Beale feels the staff at the town house should know about."

"Did Beale inform Helton about the spell in the window?" Lucivar cut several slices off a block of sharp yellow cheese, then offered the slices to her and Marian before taking a couple for himself.

"Not that I'm aware of, but I haven't been to the town house for several days." Surreal bit into a slice of cheese and wondered if Marian would be upset if she borrowed her rolling pin and beat Lucivar over the head with it to encourage him to talk instead of baiting her.

"In that case, I'll tell you about the damn window." And he did.

After almost snorting ale out of her nose at one point, Surreal gave up trying to eat while Lucivar told them about the window that swore in Eyrien and about the spell that roamed from one window to another, and how Karla had to come to the Hall with a summoning spell to coax the window's spell to a spot where the long-awaited apology could be issued to end the bit of Craft Saetan had put into a window so long ago.

"Was Daemon upset?" Marian finally asked. She picked up her fork but looked like she wasn't sure what to do with it.

"Eat," Lucivar said, concentrating on his own meal. "I think he's feeling grateful that he has stout locks on his study door—and that Holt and Beale have seen this before and keep assuring him that it could be worse."

"That's not much comfort," Surreal said.

Lucivar smiled. "Apparently he's been given a reason to believe it is."

Saying *I'm so glad I'm not living there* would have been heartfelt but maybe not tactful.

Speaking of tactful . . .

She waited until Lucivar had cleared the table and Marian made coffee.

"Several things," she said, turning to Lucivar. "First, Saetien wants to locate Wilhelmina Benedict."

"Why?" Lucivar growled.

"Because a broken Black Widow said this is something she needs to do." She waited for Lucivar to stop swearing. "I'm sure Geoffrey will have the information, but I don't want to go to the Keep, because I don't want to call attention to this request. You're there all the time talking to Karla, so your presence wouldn't be noted as unusual."

"You still pissed about Witch sending the girl to Briarwood? Or the memory of Briarwood?" Lucivar asked.

"Sometimes," Surreal admitted. "I'm grateful to Witch for many things. I'm even grateful to her for that, since the alternative would have been Saetien's execution. But I'm not ready to go up there and see her."

"You wouldn't have to see Witch. People go to the Keep for information all the time."

Funny how this aversion had come on slowly, quietly. "I don't want to go to the Keep."

Lucivar studied her for a long moment. "All right. I'll talk to Geoffrey and find out what I can. Anything else?"

Surreal eyed his mug of coffee. "You might want to add something to that. Something with some kick."

Marian sat up, looking alarmed. "Has something happened?"

She looked at Marian. "Jillian is ready for her Virgin Night."

"Oh," Marian breathed.

Neither of them looked at Lucivar, who was completely still in an absolutely terrifying way.

"She's considered it a couple of times, but when the men who perform that service found out she was the Demon Prince's daughter, their enthusiasm, to say nothing of their ability, withered on the vine." Since Marian looked confused, Surreal held up a forefinger and then curled it.

Marian burst out laughing.

"Why now?" Lucivar said. "Who's the prick who wants her under him?"

Oh, no. That wasn't part of *this* discussion. "Now is because Jillian is also ready to make the Offering to the Darkness, and if she reaches the full potential of her mature strength, she'll wear Sapphire—and it will be more difficult to find someone who can see her safely through her Virgin Night."

This is hard for him, Marian said on a distaff thread. *Especially after seeing Daemon's report on how many girls the coven of malice destroyed.*

I know, Surreal replied. Then she turned to Lucivar. "This is what I'm proposing. There is an establishment in Amdarh that can accommodate this rite of passage. It has the advantage of being a place Jillian isn't likely to visit again, so she won't have to associate a place she usually visits with her experience of that night. I will go with her, and help her if she runs into any trouble. I can do that without scaring the man into impotence."

Lucivar snorted. "Only if he doesn't know you."

True. "You and Daemon can wait for us at the town house. Then we can all have a celebratory dinner and acknowledge that Jillian is now a woman who can take a lover."

"We can acknowledge that when the sun shines in Hell."

Marian huffed out an exasperated breath. "Lucivar! She's grown up. She's reached her majority, and she's ready to have sex. This is no longer your decision."

He stared at his wife.

"And Jillian would like Marian and Nurian—and me—to accompany her when she goes to make the Offering to the Darkness."

Lucivar said nothing. He simply pushed away from the table and walked out of the kitchen.

"He feels excluded," Marian said quietly.

"He's too strong. So is Sadi." Surreal breathed out. "The Darkness only knows what their presence might do during the Offering. Not that they would interfere, but the Offering tests everything you are, and you can't afford to be thinking of anyone else—or feeling the presence of anyone else. I might decline to join her for that reason. I was alone when I made the Offering. I'll ask around, find out if someone else's power is really a concern. I'll stay with Lucivar while you and Nurian are with Jillian. Help keep him steady—or at least keep him from trying to break walls with his fists."

Marian sighed. "That would be good." She hesitated. "My father never cared about me enough to be concerned about any of these things."

"And I didn't want mine anywhere near me. We'll just have to help him as best we can."

Lucivar stayed focused on driving his fists into one of the punching bags that had been hung in the communal eyrie. They'd been acquired recently as a way for the Eyrien warriors to keep their skills honed without damaging another person. He knew the moment when Rothvar, his second-in-command, entered the eyrie, but he kept his fists—and his temper—focused on the bag.

"You want to spar?" Rothvar asked.

"No. Stay away from me."

Rothvar kept his distance but didn't leave. He just

waited, saying nothing for a minute. "I felt the Gray arrive in Ebon Rih. Lady Surreal?"

"Yeah."

"Is there a problem?"

Lucivar beat on the punching bag for a minute before he could answer the question. "Jillian says she's ready for her Virgin Night."

"Hell's fire." Rothvar blew out a breath. "She's at the age . . ."

"To let a man do with her what you or I do with a woman?"

Rothvar paced and swore for a minute. "That's different."

"I don't think either of us is going to be able to explain that to our girl." He wasn't sure he could explain the difference to anyone who had breasts—including his wife and his Queen.

Rothvar continued to pace while Lucivar slammed his fists into the punching bag.

Finally Rothvar stopped pacing and Lucivar stopped punching.

"She have her eye on someone?" Rothvar asked.

Lucivar nodded. "I'm sure Surreal knows who it is, but she won't say. Not to me." He could ask Daemon to find out, but there was always a chance that the Sadist would dislike Jillian's choice enough to . . . remove . . . him from the living.

"Gotta find someone trained who will see the girl through this," Rothvar said.

"Surreal is going to take care of that. And she's going to stand as Jillian's escort." Lucivar snarled. "Apparently no one's cock will stand up long enough to do the job if the Demon Prince is nearby keeping watch."

Rothvar coughed. "I'd take you over Surreal any day."

"Yeah, well, an assassin does things quietly, so it's easy not to see how dangerous she is."

"Probably for the best." Rothvar rubbed the back of his neck. "I think Nurian will be relieved to have it done. It's a risk. It always is. But it's one night instead of Jillian being vulnerable every day."

He knew that. He did. "After that, she'll make the Offering to the Darkness. She says she's ready."

"I guess we're going to have to strap some steel to our spines and not get in her way."

Lucivar rubbed his sore knuckles and sighed. "I guess we'll have to do that."

TWELVE

Surreal checked into a room at The Tavern. Marian had invited her to stay with the family, but the guest rooms in the Yaslana eyrie held too many difficult memories that she didn't want to deal with. The rooms at The Tavern held memories, too, but the Rihlanders were a short-lived race, and each generation "freshened" the look of the rooms. Same room but not the *same*.

Ebon Rih also held a lot of memories for her, both good and bad, but there was room to move there, room to breathe.

After arranging with Marian and Nurian to have dinner at a dining house that specialized in seafood, she'd gone down to Riada—and The Tavern. On her own for a few hours, she wandered the village streets. She'd been thinking about purchasing a house for herself somewhere, a residence that wasn't part of the SaDiablo holdings. She'd toyed with the idea of settling into a village, but she hadn't found any village or any house that called to her.

The truth was, she liked living in Amdarh, liked living in the town house. Dhemlan's capital city had neighborhoods, and she could take a healthy walk to some of her favorite shops if she didn't want to use the family's conveyances or hire a horse-drawn cab. She liked the feel of the city and the variety of talks and entertainments available. She liked all the theaters.

But the town house wasn't hers, and if she purchased one in the city, that news would be all over Amdarh before the ink was dry on the deed, and whatever protection her wedding ring provided for Daemon would be lost. That would be dangerous for everyone, especially now that Sadi's Queen was once more in residence at the Keep.

She'd figure things out. In the meantime, she was here to request information about someone who was never mentioned.

She didn't know what had happened between them or exactly when it happened. She remembered just that Wilhelmina Benedict had made a choice—and Jaenelle Angelline had accepted it.

Surreal stopped in front of a store window and pressed a hand to her chest, trying to ease the ache there. Years ago, Witch had helped her release the burden of all the girls she hadn't been able to save—including herself. Maybe, if she helped Saetien on this part of the girl's journey, it would help this new wound to heal.

Nurian and Marian arrived together and knocked on the door.

"When Lucivar heard about our dinner plans, he arranged for us to ride in a fancy aristo carriage drawn by two horses and including a driver who is exclusively ours for the evening," Marian said, laughing.

"Hell's fire." Surreal stepped back to let them enter her room. "What does he think we're going to do besides eat dinner? Drive around the village, drinking sparkling wine while singing bawdy songs?"

"Now, there's a thought," Nurian said. "And I'll apologize now for any remarks I may make about food you leave on your plate. I haven't had a dinner with just adults in a long time."

"The three of us should take a couple of days in Amdarh to go to the theater and some place that's a female indulgence," Surreal said.

"That would be lovely," Marian said with a sigh. Then she called in a sealed paper and held it out. "Lucivar brought back an answer from the Keep just before I was ready to leave. And he said to tell you he'll accept whatever arrangements you and Jillian make for her Virgin Night."

"Do you want us to wait outside?" Nurian asked when Surreal hesitated to take the paper.

Surreal shook her head, took the message, and broke the seal.

> *After a brief stay at SaDiablo Hall, Wilhelmina Benedict resided on the Isle of Scelt for the rest of her life. If more information is required, the Seneschal and I suggest that the person looking for answers should begin the journey in Maghre.*
> *—Geoffrey, historian/librarian*

"Did you get the answer you wanted?" Marian asked.

Surreal handed her the paper and waited while she and Nurian read it.

"That's . . . sparse," Nurian said. "Wouldn't the Keep have more information about one of the Blood?"

"I'm sure they know a great deal more than that," Surreal replied. "But I think the answer underneath these words is this: anyone who wants to know about Wilhelmina Benedict will have to earn the information. And the first step is going to Maghre."

As the women went out to the carriage, she wondered how Sadi was going to respond to his daughter's request to travel to the other side of the Realm.

THIRTEEN

Daemonar dealt the cards and wondered why Lord Morris, one of the instructors teaching at the Hall, had insinuated himself into this social evening of playing cards. He couldn't kick about an instructor being present, since Raine was also at the table, along with Mikal, Holt, and Weston, but tonight there was a forced friendliness about Morris that seemed . . . off . . . in a way that made Daemonar uneasy.

Either Uncle Daemon had missed something when he interviewed Morris for the instructor's position, or Morris was very adept at hiding some things about his nature—even from a man who had razor-sharp instincts when it came to assessing other people.

Or whatever was off about Morris was something Uncle Daemon did know about and considered a personal flaw rather than a potential threat.

I think he's a gambler, and that could be the reason he resigned from his last position—although there was nothing in his references to indicate he wasn't suitable for teaching at the Hall, Holt told Daemonar on a personal psychic thread, as if his thoughts were following the same path. *He's been unhappy about how strictly the betting limits are enforced when the staff play games of chance.*

He could try his luck in Halaway, Daemonar pointed out.

*And have someone who serves Halaway's Queen sitting at the table, who will then make a comment to his Queen about the amounts Morris was wagering, and have *her* voice a concern to Prince Sadi? I don't think Lord Morris is willing to risk that—yet.*

We can't control other people's lives. Not to the extent of taking away choices. His father and uncle were firm about that, since Warlord Princes—and Scelties—were sometimes *too* helpful when it came to herding someone into making the correct choice, and it required experience and training to know when to draw a line and when to let someone make their own mistakes.

No, Holt agreed, *but we can wonder if a man prone to making large bets—and acquiring large debts—might be tempted to sell information to cover his markers.*

Yeah, he was beginning to wonder the same thing. And he wondered if Morris had invited himself to this game tonight because Uncle Daemon was having dinner with the Queen of Halaway, her Steward, and her Consort and wouldn't be anywhere near this part of the Hall—or be one of the men playing cards.

Whatever reason Morris had for getting into this game wouldn't be a problem now, because of the other male who had joined them tonight. Liath wanted to learn a human card game, so the original playing cards were removed from the table, and Daemonar produced the deck of cards for hawks and hares—a card game played by Eyrien children. Since he was the only one familiar with the game, Daemonar dealt the cards while he explained the rules.

The Sceltie Warlord Prince sat on the chair to Daemonar's left, his front paws resting on the table and his cards floating on air in front of him—and curved in a way that prevented any curious human from seeing the cards.

Did Liath assume humans would cheat? Or had he *observed* a human cheating?

"All right, gentlemen, here we go." Daemonar set the remaining cards on the table and turned over the top card. It was a simple enough game, the object being to collect the most hares either by matching a pair of hares or by having a hawk "strike" and take a hare.

After the players had all taken a turn, Weston said, "Liath, I was wondering how the Scelties who are helping Prince Sadi were chosen."

Are you sure you want to know? Daemonar asked Weston on a psychic thread. He used one of his hawks to "strike" a hare and took that card.

He's a Green-Jeweled Warlord Prince, Weston replied. *Don't *you* want to know?*

Actually, he did. The Sceltie had gone through the Offering to the Darkness, and the Green was his Jewel of rank. That maturity, compared to that of the other Scelties currently in residence, made him the pack leader. That maturity and Jewel also made him an adult male who could be reasoned with, up to a point, but who wouldn't back down from a fight, because a Warlord Prince was a Warlord Prince whether he walked on two legs or four.

We are needed, Liath replied on a general communication thread they could all hear.

"Yes, but why were *you* chosen?" Weston asked.

Liath stared at his cards before using Craft to put down a matching hare and collect the pair. Finally he said, *There is a human girl who lives in Maghre near the Sceltie school. She was hurt when she was young. One leg doesn't work right and she has . . . puppy brain . . . and wears a Yellow Jewel.*

Daemonar translated that to mean there had been some serious injury to the girl's brain that the Healer wasn't able to repair, and the girl was, in some ways, simple and most likely would never be able to do more than basic Craft.

A bad male came to the village. Many females liked him, but Lord Kieran and other human males did not, so the Scelties kept watch over the younger females in the village, since that male wanted to sniff around them more than the adult females.

Hell's fire, Daemonar thought, discarding a hare and taking a card from the deck when it was his turn.

He found the Caitie girl picking flowers in a field and tried to mate with her. Liath put down a hare matching the one Daemonar had just discarded and collected the pair. *She was on the ground crying and didn't want to mate, but he pushed his pants down and ripped her clothes. She said "stop" and "no," but he didn't, so I bit him. He screamed a lot and held his male sac. I got the Caitie girl away from him and summoned the human guards, who took him to the Healer because he was bleeding.*

Daemonar glanced around the table. Morris looked like he was going to be sick. Raine had lost all color in his face. Even Mikal, who had plenty of experience with Scelties, and Weston, who was a sword and shield, looked a little woozy.

"You bit off his balls?" Daemonar asked, struggling to sound unconcerned—and struggling equally hard not to put a shield around his cock and balls. But that would attract Liath's attention and make the Sceltie wonder about the reactions of the humans around him.

Just one, Liath said.

Morris knocked over his chair in his haste to get out of the room. Daemonar hoped the man made it to the nearest toilet before throwing up.

Liath, clearly confused by Morris's reaction, looked at the rest of the men. *The Healer said the other ball would work well enough that the male would be able to make puppies if there was a female anywhere in Scelt who would want him for a mate.*

"You didn't stay to become the Caitie girl's special friend?" Daemonar asked.

There is a colt who is the Caitie girl's special friend, and Lord Kieran thought I would be more useful here. Prince Sadi agreed.

Yes, Daemon Sadi would definitely view a Green-Jeweled Warlord Prince who wouldn't hesitate to castrate any male who got too frisky around the girls as an asset. And Lord Kieran had probably breathed a sigh of relief at getting this particular Sceltie away from his own village.

A nearby flash of female fear, of panic. Someone close by was in trouble.

Before Daemonar and Weston could push away from the table, Liath leaped out of his chair and ran out of the room. *The Alvita boo-hoo girl is attacking Allis and Breen!*

Daemonar was only a few steps behind the Sceltie, and Weston was right behind him. He saw Alvita fiddling with the door of Uncle Daemon's sitting room, felt the clash of Allis's Rose Jewel with Alvita's Rose Jewel, heard Breen's frantic barking.

Daemonar wasn't sure there was anything he could do that wouldn't cause an explosion of power if his Green tangled with Liath's while the Sceltie formed a Green shield in front of the door. But instead of forming a shield, Liath charged the girl. Daemonar saw Alvita notice the dog and raise an arm as if to release a blast of power from the Rose Jewel in her ring.

And he watched, because he hadn't understood the intent behind Liath's charge, as the Sceltie launched himself at the girl and closed his jaws around her wrist. Liath twisted in the air, Alvita screamed as the Sceltie's move knocked her off her feet, and when she landed on the floor, she showed everyone the lacy bra and panties that were the only garments she was wearing under her robe.

Fool, Daemonar thought as his heart pounded and the girl wailed. Aware of Weston standing a few steps behind him, snapping at someone to stay back, he pointed at Liath, who was snarling and worrying the girl's bleeding wrist. "Back off now, Prince Liath. Let her go, and *back off.* We'll deal with her now."

"Will you?" a deep voice purred.

The air in the corridor turned so cold, it hurt to breathe. The blood dripping from Alvita's wrist froze before it hit the floor.

Liath released the girl and backed away, growling to let everyone know he was *angry.* But a Green-Jeweled Warlord Prince wasn't the biggest threat right now.

May the Darkness have mercy on us, Daemonar thought as the Sadist dropped the sight shield and stood on the other side of the girl.

The Sadist stared at Alvita, his gold eyes glazed and sleepy—the only warning that his cold rage was viciously sharp and lethal. Then he looked past Daemonar and purred, "Lord Beale. You'll handle this?"

"I will, High Lord," Beale replied. "You'll want the Coach first thing in the morning?"

"I will." The Sadist looked down at Alvita again and said too softly, "If the bitch harmed the puppies, she'll forfeit her skin." Then he stepped around the girl, carefully opened the door to his sitting room, and slipped inside.

Footmen arrived with a stretcher to take Alvita to the healing room, where Lady Nadene, the Healer who looked after the Hall's residents, already waited.

"I'm supposed to go," Arlene said. "Lady Nadene requires my presence."

"She has summoned the three Healers in training," Beale said, looking at Weston when the sword and shield hesitated to allow Arlene to pass.

Weston stepped aside enough for Arlene to slip past him, but blocked Zoey, Titian, and the other girls.

"What's going on?" Zoey asked. "Can we help?"

"No," Weston said.

"The best thing you can do is stay in tonight," Daemonar said, meaning the girls should stay in their square of rooms.

Zoey looked toward Sadi's sitting room door. "But . . ."

The door opened just enough for Allis to slip out. She rushed over to Liath, not Zoey. The Sceltie Warlord Prince gave the young witch a thorough sniff and a lick on her muzzle. Satisfied, Liath trotted off and Allis leaped into Zoey's arms.

Helene and some of the senior housemaids arrived to clean the corridor and deal with the blood soaking into the carpet. The Hall's housekeeper gave the men a sharp look and said, "Don't you have somewhere else to be?"

"Yes, Lady," Mikal said.

They retreated to the room where they'd been playing cards.

"Any guesses why Liath attacked the way he did?" Holt asked, looking at Mikal. "His Jewel is a lot darker than Alvita's. He could have put a shield in front of the door to keep her out." Now he looked at Daemonar. "You hesitated because you expected him to shield the door and keep her from getting into the room, but he was savage."

"He said she was attacking Allis and Breen," Daemonar said.

"But she wasn't *attacking*. She was trying to get into a room she had no business entering—and thank the Darkness she didn't cross that threshold—but Liath's response was not appropriate unless there is more to this than we're aware of." Holt called in a bottle of whiskey and some glasses. He poured a couple of fingers in each glass and passed them around.

Weston blew out a breath and said, "Speaking as a sword and shield, if a threat has been made, you respond to the adversary's next move as an attack. You don't wait; you don't hesitate. If you do, the Queen you're protecting could be harmed."

Mikal downed his whiskey and set the glass on the table. "I'd better locate the rest of the Scelties and find out if there had been a previous threat that they didn't tell me about. And then I need to get home." Home was a cottage in Halaway that he shared with Daemon's mother, Tersa, and Keely, the Sceltie who was a journeymaid Black Widow.

"You'll let us know if there's more trouble on the horizon?" Daemonar asked.

Mikal nodded and left.

Raine sank into a chair. "Perhaps tomorrow all the Warlord Princes in residence should have a discussion about appropriate responses." He looked at Daemonar and tried to smile. "Like those 'what if . . . ?' exercises you're so fond of."

"I'd like to sit in on that lesson," Weston said, looking thoughtful. "I didn't see it clearly until tonight. We've all been so busy settling into the new arrangement, I didn't appreciate the real intent." He looked at the other men. "This isn't a school, despite the subjects being taught. This isn't just protection for the youngsters who were targeted by the coven of malice and might still be targeted by someone who wants to destroy young Queens. This is a training ground for Queens and the Blood who might serve in courts. Five Queens living here, each with a group of friends who are drawn to a particular girl. Being here is the equivalent of doing an apprenticeship in an established Queen's court, but more demanding because they're all young and learning together."

"Yes," Holt said. "And more demanding because they're living under the hand of a Black-Jeweled Warlord Prince who has seen the best—and the worst—of what Queens and their courts can do. Everyone who works at the Hall is part of the training because aristos aren't the only people who will live in a Queen's territory, and a Queen and those who serve in her First Circle need to learn how to interact with all her people."

"Including the kindred," Daemonar added.

Weston set his glass on the table. "I'll check on Lady Zoela. I'm sure she has questions about what happened. Allis will have told her what she knows from a Sceltie's point of view, and I'll tell her what happened on the other side of the door."

Holt turned his head, as if listening to something. Then he sighed. "Messenger bag coming in from one of the estates. I'd better go down and sort through what was sent, in case there is something that requires the High Lord's attention before he leaves in the morning."

Raine and Daemonar left the sitting room and went out to the open courtyard that made the square's interior space.

"Not what you expected when my uncle offered you this job, is it?" Daemonar asked quietly.

"No," Raine replied just as quietly. "But it occurs to me

that this was Prince Rainier's life. From the things my father and aunt told me about our family's history, Rainier's close family members were uncomfortable around him because he was a dark-Jeweled Warlord Prince. I think some of them felt guilty about that, but they couldn't put aside their gut-level fear and he became this . . . blank. An empty chair at family gatherings. The name unspoken. And yet he knew, *really* knew, some of the most powerful Territory Queens who ruled in Kaeleer."

"He more than knew those Queens, Raine. He was a friend. He became part of this family. You should talk to Holt. Rainier was Uncle Daemon's secretary before Holt took on the job." Daemonar looked up at the night sky. "Weston's right. This is a training ground—and it's very important to pay attention to the lessons that aren't in the books as well as the lessons that are."

Zoey and the other five girls listened to Weston's report. Concise and factual—and very unsatisfying.

"*Why* did Liath attack that way?" When she was younger, she'd had a Sceltie Prince who had been her special friend, and now there was Allis, and she'd never thought a *Sceltie* would *attack* a human. She'd gotten only a glimpse of Alvita, but Arlene, who had sent one message on a psychic thread before Lady Nadene began the healing, said the damage to Alvita's arm was very bad.

"Liath believed she was a threat to Allis and Breen," Weston replied. "He dealt with the threat."

"You wear Sapphire," Titian said. "You could have stopped him."

"Ladies, Warlord Princes are a law unto themselves, and Liath is a Green-Jeweled Warlord Prince who has been trained to defend, to protect, and to fight. He could have torn out her throat. He could have hit her with a blast of Green power that would have exploded her chest and splattered her all over the corridor. He didn't do that. But it's my opinion that Liath's attack spared Alvita from whatever the High Lord's response would have been to her outrageous behavior."

He's angry, Zoey thought. *At Alvita? Or at us for not understanding something about Liath's response?* "What happens now?"

"She crossed a line, Lady Zoela," Weston replied. "Lady Nadene will do the healing tonight to repair the damage, and tomorrow Alvita will be taken home—and I doubt she will ever be welcome in this house again. And I think there will be several young men who will feel grateful for that decision."

Zoey winced. She *had* noticed that all the boys who weren't friends with Dinah and her coven avoided Alvita as much as possible without being scolded for being discourteous or flat-out rude. "Thank you for explaining things, Lord Weston. We'll be staying in this evening."

Jhett made a soothing brew, and Titian sent a request to the apprentice cooks who were tending the auxiliary kitchen. When they had steaming mugs in front of them, and plates of pastries, cheeses, crackers, and grapes to nibble on, Zoey ventured onto what felt like dangerous ground. She was friendly with the other four Queens in residence, but it did seem like the girls had separated into distinct groups while the boys mostly flowed in and around the groups, not displaying more loyalty to one Queen than to the others. Even Daemonar didn't show a preference. Well, *maybe* he showed a little preference for her, but that was because she and Titian were close and he treated her like another sister instead of a Queen.

"Dinah is going to be upset about this," Zoey said. "Alvita was one of her friends."

"Do you think Dinah will be blamed?" Laureen asked. "Alvita did brag about flirting with some of the boys and didn't care who overheard her, but flirting isn't bad. It's hard *not* to flirt a little when you like someone and would like him to pay some attention to you."

"Flirting with words isn't the same as lifting your skirt and showing off your 'womanly parts' to tease the boys,"

Jhett said. "Especially when you're years away from safely having your Virgin Night, and your taunting them could end with them being executed for trying something they're forbidden to do."

"Flirting with words also doesn't break any of Uncle Daemon's rules," Titian pointed out. "We all signed an *agreement* with him that spelled out the rules of living at the Hall and the consequences of breaking them. *Especially* the rules about sex."

Banishment being at the top of the list of possible consequences for breaking the rules.

Titian slipped her hand into Zoey's and squeezed lightly. She looked worried about Zoey's reaction to Liath's actions.

"Warlord Princes are born to stand on killing fields," Zoey said. "They are fighters. Predators. That is what they are. Even when they're relaxed and friendly, that doesn't change their nature."

There were five Warlord Princes in residence. Seven if she counted Prince Sadi and Prince Liath. Predators. Killers. Her grandmother Zhara, who was the Queen of Amdarh, often said that Warlord Princes were dangerous assets in a court, and holding the leash on one of them required great skill—and great care.

Zoey had known Prince Sadi was dangerous. *Everyone* knew he was dangerous. But that hadn't stopped Alvita from trying to sneak into his suite and . . . do what?

"Should I have done something? Said something about Alvita's flirting?" Zoey whispered.

"Would she have listened to you?" Jhett asked. "She had been given two warnings already for inappropriate behavior. We all thought her actions were minor things, stupid things. But showing up at Prince Sadi's door dressed like that would have earned her banishment even if she had done nothing else. For one thing, he's *married*, and nobody who wants to stay alive propositions a married Warlord Prince. Hell's fire, girls our age should *know* that."

"You're right. She shouldn't have tried to get into his

private suite—unless she'd done something else and was hoping to use her state of undress to convince him to ignore her other indiscretion," Zoey said. *Or intended to use being alone with him as a way to compromise his honor?*

Titian shuddered. "If Alvita intended to claim he'd invited her to his suite and then accuse him of being inappropriate unless he did what she wanted, she wouldn't be going home now. She'd be going to Hell—or to Ebon Askavi to answer to his Queen."

They nibbled pastries and considered that for a few minutes.

"We'll have to be careful tomorrow," Titian said. "Uncle Daemon will be gone and Beale will be the dominant male at the Hall, so everyone else will be on edge because . . . you know."

Because the last time Beale had been left in charge, Jaenelle Saetien had overruled him and people had died.

Yes, they had to be careful. *She* had to be careful. Alvita's banishment was a harsh reminder that the protection given at the Hall could be forfeited by a girl who crossed a particular line. But how could you learn if you didn't try new things?

Zoey looked at Titian. "Do you think your aunt Surreal would be willing to talk to us about flirting?"

FOURTEEN

VILLAGE IN DHEMLAN

Daemon half listened to Alvita's parents' protests and justifications. What they said wouldn't change his decision any more than the girl's tears and pleas and delusional variations of "but you *could* want me" that he'd listened to while he drove the Coach to the girl's home village.

He was far more interested in the District Queen who didn't seem surprised at the girl's behavior and wouldn't meet his eyes. Yes, Alvita had been on the list of young witches who were targets for the coven of malice. Yes, she had the potential to wear an Opal when she reached her mature strength, and that had been taken into account, along with the District Queen's letter of recommendation. Which is why that Queen was also here this morning. He hoped she had a good reason for that letter. He really did.

"Enough," Daemon said, using Craft to make his voice roll through the room like soft thunder. "SaDiablo Hall is not a private school. You did not pay tuition for your daughter to be there. You do not pay room and board. You don't contribute to the salaries of the instructors. You don't pay for anything except to provide your daughter with money for her personal expenses, since I will not cover those. But SaDiablo Hall is *my home*, and my rules are absolute. You reviewed all those rules and signed an agreement *with me* that would hold you accountable for any misconduct on the part of your child. *She* signed an agreement *with me*, acknowledging my rules and the penalties for breaking those rules—especially the rules about sexual conduct. Do *not* complain because she knowingly broke the rules and I am now enforcing the penalties."

"But you *do* want me!" Alvita wailed, touching the sling that held her still-healing arm, as if to remind all the adults that she had *suffered*.

The leash on his temper snapped, and the room turned blood-freezing cold.

The Sadist smiled a cold, cruel smile, and purred, "The only way I would want to use your body is to feed it to Hell's flora and fauna. And that could be easily arranged."

Silence.

It took effort—too much effort—to step back from that delicious possibility, and the only way he could was by imagining Witch pointing out to him that the girl hadn't actually touched him, so his reaction might be a little extreme.

"Your daughter is no longer welcome at SaDiablo Hall—for any reason," Daemon said. "I suggest you find a private school—and check the credentials of the administrators and staff carefully—or hire tutors to allow the girl to continue her studies at home. I also recommend that you keep her away from Warlord Princes, and keep her on a tight leash where any males are concerned. If you don't, she may not survive to reach her majority." And if she didn't and she made the transition to demon-dead, her time in Hell would be short. He'd make sure of it.

As he turned away from the girl and her family, he looked at the District Queen and said, "Lady, with me. Now."

He walked out of the house and headed for the small Coach he'd used to convey the girl back to her home that morning.

"Prince . . . ," the Queen began.

"When I return in a few days, you and your triangle will give me an explanation for your letter of recommendation and exactly what favor you owed that girl's parents."

"It isn't easy being around Warlord Princes."

"I'm aware of that. And you were aware of who lives at the Hall, and you should have said something if you didn't think the girl could handle being in the same residence." He reached the Coach but didn't enter. He had one more thing to say. "You rule three Blood villages and two landen villages. You and your First Circle should consider which village you would want to keep under your hand, because if I'm not satisfied with your explanation, you will forfeit the others." Which meant she would also forfeit the income from the tithes that came from those villages.

"Prince!"

The Coach's door opened, but Daemon turned to look at her. "I am not my father. I carry scars he could barely imagine, and that has left me with very little mercy. But I will not make a decision about your future until I hear your explanation. When you discuss this with your First Circle, you should be more honest with them than you were with me—for their sakes as well as yours."

He left the District Queen weeping as he lifted the Coach off the landing web, caught the Black Winds, and headed for the next difficult meeting.

FIFTEEN

Saetien studied her face in the mirror. Jillian had assured her the simple lines and color of the dress she'd chosen flattered her, but what about her hair? It was black and straight—typical of all the long-lived races. Should she pull up the sides to show her delicately pointed ears? Or would that be seen as a ploy to remind her father of his wife—and would that remind him of his conflict with Surreal and destroy any possible permission for what she wanted to do?

She'd leave her hair down to flow over her shoulders.

A knock on her door.

Saeti? Where are we going? Shelby asked, ready to go out and help the humans.

"You're staying here to have your lessons with the other Scelties," she replied. "I'm going to the estate with Lady Jillian to talk to my papa."

I can talk too. Shelby wagged his tail. *He will pet me and be happy.*

Saetien crossed the room and opened the door as she said, "I'm sure he would be happy if he petted you, but I need to talk to my papa by myself."

Shelby whined, a sound that always made her feel guilty, even when she *knew* she shouldn't give in.

Jillian gave her a sympathetic smile. "Your father has arrived at the estate and is waiting for us."

Jillian seemed a bit nervous about this meeting. Why would she be nervous?

"Come on, Shelby," she said.

He followed her out of the room, looking woeful.

"Sometimes human females need to talk about private things," Jillian said. "And it's important to know when to give them private time."

Scelties learn this?

"Yes, they do. Special friends need to learn this important lesson even more than other Scelties."

Then I will stay here and learn Sceltie lessons. It was a declaration that had Shelby trotting ahead of them, eager to learn about this human female behavior.

"Thank you," Saetien whispered.

They left Shelby with the other Scelties who lived at the sanctuary and drove to the estate in a simple pony cart.

"I have a couple of things to discuss with Prince Sadi when you're done, so you'll have to wait for me or ask someone from the estate to escort you back to the sanctuary," Jillian said.

She was tempted to point out that she was old enough to walk through the village on her own, but girls who lived at the sanctuary were never on their own when they went into the village. They'd been broken and were rebuilding their lives—or were like Teresa, whose mind was shattered and who walked the roads of the Twisted Kingdom. If she went off on her own, it would be another way of reminding the rest of the girls that she wasn't like them. Yes, she'd lost a lot of the power she'd once had, but she wasn't broken and could regain some of that power when she reached her mature strength.

She didn't know much about this estate except that it grew grapes and made wine. Jillian mentioned that part of the house was set aside for the SaDiablo family—or the Yaslana family, since Lucivar Yaslana owned this estate—and the rest was the residence of the estate manager. Should she have known this now that she was living in the same village?

When Saetien and Jillian arrived, Saetien was escorted to a sitting room. She was so used to dealing with her father in a study that it took her a moment to see the father instead of the man. Thick black hair silvered at the temples. Gold eyes and golden-brown skin. A well-toned body beneath a perfectly tailored black suit and white silk shirt. And a beautiful face that could melt a woman's caution and self-preservation and let him do whatever he wanted to do with her. To her.

Saetien blinked and saw her father—and sucked in a breath. It was his sexual heat that was affecting her. During that fight at SaDiablo Hall when the coven of malice tried to hurt Zoey and the other girls, Daemon Sadi's heat had flooded the Hall, and whatever protection a daughter had against a father's heat had broken under that flood— and the cold rage that had been carried with it.

"Hello, Father."

She saw him start to shape the word "witch-child" and then catch himself. His father had used that word with the Queen. Knowing how she detested any comparison to the Queen who ruled her father's life, Daemon gave Saetien the courtesy of no longer using it with her.

She missed hearing it, but she wouldn't tell him that. Couldn't tell him that.

"Hello, Saetien," Daemon said. "I received your request for a meeting. Your explanation was a bit sparse."

A quick knock on the sitting room's door before the housekeeper brought in a tray—wine for him, fruit punch for her, and sandwiches. Everything was set out on a table between two chairs. Then the woman was gone, closing the door behind her.

Daemon waited until Saetien took a seat before settling into the chair opposite hers.

"What's on your mind?" he asked.

She sipped her punch and selected a couple of the small sandwiches. Stalling. Trying to figure out how to tell him this was important without admitting that she didn't know *why* it was important. Saying her future depended on it sounded so dramatic, even if it was true.

She called in the drawing Teresa had made for her—of her. She also called in the response to the query sent to the Keep. She handed the pages to Daemon and waited.

He drank the wine—and said nothing.

"Teresa said I needed to find her," Saetien finally said. "Or find out about her."

"Why?" he asked too softly.

"Because I won't understand myself until I know about her." Part of her wanted to bubble up and argue that she deserved to find out and she shouldn't have to explain why. Part of her was tempted to tell him she would go to Scelt with or without his permission. But those were feelings born of impatience. The rational part of her mind recognized that challenging him would spur him into refusing her request.

"Why?" he asked again.

Saetien looked him in the eyes and had a feeling she wasn't talking to her father anymore. "Because she is sadness and truth."

He used Craft to float the pages back to her. "I'll consider it. However, if I do permit you to go to Scelt, there will be conditions, and if you defy me, I will make sure that the answers you seek will no longer be within your reach. Is that clear, Lady Saetien?"

She definitely wasn't talking to her father. "Yes, sir."

"Then I'll be back in a few days with my answer."

She wanted to ask why he needed that long to decide, but she held her tongue. Problem was, she couldn't think of anything to say to him now. Small talk about her classes? About the food at the sanctuary? About Shelby? She could probably talk about the Sceltie, but she felt awkward and uneasy and really wanted to get out of the room.

"Jillian is waiting to talk to you," she said.

"Is she?" Some dark amusement in his voice that she didn't understand.

When he stood, she leaped out of her chair, then hesitated. Should she hug him? Kiss his cheek? Would he expect it and feel insulted if she didn't? She didn't know what to do with him anymore.

"Why don't you tell Jillian to come in?" he suggested gently.

"Yes, sir." She practically ran to the door, then stopped and forced herself to turn back to him. "Thank you for considering my request."

"You're welcome. I will give it serious consideration."

She nodded and left. The housekeeper led her to another small room, where she sat quietly and wiped away tears—and wondered how many other things would crack in the wake of her previous bad choices.

Jillian walked into the room, followed by the housekeeper, who removed the glass of fruit punch and the plate of uneaten sandwiches, then added clean plates and three wineglasses to the remaining dishes on the table and retreated, leaving the door open.

"Prince Sadi," Jillian said, taking the seat opposite him.

"Lady Jillian."

They watched as a young Prince, a vintner at the estate, walked into the room carrying a case of wine bottles.

"Stefan has created a new blend of wine from the grapes grown in the vineyards here," Jillian said, sounding a little breathless.

"The master vintner only recently gave his approval to make it available in the village, but I thought you might like to try a glass," Stefan said.

"I'd be delighted." Daemon set aside the glass of wine he'd already been given while Stefan drew the cork from a bottle and poured wine for the three of them.

Daemon took his time tasting the wine before making a quiet sound of approval. "Is that case for me to take back to the Hall?"

"Yes, sir, if you like it."

"I do." He savored another swallow of wine.

If the man kept drinking wine and delaying this necessary discussion, she was going to burst out of her skin—or slug him.

Daemon's gold eyes warmed with amusement as he looked at her. Then he smiled at Stefan. "So, you're the reason our Jillian has decided it's time to have her Virgin Night."

Jillian and Stefan looked at each other, then at him.

Knowing who and what he was, she couldn't tell Daemon she'd already taken care of her Virgin Night, not while Stefan was in the room and would be such an easy target if Sadi's temper snapped the leash.

"Yes," Jillian said. "We're ready to . . ." She hesitated.

"Have a full romantic, intimate relationship?" Daemon suggested.

"Yes."

"We haven't known each other long, but our feelings are strong enough to make this choice," Stefan said. He breathed in, breathed out. "I've been careful, Prince. I'm not without some experience, but there is no tarnish on my reputation or honor."

She and Stefan had talked about acknowledging that he'd had lovers. For men, there was a delicate balance between too little experience and too much.

"I'll explain things to Lucivar," Daemon said. "Now, Prince Stefan, I believe I have something else to discuss with Lady Jillian."

Stefan bowed to Daemon, smiled at Jillian, and left the room.

"Are you concerned about Saetien wanting to go to Scelt?" Jillian asked.

"Yes, but we're here to discuss your Virgin Night."

"Why? Lady Surreal is making the arrangements."

"I'm delighted to hear that. However, Lucivar and I will be at the town house in Amdarh that night. This is too important to him for Lucivar to keep his distance—just as it's important to you to have it done safely."

She should tell him now, before the arrangements went any further. Sadi wouldn't bounce off the ceiling like Lucivar would. He would . . . quietly shred whoever had helped her do it without informing the High Lord and Demon Prince.

Hell's fire, Mother Night, and may the Darkness be merciful.

"But . . . Lucivar will get so exercised while it's happening that he'll scare every man in the city into impotence." She waited—and, when Sadi didn't disagree with her, felt a weird vindication about her decision to withhold information.

Daemon looked uncomfortable. "Before he became Marian's husband, Lucivar saw a witch through her Virgin Night. Would it help if you talked to her? Not about the sexual details, of course, but maybe it would help you understand why this is so important to him?"

Hearing Daemon Sadi stumble over any discussion about sex was like watching a mountain fall down. Hell's fire, when she'd asked him to explain oral sex a few years ago, he hadn't even blinked before calmly describing that particular act from both sides of the give-and-take. But he was stumbling now?

"Yes," Jillian breathed. "That would help." If nothing else, the woman wouldn't be family and, maybe, could offer advice about how to explain her decision—because Daemon and Lucivar had to be told *before* she had this second Virgin Night.

"Then I'll ask her to drop by your cottage one evening very soon."

He abruptly changed the subject—another sign of nerves—and asked about the cottage and how she was settling in. After reassuring him that she wasn't doing without anything she truly needed, he made his farewells, returned to the Coach, and caught the Winds, explaining that he had some business in Amdarh.

SIXTEEN

S urreal felt the presence of the Black as soon as the Sa-Diablo carriage approached the town house, but when she entered the residence, there was a noticeable absence of Sadi's psychic scent and sexual heat. There was also a noticeable absence of Helton, the town house's butler.

Shaking her head at the footman who wanted to take her lightweight coat, she walked into Sadi's study—and stared at the empty room. Furniture, carpet, books—everything gone.

She rushed up the stairs and into his bedroom, not giving herself time to think about the dangers of being in his private space. The bed was stripped down to the mattress. No clothes in the wardrobe or dresser. No toiletries in the bathroom.

And yet she *felt* the Black.

She rushed back down the stairs, almost plowing into Helton.

"Where is Prince Sadi?" she asked.

Helton looked uncomfortable and yet relieved. "The Prince is on the other side of the town house."

She didn't wait for further explanation. Out the front door on this side of the town house, in through the front door on the other side. She charged into the study, because where else would he be?

"Sadi, what in the name of Hell is going on?"

Daemon turned away from the bookshelves and smiled at her. "Ah."

"Ah? Try again."

He took a few steps toward her, then leaned against the front of the blackwood desk. *His* blackwood desk.

"You hadn't found a residence of your own, and the town house in Amdarh has always been more your home than mine, so I moved my things over to this side, giving you the other side as *your* residence here in the city. Lucivar doesn't care about me using this side when I'm in Amdarh, and since both sides share the staff and they can retreat to your side, my heat won't be as difficult for everyone to endure." He smiled dryly. "Besides, if you purchased a town house of your own, Helton would give his notice and go with you, and butlers of his caliber are hard to find."

It made her heart ache a little that he would do this for her so that she didn't have to give up a place that felt like home.

Surreal nodded. "Makes sense, and I appreciate not having to fight with you over who gets to keep Helton. But tell me, sugar. What happens when your wife would like her husband's company? Are you going to walk out of your town house and knock on the door of mine? Or use one of the connecting doors in the staff's part of the building to sneak up to my bedroom?"

"I could always go out to the back garden and climb over the wall."

Surreal hooted. "Yes, that would be subtle."

Daemon gave her a wicked smile. "It would certainly give our neighbors something to talk about. Should I give it a try?"

SEVENTEEN

SaDiablo Hall

"H ell's fire," Daemonar grumbled to the other Warlord
Princes as they headed away from the square that
housed four of the Queens and their covens. "If this is
what Queens are usually like when there are more than
two of them in the same place, I'm beginning to understand why my father used to toss females in the lake whenever they annoyed him."

"He tossed . . . *her*?" Trent asked, sounding scandalized.

"He tossed anyone and everyone." Maybe he should
find out just how pissed off Uncle Daemon would be if he
used Lucivar's solution to dealing with spats involving
Queens and the friends who made up their current covens.
He wouldn't have to drop any girls in the lake. He could
just throw a big bucket of very cold water on them. Shriek-
ing would replace quarreling, but he'd be okay with that.

"It wasn't fair to gang up on Zoey during classes today,"
Raeth said. "It wasn't *her* fault that Alvita was sent home."

"Yeah, that made no sense, since she didn't have anything to do with it," Daemonar agreed. He made a note of
which girls were making spiteful remarks or displaying
outright bitchiness toward Zoey or her friends. He didn't
think Weston and Beale were aware of the bitchiness,
since the girls were careful not to cross that line when an
adult was present. Then again, Beale was aware of a great
many things at the Hall. Maybe not as many as Uncle Dae-

mon, but very little got past the Hall's Red-Jeweled butler. "If anyone is to blame, it's Dinah. She's a Queen, and she should have told her friend to stop doing things that were bound to cause trouble."

"Maybe Dinah wanted to see how far one of them could go before being tossed out the door," Trent said.

"Well, now they all know."

"Daemonar!" Zoey called.

Daemonar stopped and took a breath before he turned to face Zoey and deal with her distress. The other four boys stepped aside, giving the young Queen a clear path to the darkest-Jeweled Warlord Prince.

Sometimes being the strongest and oldest sucked rotten eggs—a phrase he'd learned from the Dharo Boy and would never ever say in front of his mother. Or Mrs. Beale. He was beginning to appreciate why in a court there was always a room set aside for the males so they could have some peace and time away from daily female drama.

"Zoey," Daemonar said.

A flicker of something approaching the Hall. Someone just arriving at the landing web and now walking up to the front door?

"Could we talk?" Zoey sounded tearful.

Why wasn't Titian with Zoey? For that matter, where was Allis? Shit. Was Titian holding on to Allis to prevent the Sceltie from biting one of the other Queens for upsetting her special friend Zoey?

"Of course," he replied automatically as he sent out a quiet tendril of Green power to try to identify what scratched at his instincts. With Uncle Daemon being away this evening, anything unknown couldn't be shrugged off—not when there were five young Queens in residence.

His Green probe brushed against . . . Power. Female. Sapphire.

And an unknown Warlord Prince.

"Zoey, go back to your room," Daemonar said. He pointed at the other four Warlord Princes. "You go back to the Queen's square and stand guard. And alert the other boys to stay sharp for any strangers in that part of the Hall."

Moving at a fast walk, the boys headed back the way they'd come.

"What's going on?" Zoey trotted after Daemonar as he headed for the great hall.

Weston! You're needed at Zoey's square of rooms, Daemonar called on a spear thread. Then to the Queen dogging his heels he said, "Hell's fire, Zoey. Go back to your room and stay near Weston."

"Tell me what's going on! Can I help?"

She sounded desperate to do something, prove something. What *she* needed was quiet time for her emotions to settle. What *he* needed was her staying out of the way so that he could help Beale with . . . whatever.

"No, you can't help." He didn't know what was going on, but he sensed Liath heading in the same direction, and he felt Beale's Red presence in the great hall. He couldn't get a feel for the unknown Warlord Prince's strength, and that was a worry, because that Sapphire witch could be serious trouble, even for two Green-Jeweled Warlord Princes.

He rushed down the stairs in the informal receiving room so fast, he had to spread his wings to maintain his balance. As he approached the door that opened to the great hall, he looked over his shoulder and snapped at Zoey, "Stay back."

Top of his list for tomorrow's lessons was a frank discussion of how to get a Queen to do what you needed her to do without smacking her head against a wall to encourage her brain to work.

Stepping into the great hall, Daemonar glanced at Beale. Liath was nearby. Probably sight shielded. Good.

A knock on the Hall's front door. Almost timid, considering the person knocking wore Sapphire.

At Beale's nod, a footman opened the door and stepped aside.

Daemonar sucked in a breath.

A girl walked into the great hall. Tawny skin with dark

stripes. A dark mane that wasn't quite hair and wasn't quite fur. Hands that had retractable claws. And a Sapphire Jewel hanging from a gold chain around her neck.

Mother Night, she's one of the Tigre.

Walking in next to her was a tiger. Still a kitten who wasn't old enough to have gone through the ceremony to acquire his Birthright Jewel.

As for the girl, Daemonar guessed her to be the equivalent of Titian's age, whatever that was in years for this short-lived race. She trembled visibly, and he wasn't sure if that was from fear or exhaustion.

Taking his cue from Beale, he stayed still and quiet, giving the girl and kitten a chance to settle. And she *was* settling as she looked around the great hall. Every breath she took seemed to be telling her something that reassured her.

"She lived here," the girl said softly. "Power still here. I was told go this place for . . . help. For . . . safety."

No question about who *she* was. Not when Witch's hands and gold mane must have come from the Tigre, whose dreams, so many generations ago, had been part of the making of the living myth.

Then bright, eager Zoey shoved past him and said, "Hello. I'm Zoey. Can we help you?"

The girl recoiled and looked ready to bolt—or attack. She bared her teeth and hissed. So did the kitten. They'd been fine as long as they were dealing with him and Beale, and everyone was quiet, but something about Zoey was seen as a threat. That she was a Queen?

"We'll take care of it, Lady Zoela," Beale said, his voice quiet but carrying through the great hall—and leaving no doubt the words were a command given by a Red-Jeweled Warlord who was, at that moment, representing Prince Sadi.

"We shouldn't leave her standing there," Zoey protested. "She can come with—"

"We'll take care of it." Daemonar kept his voice quiet so the girl and tiger wouldn't panic and run, but there was a knife-sharp warning in his tone.

The girl took a step back, shaking her head, her hands

flexing to reveal her claws. The footman hadn't closed the door, probably on Beale's orders. You didn't close in some-one who was that strong and that frightened. The tiger might be a kitten, but he was also a Warlord Prince who would attack if he felt threatened.

And still Zoey persisted. "She can—"

Everything has a price.

Grabbing Zoey's arm, Daemonar shoved her back into the informal receiving room, spreading his wings to block anyone from seeing more than his back.

"If you don't want to find out just how mean I can be, stop being a nosy brat and do as you're told. Go. To. Your. Room. *Now.*"

She looked as shocked as if he'd given her a fist in the face. Then she turned and ran, stumbling up the stairs be-fore she headed in the direction of her bedroom—and the comfort and sympathy of her friends.

Having returned to the great hall and the girl who might be a threat or was in desperate need of help, Daemonar waited. When he didn't get the feeling that the girl would bolt, he said, "I'm Daemonar Yaslana."

"Yaslana." She stared at him, then frowned. "Lu-ci-var."

"My father." He wondered what stories the people in Tigrelan told about Lucivar Yaslana.

The tension in her eased, so he must be saying the right things.

She called in two sheets of paper and held them out. "We have bloodlines."

Beale was the dominant male at the Hall right now. By rights he should be dealing with her. *She* should be dealing with him. But the butler remained watchful and quiet, let-ting him take the lead.

Daemonar moved toward her slowly. Before he was close enough to take the papers, the kitten lashed out, his claws just missing Daemonar's legs.

That's when Liath dropped the sight shield and growled at the tiger, his Green power demanding that this oversized fur ball acknowledge his dominance.

The girl froze. So did Daemonar. If the tiger was willing to challenge him . . .

The kitten made unhappy sounds, then rolled over to expose his belly. Liath sniffed the tiger thoroughly before giving the kitten a lick between the eyes.

Well, Daemonar thought. *I guess we all know whose orders the kitten will follow.*

Taking a step toward the girl, he accepted the papers and scanned the names, feeling a jolt as he came to two names he knew from his study of Kaeleer's history—and his study of the Dark Court that had stood at Ebon Askavi. He felt another jolt when he recognized a name in the tiger's bloodlines.

"You're Lady . . . ?"

"Grizande. Named for Tigre Queen who served living myth. He is Jaalan."

No doubt given that name because the kitten could trace his bloodline back to Jaal, the Green-Jeweled Warlord Prince who had also served in the Dark Court. A shadow of that Jaal sometimes roamed the Hall, along with a shadow of Kaelas, the white-furred Arcerian Warlord Prince who had also served, and loved, Witch.

"Prince?" Beale said. "A room has been prepared for your guests, and a meal will be waiting in the sitting room for all of you by the time you get there."

"Thank you, Beale. Could you put these in Prince Sadi's study?" Daemonar handed the papers containing Grizande's and Jaalan's bloodlines to the butler. Then he smiled at the girl as if he wasn't sharply aware that her Jewel was darker than his and a fight could leave both of them injured—or dead. "Shall we go up?"

She nodded and started to follow him, then looked back at the kitten, who seemed attached to the floor. When Liath gave the tiger a nudge, Jaalan leaped up and the two kindred led the way to the square of guest rooms that were used for people who weren't given access to the rest of the Hall.

"Your . . . guests?" Grizande sounded puzzled. Unsure. Something about the way she said words gave him the impression she didn't know much of the common tongue that was spoken by the Blood throughout the Realm, and that what she did know had been learned recently.

"Prince Sadi is my uncle. This is his home. He's not here this evening, so I am standing in his place, and that makes you and Jaalan my guests."

"That . . . other?" Wariness. Some fear, despite the Jewels she wore.

What would make a Sapphire-Jeweled witch afraid of an Opal-Jeweled Queen?

"Lady Zoela lives here now. She's a Queen in training."

Grizande stopped moving. The look in her green eyes reminded him of a warrior searching for an enemy before he stepped into a fight—or deliberately walked into an ambush in order to flush out his enemies. Watching her, he guessed she was a fighter like the Dea al Mon more than an Eyrien—and he wondered how much she already knew about fighting with a knife, *if* she used a knife instead of her claws.

"More . . ." She said a word in her own language.

"Five Queens live here, plus some Healers, Black Widows, and witches," Daemonar said. "There are also Warlord Princes, Princes, and Warlords. We're all here to study Craft and Protocol from Prince Sadi and to learn the workings of a court."

"He is . . . teacher?"

Oh, *that* sparked her interest.

"He is." When he continued toward the sitting room where a meal had been laid out, she matched him stride for stride, whatever concern she had about being in a place that contained Queens momentarily forgotten.

Unhappy sounds came from the sitting room. Daemonar lengthened his stride and wrapped a tight Green shield around himself. Not because he thought he would need it but because he didn't want to get his ass kicked for *not* doing it.

He stopped a few steps into the room.

Food on the table. A Green shield around the table. One

stern and growling Sceltie Warlord Prince—and one grumbling kitten standing on his hind legs to see the food out of his reach.

"Jaalan is hungry," Grizande said softly. Apologetically. As if there was some shame attached to the young tiger's hunger.

So are you, Daemonar thought as he studied her. Both of them were exhausted and half-starved. What had it cost Grizande to get herself and Jaalan here? She said she had come to the Hall for help, for safety, but why bring the tiger?

"Over here," he said, leading her to a door.

She followed him, casting glances at the food on the table.

How to ask questions without making her feel inferior? "Do you know this kind of plumbing?" he asked when he led her into the bathroom adjoining the sitting room. When she hesitated, he turned the water taps on the sink. "Hot water and cold water." He turned those off and lifted the toilet lid. "Toilet for pee and . . ." If she'd been male, he wouldn't have hesitated to talk about bodily functions, but he wasn't sure if that was considered taboo among her people.

Grizande's lips twitched. "Pee and other."

Daemonar grinned. "Yeah. That." He stepped out of the bathroom. "We'll have something to eat when you're ready."

As he approached the table, the kitten looked more than willing to pounce on him to convince him to give up some of the food. Until Liath growled again. The kitten was bigger than the Sceltie, but that didn't seem to matter. As far as Jaalan was concerned, Liath was in charge—of all of them.

Beale? Daemonar called on a psychic thread.

Prince? Do you need assistance?

No, we're fine for now. But I think Lady Nadene should take a look at our guests if you can think of a way to make that happen without causing distress.

We can do that, Beale replied.

Daemonar closed his eyes. Quiet. Confident. Easy. He

swallowed the emotions churning inside him, leashed the instincts that demanded he give more forceful help to this female who needed the safety he—and Beale— could provide. What he felt didn't matter. Not right now.

Grizande came out of the bathroom. Daemonar hadn't heard the toilet flush, so he wasn't sure if she hadn't used it or didn't know how to flush the waste. He'd let Helene know.

"Thanks, Liath," he said. "You can drop the shield now."

He'd been prepared for the kitten's leap to grab some food, but Liath was faster. The kitten hung in the air before being set down near the table.

Grizande said something that sounded like a scold, but it was the sadness under that scold that scraped at Daemonar.

"I am . . . sorry," she said as she approached the table.

"No need to be," he replied as he poured water into a shallow bowl and set it on the floor for the kindred dog and kitten. "I have a little brother who does much the same thing."

She smiled and took a seat.

Daemonar eyed the food and realized the bowl of raw meat wasn't meant for him and Grizande. At least he assumed it wasn't. Taking a small plate, he filled it with a quarter of the chunks of raw meat and used Craft to set it on the floor near the table.

Liath growled. Jaalan didn't make any move toward the dish, but he did make sounds that Daemonar figured would have kicked the instincts of an adult tiger into giving up some food. Too bad the kitten was dealing with a Sceltie.

Liath approached the dish, carefully sniffed the meat, took one chunk, then stepped back—a signal for the kitten to eat. The meat was gone in seconds.

Daemonar moved the roasted chicken within Grizande's reach. She ripped off a whole leg with a speed that startled him because the move looked . . . and felt . . . feral. And desperate.

"Easy," he said, placing his hand over hers.

She immediately dropped the chicken leg and looked . . . ashamed?

"You can have as much food as you want," he said gently, "but I can tell you from experience that if you eat too fast when you're empty, you'll end up with a bellyache." He released her hand, then tore off the other chicken leg and set it on his plate.

"You have been hunger?" She sounded like she didn't quite believe him.

He thought for a moment before nodding. "Because I was focused on boy things and food wasn't immediately available, not because there wasn't any. So I came home very hungry, ate too fast—and learned about bellyaches."

She bit into the thigh, and he could see the effort it took for her not to gulp down the meat as fast as possible. Had speed been essential to getting *any* food because there was competition for what was available—or because there was fear that it might be taken away?

Who was this girl who could trace her bloodline back to Grizande and Elan and yet arrived at the Hall frightened and starving?

She took another bite. Chewed. Swallowed. "Boy things?"

He grinned. "My grandmother's term for all the objects and adventures that male children find fascinating."

Liath and Jaalan's plate, licked clean, rose up to the height of the table.

Daemonar? Liath said. *We are ready for more meat.*

Nodding, he filled the plate with another quarter of the raw meat and used Craft to set the plate on the floor, just in case the kitten forgot his manners.

Same steps. Liath sniffing the meat and taking one chunk before Jaalan ate the rest.

Grizande had devoured every scrap of meat off the chicken leg and now eyed the rest of the chicken, her battle between hunger and manners visible on her face.

Daemonar took two biscuits out of a basket and broke them in half. He spread one side of one biscuit with a creamed cheese. He spread the other side with a thin layer of butter and . . . "This currant jam comes from Tigrelan. You won't find it in any of the shops here. My uncle buys it directly from whoever makes the jam in your Territory, so

it's a special treat, not something that shows up on our table every day." He set the two halves of the biscuit on a
small plate and set it in front of her before fixing his own
biscuit and taking a bite.

She took a small bite of the half with the creamed
cheese, made a face, and set it aside. He'd bet his quarterly
spending money that she wouldn't have set it aside yesterday, whether she liked it or not.

She savored the half with the currant jam. "I not have
like this. We pick berries and eat."

"I've never had the berries right off the bush. Are they
good?"

"Good."

"More chicken?" When she nodded, he sliced the meat
off one side of the breast and put it on her plate. Then he
refilled Liath and Jaalan's plate before forcing himself to
eat a few bites. He was hungry, but he felt too tense, too
tight, to put much food in his belly.

He swallowed a couple bites of chicken before easing
into what he and Beale needed to know. "How did you find
the Hall?"

She made a shape with her hands and said a couple of
words in her own tongue.

Daemonar shook his head. "I don't understand."

She thought for a moment, made the shape again, and
said, "Sister." Then the two words she'd said before.

Sister. Older sister, if the female had that shape?
Or . . . "Hourglass. Sister of the Hourglass. Black Widow."

Grizande nodded. "Black Widow. Web seeing. Says
Jaalan and I must find Witch home or die. Helped me.
Helped us before . . ."

"Before someone came hunting for you," Daemonar
finished quietly.

She nodded. "Tigre Black Widow not know where to
find Witch home. Took many days to find. Took asking
many people. Some worked for bad Queens, and I had to
fight to escape again. Always running from bad Queens
and males who hunt. Finally found woman who knew this

place. Said I find Witch home here." She looked at the remaining food with regret and sat back in her chair as a sign that she was done eating.

He wondered if the woman who knew this place quietly sold jars of currant jam for the SaDiablo table. He didn't know what Grizande had experienced, but he had a feeling that his father would understand all too well. "You don't have to say more tonight. Prince Sadi will want to know all of it, but those are words for tomorrow."

A knock on the door before Helene and Nadene walked into the room.

"This is Lady Helene, the Hall's housekeeper," Daemonar said. "And Lady Nadene is the Hall's Healer."

Grizande pushed away from the table, alarmed. "Healer?"

"A rule of the house," Helene said briskly, as if she hadn't noticed the girl's rising panic. "Every guest is checked over by the Healer to assess the scrapes and bruises they have when they first arrive." She gave Daemonar a pointed look.

"Hey," he protested, understanding what she wanted from him. "I don't *always* show up with scrapes and bruises."

"Not anymore." Helene sniffed. "There was a time when you couldn't get from the landing web to the front door without looking like you'd been on a three-day march through rough country. Which is why the rule was established and has not changed."

He turned to Grizande. "I was *little*."

Damned embarrassing, but the girl almost smiled, so it was worth the price.

"House rule," Helene repeated, holding out a hand. Then she glanced at the kitten. "Come along. Bath and bed, I think. You've both had a long day."

"Welcome to the Hall, Grizande," Daemonar said. "I'll see you in the morning."

"In morning." Grizande hesitated a moment, then walked up to Helene and slipped her hand into the housekeeper's. The girl's retractable claws could rip Helene's arm to the bone, and they all knew it—and they all pretended that nothing would frighten the girl or the kitten so much that it would happen.

Daemonar waited until two maids came in to clear the table and tidy the room. After suggesting they check the bathroom in case he'd left out some instruction their guest needed, he made his way to his own room, where he would have the privacy to release all the churning feelings he'd held back while he'd been with Grizande.

His stomach ached, but he couldn't tell if it was because he hurt for Grizande and Jaalan or because he was hungry. He just knew he couldn't sit at a table with children tonight, couldn't remain civil while they speculated about Uncle Daemon's guests. And as sure as the sun didn't shine in Hell, he did not want to deal with Zoey.

But it looked like he was going to deal with his sister.

Titian stood in front of his bedroom door, her expression a mixture of distress and fury.

He couldn't remember ever seeing fury before. And this display of her temper frayed the leash on his when he already felt raw.

"You owe Zoey an apology," Titian said.

"No, I do not."

"She's been *crying.*"

"Too bad."

Titian looked outraged. A year ago, she wouldn't have shown that much steel. She'd had it in her, but she wouldn't have shown it. "I'll tell Father."

His temper snapped the leash. "Go ahead. I gave Zoey a verbal slap for what she did. Father would have given her a fist in the ribs."

Her mouth fell open in shock. "She was trying to *help.*"

"But she *wasn't* helping, Titian. Her presence was causing that girl pain, and if I hadn't stopped Zoey, Grizande might have run, because right now she's just too tired to fight. And if she ran, she could have died." *That* was one of the things that was chewing at his gut—the certainty of how close a Sapphire-Jeweled witch had come to dying because of Zoey. "Beale told Zoey he would take care of Prince Sadi's guest. *I* told her we would take care of her. But Zoey was so determined to do things *her* way that *she didn't listen.*"

Daemonar moved Titian to one side and opened his door. Then he looked at his sister. "If you want to give Zoey hugs and pat her hand and say *there, there*, you go right ahead. But don't you kick at me for doing my duty to the patriarch of this family and the Warlord Prince of Dhemlan." *And my Queen.* "Don't you ever do that again."

He walked into his bedroom and slammed the door in Titian's face. Then he pressed his hands against his face and allowed himself to feel all the things he'd chained under the pretense of easy manners while he'd talked about food and currant jam, while he'd played the game with Helene to lighten the mood and make it possible for Grizande to trust all of them enough to receive the help she needed.

Fear. Pain. Where had this girl been that she didn't know the common tongue among all the Blood?

Fierce. A fighter. But how long can someone fight before they have nothing left and break?

Lucivar would know. So would Daemon. Except they had forced themselves to stand and fight again, even when there was nothing left. Had Grizande done that?

A tap on the glass door that opened onto the balcony that ringed the courtyard.

Holt.

Daemonar crossed the room and opened the glass door.

"Rough?" Holt asked quietly.

"Rough," Daemonar agreed.

"Did you get any food?"

"Not much."

"You want some?"

He shook his head. "Not right now. Wouldn't sit well." He tried to smile. "They need help, Holt. They really do."

"They'll get it." Holt hesitated. "Beale has already informed Lord Weston that, regardless of Lady Zoela's feelings, Weston can have no quarrel with you."

A warning to Zoey's sword and shield that Daemonar hadn't crossed any lines.

Holt rested a hand on his shoulder, a moment's touch. "Get some rest. We'll take care of whatever else is needed tonight."

"Thanks."

A hot shower eased the soreness in his tense muscles but did nothing to soothe the raw churning in his gut or the ache in his heart. He'd never lashed out at Titian like that before. Hadn't thought it possible. But . . .

Fear. Pain. *Grizande, what did they do to you?*

When all the young people had retired for the evening, leaving the staff free to take care of preparations for the next day, Beale waited in Prince Sadi's study for the senior members of the staff to join him and make their reports. He'd chosen the Prince's study because it would be private—and it was large enough to hold all the people who needed to be present.

Mrs. Beale arrived first. "The Dharo Boy is looking through my books to find the recipes I used for the Tigre during the Lady's time here. The girl can't live on currant jam and chicken." She frowned at Beale. "Did Prince Yaslana request a meal from the auxiliary kitchen? He ate next to nothing while talking to the girl."

His wife knew as well as he did that Daemonar hadn't requested any food. If the boy turned down food in the morning, something would need to be done. Daemonar had stepped up to the line, and Beale had let the boy take the lead because the girl had responded to his name, had *trusted* his name.

The girl hadn't trusted Lady Zoela. Had looked at a Queen and seen an enemy.

And Daemonar had done what needed to be done to protect both girls—and had received an emotional hit on behalf of one of those girls as thanks.

Something else he would mention to Prince Sadi, along

with what he'd gleaned about the spitting and spatting going on among the females today. Another day of that and the boys would be pulled into the scrapping, arguing with the girls and with one another about who was right and who was wrong when what they *should* be concentrating on was who would get their asses kicked for this excess of emotions.

Holt, Helene, and Nadene entered the study. Holt locked the door. Beale put a Red aural shield around the room.

"What does Prince Sadi need to know about his guests?" Beale asked.

Helene and Nadene exchanged a look before Nadene said, "Lady Grizande was tortured. More than once, since some scars are older than others. Scars on her back are from a whip." She swallowed hard. "Burns on her legs, like a hot knife had been pressed down on some of the dark stripes in her skin. I'd say there has been little formal education, based on how she speaks the common tongue. The way she does some basic Craft is different from how we teach our young, but that could be cultural—or it could be she's had to figure things out on her own. She hasn't had enough food for too many days, and she's exhausted. I didn't detect any illness or other cause for concern."

"Her clothes are little more than rags," Helene said. "I think she's spent a good part of her life pretending not to care about such things, but I think it's weighing on her now to appear before Prince Sadi like a beggar. We have enough spare clothes on hand that I put together a couple of outfits for Lady Grizande to use—or keep."

Tortured. The girl had been tortured. Beale forced himself to ask the next question because it would be Prince Sadi's first question. "Sexual torture?"

Nadene shook her head. "She was spared that."

Or she managed to escape before it happened.

"And she's still a virgin," Nadene added.

"I expect the Prince to return in the morning," Beale said. "I'll inform him then."

"It might be prudent to make him aware that we do

need him here in the morning," Holt said. "In case some-one else requests his attention."

"Yes."

Holt opened the door for the women, then closed it again and looked at Beale. "You have to tell her."

Beale released his breath in a long sigh. "It was a small indiscretion, and Lady Zoela intended no harm."

"Lady Saetien hadn't intended harm either, but people died that night because of her lack of judgment and her refusal to acknowledge your authority," Holt replied.

Beale nodded. He liked Lady Zoela and he regretted the storm of fury he was about to unleash on her. "I'll take care of it tonight."

"Unless you need something, I'll do a quick check on everyone on my way to my suite."

"Good night, Holt."

Beale waited until he was the only one in this part of the Hall. Then he called in a gold coin. One side was etched with a unicorn's horn laid over Ebon Askavi. The other side had an *A*.

If anyone challenges your authority again when you stand for Daemon, I want to know. I don't care who they are or why they did it; I want to know. This is more than a request, Lord Beale.

Shortly after that awful night when the coven of malice had used a house party at the Hall as the cover for attacking Lady Zoela and her friends, he thought he had dreamed of a place so deep in the abyss that no one could reach it and survive. But he'd found himself there, in that place of mist and stone—and power—and he'd seen the dream that had lived beneath the flesh he'd known as Jaenelle Angelline.

He'd thought she would tear him apart for failing to protect the Hall. But that wasn't the girl or woman he'd known. She looked different in this place, but she wasn't different. Not really. She'd been angry on his behalf. She'd been angry about the lack of respect for who he was and the Jewel he wore and how that disrespect had put him in such a difficult position. So she'd given him a gold mark as a way to reach her—and she'd given him one of her rare commands.

Beale called in a small knife and nicked his left thumb. He pressed the bead of blood against the Queen's gold mark. *Lady.*

He waited. Almost hoped nothing would happen and this would be left for Prince Sadi to handle. Then . . .

Lord Beale?

I regret to inform you that a young Lady residing at the Hall ignored my authority and almost put another young person at risk.

A silence that held feral ice before Witch said, *Tell me everything.*

EIGHTEEN

With Surreal beside him, Daemon stepped off the landing web, then dropped the Black shield he'd wrapped around her so that they could both travel on the Black Winds.

He'd asked her to come with him because Beale's message last night had been lacking in information, considering that the Hall's butler had said his presence was *required* this morning. A quick psychic scan of the Hall's residents revealed a great deal of emotional turmoil but little information of use. With one exception.

Daemonar felt . . . wounded. And Daemon's temper went cold in response to the boy's pain.

Surreal gave him a sharp look but didn't move away from him until they started walking toward the Hall's front door. Then she took a long step to the side and would enter the Hall a couple of steps behind him.

Fighting room.

Beale waited for him in the great hall. He'd expected that, but he didn't expect his butler to look tired—or regretful.

"Beale." Daemon's voice was filled with a quiet warning. "Are you well?"

"I am well, Prince," Beale replied. Meaning he had no physical injuries or serious emotional trauma.

"And Daemonar?"

"Physically, he is well." Beale hesitated. "Although he barely touched his breakfast."

Daemonar wasn't eating? What in the name of Hell had happened? And who . . .

"We have guests?" Daemon asked too softly.

"Lady Grizande and Prince Jaalan." Beale called in two sheets of paper. "Their bloodlines."

"Grizande?" Surreal stepped up to stand beside Daemon. "Wasn't she . . . ?"

"The Queen of the Tigre and a member of the Dark Court's First Circle," Daemon replied. "This witch is a descendant of Grizande and Elan." And the Warlord Prince came from Jaal.

Hell's fire.

"They came to the Hall last evening, looking for help and safety." Beale hesitated again. "The girl has been tortured. I don't know about the kitten."

It took effort to keep the Sadist leashed. "Sexual?"

"No. Lady Nadene confirmed that Lady Grizande is still a virgin."

Sexual torture didn't require a loss of virginity, and if the girl was the unfamiliar Sapphire his psychic probe had picked up, someone would have tried to break her before she grew into her strength. Unless that person died trying and the girl had escaped.

Daemon pushed those thoughts aside since they called to the Sadist.

"I am sorry, Prince, but . . . Her will." Beale held out a pale gray paper, folded and sealed with black wax. "It was a small indiscretion, but since you weren't at the Hall, it fell within the boundaries of her command."

"Shit," Surreal whispered.

Daemon took the paper, broke the seal, and read his Queen's command.

"Hell's fire," Surreal said as she read the note. "I've known women to spritz a bit of their signature perfume on a letter, but I didn't know anyone could infuse the feeling 'I am seriously pissed off' into paper and ink."

"Yes," Daemon said. "The Lady is not pleased." He read the names of the individuals who had been summoned to the Keep; then he looked at Beale. "Who crossed that line?"

Beale sighed. "Lady Zoela."

That's what he figured, based on the names. If it had been Daemonar, Witch would have dealt with her erring nephew directly. This formal summons was meant to scare the shit out of everyone. Especially a young Queen.

Daemon folded the summons and vanished it.

"What else is going on?" Surreal asked.

"Squabbles among the young Queens," Beale replied. "Nothing connected to the guests."

"But connected to whatever prompted Zoey to cross a line?" she suggested sweetly.

Beale didn't answer—which was an answer.

"Have a Coach brought around to the landing web," Daemon told Beale. Then he looked at Surreal. "With me."

They went to his study.

"You want me to stay at the Hall while you get this settled," Surreal said.

"Yes," Daemon agreed. "You don't have to interact with the youngsters if you don't want to get entangled in their . . ."

"Bitch drama-trauma?" she supplied cheerfully. "Actually, sugar, I think I will wade into that and show them what a real bitch looks like."

He choked on a laugh. "Yes. That." He sobered. "I'm making the request because you're my second-in-command and you wear the Gray."

"And someone might come looking for the girl while you're at the Keep."

"Yes."

"Well, the staff here has had plenty of experience cleaning up ponds of blood, so we'll be fine."

Her enthusiasm for the possibility of another pond was a little alarming. "Do you want to come with me to meet our guests?"

Surreal studied him for a long moment before shaking her head. "Not right now. The Tigre witch came here seeking help from you. Prince of the Darkness, High Lord of Hell. One side of the Queen's Triangle. Time enough for her to meet me."

Queen's Triangle. As Daemon walked to the guest room, he wondered if that was as significant as Surreal seemed to think. He and Daemonar were two sides of that triangle. How would Grizande react to Lucivar, the third side?

Maybe they should find out before he made any decisions about the girl.

Assuming *he* would be making any decisions.

As he approached the room, he released a thread of psychic power. He'd expected to feel the girl's Sapphire and the kindred tiger. But . . . Green?

He rapped on the door and walked in.

Prince! Liath gave him an enthusiastic tail wag. *I am reading to Grizande and Jaalan to help them learn the human words.*

Daemon recognized the book floating on air. *Sceltie Saves the Day.* Well, generations of four-footed youngsters had learned how to read using those books.

The Tigre witch leaped to her feet. Fearful. Wary. Hopeful. Uncertain.

"Lady Grizande." He slipped his hands into his trouser pockets, giving the impression of being totally at ease, despite the way his heart ached for this girl who had such *need*. "I knew Grizande and Elan. You come from a strong line, witchling. As does your little brother." He tipped his head to indicate the kitten.

Her fingers touched the tunic she wore. "Helene gave. I not take."

"I know," he said gently. "Did she give you more than one outfit?"

She nodded.

"We have been summoned to the Keep." He watched her. A moment's panic eclipsed by excitement—and hope. "We'll leave in about an hour. Liath? Can you escort Lady

Grizande and Prince Jaalan to the great hall when it's time?"

I will escort them.

Badger and herd was closer to the truth, but everyone learned about dealing with Scelties in their own way.

"Have you had breakfast?" Daemon asked. Then clarified when she looked confused: "Food?"

"Yes." She seemed to be gathering herself to ask a question. "Daemonar. He said in morning. I not see."

"He'll be coming with us." That didn't explain why the boy hadn't come to check on her, but it did confirm that Daemonar was Grizande's touchstone. For the time being, anyway.

Daemon gave the girl a warm smile, then headed for his nephew's room. The boy wasn't eating, wasn't honoring a promise to see someone who clearly needed some help?

He rapped on Daemonar's door, and this time he waited for permission to enter—and he wondered who the boy was keeping out by putting a Green lock on the door and a Green shield around the room.

He released a drop of Black power, rippling it across the Green shield in a way that would let Daemonar know who was outside his room without breaking the shield.

The door opened. Daemonar stared at him, then stepped back.

Daemon walked into the room and closed the door—and found his arms full of a boy who'd received an emotional kick in the gut and hadn't regained his balance yet.

"What happened?" Daemon asked as he massaged the back of the boy's neck and added a soothing spell to quiet some of the emotional turmoil. "Report." A word that required a recitation of actions but didn't require any explanation of the feelings connected to those actions.

Daemonar took a breath, released it in a shuddering sigh, and told Daemon everything he had done to settle Grizande—and told him about his clash with Zoey.

"You danced on a knife's edge, and you danced well," Daemon said when Daemonar finally stopped talking. The boy had done everything right, so why was there still this distress?

Daemonar rested his head on Daemon's shoulder. "Titian is mad at me."

Ah. That explained the boy's lack of interest in breakfast. "Every girl can be a bitch some days. Every boy can be a bastard or a prick. We are not sweet and eventempered all the time."

Daemonar snorted.

"We've been summoned to the Keep. We'll leave in an hour."

Daemonar raised his head and stepped back. "Summoned? By Witch or Auntie J.?"

Daemon swallowed a laugh. "I think most of us will be dealing with Witch. You? No guarantee which side of her *you're* going to be dealing with."

"Hell's fire."

"And may the Darkness be merciful." Daemon kissed the boy's forehead. "Why don't I arrange for scrambled eggs and toast to be brought to your room? You should have something under your belt before you get a scolding from your auntie J."

"I guess I should." Then, "Is Father going to be at the Keep too?"

Oh, I'll make sure Lucivar's there, Daemon thought as he stopped at the auxiliary kitchen to request that a plate be brought to Daemonar's room.

One more chat before he met with Holt, Helene, Nadene, and Beale to receive their reports.

He found Zoey and Titian in the sitting area of Zoey's room. The plates on the small table held nothing but crumbs. That they could dismiss what happened yesterday easily enough to enjoy breakfast while Daemonar struggled pissed him off, so he gave them a cold smile.

"Lady Zoela."

"Prince Sadi." Zoela lifted her chin. "I want to—"

"You disappoint me." He watched her crumple under the lash of those words. "We've been summoned to the

Keep. We leave in one hour. Be down in the great hall by then. You, too, Titian."

"I've been summoned to the Keep?" Titian squeaked.

"No, but I expect your father is going to want to have a little chat with you."

He walked away. He didn't need to say more. Neither girl had any comprehension of the fury waiting for them at Ebon Askavi.

But they would learn.

Standing with Beale and Holt, Surreal watched the combatants gather in the great hall. Zoey and Titian. The Tigre witch and the tiger Warlord Prince. And Daemonar, looking like he'd flown through a storm, standing alone—and standing exactly halfway between the two pairs, seeming to take no sides.

But you took a side, Surreal thought as she watched him. *You just never imagined you would need to side against your sister, or that she would turn on you, and that hurts you.*

But Hell's fire, a girl who already wore Sapphire had the potential to wear Ebon-gray when she made the Offering to the Darkness. What had the Tigre Queens been thinking to condone any kind of abuse, let alone torture?

Daemon walked into the great hall with Liath. The Sceltie eyed the groups, seemed satisfied with the arrangement, and trotted off to perform his other self-appointed herding duties.

Sadi looked at her, Beale, and Holt. He gave them a nod, said, "Let's go," and walked toward the front door. A footman sprang to open the door for the Warlord Prince of Dhemlan—or the High Lord. Surreal wasn't sure which level of Sadi's temper was currently leading. Not the Sadist, thank the Darkness.

Zoey and Titian followed Sadi out the door. Daemonar stepped forward, offered Grizande a smile, and walked out of the Hall with her and the kitten.

The footman closed the door.

Surreal turned to Beale and Holt. "So. Tell me the reason for the bitch drama-trauma."

Beale blinked. Holt choked on a laugh before sobering abruptly.

"Jealousy," Beale said.

"Resentment that Zoey is Prince Sadi's favorite," Holt said.

"I would have thought that was Titian, at least among the girls," Surreal said.

"Titian is family," Beale replied. "A relationship that gives her an acknowledged advantage when it comes to receiving the Prince's time and attention. That's the perception, but Titian has to request an audience with her uncle the same as any other girl."

"But he will go out with Zoey and Titian for an early morning ride," Holt added. "He doesn't invite them to join him every time he goes riding, and he does go out riding with other groups of youngsters, but the other girls, especially some of the other Queens, are of the opinion that Zoey receives special treatment, and they were expressing their . . . opinions . . . about it yesterday."

"Which provoked Zoey into trying to prove she deserves special treatment?" Surreal guessed. She called in a small stoppered bottle and held it out to Beale. "Please ask Mrs. Beale to fill this with a thick dark liquid. Something that tastes bitter and has a scent that stings. She could ask Nadene to assist. A Healer would know how to brew up something like that."

Beale took the bottle. "When do you need it?"

"As soon as possible." Surreal gave the men a knife-sharp smile. "The Ladies and I are going to have a chat before they all start their formal lessons this morning."

Zoey and Titian sat in the front seats of the Coach. Grizande and Jaalan sat in the back seats. Since Uncle Daemon was driving the Coach on the Black Winds, Daemonar took the middle ground—a physical barrier of pissed-off male that discouraged any discussion. Time enough to discuss things when they arrived at the Keep.

Sitting in a chair that faced three rows of chairs that had been curved and spaced so that everyone could see the instructor, Surreal watched nineteen witches file into the room and hesitate when they saw her.

She hadn't been at the Hall much since the youngsters arrived a few weeks ago. Even when she stayed at the Hall overnight to talk to Sadi about Dhemlan's business or keep him informed about the sanctuary she ran for witches who had been broken, she had kept to the family wing, preferring to eat in her suite rather than deal with adolescent girls.

She accepted that what had been broken inside her would never fully heal, but the wounds her daughter had inflicted were still too raw for her to want to be sociable with girls that age.

She wasn't sitting in this room to be sociable.

"Queens in the front row," she said, holding up the stoppered bottle of dark liquid and tilting it one way, then the other. "Black Widows and Healers in the second row. The rest of you in the third row."

Yes. The seeds of five courts. She watched the girls. She recognized Jhett and Arlene, who were friends of Zoey's, as well as the other three girls who had been at the house party that had given Sadi the proof he needed to destroy the coven of malice—and had cost her family so much in so many ways.

"In case some of you don't know who I am, I am Surreal SaDiablo," she said pleasantly, tilting the bottle back and forth, drawing the girls' eyes to what she held. "In case you haven't heard about me, when I lived in Terreille centuries ago, I was one of the highest-paid whores in that Realm. I was also one of the highest-paid assassins in that Realm. I retired from whoring before I came to Kaeleer." She gave them a sharp smile and let silence tell them a truth about her other profession.

The girls shifted in their chairs and looked longingly toward the door.

"You want to play the bitch, do it somewhere else," Surreal continued. "Sadi has a cold hatred for bitches, and he has good reason for that hate. You continue that way and come to the age when you can set up a court? If you try to play the bitch with him then, the High Lord of Hell will declare war on your court. That war will be swift, it will be messy, and he will leave no survivors." She watched every girl in the room turn pale—and she noted the one Queen who, despite turning pale, wasn't sufficiently alarmed by that statement. "I understand there was some bitchy drama going on yesterday between all the Queens, and the squabbling extended to the rest of you. Here and now, I'm giving you a chance to voice all your complaints and concerns without penalty. What you say to me, here and now, will go no further. After today?" She shrugged. "You'll take your chances with cold rage."

Surreal crossed her legs and continued to play with the bottle of dark liquid. "Names first. Then we'll begin." She focused on the Queens: Dinah, Kathlene, Felisha, and Azara.

"We're Queens, but *Zoey* is treated like she's special," Azara said.

"Because she's tonguing a Yaslana," Dinah said, sneering.

Well, you won't last long here, Surreal thought. "That's not the reason she's special. Do you all realize that Zoey is the reason you're here? That she's the reason this protected training at the Hall was set up in the first place?" She waved a hand at the four Queens. "Did any of you know that?"

All four shook their heads, and Dinah looked miffed that she might owe Zoey anything.

Surreal wasn't sure if they truly didn't know why the Hall had become a training ground or if they didn't want to admit knowing they were chosen to be here because they'd also been targeted by the coven of malice.

She looked at the four Queens, one by one, and held up the bottle of dark liquid. "Want to be special like Zoey?"

All the girls looked at the bottle.

"*Safframate*. A powerful, vicious aphrodisiac. One teaspoon of this, in this concentration, will guarantee you about seventy-two hours of agony and suffering and sexual need so fierce you'll be begging and screaming for the boys to mount you and ram their cocks into you hour after hour after hour after hour. You'll be torn and bloody and half mad from the pain, not to mention that your power will be broken and you'll no longer wear a Jewel, and it still won't be enough. But you won't have to worry about that if you want to try a dose here. I'll put a Gray shield around your room so the boys can't reach you. I can't say whether ramming a dildo between your legs and breaking the hymen will break your power the same as a flesh-and-blood cock, but I wouldn't advise trying it. Of course, if you pound on the walls of the room until the bones in your hands break and the tendons in your shoulders tear, well, those things can be healed almost as good as new. You're young and healthy, so the odds are good that your body won't give out before the drug finally burns out of you. And if you spend weeks or months or years having nightmares, if you startle when someone approaches you without warning, if you flinch because of the lightest touch? Well, everything has a price, doesn't it? You may still be a virgin who will have to go through her official Virgin Night; you may still have your power; but you won't be innocent. You won't be who you were. This will change you, will scar your body, mind, and heart."

Smiling, Surreal waggled the bottle and looked at Kathlene, the Queen directly in front of her. "Want to have your life ripped apart in order to be special like Zoey?"

Kathlene swallowed hard. She shook her head.

Felisha shook her head. Azara hesitated, then shook her head. Dinah stared at the bottle.

Surreal stared at Dinah. "You have some romantic notion that Sadi would service you in order to see you through those seventy-two hours?" She shook her head. "If you were dosed by someone else at the Hall, he would do what was required to help you by arranging for trained individuals to walk with you, run with you, spar with you, as a way to help you burn out the drug. They would do that for hours, until you were too physically exhausted to stand. And while those individuals were giving you that help, Sadi would be taking apart the person who drugged you, layer by layer, piece by piece, body and mind—and he would find out *everything* that person knew, including any possibility of collusion on your part. And if you should be so foolish as to take the drug yourself in a misguided attempt to get him into your bed? Sugar, he would stand there and watch you suffer for the whole seventy-two hours, without any help from anyone."

She looked at all of them. "Any questions? No? Then you should go on to your classes."

They scurried out of the room—except Zoey's five friends. Three hung back, leaving Jhett, the Black Widow, and Arlene, the Healer, to approach her.

"What happened to Zoey was private," Jhett said. "It wasn't fair to tell the rest of them without her consent."

"You think no one has noticed how she reacts to an unexpected touch?" Surreal countered. "You think some of the girls haven't done exactly that, coming too close to her without warning, just because they *know* how she'll react even if they don't know why? People, especially Queens, need to understand that there is a price for being special, and that price is usually very high. Zoey receives extra care and attention because she is still healing. Those other girls attacking her, whether they use words or fists, because she is still healing? Zoey's friends should have had a quiet word with Lady Nadene or Lord Holt or Prince Raine to make them aware of what was happening, especially if yesterday wasn't the first time the other Queens took a swipe at her. Protecting your Queen is one of the duties of members of a First Circle. It's not tattling or bitching or whatever else someone might want to call it. It is your duty."

"Would reporting it make a difference?"

She vanished the bottle. "Well, I'm here—aren't I?—having this little chat with all of you because someone *did* report what happened. And you should all be grateful that Sadi is not here today."

"You wouldn't have let anyone take a dose of that," Arlene said. "Since it's so awful and possibly lethal, you wouldn't have let anyone try it. Would you?"

Surreal just smiled—and walked away.

NINETEEN

Lucivar prowled one of the sitting rooms near the Queen's part of the Keep, working to keep his temper leashed.

Children made mistakes. They were children, after all. But for this mistake? He needed to wrap a hammer in velvet in order to deliver the correct blow for *this* child.

He felt the presence of the Black, knew the moment Sadi set the Coach on the landing web closest to that part of the Keep.

Bastard? he called on a spear thread.

Prick?

The Queen wants to see Daemonar first. But I want a word with the boy before he stands before her. He waited a beat before adding, *I'll deal with my daughter my way.*

He felt Daemon's hesitation, and appreciated that his brother wanted to soften the blow heading toward the family's sensitive child. Then something changed—and a chill filled the link between them.

Yes, Daemon purred, *better if you deal with her.*

Daemon broke the link.

Lucivar continued prowling the sitting room. Before leaving the Hall, Daemon had contacted him on an Ebongray psychic thread and told him Titian had crossed a line and had behaved in a way that wouldn't be tolerated in an actual court, and Daemonar was hurting because of it.

That told him enough, especially since Daemon was coldly displeased with Titian.

Daemon arrived a few minutes later, escorting all the troublesome children into the room.

Zoey and Titian took the chairs nearest the door. Tigre and tiger moved to the far side of the room, close to the windows. A way to escape if things soured.

Hope soiled by the expectation of pain. That was what he picked up in the Tigre witch's psychic scent. But there *was* hope in that girl. He and Daemon could work with that.

First things first.

"Prince Yaslana, with me." Lucivar walked out of the room, leaving Daemon to enforce civility among the girls.

He didn't bother going to another sitting room. After stepping into the corridor and closing the door, he faced his son and asked one question. "Were you wrong?"

A thoughtful silence rather than a hesitation. Finally, Daemonar said, "I may have been too harsh in what I said to Lady Zoela in order to get her to leave and let Lord Beale and me deal with Lady Grizande. But I wasn't wrong."

Titles. Formality. The boy's use of both told him where Daemonar had drawn the line.

"All right," Lucivar said. "The Lady wants a word. You know the way."

"Yes, sir."

Unhappy and heart bruised. Well, his first-born wouldn't be the only one feeling that way today.

Lucivar tracked Daemonar's progress through the Keep until the boy's Green power disappeared beyond the ornate metal gate that separated the Queen's residence from the rest of the Keep. Then he went back to the sitting room to summon his daughter.

Daemonar approached Witch, stopped at the correct distance for a member of the Queen's Triangle, and bowed. "Lady."

Witch closed the distance between them. Those ancient, haunted sapphire eyes looked through him, into him, seeing . . . Well, she was Witch. Who knew what she saw?

Her hands rested on his shoulders. She leaned in and kissed his cheek. The feel of her lips against his skin startled and soothed.

She eased back and smiled. "I'm proud of you, boyo. Even though it cost you, you did what was right."

"She needs help, Auntie J.," he said. "*They* need help."

"I know. Are you comfortable with providing some of that help?"

"Yes." Daemonar smiled. "If nothing else, I can be an alternative to Liath when it comes to the kitten learning Craft and . . . boy stuff."

"Well, it will be better for all of you if a tiger doesn't grow up thinking he's a Sceltie," Witch said dryly.

Daemonar choked. "Hell's fire." When he caught his breath, he added, "At least the kitten doesn't have a herding instinct."

"No, but he does have the Warlord Prince bossiness and an instinct to pounce." She gave Daemonar a bright, bright smile.

"You are not helping." Or was she giving him a friendly warning based on experience?

His auntie just looked at him. The amusement and hint of mischief in her eyes lightened his heart—and terrified him a little bit.

She approved of the choices he'd made, and that was all he needed to know.

As he walked back to the sitting room, he wondered if there was anything to eat.

Lucivar sat across from Titian. This sitting room was smaller than the one on the other side of the corridor. Almost intimate—or claustrophobic, depending on who was in the room with you.

"Tell me what you witnessed in the great hall when Zoey and Daemonar had that clash of wills," Lucivar said.

Titian sat forward. "Zoey said—"

"I didn't ask what Zoey said. She only knows her side of it. I asked what *you* witnessed."

She blinked. Hesitated. "I wasn't there, but Zoey—"

"Either didn't understand what was really happening in the great hall when that girl arrived, or she chose to ignore what was happening for her own gain."

As he expected, the choice of words pricked enough that Titian leaped to defend her friend.

"She was just trying to *help*," Titian insisted.

"Was she? She put herself in danger, and she put Grizande in danger. How was that helping?" He kept his voice quiet and even. He wanted his girl to think, not crumble.

"Danger?" She didn't sound sure anymore.

"Beale had two conflicting duties," Lucivar explained. "The first was to keep you all safe. The second was to assist a girl who had come to the Hall for help. Zoey trying to push in and take charge put both girls at risk—and she showed a blatant disregard for Beale's authority as a Red-Jeweled Warlord standing in for your uncle. Do you recall someone else who challenged Beale's authority because he was only the butler? You should remember. It wasn't that long ago."

Titian looked horrified. "It wasn't like that! Zoey wasn't doing what Jaenelle Saetien had done."

"From where I'm sitting, witchling, Zoey tried to do exactly the same thing that Saetien had done. The reason might have been different, but the result could have been Zoey or Grizande dying because *Zoey didn't listen*. Beale told her he would take care of it. Daemonar told her they would take care of it. What part of those words didn't she understand?"

"But—"

"Did Zoey tell you that Grizande has no liking for Queens, that she viewed Zoey's presence as a threat? Did

Zoey tell you Grizande had been tortured more than once, most likely at the orders of a Queen? Do you want me to take off my shirt and show you my back so you get an idea of what was done to that girl?" Quiet voice, but the words were a hammer.

"The moment Daemonar saw Grizande's reaction to Zoey's presence, he knew Zoey had to get out of the great hall, had to get out of sight," Lucivar continued. "She wouldn't listen to the courteous words, so he gave her a verbal punch designed to drive her away. Did she tell you any of that?"

Tears filled Titian's eyes and ran down her cheeks.

"And what did you do when Zoey returned to her room upset because Daemonar had been mean to her? Probably comforted your friend, which is understandable even if you didn't know what was going on. Then you lashed out at your brother because he'd taken a stand to protect Zoey as well as Grizande. If you'd wanted to know what happened, you could have told him that Zoey was upset and asked him politely to explain why he had done what he'd done. He would have told you, just like any First Circle Warlord Prince would have told you. But, my darling, if this had been a real court and you'd lashed out that way at a Warlord Prince who *wasn't* your brother? He would have slapped you down so hard you would have needed help getting off the ground."

Lucivar sat back, offering no sympathy or comfort while she cried. It ripped at his heart, but he wasn't going to let Titian shift the blame because she wanted Zoey to be right.

"If Grizande is so dangerous . . . ," she began.

"No," he said sharply. "You will not blame someone else for Zoey's mistake. And now is the time for you to understand that loving someone doesn't mean blindly thinking they're always right. People make mistakes, Titian. Even Queens. And sometimes loving someone means being willing to fight them into the ground if they're putting themselves in danger or doing something wrong."

"What if the person wouldn't forgive you for not taking her side?" Titian's voice was a pained whisper.

"Everything has a price," he replied softly. "You take the chance of learning that the person wasn't worthy of your loyalty or your love."

He wondered if Zoey expected blind loyalty, or if this was an unfounded fear of Titian's and just something each person learned at some point—the cost of making the choice between being loyal and doing what was right.

"Papa." A little girl's plea.

Lucivar stood and opened his arms, gathering her to him.

"I'm s-sorry."

"I know, witchling." He kissed the top of her head. "Make things right with your brother. You hurt him."

He held her while she cried. She'd be heartsore as she worked things out for herself, but she would work things out.

Prick?

Bastard?

I'm taking Grizande and the kitten for their audience with the Queen. Zoey will be alone in the sitting room.

Daemonar?

Amusement. *I think your boy was waylaid by the scent of food.*

He must be feeling better.

It would seem so.

When Daemon broke the link, Lucivar said, "Come on, witchling. There's a washroom attached to that other sitting room. You can tidy up there."

After leading Titian back to the sitting room and pointing to the washroom door, Lucivar looked at Zoey and saw a scared young girl who was trying to be brave but was starting to wonder if she had been wrong.

Wondering was good.

This wasn't the best way for Zoey to meet Witch, but he was sure it was a meeting the young Queen would never forget.

✦ ✦ ✦

Daemon walked into the sitting room that was opposite the Queen's and Consort's suites in Witch's part of the Keep. Grizande trailed behind him with the kitten following her.

As he approached his Queen and bowed, he wondered about the change in her dress. This dress was black and sleeveless, as usual, but instead of ending around midthigh, it fell to her ankles—or hocks—revealing the hooves. He doubted she was as calm as she looked, but she stood absolutely still while the girl approached, step by trembling step.

What do you see, Jaenelle? What do you want me to do with this Sapphire-Jeweled witch who came seeking help?

He knew what he wanted to do, what everything in him *demanded* he do. But Witch's will was his life, and he would obey.

Daemon called in two sheets of paper. "Lady Grizande brought her bloodlines, as well as the bloodlines for Prince Jaalan."

"I don't need to see them." Witch's haunted sapphire eyes focused on the girl. Then she smiled. "Blood sings to blood, and I can hear a little of my friends' song in the blood that runs in your veins."

He wondered if she was being poetic or literal. With Witch it was hard to tell.

Witch held out a fair-skinned hand and flexed her fingers, revealing the retractable claws. "Your people were among the dreamers."

Grizande raised her hand—tawny skin with dark stripes—and flexed her fingers, revealing claws. Common ground.

The look in the eyes of a girl who had already seen too much was also common ground.

"The Keep is important as a sanctuary and as a place of learning, and it is my home, but it is not the best place for a witch your age to spend a lot of time," Witch said. "If you are willing and comfortable being there, I suggest that you stay at SaDiablo Hall, where you can meet a variety of people and receive an education in many areas that will be useful, including improving your command of the common tongue."

Grizande looked ashamed and lowered her eyes.

"It's foolish to feel ashamed simply because you didn't have the opportunity to learn something." The sudden anger in Witch's voice was a distant thunder that warned of a rising storm. "It's even more foolish to let anyone try to make you feel ashamed. Some will. Take note of them. They are not worthy of your time."

Grizande looked up—and Daemon wondered how many people had tried to make her feel ashamed as a way to control a witch whose power would have few equals when she came of age.

"You and Lady Zoela did not start out on easy ground, but I would like you to consider residing in a room in the same square in the Hall. There are seven young women in that square, and occasionally Lady Karla. You may like some of those women or none of them, but those rooms are close to Prince Sadi's suite as well as Prince Yaslana's, so the men would be in easy reach if you needed help." Witch waited until it was clear the girl wasn't going to respond. "Or you can reside in another square of rooms, where you wouldn't have to deal with the other people who live at the Hall. I ask that you try to live among the others before choosing solitude. I think in many ways you've been alone too long already."

"Jaalan?" Grizande asked, lowering her hand to touch the kitten's head.

"He has lived with you?" Witch asked.

Grizande nodded.

"He is an orphan?"

The girl touched her chest. "We . . . orphan."

"Then he will stay with you and learn the rules of the house and receive his own training."

Grizande looked wary. "Liath?"

"Among others."

Big sigh. "Liath. Bossy stern teeth."

Witch's silvery, velvet-coated laugh filled the room. "Well, you've already learned that much."

Grizande nodded—but for the first time, Daemon saw a hint of amusement in the girl's green eyes. Then the amusement faded.

"I live around Queen," Grizande said. "Must . . . obey?"

"You answer to no other Queen than me." Amusement forgotten. The distant storm was rising again. Getting closer. "However, at the Hall, you are under Prince Sadi's hand, and I expect you to obey him. Usually."

Daemon raised an eyebrow.

Witch shrugged. "No one is obeyed *all* the time. Even Saetan didn't expect *that*."

"Saetan was dealing with you when you were Grizande's age," Daemon said sweetly.

"Exactly." She gave him a bright smile before turning back to Grizande. "Can you agree to that?"

"I live at Hall?" Grizande asked. "Learn?"

"Yes," Witch replied.

"Jaalan too?"

"Yes."

The girl said something in her own language, which Daemon assumed indicated agreement. Grizande was surprised when Witch responded in the same language. He didn't understand what was said, but the rhythm of the Queen's words held a formality that resonated through him. Ritual. Protocol. The claim Witch made just now put Grizande beyond the reach of everyone except those who also served the Queen.

Daemon opened the sitting room door and, with a graceful move of his hand, indicated that Grizande and Jaalan were to leave.

"Wait for me," he told them. "I'll escort you back to the other room in a minute."

Closing the door, he returned to Witch.

"You'll teach her?" Witch asked.

"I will teach her. And I'll keep her safe."

Jaenelle suddenly took great interest in the carpet's pattern. "A tiger needs to learn how to hunt like a tiger."

"So . . . ?" Easy enough to guess what was coming.

Daemon tucked his hands into his trouser pockets. Less temptation to try to strangle her. Not that he'd succeed. Her form was a shadow, an illusion made of Craft and power.

"You do have access to a tiger. An appropriate one, considering Jaalan's bloodlines."

"You want a shadow of Prince Jaal to teach that kitten how to hunt?"

"Can you think of anyone better?"

Daemon stared at her. She smiled at him. Bright, bright smile.

Pick your battles, old son. You've already lost this one. He sighed—and surrendered. "Fine. Maybe shadow Jaal will balance what the kitten learns from Liath."

He took a step closer. "You asked Grizande if she was willing to do this. You didn't formally ask me."

Witch laid a hand against his cheek. "I didn't have to ask. I saw the look in your eyes when you walked in the room. You'd already decided to protect them before you arrived at the Keep. I simply acknowledged your choice— and gave Grizande a way to be around Queens without feeling threatened."

"A witch her age who wears Sapphire needs careful handling."

"And the rough-and-tumble handling of an Eyrien boy and Scelties, along with adult supervision and encouragement to learn the things that will help her. She will be formidable and dangerous."

"She already is those things," Daemon replied.

"Yes." She lowered her hand, let it rest on his chest for a moment.

"We'll all be going to Lucivar's eyrie, but I'll be staying at the Keep tonight. When I return, I need to talk to you about Saetien."

"All right." Witch stepped back. "I think Lady Zoela has had enough time to stew—don't you?"

"I'll bring her to you."

Daemon almost escorted Grizande and Jaalan back to the sitting room where the others waited, but Daemonar

suddenly appeared in another doorway holding a plate
with a huge piece of steak and ale pie.

"There's more." Daemonar waved a fork at something
over his shoulder as he looked at Grizande. "You want
some?" Then he looked at the kitten and growled, "No
pouncing."

Grizande glanced at Daemon.

"Go ahead," he said, keeping his voice mild. He stared
at his nephew. "Just remember that your mother expects
you at dinner, so don't stuff yourself."

The boy snorted and stepped back. As soon as Grizande
had walked past him and couldn't see, Daemonar winked
at his uncle before returning to the table filled with what
Daemon hoped was enough food for the three of them.

Zoey didn't know what to expect as Prince Sadi led her
past an ornate metal gate and opened the door to a room.

She hesitated. "You're not coming in?"

"No," he replied. "This is between you and Witch."

Mother Night.

She walked into the empty room. Prince Sadi closed the
door.

The room turned cold and was no longer empty. What
stood before her . . .

Human. But not human. Delicately pointed ears. A tiny
spiral horn in the center of her forehead. A gold mane that
wasn't quite hair and wasn't quite fur. Hands that had retractable claws instead of fingernails. Hooves. And sapphire eyes that looked like a window into a place that held
so much power, a person couldn't hope to survive there.

Couldn't hope to survive her.

I'm a Queen, Zoey thought desperately. *I. Am. A. Queen.*

"There's something you want to discuss with me?" Her
voice shook. So much for bravado.

"Yes, there is." A midnight voice. "I want to discuss
how a Queen could reach your age without any education
or training in the workings of a court—and without any

knowledge of the basic Protocol you should have begun learning as soon as you acquired your Birthright Jewel."

Zoey blinked. "What?"

Witch stepped closer. Her fury became a smothering storm. "How dare you challenge Lord Beale's authority? He wears the Red; you wear Opal. *How dare you* ignore an order from him and put yourself and another girl at risk?"

"I—I didn't!"

"Did you learn nothing from what happened at that house party when Saetien overruled Beale?"

"This wasn't the same," Zoey cried.

"How do you know?" Witch demanded. "You're a Queen *in training.* That means there are a great many things you *don't* know. What if that girl had been sent to kill you, or any of the Queens in residence?"

"But she wasn't!"

"How did you know? She could have been hired by one of the families who would like to blame you for their off-spring being executed. When Daemon is conveniently absent, a stranger comes to the Hall, asking for help, for sanctuary. Maybe the need is sincere. Maybe it's a way to get inside."

"But—"

"Maybe you should ask Lady Surreal how she got into places when she was hired as an assassin. You might find it illuminating."

"I was trying to help!" The words came out as a plea.

"Beale told you he would take care of it. Daemonar told you they would take care of it. If you don't understand what that phrase means within a court, then you have missed an important lesson."

"But the Hall isn't a court."

"Child, what do you *think* it is? It's a training ground, no different than if you were apprenticing in another Queen's court. The senior staff at the Hall should be considered the equivalent of a First Circle. They are adults. Their experience counts. You tried to blunder in for who knows what reason and could have gotten yourself and that girl killed. She wears Sapphire. You wear Opal. You would stand no chance against her in a fight."

Zoey's legs trembled. She wished she were allowed to sit down.

She wished she had the courage to ask if she could.

"But let's suppose that Beale had abandoned all sense of duty and allowed you to have your way, and let's suppose a witch like Grizande, who loathes Queens, wouldn't have eviscerated you as soon as she got close enough. What were you going to do? A powerful witch arrived at the Hall, exhausted and frightened because of what she's endured. What were you going to do? Invite her to your square of rooms, where she could sit quietly and have some food? Sit quietly with you? Only you?"

Zoey didn't answer. Didn't know how to answer.

"Or would you have invited Titian to meet a girl who is just learning the common tongue and feels self-conscious about the struggle to communicate? Now there are two girls trying to be friendly. Talking and talking. And the rest of your coven? If they became curious about someone from a people that has rarely been seen in centuries? Would you have told them they had to stay away? They're all friendly, too, aren't they? Would you, having taken responsibility for this girl's well-being, to say nothing of a young tiger who would be uneasy around strangers, have done your duty as a Queen and told your friends to stay away? Even Titian? Even if they pushed to meet the girl? Would you have stood for her as a Queen, disappointing your friends?"

"I didn't think . . ." Tears ran down Zoey's face.

"No," Witch said gently, "you didn't think. You followed the instincts of a Queen, and usually there is nothing wrong with that. But in this case you chose to ignore the experience of two men who understood the dangers and needed you to leave so that they could help the girl without compromising your safety and the safety of everyone else in the Hall. The moment Beale said he would take care of it, you should have retreated. If you wanted information, there are ways to ask for it—and Beale would have come to you when everything was settled and answered your questions. As it was, you put Daemonar and Beale in a difficult position. While your intentions weren't the same, your attitude about Beale's authority was not that different from Saetien's—and look at the price so many paid for that. Including you."

Zoey called in a handkerchief and cried as quietly as possible. She wanted to wail, but she wasn't a child anymore.

"You probably never did anything wrong," she said in a small voice.

A silvery, velvet-coated laugh filled a room that suddenly warmed. "Oh, I sat across from my father more times than I want to count, receiving a sharply worded lecture on why a Queen doesn't do whatever it was I did. Although sometimes I—and other members of the coven—sat across from him and tried to explain something like a spell that had gone wrong, which was difficult since we were usually summoned to his study before we'd figured out that part."

Zoey wiped her nose and vanished the handkerchief.

"A natural Healer instinctively knows how to do some things, how to heal some wounds. She still needs training. The same is true for a Queen. A good Queen—a potentially great Queen—needs to harness instinct to training and experience. You have the instinct, Zoela. You're just beginning to acquire the training and experience. You'll make mistakes—and you'll face consequences. That's part of the experience. And if someone is trusted to stand for you and protect you, don't ignore what they're telling you."

She sighed. "The other girls were jabbing at me for being treated like I'm special."

"You are special," Witch said quietly. "You survived."

You survived. Two words that encompassed physical pain and still-recurring nightmares.

"Fortunately, you have a friend who isn't going to hesitate to slap you down if you get stupid."

Zoey looked into those sapphire eyes and knew that

something even more terrible than what she'd endured had happened to this Queen. "Did you have a friend like that?"

Witch gave her a dry smile. "If you think Daemonar can be a prick about things, you should try tangling with Lucivar."

Zoey responded to the smile. "Training and experience?"

"Uh-huh."

"Mother Night."

"And may the Darkness be merciful."

She sighed. "I owe Daemonar an apology. And Lord Beale."

"Yes, you do." A beat of silence. "Grizande and Jaalan will have a room in the same square as you and your co-ven. She is not yours to command. She is mine, Zoela. She may never be easy around other Queens, but it is important for her to become acquainted with other people."

"I'll try not to be a Sceltie."

"Liath has already filled that position."

"Oh." Zoey wrinkled her face in sympathy. "Is that a good idea?"

"Do you want to tell him he's not going to help teach the kitten?"

"Noooo."

"Which indicates you are at least as intelligent as every-one else at the Hall, because no one else is going to tell him."

The sitting room door opened. Prince Sadi stood in the corridor, waiting.

Zoey hesitated. "Can I still have the lessons?"

"Yes, you can."

She bowed. "Lady."

"Little Sister."

Zoey walked out of the sitting room. The door closed. Prince Sadi said nothing.

"I got scolded," Zoey finally said.

"Did you think you wouldn't?" he asked mildly.

"She's . . ." *Terrifying. And yet . . .*

"Yes, she is."

As they walked back to the sitting room where the rest

of their group waited, it occurred to Zoey that Witch was the Queen of Ebon Askavi—and Daemon Sadi had been married to her.

If he could be married to *her* . . .

She began to appreciate just how dangerous he was.

TWENTY

Daemonar landed in the flagstone courtyard outside his family's eyrie. He appreciated not being stuck in the Coach with the girls, especially since Grizande was the only one who didn't look ready to fall on him weeping and wailing. Lucivar was acting as the barrier between the girls on the short trip from the Keep to the eyrie—and may the Darkness have mercy on any girl who crossed *him*.

"Mother?" Daemonar called as soon as he walked into the eyrie's large front room. "Mother?"

His brother Andulvar would be in school for another hour or so. It was possible Marian was in Riada doing some extra shopping to accommodate guests tonight.

Had anyone told her about the tiger?

I'm getting the guest rooms ready, Marian said before Daemonar released a Green psychic probe to locate her. Women, including mothers, could get fairly exercised about having a male track them down when they wanted some privacy.

Boyo, unless there's a reason to assume she's in trouble, give your mother a minute to respond. And if you're going to use Craft to locate her, be subtle about it or risk getting whacked upside the head.

His mother wore Purple Dusk; he wore Green. Even so, it had taken him a while—and a few whacks—to figure out how to be subtle.

He headed for the part of the eyrie that held the guest rooms. He found her in the best guest room, smoothing the covers on the bed.

"Uncle Daemon said he's staying at the Keep tonight," Daemonar said.

"So I was told," Marian replied.

He frowned at the bed. "You're giving Zoey the best room?"

"Zoey is staying in the guest room close to Titian's room, where the children's guests usually stay."

If Zoey and Titian weren't romantic, a cot would have been set up in Titian's room so the girls could stay together. But romance—and sex—had strict rules, at least within the family, so Zoey slept in her own room.

"You're giving this room to Grizande?"

Marian gave him a look that had a sharp edge. "You have some objection to that?"

"None at all." A challenge. His mother was a bit riled about something. "Did Father mention the tiger kitten?"

"He did." Marian stared at him. "No guest will be made to feel unwelcome in our home."

Whoa. Seriously riled.

He suddenly stood on slippery ground and had no idea why.

Daemonar blew out a breath. "I like her. I like them. I have no quarrel with Grizande and Jaalan."

Marian sighed, walked up to him, and kissed his cheek. "My apologies. Some things stir up old memories." She hesitated. "Old wounds. When I first arrived in Kaeleer, someone made me feel unwelcome, encouraged me to feel inferior. Unworthy of time and attention even though I deserved both."

Daemonar put his arms around her. "What can I do?"

She hugged him hard, then eased back and smiled. "Just be your father's son."

As soon as Daemon set the Coach down on the landing web below the eyrie, Lucivar opened the door and gave

Titian and Zoey permission to leave. They pelted up the stairs, not giving Grizande a backward glance.

He approached the Tigre girl and the kitten from the back of the Coach. Daemon stepped out of the driver's compartment and approached from the front. Realizing she was caught between two powerful Warlord Princes, Grizande slowly rose to her feet while Jaalan pressed against her legs.

She would fight. Even knowing she couldn't win, she would fight—because she just might last long enough to get away. Maybe that's how she survived whatever had happened in Tigrelan.

The girl had backbone. He approved.

"I have noisy children," Lucivar said. "There are only three of them. . . ."

"Who sometimes sound like three dozen," Daemon added dryly.

Lucivar nodded. "If you need some quiet time, you let us know. That goes for the kitten too."

He watched the way she looked at him, then at Daemon. Thinking. Reassessing. Gambling that they could be trusted.

"I say if noisy too big," she said.

"Okay. Then let's go up to the eyrie." Lucivar walked out of the Coach.

"Do you fear heights?" Daemon asked Grizande.

"Heights?" She stepped out of the Coach. Her eyes widened as she looked around and saw the valley below them.

"High places," Daemon said. "Allow me." He wrapped a hand around one of her arms and pointed to the stairs with the other. "Lucivar's home is up there."

The kitten seemed frozen in the doorway of the Coach. Too many changes for one so young?

Rather than have Jaalan bolt and take a tumble on the mountain, Lucivar grabbed the kitten and settled him in his arms like some oversized, furry baby. Either the kitten was too startled to object or he was used to being held this way, even if the person now holding him was a stranger.

Lucivar reached the flagstone courtyard and was about

to put Jaalan down when Andulvar flew in at a reckless speed. Daemon held the girl. Lucivar held the kitten and watched his youngest barely manage to backwing and land without ending up in a heap.

"Is that a cat?" Andulvar asked, his eyes on the kitten. "I saw you arrive when I left the school eyrie."

Well, that explained the boy's hurry to get home.

"Can you say hello to our guests?" Lucivar said.

"Hello." That aimed at the kitten.

"The other guests?"

Andulvar blinked, then turned his head. "Hi, Uncle Daemon." He gave more of his attention to Grizande as he reached for Jaalan. "Who are you? Is this your cat?"

"Boyo, you're fondling the tail of a Warlord Prince," Lucivar said.

"Huh?"

"This is Lady Grizande," Daemon said. "That is Prince Jaalan."

The titles seeped into his boy's brain. "They're Blood?"

"They are Blood," Lucivar agreed. Then he sighed. The boy was focused on the cat. The kitten was focused on the boy's wings. "Come on."

Lucivar led his guests and son into the eyrie, then turned and took the kitten through the glass doors that led to the play yard. He set Jaalan on the grass and gave boy and kitten a stern look. "No teeth, no claws, no fists. Play nice or you won't be allowed to play together. Understood?"

"Yes, Papa," Andulvar said.

Lucivar wasn't sure how much the kitten understood, but the adults would soon find out. "All right. Go play." He walked back into the eyrie and looked at Grizande, who watched the kitten bound after the boy. "There are shields around the yard to keep them from falling off the mountain. They'll be all right." More or less.

"Big noisy stay outside?" Grizande asked.

Daemon chuckled.

Lucivar grinned. "Yeah. Until the big noisy is tired enough to be quiet." He sensed Marian's presence a moment before she entered the front room. "Marian, this is Grizande. Witchling, this is my wife, Marian."

He felt Grizande brace for an attack.

Marian walked up to Daemon first and gave him a kiss on the cheek before turning to the girl. "Welcome, Grizande. I have a room ready for you, if you'd like to see it." She frowned. "Where is . . . ?"

A happy shout coming from the play yard.

"Oh," Marian said. "Well, they can't get into *too* much trouble out there."

"One Warlord Prince is Lucivar's son and the other is a tiger kitten," Daemon said in a tone that sounded insincerely helpful. "How much trouble can they be?"

Marian smacked Daemon's arm and huffed while she tried not to laugh.

Grizande blinked.

"I'll keep an eye on them." Daemon sounded chastened— and amused.

Grizande blinked again.

And so your education begins, witchling, Lucivar thought.

"I'll show you to your room," Marian said, focusing on Grizande. She looked at the men. "You two do whatever you're supposed to do."

"Well, that put you in your place," Daemon said when the women headed into the warren of rooms that made up the eyrie.

"You're one of the two, old son," Lucivar replied. He watched Andulvar and Jaalan for a minute. "The girl is fairly easy with Warlord Princes but struggles with other women."

"I noticed. But she trusted a Black Widow enough to leave everything she knew and come to the Hall."

"If the girl is being hunted, do you think that Black Widow is still alive?"

The air chilled. "I'll ask some of the demon-dead to keep watch for any Tigre witches arriving in the Dark Realm. If something happened to the people who helped Grizande get away, I'll know soon enough."

You'll know when they die. But if they're captured and tortured, who can say how long they'll endure before you have an answer?

"Tigrelan is not our Territory, Prick. There's nothing we can do."

"I know. But that girl isn't in Tigrelan anymore."

"No," Daemon said too softly. "She's under my hand now."

Protected by the High Lord of Hell. And Witch.

Grizande followed the female Lucivar called wife. Same as mate?

As they walked through wide corridors carved from the living mountain, she looked for cages and traps. For betrayal.

Marian opened a door and walked into a room that held a large bed and small bedside tables, a wardrobe and dresser, a chair and floor lamp. A window without bars, but shields could also make a prison. This witch didn't have that kind of power, but if she wanted it to be so, would Prince Lucivar use his Ebon-gray to create a cage?

"This room is closer to our bedroom, in case you have any questions or wake up uneasy," Marian said. "The bathroom is just down the corridor. I'll show you." A hesitation. "Did anyone at the Hall ask you about moontime supplies? Do you need some? Or any other supplies?"

Kindness. Caring. Grizande looked around the room. Simple. Clean. But the quilt on the bed, in colors of the forest . . .

When she pressed her hand against it, she could pick up some of Marian's psychic scent. Too much scent for just handling. Scent held over from the making? "Beautiful," she said softly.

"Thank you."

"You make?"

"Yes, I did."

Memories almost forgotten out of necessity rose and raked Grizande's heart.

"Grizande?" Marian sounded concerned, as if feelings mattered.

How to explain to this woman when she didn't have the words anyone here would understand? "Mother." She waved a hand to indicate the room and what its clean simplicity meant.

"This reminds you of her?" Marian asked.

She nodded. "Dead long time."

"Ah." A pause. "Would you like a hug?"

"Hug?"

Marian opened her arms. An invitation.

The Hourglass had raised her, protected her, trained her in basic Craft, because of her bloodline. But they had kept their distance from her. It hurt now to be held by a woman, by a mother. It hurt—but it also felt good. Felt safe in a way her mind barely remembered but her body did.

"You've had an eventful couple of days," Marian said. "Would you like to stay in your room and rest or come out and join us?"

"Join big noisy."

Marian laughed. "Come on, then."

When they reached the large front room, Marian stopped and looked around. "I guess we're on our own. Oh! Daemon."

Prince Sadi appeared in an archway. "Darling, do you mind if Grizande and I use your kitchen table?"

"I don't mind as long as you don't get in the way of me making dinner," she replied.

"I would never get in the way of dinner preparations," he said dryly. "Not with your hoard."

Grizande followed them into the kitchen. Marian pulled food out of a cold box and set bowls and other tools on the counter. Humming a tune that sounded bittersweet, she began her work.

Prince Sadi took a seat at the table and indicated that Grizande should sit beside him. He placed a sheet of paper and a writing tool in front of her. He picked up another writing tool, and on the paper in front of him made careful shapes. Then he pointed to the paper in front of her. "Now you try."

She studied the shapes on his paper, picked up her writing tool, and copied them.

The Prince nodded. "That is your name. That is how 'Grizande' looks in the common tongue." He looked at her. "In Tigre?"

She wrote her name in the language of her people. He studied it, copied what she'd done, then asked, "Is that correct?"

"Yes." Her name. The Hourglass had taught her what they could of the common tongue, but they hadn't known this.

The Prince drew more symbols below her name. "Daemon."

She copied that name—and the ones that followed. Daemonar. Lucivar. Andulvar. Jaalan. Marian. Titian. Zoela. Helene. Nadene. Beale. Mrs. Beale. Holt. Raine.

When it seemed like he wasn't going to write any more, she wrote a word in her language and looked at him. When he didn't seem to understand, she pointed in the direction of the Black Mountain. "Her?"

"Witch?"

She nodded.

He wrote the word for the Queen who was more than a Queen. Who was myth and dreams. One name for her, anyway. She copied the word.

Smiling, the Prince called in a strange book of empty lined paper. "This is what students use for their studies. You write in it."

"Write important . . ." How to ask?

He seemed to know. "Whatever you want. Words you want to know. Things you want to remember. Questions you want to ask. And these"—he called in printed books and set them in front of her—"are how our young learn to read the common tongue. I think they will be a useful way to begin the lessons."

"Lessons?"

"With me. I'll be teaching you Craft and Protocol with some of the other girls. The lessons in the common tongue will be with me or with Prince Raine."

"Daemonar?"

"He can help you learn the common tongue and help you practice the lessons you learn from me." The Prince paused. "And I'm sure Liath will help too."

Grizande sighed. "Prince Bossy Stern Teeth."

Marian let out a hoot of laughter and stopped chopping vegetables. "Who is this Liath?"

The Prince cleared his throat. "A Sceltie Warlord Prince who wears a Green Jewel."

"Oh, Daemon," Marian said. "You didn't."

"I repeat: Sceltie Warlord Prince who wears a Green Jewel. What makes you think I had any say in this?"

"You own the Hall?" Marian replied.

"You wear Black," Grizande said, then braced for a slap. She hadn't been told she could speak.

The Prince looked at Marian, then at Grizande. "I own the Hall, and I wear the Black. Not everyone who lives or works at the Hall is impressed by those truths."

The tone was dry as dust, but his gold eyes were filled with humor.

Prince Lucivar stood in the archway and looked at the Prince. "You done with her?"

"For the moment," he replied.

"Good. Come on, witchling. I'll get you started learning the sparring warm-up."

Grizande looked at the Prince, not sure who she should obey.

"I thought you were going to help me fix dinner," Marian said.

"You have him," Prince Lucivar replied, tipping his head toward the Prince.

"Go on," the Prince said quietly. "You should learn from the best."

Grizande vanished the items she'd been given, then followed Prince Lucivar to the large front room.

Daemonar handed her a long, thick stick. "An Eyrien sparring stick." He took up a position on one side of her.

Prince Lucivar took up a position on the other side. "This is how you begin."

Daemon had known Marian for centuries, had loved her for being his brother's wife and also loved her for being Marian. He knew her moods almost as well as Lucivar did.

"Something on your mind?" he asked as he kneaded the dough for the biscuits.

"You are going to help that girl." It wasn't a question.

"I am. I'll keep her safe, Marian, along with the other girls."

"Are there Tigre in Hell?"

"Why do you ask?"

"She said her mother died a long time ago, but she's from a short-lived race and she's young, so it can't be that many years."

Daemon continued to knead the dough while he considered how to answer. "If it was a hard death . . ."

"The girl doesn't need to see the mother, although she desperately needs some affection. But I think Grizande's mother would appreciate knowing her daughter is safe. Especially if hers was a hard death."

"The Tigre are almost as reclusive a race as the Dea al Mon. We don't know what happened in that Territory that has left the descendant of a powerful Queen orphaned and uneducated—and at risk." He put the dough in a bowl and covered it to let it rise. "I'll look for Grizande's family. If any of them are still in the Dark Realm, I will let them know she is safe."

He washed his hands and didn't look at her when he asked, "Are you all right with her being here?"

"Don't be insulting, Daemon," Marian replied, her voice sharp.

Hit a nerve, he thought. "My apologies, Marian. I wasn't implying that you wouldn't welcome—"

"My father sold me to pay off some gambling debts. Did Lucivar ever tell you that? Did Jaenelle?"

"Stop. Please." He struggled to keep the Sadist from slipping the leash in response to her words. It wouldn't do any of them any good to have that side of him here tonight.

She ignored the warning. "Sold me to five Warlords so that they could rape me and kill me. For sport."

"Marian. *Please.*"

He heard Daemonar talking Grizande through the moves with the stick. He felt Lucivar at his back. Watchful. Wary.

Marian breathed out slowly, but she couldn't stop. "Titian. Zoey. Grizande. Two have been cherished since birth. One was deemed unimportant—and expendable. Maybe that's not true. Some of her people made an effort to protect her as best they could. But this stirred up memories. I want to help her heal, Daemon. I want to help her the way Jaenelle and your father helped me. The way Lucivar helped me."

He gathered her in his arms and swayed gently. "You will help. We all will. Shh, darling. It's all right."

Even centuries of being loved couldn't prevent an old heart wound from opening again and feeling as painful as when the wound had been delivered.

A brush of Ebon-gray power against his first inner barrier.

You won't find her father among the living, Lucivar said. *And you won't find him in Hell. Saetan made sure the debt Marian's father owed our family was paid in full.*

And the rest of Marian's family?

I don't know. As long as they don't come here, I won't ask.

*Then I won't actively hunt. But should our paths cross, whatever debt *they* owe will be paid in full.*

Thank you, High Lord. Lucivar cleared his throat. "You going to cuddle my wife all evening, or are we going to get some dinner?"

"Take a piss in the wind, Prick," Daemon said.

Marian stepped back and patted the skin under her eyes. "Behave. Both of you."

Lucivar returned to the front room. Marian finished preparing the stew and put the pot on the heat to cook.

"I'll take care of the biscuits once the dough rises," Daemon said. "Why don't you spend a little time in your garden?"

"Are you trying to Sceltie me?"

"No, I was making a suggestion. A Sceltie would have issued a statement and then blocked any attempt you made to do something different."

A small laugh, but it was a laugh. "Very well. Since you're *suggesting*, I would like a little time in the garden."

After Marian went out to her garden, Daemon waited for Lucivar to join him.

"Problem?" Lucivar asked.

"I have business in Scelt that shouldn't be delayed, but I don't want to leave Grizande on her own at the Hall until I have a chance to see how the other girls will react—and how she'll react to them."

"She can stay here for a couple of days."

A tempting solution to one problem. But . . . "Surreal is at the Hall, keeping an eye on things."

Lucivar stared at him. "You left Surreal with a pack of adolescent girls?"

"She does have that sanctuary now."

"She deals with girls who have been broken, not with girls who feel entitled because of their caste or because their families are aristo. And after getting the girls to safety, she doesn't deal with them all that much. At least, that's my understanding."

He couldn't deny the truth of that. Or the niggling worry about her wading into what she'd called "the bitch drama-trauma." "I had intended to be back tomorrow. I told her that she didn't have to interact with any of the youngsters, but she had other thoughts."

"Hell's fire," Lucivar said. "All right, I'll take the children back to the Hall and spend a couple of days there.

That way Surreal can leave, or we can have one of our bracing discussions."

"Thank you." Daemon hesitated, reluctant to scrape Lucivar's temper but feeling the need to explain. "Saetien wants to go to Scelt to find out about Wilhelmina Benedict."

Lucivar's silence took on the weight of stone. "You agreed to that?"

"If I can make some particular arrangements for her to stay in Maghre, then yes, I'll agree to it."

"Will Witch?"

"That's what the Lady and I will discuss tonight."

Zoey and Titian had spent the afternoon in Titian's room. Hiding. She'd been hiding; Titian had stayed with her. No one had demanded that they come out and be friendly with the Tigre witch. No one had seemed to notice that they hadn't participated in whatever everyone else had done that afternoon.

Had anyone even remembered that they were there?

She didn't want to be noticed—but she did want to be noticed. Unless it would get her into more trouble. She didn't like being in trouble.

What had the other girls thought about her leaving with Prince Sadi this morning? *Her* friends had been concerned that she'd been summoned to the Keep. Did the rest of the girls know where she'd gone? Dinah would be envious and make more sly remarks about why Zoey was favored by the SaDiablo family.

She'd been friends with Saetien since they were young girls. She'd been hurt during the house party Delora had tricked Saetien into having at the Hall a few months ago. Her grandmother was friends with the Warlord Prince of Dhemlan. *Those* were the reasons she was more familiar with Prince Sadi than the other girls.

Now she had to figure out how to be friendly with someone who didn't want to be friendly, because she and this Tigre girl would be living in the same square of rooms and would be crossing paths in the communal rooms and in their classes.

Why hadn't she listened to Beale? Had she really crossed the same line that Saetien had crossed at the house party? Saetien, who was Prince Sadi's daughter, had been *banished* for crossing that line.

"What if I'm not allowed to stay at the Hall anymore?" Zoey whispered, wrapping her arms around her knees. "What if I'm banished like Saetien?"

"You didn't do anything *that* bad," Titian replied. "We'll be friendly but not pouncy friendly."

"Pouncy friendly?" That made her smile. Then she sighed. "Being around other Queens. It feels like we're in a competition, but I don't know what we're competing for. It will be ages before any of us are old enough to form a court, and Queens are supposed to work together for the good of the Territory. Aren't they?"

"Kathlene's nice. So is Azara. And Felisha." Titian made a face. "But Dinah is a b-i-t-c-h."

"She was on the list of Queens who were targeted by Delora and the coven of malice," Zoey pointed out. "Delora wouldn't have done that if Dinah was *too* b-i-t-c-h."

Titian shrugged.

A quick knock on the door.

"Yes?" Titian said.

The door opened enough for Daemonar to lean into the room. "Mother wants the two of you to come out and help set the table. Dinner is almost ready."

Titian scrambled to her feet. "Daemonar . . ."

He gave his sister a long look. "Apology accepted. We can talk later if you want to talk."

They made their way to the kitchen. The Tigre girl was already there, watching Marian.

"We're eating in the dining room this evening," Marian said as she started handing out stacks of plates to the girls. "Titian, you show the others where to go and how to set up the table."

When they reached the dining room, Zoey looked at Grizande and was determined to say something friendly but not pouncy. Except . . . The look in the girl's eyes. Distrust. Loathing. As if everything Zoey might say was a trick or a lie. As if everything she might do was a trap that would cause pain.

That's not what Queens are supposed to be, Zoey thought.

Prince Sadi walked in, carrying stemmed wineglasses for the adults. Daemonar followed him with water goblets for the non-adults.

Four wineglasses. Four water goblets.

Zoey felt an odd jolt as she realized the significance. Daemonar was an adult. She didn't think of him that way. He was Titian's brother. He attended classes.

He also taught sparring and the first level of training in weapons.

Adult. Not all the way. Not until he made the Offering to the Darkness, but the simple fact of who had what glass suddenly made the line so clear—and made clear how much his experience and training outstripped hers.

Painfully aware that Prince Sadi was still in the room, Zoey turned to Grizande. "My apologies if I made you uncomfortable yesterday. It was not my intention. I wanted to make you feel welcome, but I didn't do it the correct way."

"Not your place to welcome." The words came out slowly, as if each had to be found.

"No, it wasn't, but I didn't think about that."

Prince Sadi glided past Grizande on his way to the door and said softly, "She, too, has much to learn." Then he was gone.

Grizande stared at Zoey, a feral look in those green eyes—a look that gradually faded. "We will learn."

"And one thing we learn," Daemonar said as he walked out of the room, "is not to delay getting the food on the table."

Daemonar wasn't sure what had gotten the girls all stirred up, but they seemed to have called a truce.

He picked up the bowl of lightly dressed greens, then handed the basket of biscuits to Grizande.

"Jaalan?" she asked, glancing toward the glass doors where Lucivar stood whistling for boy and kitten to come in for dinner.

"We have a bowl of food for him," Daemonar replied as Andulvar and Jaalan entered the eyrie and pelted toward the kitchen.

"Wash up before you eat," Lucivar said, his voice thundering enough to stop the boy.

The kitten wasn't quite as quick to give up on a possible meal, but he did stop before he entered the kitchen.

"But . . . Papa," Andulvar said, "we're *hungry*."

"And you'll stay hungry until your mother says your hands are clean enough for you to sit at her table."

Head down, shoulders rounded, the picture of a dejected boy, Andulvar shuffled toward the bedrooms and bathrooms. Jaalan, observant and learning from his new friend . . . Head down, tail down, the picture of a dejected kitten shuffling after the boy.

Daemonar didn't dare look at Grizande. "Kindred are very impressionable at that age. I learned that from the Scelties."

"Are you two going to stand there, or are you going to get the food to the table?" Daemon asked from behind them.

Daemonar led the way, but he was close enough to hear his father laughing when Lucivar went into the kitchen to wash his hands.

"Jaalan. Andulvar. It . . . funny," Grizande said, smiling.

"Oh, yeah," he agreed, grinning.

It became funnier when Marian stopped boy and kitten at the dining room doorway and said, "Let's see the hands."

Andulvar raised his hands palm out for his mother's inspection. She held his hands, turning them to inspect both sides—and the fingernails—before saying, "Clean hands. Good job." She ran a hand over his hair and kissed his forehead.

Then she looked at Jaalan. The kitten looked at her.

"Psst." Andulvar made little up-and-down motions with his hands.

Settling on his haunches, Jaalan lifted his front legs and showed Marian his paws.

She gave the paws the same careful inspection and said, "Clean paws. Good job." Then she ran a hand over the kitten's head and gave him a quick kiss on the nose. "Now we can eat."

Andulvar took his place at the table. Jaalan was shown the bowls of meat and water that were placed where he wouldn't trip anyone or get stepped on but could still see Grizande.

"We've done this before," Daemon said as he passed the basket of biscuits to Grizande.

She sat between Lucivar at the head of the table and Daemon on her right. Daemonar and Andulvar sat across from her, effectively forming a barricade around Grizande, while Titian and Zoey sat at the other end of the table with Marian. Daemonar's little brother looked like he couldn't decide whether to pounce on his food like some ravenous beast, which would earn a scolding from Marian, or pounce on Grizande with questions about tigers in general and Jaalan in particular.

Probably best that students and kitten were going back to the Hall tomorrow. Kindred wolves who were descended from Tassle still lived on the mountain and came to the eyrie to visit, but they were familiar and, therefore, not as interesting. Give Andulvar another day of playing with a tiger and he might work up to asking if they could have one come live with them.

Of course, if the boy started by asking if a Sceltie could live with them, he might wear the parents down to agreeing to a tiger as a less formidable companion.

Zoey usually relaxed and enjoyed the sensation of Titian brushing her hair, but tonight she couldn't relax, her mind too full of the things she'd heard at dinner. "Do they always do that when they're together?"

"Do what?" Titian asked in turn.

"Tell stories about the Dark Court. About the . . . Queen." How did a person reconcile the stories—especially the amusing stories—with the being who had stared at her with those sapphire eyes?

"Sometimes." Titian continued to brush Zoey's hair. "Maybe a lot. They don't talk about things that happened before they came to Kaeleer. At least, not at the dinner table and not in front of guests. There are private talks, things they tell us about living in Terreille when they feel we're old enough to understand at least some of what they're saying. That's why Daemonar, being older, knows lots more than I do."

"About things like what the girls at the Amdarh school said about Lady Surreal being a"—she ended with a whisper—"whore?"

"I guess. Mother and Father, Uncle Daemon, and Auntie Surreal tell stories about the Dark Court and the Lady when we gather during Winsol, because stories about the Dark Court are also the family stories."

"But you looked like you'd never heard these stories before."

"Saetien didn't like hearing about the Queen, so she would push for the two of us to leave and do something in another room." Titian put the brush on the dresser and looked at Zoey in the mirror. "Did you see Grizande's face?"

"No. I was sitting on the same side of the table, and Prince Sadi was sitting between us," Zoey replied.

"I think they told those particular stories tonight because it was a way to tell Grizande about her bloodline, about the Queen she was named after and the Warlord Prince who was that Grizande's Consort and husband. I think it was a way to tell stories about kindred that we all might find useful. Her face tonight . . ." Titian blinked back tears. "It was like seeing someone receive a gift so wonderful it was painful."

She understood that feeling. She'd felt that way years ago when she'd sent Prince Sadi her first report and received a reply. A brief reply, to be sure, but an acknowledgment of her duty as a Queen. She'd received support from her grandparents all the time and training from her grandmother, who was the Queen of Amdarh, but that hadn't felt the same as receiving that first letter from the Prince.

"We should try to be Grizande's friends," Zoey said.

Titian kissed Zoey's cheek. "We will. As much as she'll let us, we will."

A kiss on the lips might have turned into something much warmer if there hadn't been two sharp raps on the bedroom door—Lucivar's warning that it was time for everyone to settle down in their own rooms.

Zoey didn't see Lucivar when Titian opened the door and slipped out of the room, but she knew he was there.

She got into bed. The book she'd chosen couldn't distract her enough from the worry about what she would face when she returned to the Hall. At the school in Amdarh she hadn't noticed the opinions of the other students, except to be aware that Delora was someone she didn't like and didn't trust. She'd been content with her small group of friends—and her romantic friendship with Titian. Now she felt vulnerable, and she wondered if she would always feel that way.

TWENTY-ONE

EBON ASKAVI

Daemon walked into the sitting room across from the Queen's and Consort's suites and found Karla and Witch waiting for him. Well, he wasn't sure they were waiting for *him*. Still, finding them together was convenient.

"Karla, darling, your assistance is requested," he purred.

Karla blinked. "If you're phrasing it like that and using that tone of voice, what in the name of Hell did you do?"

"Nothing. But Jillian is ready to have her Virgin Night."

"You want us to lock Lucivar in a room and hold him until it's done?" Witch asked.

"No, that won't be necessary." He hoped. Well, it wouldn't be necessary. He'd be in Amdarh too. "Surreal is handling the details, but I thought Jillian might benefit from hearing about a Virgin Night from someone who had dealt with Lucivar."

Karla stared at him. "You want me to tell Jillian what Lucivar did with me as a way to *assure her* that everything will be *fine*?"

Daemon rocked back on his heels. "He got you through it."

Jaenelle looked at Karla. "He did do that. And anything anyone else does to see a witch through her Virgin Night is going to seem quite dull in comparison."

He felt the ground crumbling under him. "What did he do?"

They just smiled at him.

"You're not going to tell me."

"No," Karla said sweetly. "When do you want me to talk to Jillian?"

"At your earliest convenience," he replied dryly.

"Then you should send a message to Lady Jillian that someone will be at her cottage tomorrow evening to discuss Virgin Nights." A pause. "Kiss kiss."

Karla nodded to Witch, then floated out of the sitting room.

Daemon took a seat next to Witch on the sofa.

She smiled. "I'm not going to tell you either."

He wondered if dealing with Witch and Karla together was the mental equivalent of making the Khaldharon Run. He'd have to ask Lucivar.

"You wanted to talk about your daughter," Jaenelle said quietly.

He sobered. "Yes. She's struggling to find her balance and believes she needs to go to Scelt in order to find herself."

"Believes it because . . . ?"

"Because of a broken Black Widow staying at Surreal's sanctuary."

"I see."

He sighed, not sure if this would cause her pain. "Saetien was told the key to finding herself is learning about Wilhelmina Benedict."

Silence.

He looked at the Queen who was the love of his life. "If that would hurt you . . ."

Jaenelle shook her head. "You know who she'll have to see."

"Yes."

"He won't be kind if she is . . . rude."

"I know." He hesitated. "Does she really need to do this? Stir up the past like this?"

"If it had been Tersa who had told her to do this, would you be questioning the need for her to go?" Jaenelle placed a hand over his. "No, you wouldn't."

She walked over to a desk in the room, returned a minute later, and held out a stiff rectangle of paper that had her seal embossed in the lower right-hand corner. "Give him this. He'll understand."

Daemon vanished the paper. "I'll head to Scelt first thing in the morning."

Jaenelle resumed her seat. "What about Grizande?"

"Lucivar is taking the children—and the kitten—back to the Hall tomorrow. Surreal is there now, keeping an eye on everyone."

Jaenelle blinked. "You left Surreal with a pack of adolescents?"

He huffed. "Why does everyone assume the Hall will be a battleground by the time I get back?"

"Surreal. Adolescent girls, whose existence will scrape a sore spot right now. Boys with understandable but very inappropriate fantasies."

He leaned his head back and closed his eyes. "Shit."

She patted his hand. "Look at the bright side, Daemon. When Lucivar gets there, they will all be *thrilled* to see him. And after a couple of days of dealing with him, they'll be even more thrilled to see you."

"So the Black-Jeweled Warlord Prince who is the High Lord of Hell is the *benign* presence?"

"That confused Saetan too, but he got used to it. Eventually."

"Was that before or after you and the coven blew up a wall?"

She gave him that unsure but game smile. "Which time?"

TWENTY-TWO

Helene, Holt, Nadene, Raine, and Beale were waiting for Lucivar in the great hall. One look at the panic barely concealed behind their stoic expressions told him everything he needed to know.

"Prince Sadi has business in Scelt and will be gone for a couple more days. I will be here."

Still panicky but definitely relieved. Hell's fire.

Well, he'd start with the simple and work his way up to what he hoped hadn't reached deadly.

"Helene, Lady Grizande and Prince Jaalan will have a room in the square across from the High Lord's suite. Would you escort her there and make sure she has everything she needs? Also, talk to Tarl about setting up something for the kitten's toilet. He'll need something nearby while he's young."

Helene smiled and said, "This way."

Grizande hesitated.

"Go on," Lucivar said. "Get settled in." Before the girl took a step, he resumed going down his list. "Prince Raine, you will be assisting Prince Sadi in teaching Lady Grizande to read, write, and speak the common tongue. Give her an hour to get settled; then go over to talk to her. Grizande, you show him the books Sadi gave you to help you get started. Being a teacher by profession, Prince Raine will have helpful suggestions."

Raine stared at him, wide-eyed, before regaining some composure. "I'll be happy to help in whatever way I can."

"Good." Lucivar turned to the other three children. "Daemonar, you're on a two-day rest."

"But . . . ," Daemonar began.

"If you don't understand why, I will explain it to you later."

"Yes, sir."

"Zoey and Titian. You go get settled in. When Prince Raine meets with Grizande, he will also let you know what to study for tomorrow's lessons."

"Besides survival?" Raine muttered almost under his breath.

Lucivar ignored the mutter. "Go."

They hustled out of the great hall, leaving him with Holt, Nadene, and Beale.

Nadene next. "Anyone end up being gutted, having broken bones, or being skinned because they tangled with Surreal?"

More wide eyes. "No," Nadene replied. "Would she do that? The skinning part?"

Daemon would kill him flatter than dead if the resident Healer bolted, but although Nadene had grown up in a town near one of the family estates and had *heard* about the SaDiablo family, she hadn't dealt with any of them until now, and she needed to understand the temper behind Surreal's Gray power.

"Well, Surreal and her mother skinned her sire while he was still alive, and then fed him to the hounds of Hell. So I know she's done it at least once." He gave Nadene that smile that always meant trouble. "Then again, so have I."

She turned and walked away. He took it as a promising sign that she headed into the Hall rather than out the front door. But just in case . . .

He waited until she was out of hearing range before saying to Beale, "If she starts packing her trunks, I need to know."

"Neither you nor Surreal are in residence that often,"

Holt said. "She's comfortable enough around Prince Sadi, so I think she'll stay."

Lucivar blew out a breath. "Where is Surreal?"

Hesitation. That flicker of panic.

"She's out on the back lawn with the young Ladies," Beale finally said. "The young gentlemen are on the terrace. They seem unwilling to attract her notice."

"We're not sure what inflamed Surreal's temper, but I think Lady Dinah said or did something to provoke her," Holt said. "She ordered all the girls out on the lawn . . ." He looked at Beale.

"Where she has been testing the girls' shields to the breaking point," Beale finished. "She has not yet drained her Gray."

Lucivar nodded in understanding. Red against Gray would be an ugly fight, and Red would lose. Once Surreal had to drop back to her Green Birthright Jewel, Beale could wrap her in Red shields and contain her while he sent out a call for reinforcements. Until then, the prudent thing to do was wait unless it became clear that her intention was to kill one or more of the girls.

"I'll deal with her." Rather than travel through the Hall's endless corridors, he walked out the front door, spread his wings, and flew over the Hall to reach the back lawn. When he landed, he noticed two huddles of girls being guarded—or penned—by Liath. They'd each used most of the reservoir of power in their Jewel and looked frightened and exhausted but unhurt.

He looked at the boys huddled on the terrace. The four Warlord Princes had the toes of their shoes just beyond the flagstones, but that was as far as they'd gone. Well, none of them wore a darker Jewel yet, so he could understand their reluctance to tangle with the Gray.

He settled on the Warlord Prince who would be the next dominant after Daemonar. "You are?"

"Raeth, sir."

"Report."

"Don't know what started it, but Lady Surreal has been

testing the girls' shields," Raeth said. "At least, that's what it looks like she's doing. But she's been shattering their shields and draining their Jewels to one drop away from the breaking point."

Not that different from what had happened during that disastrous house party when Delora tried to kill Zoey.

"Divide up your men to stand as escorts for five groups of girls." Lucivar pointed. "Start with the two groups Liath has under control. Get them back to their own rooms and tell them to stay in their rooms until I summon them. Tell them that's an order, not a request. Disobedience will be considered a challenge, and they will face me—and if that happens, they should be ready to die."

He watched the color drain out of every boy's face when they realized he was serious.

When they realized that the stories about him weren't stories.

"Yes, sir," Raeth said, and swallowed hard.

Leaving Raeth to sort out the other males, Lucivar wrapped himself in two Ebon-gray shields as he strode over the lawn. He closed in on Surreal as a girl's shield exploded and the girl fell to the ground. Not broken, but seriously drained of power.

All of them had been drained.

Surreal swung a club against the last remaining shield. It exploded like the others, the young Queen's Jewel drained of power. Not the strongest girl, but the one who had been kept for last so that she had to watch the rest of them go down, knowing she had no hope of surviving this kind of attack.

Lucivar let out a sharp whistle.

Surreal spun. By the time she faced him, the club had been exchanged for her crossbow, which was aimed just above his belt.

"Threaten, threaten, blah blah blah," he said—and watched the wild look in her gold-green eyes become wilder. "We're done here. If you need to work off more temper, take a knife to a straw dummy until you rip it apart. Or you can spar with me until you're tired enough to hit the ground and not get back up. Your choice."

"Take a piss in the wind, Lucivar," Surreal snarled.

"Your choice," he repeated.

"If that little bitch makes a play for Sadi, I will rip off her skin."

"Understood. I will let the High Lord know."

"And the next one who says or implies that girls who were broken must have done something to deserve it will forfeit her tongue."

And there was one reason for her fury against all these girls—even the ones who had said nothing. "You going to use a knife for that?"

"Unlike your way of *ripping* it out?"

Lucivar gave her a lazy, arrogant smile. "Yeah."

Surreal vanished her crossbow. "I'll use a dull knife so I have to hack at it." She walked away from the Hall.

Lucivar watched her until he felt confident that she wouldn't turn back and attack. Then he looked at the boys Raeth had assigned to lead the two groups of girls Liath had already separated from the herd. Raeth, along with Liath and the rest of the boys, headed toward him. He waited until they could hear him. Then he focused on the remaining girls.

"Lesson and warning," he said. "Whether you're allowed to remain at the Hall for your training or are sent home, this is the only warning you'll receive. The next time any of you play the bitch and come at one of us in any way for any reason, we will eliminate the threat." He stared at the young Queen who, he suspected, was the cause of all of this. "And if you're thinking of making a play for Sadi, either as a lover or as his Queen? May the Darkness have mercy on you, because he'll respond by breaking you apart, piece by piece—and you will thank him when he allows you to die."

Lucivar looked over all of them. Based on experience, he would recommend sending home a couple more girls besides that Queen. It might be the only way to keep them alive long enough for them to mature out of the bitch stage.

"Not everyone is suited to serve in every court. If you don't fit with the rest of the individuals who also serve, you don't belong. You don't have to be good friends with everyone else in a court, but you have to be able to work together, have to be able to be courteous to each other. Some Queens will ignore backbiting and whispered slurs if those things are done by their favorites. Good Queens will not. Probably best if I don't know exactly what was said, since I have a feeling my response would be similar to Surreal's. Just know, here and now, that if you cross some lines there is no going back, even if you're just being mouthy. A young Eyrien Queen living in Ebon Rih crossed one of those lines a few months ago. She was banished from Askavi and sent back to Terreille. She wasn't there very long before she enraged some Eyrien warriors by playing the bitch. I was told her execution was savage even by Eyrien standards." He breathed out slowly. "You all have until Sadi returns to decide if you're going to continue to cause trouble or if you're going to make an effort to grow up and meet the expectations of this house."

Lucivar turned to Raeth. "Get them all back to their rooms. Let them walk."

Raeth eyed the girls, then leaned in. "Some of them don't look like they can walk that far."

"Then let them crawl."

He watched the boy's eyes widen. And he wondered where Raeth would draw a line between obeying and helping someone even if there was a price.

He'd have to find out if these boys had learned to air walk yet or float an object—including a person—on air to move it easily. If they didn't know how, he'd spend the next couple of days teaching them.

He'd let things settle for a day before deciding what to teach the girls that Surreal hadn't already taught them.

Grizande explored the room she'd been given—the room once occupied by the Tigre Queen who had served in the

Dark Court. The bedding and curtains were fairly new, but the furniture carried the feel of age, and all of it had carvings and decorations that were traditional to the Tigre people. A dressing table with a mirror. Aristo females used such things, not a witch who had been moved from one small village to another and hadn't been taught anything that wasn't useful for her survival. But she didn't want to shame the Prince who had granted her sanctuary in the place where the Queen who was more than a Queen had lived, so she would need to learn some female things and try to fit in with the other girls.

Helene offered a practical kindness more like the Sisters of the Hourglass than Marian mother. At least it seemed that way. Perhaps affection was reserved for girls who worked for her. Either way, the woman had taken time to show her the room and the bathroom she should use. She introduced the maids who took care of this square of rooms. She introduced a Warlord named Tarl, the head gardener. He in turn introduced some men who worked under his command—men she would see working in the courtyard that provided open ground for these rooms—and then showed her a large shallow box that held a mixture of sand and dirt where Jaalan should make his poops.

While she waited for the other man who would be her teacher, she thought about why Helene and then Tarl had introduced her to so many of their people, and she realized they wanted her to know these were people she should expect to see working in and around the space that was, in its own way, her home territory now. They were not threats.

Now all she had to do was learn to tolerate the presence of a Queen who could claim the same home territory.

The man who knocked on her door was a Prince named Raine. A teacher who said he was from the Territory of Dharo but had come to Dhemlan to teach because he wanted to learn about different peoples.

She showed Raine the books the Prince had given her and the book of empty lined paper. He asked her questions about the Tigre way of teaching but didn't ask why a witch who wore Birthright Sapphire hadn't been taught to read the common tongue and had limited ability to speak it. He wondered; she could see the questions in his eyes. But he didn't ask.

He didn't stay long, but the weight of how much she needed to learn while she was allowed to stay here felt crushing.

She was looking around the room, not sure what she should do, when someone else knocked on her door.

Strange custom to intrude on a private den. Or was she the only one who was expected to surrender privacy, because she was an outsider?

Except this visitor was welcome, if unexpected.

"You not resting," Grizande said, stepping back to let Daemonar enter her room.

She glanced at her bed and wondered if he had come expecting her to oblige, even if she hadn't had her Virgin Night yet.

"I need your help," Daemonar said, heading to a small table with two matching chairs. "Where is Jaalan?"

"Outside with Bossy Stern Teeth and a female bossy named Allis."

He grinned. "They're called Scelties." His grin faded. "Calling them bossies instead of the proper name is . . ."

"Unkind," she finished. "Scelties. I will remember."

"I know you will."

He called in a tray that held a greater variety of foods than she'd ever seen at one time. Fruits in a bowl. Cheeses on a cold-spelled dish. Sandwiches full of thinly sliced meats. A pot of coffee and a pitcher of water. Different kinds of bready sweets?

"You haven't met Mrs. Beale yet," Daemonar said. "She's an excellent cook, but she's a bit scary. Okay, sometimes a lot scary, even if she only wears a Yellow Jewel. Anyway, if I don't eat enough of this food, she'll be insulted—and all of this is to keep me from starving while I'm resting *before* the evening meal."

Grizande stared at him. This much food *before* a meal?

He nodded as if she'd said something. "Help me eat enough of this so I won't get into trouble."

Once they were seated at the small table, she wasn't sure what to choose. Daemonar picked up half of a meat sandwich and took a big bite. Chewed. Swallowed. Sighed with pleasure.

Feeling brave, she took the other half of the sandwich. "Good," she said after the first bite.

"There are some apprentice cooks and a few assistant cooks." Daemonar cut a couple of slices off one of the cheeses, then took a slice, leaving the other for her. "There is an auxiliary kitchen across from the High Lord's suite. There's usually someone on duty there to give you a bowl of soup or stew or make you a sandwich. Apprentices are cooks in training, so the food they make is edible but not always up to Mrs. Beale's standards."

"Feed lower ranks?" Orphans were often allowed to eat what no one else wanted.

"If you mean the students, yes." Daemonar selected another sandwich. "When they're hungry, boys will eat just about anything. And anyone who works at the Hall is welcome to get some food when they're taking a break from their tasks."

She wondered if he would let her keep some of the fruits and sweets to eat later. Right now, she had another priority.

Could she trust him with this secret? The Sisters of the Hourglass had been as vehement about her making use of this as they had been about her keeping this a secret—and yet there had been a false note in their concern for her, as if this protection against Warlord Princes came at a cost the Black Widows wouldn't share with her.

Because the cost might be too high? Or because the Warlord Princes who knew the Queen who was more than a Queen would understand too much about this secret?

One way to find out.

Taking the mug, she filled it partway with water, then used Craft to heat the water until it began to steam.

"Something you need?" Daemonar asked.

Grizande called in a jar full of coarsely ground leaves. After filling a tea ball with leaves, she set the ball in the steaming water—and looked at him. "Special tea. Quiets heat."

"Quiets . . . I don't understand."

She didn't have words for this, not in the language he knew. "Warlord Princes. Strong." She made a hand gesture to convey something about the nature of his caste. He must have understood enough, because his eyes widened.

"Virile?" he suggested.

She wasn't sure that was the word she'd intended, but it would do. "Dark Jewels much sex heat. Sometimes too much. Males need virile, need heat to find mate, make children. After, females drink tea, not feel heat so much."

He stared at the mug, stared at the jar. Finally he stared at her. "The Tigre have found a way for women to quiet their reaction to a Warlord Prince's sexual heat?"

She nodded. "Some Tigre know. Hourglass secret."

He pushed back from the table. "Come on. We need to talk to my father."

He reached for the jar of leaves for her special tea. She vanished it before his hand touched it—before he thought to vanish it and keep it from her.

"Grizande," Daemonar said quietly. "You know something we don't. This could help my mother. Please."

Help Marian mother? Maybe. And yet the false note in the Sisters' concern for her troubled her—more for Marian mother's sake than for her own.

Daemonar sat in the chair, waiting for her to decide.

If she was going to be in a room with Ebon-gray . . . Although being in a Coach with Ebon-gray and Black hadn't bothered her. She'd noticed their heat, but it hadn't bothered her. Still, she'd learned to be cautious in order to survive. "Drink tea first. Not waste."

He nodded.

She drank the tea and felt . . . veiled, as if all her senses had been dimmed somehow. The Sisters of the Hourglass had told her that was how she *should* feel after drinking the tea. Their words had sounded true, but now she wondered about something else.

Marian mother wore Purple Dusk. If she didn't know about the special tea, how had she survived living with Ebon-gray?

Surreal hadn't wanted to talk to Lucivar about whatever had set her off to the point where she'd drained the reservoirs of power of the Birthright Jewels of the resident Queens and their female followers. Lucivar didn't care if she talked to him or not, but it was better for everyone at the Hall if he escorted her to her suite in the family wing, where she planned to enjoy a solitary dinner.

He, on the other hand, would be eating in the large dining room tonight, with the instructors and anyone else who was capable of coming to the table.

He and Surreal had almost reached the square he still thought of as the Queen's square when Daemonar turned a corner and spotted him. Grizande trailed behind his boy, looking uncertain.

Fortunately for his first-born, Daemonar looked relieved to see him instead of apprehensive.

"Father, we need to talk to you," Daemonar said. "You should hear this too, Auntie Surreal."

"That might not be a good idea today," Surreal replied.

"You should hear this. We can talk in my room."

Daemonar backtracked a few steps to his room. He opened the door, then waited for the others to enter before he walked in—and locked the door.

"Grizande needs to tell you about a special tea the Tigre make," Daemonar said.

Grizande didn't look eager to tell him anything. "All right. I'm listening."

It wasn't just the struggle of explaining something with her limited vocabulary in the common tongue. Fear came close to choking her as she tried to explain something secret. Something . . . forbidden? But every time the girl stumbled, Daemonar filled in the words until she could continue.

A tea that could quiet the impact of sexual heat, dull it enough for a woman to live with a man like him? Make it possible for him to be home more days without overwhelming Marian?

Grizande called in her jar of special leaves. Surreal reached for the jar. Lucivar stopped her from touching it. Her life—and Daemon's—might have been different if she'd had a tea that could quiet even some of Daemon's mature sexual heat, but people had been taking things from this girl for a long time, and he wasn't going to let that happen here.

"Do you know what's in the tea?" Lucivar asked.

"Hourglass made list. Say only show to Black Widows to make more tea."

He wasn't a Black Widow, so he waited. Grizande needed to decide for herself if she would trust him.

Finally she called in a sheet of paper and held it out to him.

Yes, it was a list of herbs or leaves or whatever else had gone into the tea. But it was in the language of the Tigre. Of course it was.

He handed the paper back to her. "Can you make two copies of that list for me? And are you willing to give me two doses of that tea?"

Grizande hesitated, then nodded. Daemonar suddenly held two small white bowls, no doubt called in from the auxiliary kitchen. The girl poured two generous portions of the tea into the bowls—more than two doses, he suspected. Then she vanished the jar while she avoided looking at Surreal.

Aware of Surreal's churning emotions, Lucivar leaned forward, held his hands over the bowls, and vanished them.

"Thank you," he said.

"I drink, maybe okay," Grizande said in a rush. "No others drink until Queen say okay."

In other words, Witch might know something about the tea the rest of them didn't. "I will ask the Lady for her wisdom concerning the tea."

Grizande sighed with relief.

Daemonar cocked a thumb over his shoulder to indicate the square of rooms across the corridor. "We were enjoying some nibbles Mrs. Beale provided when Grizande told me about her tea."

Lucivar eyed his son and considered the message under the words. Yes, Daemonar was right. The girl had risked enough by offering information about the tea and needed her own kind of rest. "I appreciate you delaying your enjoyment of the nibbles in order to tell me about this. Once you fortify yourselves, I would like those copies of the list."

"Yes, sir." Daemonar stood. The girl leaped to her feet, anxious to get out of the room.

Lucivar sat back, looking easy, but he had a skintight Ebon-gray shield protecting him from whatever response Surreal would have to this revelation.

"Did she know?" Surreal finally asked. "Did Witch know there was a way . . ." Her hands curled into fists.

Hearing the bite and bitterness in her voice, he tightened the leash on his temper. "You're not the only one who has had a hard time dealing with the sexual heat. If Jaenelle had known about this, she would have said something—if not for your sake, then for Marian's."

Unless Witch knew something about that tea and had a reason to keep silent.

Surreal raked her fingers through her hair. "Dinah is going to be a problem. The other Queens seem solid enough—and sensible enough—but she . . ."

A change of subject? "What did she say that pissed you off so much?"

She bared her teeth in a vicious smile as she turned to look directly at him. "If *Dinah* had been invited to the house party, *she* would have dealt with Delora and wouldn't have succumbed to a little inconvenience the way *Zoey* did." She stopped smiling. "What the little bitch didn't actually say but implied was how grateful Daemon would be for how she'd taken charge—and how he would show his gratitude. Of course, everyone was so enthralled—or appalled—at her assertions that no one noticed me until I stood directly behind her."

"And that's when you gave all the girls a taste of what the fight would have been like."

Surreal nodded.

"Your assessment and recommendation is to send Dinah home. Anyone else?"

"None of the Black Widows or Healers are among her followers. I think that pisses her off. Her friends are potentially strong witches, yes, but not necessarily influential. Without Dinah's presence they might settle down here." She blew out a breath. "I was hard on Zoey's friends, and they didn't deserve it. Interesting, though, that those five girls didn't shield individually. Well, they did—you would have kicked their asses if they hadn't—but they layered shields around their group. Two sets from darkest to lightest. Kathlene and her friends saw what Zoey's friends were doing and tried to do the same. They weren't quite as successful, but if any of the boyos had thrown themselves into the fight, I might have had trouble breaking all those shields. The rest of them didn't believe they could be stripped of power and left vulnerable that fast. They were wrong."

"Well, I know what I'll be working on with them."

Surreal batted her eyelashes at him. "Are you going to help those boys grow some balls?"

He snorted a laugh. "Yeah, that too. Although Raeth did a good job of carrying out the orders I gave and dividing his men for the task."

"As good as Liath?" she asked.

"Oh, Hell's fire, no. That Sceltie could have run rings around those boys when he was still a puppy. They aren't close to his fighting and herding skills."

She shifted in her chair. "Let's swap. We both want to know about that tea, so I'll go to Ebon Askavi and ask

Witch while you stay here and herd the children. I can get a room at The Tavern or stay at your eyrie to keep an eye on things until you get back."

"You usually avoid the Keep."

"Tangled feelings. But I'd like to know about this tea, and I'd rather have this meeting while Sadi is in Scelt."

"All right." Lucivar thought for a moment. "You might be dealing with just Witch by the time you reach the Keep. Karla will be discussing Virgin Nights with Jillian this evening." *And may the Darkness have mercy on me.*

"Karla? Why? I'm making the arrangements for Jillian."

"Why? Because my brother had the bright idea to have Jillian talk to the witch who dealt with me on her Virgin Night."

She just stared at him.

"You go on. I'll stay here—and we'll see who's left at the Hall when Daemon returns."

"You were less scary when you were just killing people."

"Same could be said about you."

Surreal laughed. "All right, sugar. We'll both do what we do."

She left Daemonar's room. Lucivar stayed. Standing at the glass doors that opened to the balcony, he let his Red power quietly flow beneath the courtyard and the rooms.

Holt. Raine. Weston.

He let his Red power flow through the rest of the Hall. Plenty of people here he didn't know, but there was an odd . . . something . . . that felt familiar.

Daemonar returned and handed him two copies of the list of ingredients for the special tea.

Vanishing them, Lucivar asked, "Is someone missing?"

"Weston wanted an introduction since Grizande is going to be living in the same square as Zoey," Daemonar replied, not actually answering the question.

"Makes sense. Who's missing?"

Daemonar sighed. "Weston said Lord Morris resigned this morning. Morris wasn't sure about staying after Liath told us about biting off a man's ball . . ."

"Ball? Just one?"

"Just one. Anyway, it looked like Morris was going to stay. Then Auntie Surreal called in a whetstone at the breakfast table and started sharpening her knives. She kept looking at Morris and smiling. Weston said Morris threw his resignation at Beale as he bolted out the door."

Lucivar ran his tongue over his teeth. "Your grandfather experienced a lot of instructors running out the door after spending an hour with Jaenelle and the coven. Looks like Daemon will face the same challenge. Eventually he'll find people who won't run."

"I understand being rested after an assignment, but until Grizande makes some other friends . . ."

"Yeah, I know. I'm going to work with the rest of the children tomorrow. Pick one of Zoey's friends to go with you and escort Grizande to the village. She'll need more clothes than she has now. Practical garments for classes, and a couple of dresses since Daemon follows the family tradition of dressing for dinner."

"Shopping?"

The boy sounded so pained, he wanted to laugh. "That's your assignment for tomorrow. Deal with it." He waited a beat. "Besides, the girl should know how to find other shops too."

"Yeah." Daemonar looked happier. "Yeah, she should know how to find some things on her own." Then he looked uneasy. "Maybe I shouldn't do that. She doesn't have . . ."

Lucivar called in his wallet and removed some gold marks. "Daemon will figure out what to do for her, but this is a welcome gift from us so that she has some spending money. Any clothes she buys tomorrow? Tell the merchants to send the bills to the Hall. I will pay them if Daemon doesn't."

Daemonar fanned the marks. "A hundred gold marks?"

Lucivar vanished the wallet and studied his son. "Are you thinking too much or too little?"

"I don't think Grizande has ever seen this much money."

"Then ask Holt to exchange some of those marks for

smaller denominations, along with some silver marks."
Lucivar probed the rooms in the square and confirmed
they were still alone. "For Daemon, money meant freedom. Limited freedom, but even with all the restrictions
put on him as a pleasure slave, he had a skill for making
money, investing money, and making more. His clothes
were outrageously expensive—and still are—but they
were the sheath for his sharpest weapons. He would bribe
Queens to look the other way when he disappeared for an
evening and stayed at one of those flats he kept in order to
have a little solitude, some needed peace. Money was a
weapon, and he knew how to use it.

"I had nothing. A half-breed bastard in one of the Eyrien
hunting camps, wearing discarded clothes and using cast-
off weapons. Still fought everyone into the ground, but if I
coveted anything when I was young, it was weapons that
would fit my hand, that would hold an edge for a killing
field. After I was sent away from Askavi because they
couldn't control me, even with a Ring of Obedience, I met
this silky, court-trained, arrogant bastard named Daemon
Sadi. I thought he was a prancing cock until I watched him
crush a bitch with nothing but a seduction spell and words.

"We were with our respective owners, who were guests
of that court. One morning he crossed my path, took my
arm, and we walked out the doors. 'No one will ask questions,' he said. 'No one will dare.' I didn't know then and I
still don't know what he did to make sure no one asked, but
he was right about that. We went into the town, to the
smithy. The blacksmith's brother made weapons. Daemon
said he wanted to buy the best blades available. What
would I recommend?" Lucivar snorted softly. "Recommend? I thought he was taunting me, and I wanted to beat
him bloody, but I reviewed the weapons available and chose
the best. He paid for them—and then gave them to me.

"They were the first good weapons I'd ever owned. I
still have one of the knives. I don't use it anymore. It's not
the same quality as the weapons I have now, but I still have

it." Lucivar smiled. "His Queen left the next morning, and he was gone with her. But I found a leather wallet tucked in with my clothes. Ten thousand gold marks and an unsigned note that said, 'Money is also a weapon. Use it well.' I bought my first good Eyrien war blade with some of that money."

Lucivar ran a hand over Daemonar's hair. "Money as weapon. Money as freedom. Money as some measure of safety. I think Daemon's mistake with Saetien was wanting her to have the reassurance that she had the means to reach safety and not understanding that she didn't need it. She was already safe. Maybe too safe. Grizande needs to believe she is safe here, but she also needs to have the means to take care of herself and Jaalan."

"Maybe I should take her to the weapons maker in Halaway and help her buy a good knife," Daemonar said quietly.

"Yeah," Lucivar replied. "Maybe you should."

TWENTY-THREE

Daemon loved the old house in Scelt because it had been Jaenelle Angelline's home in a way no other residence had been. When she reached her majority, Saetan had leased this house for her to give her a place of her own. The cabin in Ebon Rih had been another kind of retreat, but this had been Jaenelle's personal residence in the village of Maghre on the Isle of Scelt. Morghann and Khardeen had been her close friends and neighbors, as well as the rulers of the island and village, respectively. Jaenelle had created the school for Scelties here, and for a few days each season she could pretend she was just another witch living in a charming village surrounded by beautiful countryside that seemed made for a long gallop on a strong horse.

Even when she no longer wore the Black and was no longer the Queen of Ebon Askavi, she was still a Queen. Still *the* Queen, as far as the Shadow Realm was concerned. Daemon had tried to give her that extraordinary ordinary life she'd always wanted, as much for himself as for her, and while the people around them, out of affection, pretended he and Jaenelle were just aristos coming to spend a few days in their country house, they weren't *just* anything—and everyone knew it.

He continued to renew the long-term lease on the house to give Morghann and Khary's descendants income from the property instead of purchasing the place outright. In return, Lord Kieran and his parents kept an eye on the place and helped solve any problems the small staff who managed the house might have when he was absent.

He'd sent a message to his housekeeper to let her know he'd be arriving for business but wouldn't be staying overnight. The staff would be disappointed; they didn't get much of a chance to fuss over him. Not the way the servants at the Hall or any of the other Dhemlan estates got to fuss. That was why, when he arrived at the house, he agreed that he was a fair way to being hungry and would appreciate a bit of a meal before taking care of the business that brought him to Maghre that day. He'd learned the hard way that if he admitted to being *hungry*, he couldn't possibly eat enough of what was put before him to satisfy cook and housekeeper—and considering the way someone who wore the Black burned through food, that was saying something.

Having invited his housekeeper to join him and catch him up on the happenings in the village (*"Well now, Prince, I'll just have a cup of tea to keep you company. And maybe one of those scones."*), Daemon ate, praised the food, and made appropriate sounds in response to the village's doings.

Was Prince Liath doing well, then? That was grand, finding him work to keep him busy. Everyone was fond of Prince Liath.

Yes, everyone was fond of the Green-Jeweled Sceltie Warlord Prince now that he lived on the other side of the Realm and herded someone else.

Daemon fiddled with the handle of his coffee cup, an uncharacteristic sign of nerves that wouldn't go unnoticed, although the observation wouldn't travel beyond the house.

"My daughter will be coming to Scelt for a while," he said carefully. "I'm not sure if it will be a few days or a few weeks."

"On her own?" the housekeeper asked.

"Yes."

"Staying here? On her own?"

He heard the disapproval. "No. She'll be staying with Lord Kieran and his family."

"Ah. Well, Lady Eileen runs her family with a firm hand. No doubt that will be true for any guests as well."

He was counting on that.

He rose, intending to head out for his first meeting. But his housekeeper fussed with the dishes and didn't look at him—and he felt a tickle of warning that the meal had been more than it seemed.

"There's been talk that you're training youngsters at the Hall," she said.

"We've always trained youngsters at the Hall," he countered.

"But you've got aristos there now, Queens and such, in the same way your father looked after the Dark Court when the Ladies were young. Or so the stories go."

"Yyyeess."

"Doesn't seem fair to restrict that opportunity to youngsters from Dhemlan, you being a landowner here and all."

Hell's fire. He couldn't say the training was exclusive among the staff or the youngsters receiving court training, not with the Dharo Boy working with Mrs. Beale, and Prince Raine as one of the instructors, and a Tigre witch and kindred tiger now in residence.

"Liath lives at the Hall," he said. A weak argument, but it was all he had.

"Everything has a price," she replied.

"You have a good point." And he recognized when the prudent choice was to yield. "If you should hear of anyone who would like to be considered for such . . . seasoning . . . send me their information, and I will pass it on to my senior staff to review."

"If I hear of anyone." She smiled at him—and he wondered how many packets of information were already prepared and would arrive at the Hall before he returned.

Since Kieran was descended from Morghann and Khardeen and was, therefore, his neighbor, Daemon chose to walk to the manor house. Because Morghann had been the Queen of Scelt, the manor house had been divided into a private residence and rooms to accommodate court business—including the occasional guest who was the Queen's guest rather than a family guest of Morghann and Khary. When Kieran had been officially acknowledged as the Warlord of Maghre, he'd turned the court side of the house into his residence while keeping some of the rooms for the work of looking after the village. His parents, brother, and sister lived in the family side of the house. The arrangement worked for all of them, and Daemon hoped it would work for Saetien too.

"You have business with Kieran?" Eileen asked once they were settled in the sitting room where she conducted her own kind of business. "Will you have a scone to go with your coffee?"

The question was really a command, so he said, "Thank you. They look delicious. I do have business with Kieran— and I have a favor to ask of you. My daughter has a need to spend some time in Scelt, looking for answers to some particular questions."

Eileen took her time buttering her scone. "She'll be coming on her own, your daughter? That's why she won't be staying at your house?"

"Yes."

"And who is supposed to give her these answers?"

Daemon looked at Eileen.

Her eyes widened. "I see. Does he know about this?"

"I'll talk to him this evening."

"We can put her up here, but I won't put up with nonsense."

"Whatever rules you set for your daughter you can set for mine." He hesitated. "What I am is hard for her. Who I am and whose will is my life is hard for her. This is all I can do to help her. She believes she needs these answers, but if she breaks your rules, you send her home whether she has her answers or not."

"A heart quest," Eileen said softly. "Very well."

"Thank you."

"Well, the village does owe you." She sipped her coffee, then asked so very casually, "How is Liath getting along? Doing well?"

"I've barely been home these past few days, but it's my understanding that Liath is now helping to train a tiger kitten."

Eileen choked. "Training a tiger?"

"A baby Warlord Prince with claws."

"Training him to do what?" Her voice rose to such a pitch, the butler knocked on the sitting room door to find out if there was some trouble.

"I don't know," Daemon admitted. And that was something he needed to find out very soon.

Daemon found Kieran leaning against the rails of a fence, watching Ryder and Kildare working with some of the young kindred horses. At thirty years old, Kieran was the oldest child of Eileen and Kildare. A lean man with curly brown hair and blue eyes that always held a hint of mischief, he had been the Warlord of Maghre officially for the past five years. Unofficially, his rule began when he was twenty, after he'd made the Offering to the Darkness and come away wearing the Red.

Daemon joined Kieran at the fence.

"Mother tapped me on a psychic thread and told me that your daughter will be staying with us for a while," Kieran said, watching the horses.

"Yes, she will. She's looking for some answers."

Kieran nodded. "There's an answer I've been wanting for a while now." He looked at Daemon. "I've wondered why you always seem to brace when you see me. I think we get along, you and I, and yet there's this moment of hesitation."

Gold eyes met blue. "It always takes me that moment to remember you're Kieran and not Khardeen. You have the look of him, the sound of him, the manners and the way of handling the village that is so like the way he was. He was a good friend, and sometimes it feels like there was no one in between you and him. Things are different here, as they are everywhere else in Kaeleer, but the feel of the village is the same."

"Ah." Kieran went back to watching the horses. "I'm pleased to have the answer. It's a fine compliment."

They watched Kieran's brother, Ryder, sweet-talking a filly into . . . Well, Daemon wasn't sure what she was *supposed* to be doing, but he was pretty sure she wasn't supposed to be standing on Ryder's foot until he handed over a treat.

A Sceltie witch trotted into the corral, on air, grabbed the filly's tail, and yanked.

Squeal. Kick. Bounce bounce bounce while Ryder moved out of the way of the drama and the Sceltie braced her feet on air and wouldn't release the filly's tail until *her* feet returned to the ground.

Ryder petted and soothed the filly. The Sceltie, with a single *grff* of warning, trotted to the fence and sat on the top rail, keeping watch.

Daemon pressed his lips together, fighting not to laugh—and terrified that if he laughed, he might be heading home with another Sceltie who was thought to be a bit too managing.

Kieran looked serene. "She doesn't put up with any nonsense from her own pups and sees no reason to put up with nonsense from any other kind of youngster."

"I'm not taking her," Daemon said softly.

"Of that I am sure, since you'd have to fight all the teachers at the village school in order to have her. They pay her wages to come to the school and keep order."

"Sweet Darkness."

A brief silence. Then Kieran asked oh so casually, "How is your school coming along?"

"It's not a school as such." Quick reply. Defensive reply.

Then a realization that he might as well admit defeat since he was asking for a favor himself. "Who did you have in mind?"

"Brenda."

"Your sister Brenda?"

"Aye."

"Why?"

"She wants a deeper study of Craft, and she'd like to acquire some court polish but she doesn't want to do an apprenticeship in a court, serving in a Queen's Second or Third Circle and fetching lavender water and handkerchiefs. Her words."

"Are the Queens in Scelt the kind of women who need lavender water and handkerchiefs?" Daemon asked. Granted, he hadn't met *all* the Queens in Scelt, but the ones he had met hadn't struck him as the type of woman who spent half her day on a fainting couch demanding that her First Circle fetch and carry for her.

"No, but someone serving in a court for the first time is required to observe *quietly* rather than doing—and voicing opinions," Kieran replied. "Brenda has a hard head and a stubborn will that can match a Sceltie's when she goes after something she wants. But she also has a generous heart." He hesitated. "And I think she has a reason for wanting to leave Scelt for a while."

"Oh?"

"If it had been more than disappointment and a bruised heart because someone wasn't what he'd seemed, I would have taken care of it before now. Which isn't to say that Brenda hadn't taken care of things at the time and didn't tell the family. But I think that's part of the reason she doesn't want to deal with an official court. She says that's no place for a country girl."

"Morghann was a country girl as well as a strong Territory Queen," he pointed out.

Kieran gave him a look that asked a question without saying the words.

Daemon shook his head. "Brenda wouldn't fit in with

the rest of the female students. They've lived centuries more than she has, but emotionally they're still girls. Your Brenda is a woman."

Kieran focused on the horses. "Ah. Well."

Daemon heard the disappointment beneath the acceptance. "So what can she teach?"

A hesitation before Kieran looked at him. "Teach?"

"Yes, teach. I have room for another instructor, and I see no reason why I can't share some of what I've learned about Craft with the other adults at the Hall. In fact, one of the instructors is a Prince from Dharo who has a family connection to Prince Rainier and came to Dhemlan out of curiosity about a man who had served in Jaenelle's Second Circle." Another thought occurred to him. "Lucivar's Jillian is working at a sanctuary Surreal set up for girls who need a safe place. She's . . . Well, I think she's like an older sister the girls can talk to and ask about things they might not be easy asking an adult about. Perhaps Brenda could do something like that. There are five young Queens in residence. They're not enemies, but they aren't friends with each other. Not in the way that Jaenelle and the coven were friends."

"Rivals?" Kieran asked.

Were they? "Let's just say they're still sorting themselves out."

A beat of silence. "*Lucivar's* Jillian?"

Daemon winced. "I'll thank you to forget I phrased it that way. We're just . . . Jillian is ready to have her Virgin Night, and we're feeling a bit . . . possessive."

Oh, the twinkle in Kieran's eyes. "You're having a party afterward?"

"A quiet celebration the next evening, if she's up to it then." He could feel the ground turning slippery. He just didn't know why.

"Our Brenda had her Virgin Night. Significant event in a witch's life, with her power and Jewels hanging in the balance. Father and I thought as you did—a quiet celebration with family and a few of Brenda's close friends." Kieran shook his head. "Ah, no. Brenda wanted a dance with plenty of food and music. She said she understood the importance of not having her Jewels and power always at risk, but she didn't see what all the fuss was about when it came to the act itself. The man's cock would stand at attention and do the deed, she'd bleed a little, and that would be that. Not much difference between that and a stallion covering a kindred mare the first time, and the kindred didn't make a fuss about it." He sighed. "Mother convinced her to stay in her room and rest that afternoon, to 'appease male sensibilities.' And that evening we had a party and danced until sunrise."

Daemon stared at him. "That's not . . ."

"That's our Brenda. Country girl who has grown up watching stallions cover mares," Kieran said. "The concern about a Virgin Night—and the reason for that concern— seems to be confined to the Blood in the human races. Or maybe it's that the mature kindred females provide a sharp motivation for good behavior and attack any male who tries to mate with an unwilling female. Such attacks are usually crippling and often lethal."

Daemon shook his head. "I saw too many witches who were broken when I lived in Terreille. I've seen the girls in Dhemlan who were broken by the coven of malice. I can't be dismissive about the risks."

"Nor should you be. But if Jillian is more like Brenda, she might not view the transaction with the same measure of alarm that you do." Kieran's eyes twinkled again. "Of course, knowing who's paying attention to the proceedings will make any man with a desire to live take extra care in how he performs his duty."

"Actually, Surreal is making the arrangements for Jillian, and she's the one who will be there."

"That's really not any better."

No, it wasn't. Not from a man's point of view.

And this wasn't a subject he wanted to think about. Not today. "I have a couple of other stops to make, so I'd better get on with them." He hoped the other stops wouldn't hold any surprises—or require him to add to the number of the Hall's residents. "If Brenda wants to come to the Hall, I'll find a place for her as an instructor."

"Thank you, Prince. I'll let her know."

Daemon looked at Kieran and wondered if Brenda already had her clothes packed.

TWENTY-FOUR

A long time ago, before he'd been known as Butler, he had lived in Beldon Mor, the capital city of Chaillot in the Realm of Terreille. He'd been young and alone, desperate and angry. So very angry when he'd learned a brutal truth. But he'd had no recourse against aristos who were corrupt to the very core of their Selves. He couldn't save what had already been destroyed, wasn't sure he could do anything to save himself.

Then one night, when he was drunk and sick, a young woman—a broken witch—dressed for a fancy evening wandered into the mouth of the alleyway where he'd collapsed.

"The Chaillot girl knows about the pretty poison. You should talk to her."

"They're all Chaillot girls!"

"Only one lives in the Black Mountain. At least, that's what some of the girls whispered."

He'd had sense enough left to sight shield before a man rushed up to the girl, grabbed her arm hard enough to bruise, and pulled her away from the alleyway, saying, *"Bad enough you act like a fool without you talking to yourself now."*

Only one lived in the Black Mountain.

"I need to talk to the Chaillot girl!"

When he finally reached Ebon Askavi and was taken

through the Gate to the Keep in Kaeleer, he'd shouted the words that had shaped his life after.

That Chaillot girl's ancient sapphire eyes looked through him, seeing everything. She didn't ask who he was or where he came from. She already knew. Just like she knew why he had come to the Keep looking for her. She didn't allow anyone, not even the High Lord of Hell, to ask him questions about himself or his past or how he knew the living myth, and he never chose to tell anyone.

At his request—and hers—he spent a few years studying a variety of subjects, including some that were conducted in very private surroundings. During that time, he also served short apprenticeships in a variety of courts, learning the structure of service and observing the various personalities of the Queens who ruled the Shadow Realm. After he made the Offering to the Darkness, he learned how to mask the power in his Green Jewel so that people thought his Birthright Purple Dusk was his Jewel of rank.

At one time or another, he had worked for most of the Queens who had served in the Dark Court's First Circle. He never *served* any of them, but he'd worked for them, taking on assignments for weeks or months at a time in order to be a Queen's eyes and ears—and sometimes her knife. His credentials had been as substantial as water written on wind, but they had carried the seal of the Queen of Ebon Askavi, and the Dark Court accepted that that was all they needed to know about him.

Decades later, when he was finally ready to settle down, he'd been offered an assignment that would allow him to live in Maghre. Not all his reasons for accepting were benign, but no one had known that. Still didn't know that.

Perhaps didn't know that.

He'd gone by many names over the years, but when he settled down in Maghre, he also settled on the name he'd liked the best because of the way it had sounded when she'd said it.

Butler.

✦ ✦ ✦

Butler rose a few minutes before sundown—the start of his "day"—and felt the presence of the Black. Hard not to notice when that dark power was in the village. The only question, for him, was why Sadi was there. The meetings with the Scelties and humans who ran the school followed a predictable schedule, as did the deliveries of yarbarah to him.

It wasn't the right time for a meeting or a delivery, which meant something had happened to bring Sadi to Maghre. Or was it the High Lord who was approaching the cottage that had once belonged to Lady Fiona? It had been Butler's residence for centuries, being part of the agreement when he'd taken over management of Fiona's literary works.

His next-to-last assignment—and a welcome one. But it was unusual for one of the demon-dead to stay among the living. Not unheard of, especially if you were connected to the SaDiablo family in any way, but it was unusual.

He stood in the cottage's doorway and watched that beautiful, lethal man glide toward his home. The man stopped at the front gate in the white picket fence that surrounded the cottage and the flower gardens. The property held several more acres, including pasture for the horses that used to pull the pony cart for Fiona. He'd kept the small barn in good repair, just like he'd kept the cottage in good repair, making the same improvements that were being made in other village homes. But he hadn't had a need for a pony cart or the horses, so those things were gone.

In truth, he was tidying up. It was time to go—to Hell, if that's what he wanted, or to Ebon Askavi. He hadn't seriously considered working at the Keep and extending his existence a little longer until that *power* had thundered through the Shadow Realm again, warning everyone that Witch had returned. Now he felt impatient to find a successor, but he hadn't found the right person yet.

Butler walked to the gate. "High Lord." When he didn't get a response, he said, "Or is this a visit from Prince Sadi?"

"Sadi," Daemon replied. "I've come to ask a favor."

He opened the gate. "Then you'd best come in." He led the way into the cottage, then looked over his shoulder. "I've a bottle or two of regular wine, if you'd like a drink."

"I appreciate the offer, but I've had plenty to eat and drink today" was the dry reply.

They went into the kitchen, where Butler poured and warmed a glass of yarbarah, the blood wine. "Did you keep count of how many cups of tea you drank and how many scones you ate today?"

"I'm better off not knowing."

Butler turned, intending to go to the parlor, where he usually conducted business with the living.

Daemon took a seat at the kitchen table.

Not sure what that meant, Butler took the seat opposite Sadi. "A favor, you said."

Daemon shifted in his seat, an almost unprecedented sign of nerves. "My daughter needs to regain her balance, needs to find her potential, her place among the Blood. Hopefully that will help her reconnect to her family in some way—or help her find where she belongs if not with us. It was suggested that she look for the answers here, in Scelt." A hesitation. "It was suggested that she'll find her own truths by finding out about Wilhelmina Benedict."

"No." He didn't have to think about his answer for even a moment.

Daemon called in a piece of heavy paper with a seal embossed in the lower right-hand corner and held it out.

Butler, it's time. J.

His last assignment. The one he'd been waiting to carry out. She'd said he'd know when it had arrived.

But why did it have to be this?

"So you want me to tell your daughter a pretty story about two sisters?" he asked, not bothering to hide his anger.

"No, I want you to tell her the truth uncensored," Daemon replied. "Whatever that may be."

"You don't know?"

"No. I know something happened between them, and

Wilhelmina left the Hall because of it. But we'd been preparing for war, and afterward . . ." Daemon sighed. "Afterward nothing and no one mattered to me until Ladvarian
and the rest of the kindred brought Jaenelle back. All my
father said months later was that Wilhelmina was residing
in Maghre. He arranged for her to have a modest annual
income that would be paid out while she walked among
the living and would extend to two generations beyond."

Daemon leaned back in his chair. "My father hated
Wilhelmina Benedict. He never said why his feelings
changed toward her. I know he didn't feel that way when
she first arrived in Kaeleer."

"And now you want me to stir up a past long forgotten
by most, when there are still some among the living who
are thankful it's forgotten," Butler said.

"Eileen called this a heart quest."

"You told her about this?"

Daemon nodded. "Saetien will be staying with Lady Eileen and Lord Kildare while she's here."

A heart quest. He couldn't refuse, but he wondered
whose heart would break by the time it was done. "All
right. But I do it my way."

"I didn't expect you to do it any other way," Daemon
replied.

"As long as you understand that."

"I understand that everything has a price, and the price
for the help I'm requesting for my daughter may be steep."

*But do you understand who might have to pay that
price?*

Butler, it's time. J.

Her will was his life.

"So," Butler said, wanting to end this meeting on a
lighter note. "Who's going back to the Hall with you in
exchange for your girl being here?"

"Possibly Lady Brenda," Daemon replied after a moment.

*Will some walls in the Hall crumble when she crosses the
threshold?* "Well, that's grand, but you should tell your stable

to have a box stall ready for your other guest. If Brenda is going to the Hall, Lord Shaye won't be far behind."

Daemon blinked. "And Shaye is . . . ?"

"A kindred Warlord, but not your average-sized riding horse. He's fairly attached to Brenda."

"I see."

"He got along well with Liath, so the two of them won't be at odds with each other."

"I'm delighted."

Butler swallowed a laugh. "Your father handled all this."

"So everyone keeps telling me. I'm beginning to think my father was out of his mind for taking on the coven and all the kindred who showed up. At least . . ." Daemon stopped.

"Not sure who else might have shown up on your doorstep since you were home last?" Butler guessed.

"Not sure at all."

Much later that evening, Daemon stood outside the manor house with Kieran and his family. He didn't say a word about the trunks and boxes and parcels Kildare and Ryder were packing into the small Coach he'd used for this trip. He was tempted to suggest a few more items Brenda might need for her stay at the Hall, just to be sure there wouldn't be room for the other guest who would be joining them. Kieran solved that problem by offering to drive a Coach designed to carry horses and personally deliver Brenda's friend.

Lord Shaye was . . . large . . . and pure black like his sire. Nowhere near as big as his dam, but he was definitely more substantial than a typical riding horse.

Daemon might have made a weak joke about the stud needing a ladder if the stud and the dam hadn't been in the yard to see their son off on his first adventure beyond the village and the Isle of Scelt. Somehow he didn't think a witch and a Warlord would appreciate the joke, and he couldn't assume that, being horses, they *wouldn't* understand—and be insulted by—such a comment.

They're devoted to each other, Kieran said on a spear thread. *She won't tolerate another stallion, and he won't cover another mare. They have three offspring younger than Shaye.*

Who was he to offer a comment about family? And the horses' psychic scents were too similar to Eileen's and Kildare's as they hugged their daughter and wished her well for him to think they were anything less than family.

"Lady Brenda, if you have everything you need, at least for now, we should be going," Daemon said.

"I'll write," Brenda said as she gave her mother one more hug. "I will."

Daemon met Eileen's eyes and dipped his head in a tiny nod, receiving a nod in return. Even if the daughters forgot to write, the parents would know what was going on.

He invited Brenda to join him in the front of the Coach, not because he wanted company but because there wasn't any other comfortable place for her to sit.

As he caught the Black Winds and began the journey back to Dhemlan, he wondered how many trunks and bags and boxes Saetien would deem necessary for a visit of a few weeks.

TWENTY-FIVE

Surreal paced the sitting room. The rest of the Keep felt the way it always did—full of old, dark power. Full of things best not seen in the light of day. But here on the other side of an ornate metal gate . . .

Power. And a feral presence no longer hidden by a human body or softened by human emotions.

"I'd offer you coffee, but you look like you need a large whiskey," Witch said, suddenly appearing in the room.

"Maybe a mug of this would be better." Surreal called in the jar of leaves Lucivar had given her, along with one copy of the list of plants used to make this blend.

Witch took the jar and opened it. She sniffed. Frowned as she read the list of plants. Then she focused on Surreal, and "feral" didn't begin to describe the look in her eyes.

"Where did you get this?" Witch asked too softly.

"This mixture comes from Tigrelan," Surreal replied— and wondered if she would still be among the living when she walked out of that room.

"From the Tigre? From Grizande?"

She nodded.

"Who else knows about this?"

She hadn't expected this cold rage rising from somewhere deep in the abyss. If she lied . . . No. She wouldn't lie, because there was something else besides cold rage filling the room. "I stopped by Yaslana's eyrie to tell Marian there might be a way to . . . soften . . . the effect of Lucivar's sexual heat. Nurian was there."

"And at the Hall?"

"Lucivar knows. And Daemonar." Surreal swallowed hard. "Look, sugar . . ."

"Contact Marian and Nurian now. They are to say *nothing* about this until they talk to me. I'll inform Lucivar that Grizande is not to drink any more of that tea."

Witch vanished. A moment later, Surreal fell to the floor as an arrow of dark power was unleashed and headed west. Toward Dhemlan. Toward SaDiablo Hall—and Lucivar.

Mother Night. Surreal sent out a psychic call to Marian. *Something about this tea has made Witch furious. She *commanded* that you and Nurian say nothing to anyone until you talk to her.*

Witch? Marian sounded confused. *But . . . why?*

I don't know yet. Surreal tried to get to her feet, discovered she was too shaky, and collapsed into a chair moments before Witch returned. A moment after that, a tray with a pot of hot water, a cup and saucer, and a tea ball appeared on the table near the chair.

"Do you want to try the tea?" Witch sounded terrifyingly calm.

Whenever Sadi was that kind of calm, people died.

"The Tigre witches drink this in order to quiet their response to a Warlord Prince's sexual heat," Surreal said, watching Witch. "That's what Grizande told us."

"That's probably as much as she was told. It's true that this tea muffles the response to sexual heat by dulling a woman's desire. One cup won't hurt you, and since you wear the Gray, the effects won't last for more than a few hours. Maybe a day."

One cup could reduce the lust response produced by a Warlord Prince's sexual heat *for a day*?

Surreal filled the tea ball with leaves, set the ball in the cup, and poured the hot water over it to let the tea steep. "If you've known about this tea, why didn't you say something? It could have spared . . ."

"I wasn't here when things went wrong between you and Daemon," Witch said.

The calm didn't break, and Surreal had a bad feeling that it was holding back something terrible.

"Marian, then. It's difficult for her right now."

"The webs Karla and I created to absorb sexual heat keep things tolerable for Marian when she is home—and those webs aren't that different from the webs hearth witches use to cleanse a bedroom after a Warlord Prince's rut. Since Daemon is a Black Widow, he's been able to make the webs to absorb the sexual heat in specific rooms at the Hall to make it easier for the students and staff."

"Rooms." Surreal removed the tea ball and set it in a small bowl. "This tea doesn't restrict someone to specific rooms."

"Drink it. See what it does. Then we'll talk. You've focused on the relief you and Marian might have from the heat of Ebon-gray and Black. You haven't considered the price the rest of the Blood might pay if this tea was discovered again."

"Again?"

Witch said nothing. Surreal drank the tea.

"How do you feel?" Witch asked.

She shrugged. "The same."

"Good. Now think about something besides what this means for you personally."

"Not just me. Marian."

Witch nodded. "All right, let's consider Marian. She wears Purple Dusk. Until this last phase, she was able to handle Lucivar's leashed sexual heat without being overwhelmed and certainly appreciated the way it excited her and added to her enjoyment of sex. Now the heat is too much even when it's leashed, and it will be for a few more decades, before it begins to decline. A woman from a short-lived race would endure this for a few years if her lover was a Warlord Prince who outranked her. It's harder for someone from one of the long-lived races because it has to be endured for a lot more years.

"Then a tea is discovered that quiets a woman's response to the heat, dulls her desire for sex. Doesn't affect the Warlord Prince, just her. How often does Marian drink the tea? Once a week? Twice? Does she wait until she starts to feel her husband's heat again, starts to feel sharp desire again, before brewing another cup? Don't you think Lucivar will notice that the woman who is the love of his life, the woman he's been living with for centuries, no longer wants to have sex with him, no longer wants more than a hug and cuddle?

"You wanted to use Marian as the example, so let's talk about Lucivar. If Marian could no longer have sex because of injury or illness, he wouldn't consider leaving her—and he would remain celibate, even during the ruts. But how hard would it be for him to stay if Marian chose to drink a tea that silenced desire in order to escape an intrinsic part of what he is? How hard would it be for both of them when they realized she'd castrated herself to avoid his sexual heat?"

Surreal snapped upright in the chair. "What?"

"Depending on a witch's power, drinking a couple cups of that tea every week can silence desire for good. If she hasn't been drinking it very long and stops drinking it, sometimes desire comes back in a few weeks; sometimes it takes months. And sometimes it never returns. It doesn't even take a year of drinking that tea to reach the point of never."

Surreal raked a hand through her hair. "Mother Night."

"And may the Darkness be merciful." Witch sat in a chair opposite Surreal and leaned forward. "Now think beyond the Ebon-gray and Black. A woman who wears a Rose Jewel handfasts to a Warlord Prince who wears Purple Dusk. Even leashed, his heat is going to bother her at times. But there's a tea she can get from a Black Widow or Healer that will quiet that. Does she talk to him, tell him she's going to drink this tea and why, so that it's a decision they make together? Or does she keep it a secret? What happens in a few months when he realizes she's no longer interested in his pleasuring her—or in giving him plea-

sure? Does he assume she no longer has feelings for him?
Unless she fills some other need in him, most likely he'll
choose not to renew the handfast because he'd prefer to be
alone than be with someone who doesn't want him.

"No longer living with a Warlord Prince, the woman
stops drinking the tea. She enjoys being around men and
emotionally would like another lover, but her body won't
respond. Desire was drowned one time too many. And
once Warlord Princes figure out why lovers no longer respond to them? They learn the warning signs, and they
walk away at the first sniff of that tea—especially if they
feel some affection for the woman. They don't consider a
handfast or marriage to a witch who doesn't wear a Jewel
of equal or darker rank."

Surreal shook her head. "If the tea was only provided
by a Healer when the need was acute, and no one else
knew how to make it . . ."

"Did Grizande tell you this tea was a secret?" Witch
asked.

She hesitated. "Yes, she did." And the girl had reserva-
tions about the tea.

"And what was the first thing you did when you arrived
in Ebon Rih?"

"I thought it might help Marian!"

"I know, Surreal. I know. But Marian and Lucivar love
each other, and they will get through this phase of the heat,
just as they will get through the years when Marian goes
through the physical and emotional changes that mark the
end of her fertility. They don't need that kind of help. And
you will never drink another cup of that tea again. You will
not sacrifice your ability to enjoy another man as a lover."

Surreal studied Witch. "What aren't you saying?"

"Daemon is dying." Witch looked away, something she
rarely did. "He agreed not to accelerate the process that
will bring him to the day when he no longer walks among
the living, but I had to agree not to do anything that would
postpone that day. So, you see, his sexual heat won't be a
problem for you."

Surreal sprang to her feet and paced around the room. "Dying? How? Why?"

"It doesn't matter. When it comes it will be swift, and he'll make the transition to demon-dead."

"How long? Centuries from now?"

A painful silence. "Years, not centuries."

She stared at Witch. *She doesn't want him to die. She doesn't want him to give up his time among the living. He's the one who wants this, maybe needs this. Because then he'll be free to have the one thing he wants more than anything else.*

"What can I do?" she asked.

"Nothing." Witch gave her a sad smile. "There's nothing we can do except respect the choice he has made. Hell's fire, Surreal, even Lucivar isn't arguing about it. That should tell you something."

Lucivar knew and had said nothing. Not surprising.

Surreal resumed her seat, stared at the jar of tea leaves, and started thinking like a Warlord Prince's second-in-command. Like an assassin. "Why give a girl Grizande's age this tea?"

Witch's smile turned feral. "My Sister, that's a very good question."

TWENTY-SIX

J illian hurried to the front door of her cottage in response to the second knock. The two young Scelties who lived with her didn't tend to bark. They usually used human speech to announce—loudly—when there was a visitor. In fact, they often used Craft to open the door and inspect the visitor before deciding if that person would be allowed inside. But they didn't bark in response to the knock on the door, and they didn't announce themselves or anyone else. They just stared at the door, whining softly as if uncertain about how to respond to this particular visitor, then trotted off to their beds in the kitchen—a sure sign that they knew they were too young and had too little power to deal with her guest.

Gray power on the other side of the door. Female. Not completely unfamiliar, but not Surreal. Who . . . ?

Swallowing nerves and trying to remember where she'd come in contact with that psychic scent before, Jillian put a double Purple Dusk shield around herself before opening the door. Then she blinked. "Lady Karla."

"Kiss kiss."

"Uh . . ." Jillian felt like she'd been tossed in the air by a storm-driven gust of wind. "I'm expecting . . ."

"Me."

She blinked again. "Really?"

"Lucivar. Virgin Night. You wanted to talk."

Oh, Hell's fire. She opened the door wider and stepped aside for the Gray-Jeweled Black Widow Queen.

Karla walked into the cottage. "It looks lovely. Comfortable."

"I'm pleased with it." Jillian led the way into the sitting room. "I don't have any yarbarah."

"I brought some." Karla settled into a chair, set her cane to one side, then called in a bottle and a ravenglass goblet. She poured a glass of the blood wine and warmed it over a tongue of witchfire. "I heard that your lover-to-be has a keen interest in wine."

Lover-to-be. Is that how Stefan would be seen from now on? "He's a vintner. Prince Sadi took a case of a new wine that Stefan had made."

"Tell me about him."

Jillian poured a glass of Stefan's wine for herself. "Why do you want to know?"

"Think of it as foreplay before we get to the subject we're here to discuss."

"I'd rather just find out . . ." What could she ask? Karla wasn't outside the family, so confessing that she'd already gone through her Virgin Night might not be the best idea, since she would have to explain who and how and where and why. "I don't need details about the . . . act . . . just some idea of what to expect from Lucivar."

"Typically Eyrien to be so direct. Just as well you don't want details. It was Lucivar, and he does things his own way."

Jillian gestured with the wineglass, indicating Karla's Gray Jewel. "You obviously got through the Virgin Night."

"I did, although the details I was aware of have gotten a bit fuzzy, which I'm sure is for the best. Do you know what free fall is?"

"Yes. It's . . ."

"Uh-huh," Karla said. "I made the Offering to the Darkness first. There aren't many men powerful enough to see a Gray-Jeweled Queen through her Virgin Night, and at the time, the ones who could be trusted belonged to the Dark Court. Chaosti was married to Gabrielle by then, and he would have fought going to anyone else's bed. Lucivar was interested in Marian but not formally attached in any way, so Uncle Saetan asked him to perform that duty."

"Duty," Jillian murmured. "Not exactly romantic."

"Some women need the romantic setting, with candles and music and seduction. I like candles and music with a good dinner. I just don't want it spoiled by a cock." Karla drained her glass and prepared another serving of yarbarah. "Lucivar went the other way and told me about the only other time he saw a girl through her Virgin Night, and why he'd never done it again." She looked at Jillian over the rim of her glass. "He saw her safely through, and the next morning the bitch spat on him because he was a half-breed bastard."

Jillian set her glass on the side table before she dropped it. "What? She did what?"

"Spat on him. I was riled about that too. Anyway, he and I drank the brew we were supposed to drink to make things easier, and he suggested that I open my inner barriers and allow him to create a . . . scenario . . . as a bit of distraction. I think that's what he said. Things got fuzzy."

"Yes, you mentioned that. Men create a scenario?"

"Darling, we're talking about Lucivar, not men."

"Right."

"One moment, we're in the bedroom, in bed. The next moment, we're outside and heading for the sky. Hell's fire, that man has speed. I do remember that. Then he rolled us so I had a terrific view of the ground that was so very far away—and he folded his wings."

"Free fall," Jillian said, barely breathing.

"There I am, yelling at him and watching the ground come up to meet us and wondering how big a splat we'll make when we hit and who will have to scrape us off the ground, when he *finally* opens his wings and glides to this quiet little lake and sets me down. I'm pretty sure I swore at him. I'm pretty sure I slugged him. At some point while I'm swearing, I blink and we're back in the bedroom where we started, and Lucivar is telling me it's done."

"What's done?"

"Exactly. While I was preoccupied with falling out of the sky, he took care of business. I can't say we had sex in the usual sense, since I don't remember any of that, but his cock did what it was supposed to do for a Virgin Night."

"Hell's fire." Jillian gulped her wine too fast and started to cough. When she finally could wheeze . . . "That's not . . . ?"

"Typical? No. Not even for Eyriens. But that was Lucivar."

"You had a daughter. Was her Virgin Night . . . ?"

"More traditional? The second attempt was. Or so I was told. The first attempt . . . Let's just say I was more anxious than I realized, and I informed the man that if anything happened to my daughter, I would prepare cock and balls soup and make him eat it while I melted his eyeballs. My Master of the Guard informed me that I threw the man so far off stride, there was some question about him ever standing at attention again. My Master took care of arrangements for the second time and asked me not to attend. Well, I gathered that was one of the conditions of anyone trying to perform the service."

I am so glad Lady Surreal is arranging my Virgin Night. Then again, she also wears the Gray and is an assassin. Is that any better, even for a fake Virgin Night?

"Are you feeling better about your Virgin Night?" Karla asked brightly.

"I don't think 'better' is the correct word," Jillian replied.

"My advice? Surreal will make sure the man has the experience and skill to see you safely through the act, and she will stay nearby. But Lucivar and Daemon . . . You're the first girl in the family to reach this age. Let them fuss over you, even if you think they're being silly. They need the reassurance that you're all right. Let them give you a party to celebrate."

"Somehow I don't think I want to send out 'I survived my Virgin Night, come celebrate' invitations."

"You don't need to explain anything. Invite your vintner. Give the boyos a chance to get used to the idea that he'll be warming your feet—and other things."

"Poor Stefan."

"It will be safer for him if the two of you inform Lucivar and Daemon of your intention to be lovers," Karla pointed out.

Hadn't she already done that?

"Well, I certainly have a lot to think about," Jillian said. And she would have plenty of time to think, since she was certain she wasn't going to sleep for the rest of the week.

"Then I'll take my leave. By the way, I like your hair."

At the door, Jillian said, "There's no such thing as cock and balls soup. That was a bluff, wasn't it?"

Karla gave her a long look before saying softly, "Don't ever underestimate Daemon Sadi when he's protecting someone he cares about."

TWENTY-SEVEN

Daemon set the Coach down on the village's landing web long enough to inform the guards on duty of his presence. Then, using Craft, he floated the Coach a hand span above the road, as if it were a wheeled Craft-powered coach, and guided it to the family estate.

He and Brenda had talked during the first part of the trip. He'd told her about the Hall and the young witches who were there for court training and also for protection in case Delora's coven of malice wasn't the only threat to the well-being of the Queens, Black Widows, Healers, and other strong witches who would eventually come into power in Dhemlan. He told her about the young men who were there for training, including five Warlord Princes. And he told her about the other instructors—and admitted that he wasn't sure how many would still be there after dealing with Surreal and Lucivar for a few days.

She thought he was joking. That told him she'd never met Lucivar. Or Surreal.

In her turn, she told him about the skills she had and what she could offer his young charges as well as the staff at the Hall.

Bracing. That's how he would describe Lady Brenda, assuming anyone needed any comments from him after spending five minutes with her. He had a feeling she could out-Sceltie a Sceltie—and may the Darkness have mercy on all of them. He just hoped she never turned that focus on him.

And he wondered if that strength was the reason she'd wanted to get away from Scelt in order to heal a bruised heart.

She'd fallen asleep, giving him time to think about another girl and how he should handle this permission to make a heart quest, as Eileen had called it.

How would Lucivar handle it? Yaslana would state the terms and draw the line, and then wouldn't budge. His way or nothing.

Did Lucivar lie awake some nights wondering if his way was the wrong way? Probably not.

When they arrived at the estate, he set the Coach down near the house and touched Brenda's arm.

"Are we here, then?" she asked, blinking at him.

"Actually, we're at one of the SaDiablo estates," he replied. "I have some business to take care of here. It shouldn't take long. You can come into the house with me, stretch your legs and get something to eat. Or you can stay tucked in here and sleep."

She blinked again and straightened in her seat. "I need to use a toilet before I embarrass both of us, so I'll come out with you. Besides, I'm wondering what a Dhemlan estate looks like. Are you raising cattle or sheep here?"

"Mostly they raise grapes here."

"Not much herding required, then."

"Not on the estate." The sanctuary was entirely another matter. Fortunately, the girls at the sanctuary kept the Scelties who were living there sufficiently busy that they hadn't expanded their help to the villagers—yet.

Daemon led Brenda to the door of the Coach and offered a hand to help her step down.

He looked at her, amused, recognizing her desire to be independent and step down—or jump down—on her own.

She looked at him, amused, recognizing that the gesture of offering his hand was part of the dance between distaff and spear—and something he would not surrender.

She took his hand and stepped out of the Coach.

After introducing Brenda to the housekeeper and leaving the Scelt witch in the other woman's hands, Daemon used a psychic thread to tap Jillian and Saetien, informing them that he was at the estate and expected them within the hour. Then he reached for Beale on a Red psychic thread and informed the Hall's butler that he was bringing another instructor with him, a witch from Scelt. And *she* would be accompanied by a kindred friend who would need a box stall in the stables.

After receiving assurances that accommodations would be ready for the Lady and her friend, Daemon settled in the sitting room he'd occupied a few days ago and reviewed the papers and reports the estate's manager brought in with a pot of coffee and breakfast sandwiches.

Jillian walked into the smaller sitting room, then retreated a step when she saw the unknown Green-Jeweled witch who was already in the room—an instinctive reaction, since Purple Dusk couldn't stand against Green in a fight. When nothing in the woman's psychic scent indicated an adversary, Jillian took a moment to consider this stranger— and to remember that Prince Sadi was just across the hall and had to be aware of the Green's presence. Rich brown hair with just enough curl to sensually frame a pretty face, green eyes that sparked with curiosity and energy, fair skin with a rose blush in the cheeks.

"It's a grand morning, isn't it?" the woman said cheerfully. "If you're waiting for the Prince, he and his daughter are having a talk, so you might as well tuck in to a bit of breakfast. I'm Brenda, from the village of Maghre on the Isle of Scelt. You?"

"Jillian, from the valley of Ebon Rih in the Territory of Askavi." The formal identification seemed odd, but saying less would feel rude. She sat in a chair on the other side of the coffee table and looked at all the dishes that covered the surface. "How many people are they expecting to eat this?"

"Well now, there was me and now there is you." Brenda grinned. "Maybe the girl, depending on how the talking goes. I didn't see her when she arrived, but I'm thinking her idea of how things are going to go in Scelt is very different from how the Prince and my family intend for things to go."

"Your family?" Jillian poured a mug of coffee for herself and made a selection from the various foods being offered.

"Aye. My brother, Kieran, is the Warlord of Maghre. The Prince's girl will be staying with my parents. Strict rules, and no tolerance for someone putting on airs. I'm going to SaDiablo Hall to be an instructor. What brings you here this morning?"

"Lady Saetien is currently staying at the sanctuary Lady Surreal established for girls who were deliberately broken on their Virgin Night. Those girls need an escort when they leave the grounds, so I brought Saetien here." Jillian bit into a sandwich triangle and studied Brenda. Then she added, "And I wanted to talk to Prince Sadi about a couple of concerns I have about my Virgin Night. Have you had yours?" Since Brenda was direct with lobbing questions at her, she didn't see why she couldn't be the same.

"I have. It was pleasant enough—or not unpleasant, at any rate—and I was relieved to have it done, and even more relieved that it had been done before I . . . Well, there was a man who was very good at hiding his true nature and true intentions. Never got past kisses and a bit of this and that with that one before his true nature collided with my true nature—and my fist."

Jillian laughed. "I've used my fist a time or two to explain things."

"Well then, you know how it goes. I did have a lover for a little while, and I enjoyed being with him. Was fairly on my way to falling in love and giving him my heart, and that's the truth. Then I made the Offering and came away with the Green."

"You were stronger than him?" she guessed.

"I was. I am. And suddenly the things he said he liked about me he started claiming were emasculating him, and he deserved better. 'Better?' said I. 'Maybe so, but then, so do I.' But there was some pressure from some of the Queens in Scelt for me to do a formal apprenticeship in one of their courts, and he was a favorite with some of those same Queens, and I didn't need reminders. Then this opportunity to work at the Hall and get a kind of informal apprenticeship opened up, and that's where I'm headed."

"I'm a kind of counselor at the sanctuary—and I teach the girls how to fight."

Brenda leaned closer, the sparkle in her eyes more intense. "I've heard Eyriens have those war blades they use on a killing field. Do you have one?"

Jillian called in her war blade. "It's balanced to my hand and sharp enough that I can cut halfway through a person just by resting the blade against skin and relaxing my grip."

"A warrior's blade."

"Yes." She was a warrior in her own way. "There are other Eyrien weapons that are better suited for young women who want to be able to defend themselves. An Eyrien club, for example. And there are the sparring sticks. Those moves could be made with a broom as well. If you're interested, you should talk to Daemonar Yaslana when you get to the Hall. He's been teaching others how to use the Eyrien sparring sticks."

Brenda jumped up. "Come on, then. Show me a couple of moves so I don't feel like a complete fool when I get there."

By the time Saetien joined them, they'd gone through the first moves of the warm-up a couple of times.

Saetien had barely been awake when her father had tapped her on a psychic thread and summoned her to the estate for this meeting. Now she sat in the same sitting room, even the same chair, where she'd made her request. Now she tried not to fidget, tried not to explode with a demand for an answer, as if getting an answer a minute from now would be different from getting an answer *right now*.

"I've made arrangements with Lord Kieran's family for you to stay with them while you're in Scelt," Daemon said.

He was going to treat her like a baby? "You have a house in Maghre. Why can't I stay there?"

"You're not old enough to stay by yourself. Therefore, you'll stay with Kieran's family while you search for your answers."

"What if I don't like them?"

"Then Kieran will escort you back to the sanctuary here, and that will end your quest."

"Your way or nothing?"

"Yes."

Why was she fighting about this? Once she arrived in Scelt, she could do what she liked. "Can I have some money for new clothes?"

A beat of silence as the air in the room chilled, warning her that she had, once again, crossed a line with him. Sometimes it felt like she was in a bad play and fell into her part the moment she was with another actor. But she'd written this particular play and kept falling into the role she'd created. She just didn't know anymore how to be someone else when she was around her father.

"No," Daemon said softly. "Maghre is a country village. You have a wardrobe stuffed with clothes. I'm sure you already have anything you'll need."

"What about expenses?"

"The spending money I already provide is more than sufficient. You'll be there a few days, a few weeks at the most."

She didn't want to arrive in Scelt like some *child* with a *project*. "I don't need minding by some strangers." *Stop acting like a brat. Stop it.*

"It's been years since you were last in Scelt, so I suppose everyone in the village will be strangers. Whether you stay here or go is your choice—as long as you abide by my terms."

"I could just go there on my own. How would you stop me?" She was playing to an audience that already hated her performance, but she couldn't seem to hold back the words.

The room turned icy. His eyes glazed—and he smiled a cold, cruel smile. "If you're gambling that I wouldn't physically hurt you, then you're probably right. But I could—and would—hurt anyone who helped you defy me, and everyone on Scelt knows that. Also, you would forfeit any additional funds that come from me. I wouldn't strip you of the money already in your account, but that would be the end of it. Instead of having free time, you'd have to find work that would provide you with income for food and lodging."

She *did* want to go to Scelt. *Needed* to go to Scelt. So she had to accept his terms.

"Fine," Saetien said. "I'll stay with this Kieran and his family."

"I'm delighted," Daemon replied, the words holding a sharp edge. "I'll return in three days to pick you up and take you to Scelt."

"I can—"

"Be ready first thing that morning. I'll talk to Helene about sorting out some clothes that will be appropriate for a stay in Maghre—unless you would prefer to write to her and make that request."

Having Helene and a maid going through her clothes to choose some outfits wasn't any different than having a maid put clothes *into* her wardrobe and dressers after wash day, but it felt more intrusive somehow. But she was banned from the Hall, so she couldn't go through the clothes there anyway, and if she sent a written request, she'd lose a day or more before Helene received the message.

"Thank you, Father. If you talk to Helene, that will give her time to find the proper outfits."

She left the sitting room feeling churned up and un-happy instead of excited. And she knew without a doubt that she had brought that unhappiness on herself.

Daemon wanted nothing more than to collect Brenda and head to SaDiablo Hall. And Hell's fire, he needed some sleep, but he had no idea what was happening at the Hall. Beale had been reticent about what had been going on, saying only that Lucivar was still in residence and Surreal was not. And one instructor had resigned, so it was fortunate he was bringing someone new.

One more to go, he thought as Jillian walked into the room.

She stared at him. He tried very hard not to stare at her short spiky black hair.

"Lady Karla?" Jillian's wings flared to their full span before settling back to their usual position. "Free fall? What were you thinking?"

What was she talking about? "Free fall?"

"Karla. Virgin Night. Did Lucivar actually *tell* you about that night?"

"Well . . . no." Maybe he should have asked Karla before he suggested she talk to Jillian.

He looked at her spiky hair. Maybe he should *stop* suggesting that Jillian talk to Karla. For his own sake.

"Fortunately, Brenda was more forthcoming about what to expect."

Hell's fire, Mother Night, and may the Darkness be merciful. "Oh. Good. I'm delighted." Daemon wanted to put some distance between himself and this witch who was sounding a bit . . . exercised. But he was a Black-Jeweled Warlord Prince, and backing down wasn't an option.

"I think having the party the following evening would be sensible. Give me a little time to adjust. What do you think?"

"Quite sensible," he agreed, grateful that she was back to sounding like the Jillian he knew. "Inform Surreal to send me the date you'll be going through this rite of passage, and Lucivar and I will arrange to have a party at the town house the next evening."

"Nothing big. Just family and a few good friends. I'd like Brenda to come, if she's interested and can get away for an evening. And Stefan, of course."

"Of course. We'll take care of it."

Jillian gave him a bright smile. "I'd better get Saetien back to the sanctuary, or she'll be late for her morning classes."

"You do that."

Daemon waited until Jillian left the room. Waited until he was sure no one else was going to come bouncing into the room with other thoughts, demands, opinions. Then he scrubbed his hands over his face and muttered, "Jillian and Brenda. May the Darkness have mercy on me."

TWENTY-EIGHT

Daemonar felt self-conscious about leading the adult men through the warm-up and workout with the Eyrien sparring sticks when his father was one of those adult men. How was he supposed to comment about *Lucivar's* fighting skills?

The second time Daemonar almost missed blocking one of Weston's moves because he wondered what Lucivar thought about the way he'd taught the other men to use the sticks, his father's sharp whistle called a halt to the workouts.

"You can't be thinking about my opinions when you have an opponent in front of you," Lucivar said when the other men left the room. "You do that, you're going to be kissing dirt—or nursing bruised ribs."

"You should be leading this workout," Daemonar said.

"No, I should not. That's one of your duties. From what I've seen, you taught those men the moves as they should be done, and the only thing they need is practice to hone their skills."

"Is your ankle bothering you?" He'd noticed a couple of moves that weren't fluid and gave Lucivar's opponent a potential opening.

"Is that why you retreated from Weston's advance?" Lucivar gave him a knowing look. "So you'd be close to my left side? But you didn't comment about the misstep. An instructor should have."

"You did that deliberately?"

Lucivar smiled. "A different kind of lesson, just for you. You made the right move for a battlefield or a killing field. But here? You should have called me on it—if for no other reason than to prevent a potential injury. You would have if I'd been anyone else."

Daemonar sighed.

Lucivar laughed. "It's not easy giving orders to someone who outranks you and is usually the one giving *you* orders. But sometimes, boyo, that's what you need to do. I had plenty of opportunities to learn *that* lesson with your auntie J." He wrapped a hand around the back of Daemonar's neck and kissed his forehead. "Get cleaned up and get some breakfast. You have other duties this morning. I'll take the rest of the sparring lessons."

"It's the girls this morning. There will be whining."

Lucivar gave him a lazy, arrogant smile. "Then I will give them a reason to whine."

Oh, shit.

Daemonar hurried toward his room, then stopped when he spotted Zoey and her coven heading for the main dining room. He gave Zoey and Titian a nod, then said, "Lady Jhett, your assistance is required."

Jhett's eyes widened at the formal request that was actually an order, since he was a Warlord Prince who outranked her. She glanced at Zoey, who had stopped walking the moment she heard the words.

"Is there something we can do for you, Daemonar?" Zoey asked.

"I just need a bit of help from Jhett."

But not from me, Zoey said on a psychic thread, sounding disheartened.

Not today.

Zoey hurried away, followed by the other girls. Titian gave him a worried look but said nothing as she linked arms with her friend.

Zoey had stumbled the night Grizande arrived, and she hadn't regained her balance, and that was a concern. He

wasn't sure why making a mistake had hit her so hard—
and that was something he needed to mention to Uncle
Daemon.

"What kind of help?" Jhett asked.

"I'm supposed to take Grizande to the village this
morning and show her around. And she's supposed to purchase some clothes. All kinds of clothes." He had a mother
and a sister. He'd seen his share of female underwear being
dried on wash day. But he wasn't his uncle, and helping a
girl he barely knew purchase underwear . . . No.

"Ah." Jhett nodded. Then she gave him a sharp look.
"Why me?"

"You're a Black Widow. Grizande grew up around the
Hourglass. I think she'll be more comfortable around you
than with any of the other girls. Also, you live in the same
square of rooms. Getting to know you might help her relax
around the other girls in Zoey's coven."

Jhett nodded again. "Do I have time for breakfast?"

"Sure. I'll tell Grizande about our plans, and we'll meet
up in an hour?"

She hesitated. "Let's meet up in the great hall. Zoey is
my friend, and she's still feeling raw about Grizande's re-
jection."

How much to say? "Because of things that happened to
him in Terreille, my father doesn't have much use for Queens
as a caste. Grizande doesn't have much use for Queens either. I suspect her reasons for feeling that way are much the
same as his. Pain is a harsh teacher—and scars make sure a
person doesn't forget the lessons."

Jhett sucked in a breath, confirming that she understood
what he was saying. "Does anyone else know about Grizande?"

"The adults who serve Prince Sadi know. My father
knows. But the students?" He shook his head. "She'll
choose who she tells."

"It helps that you told me—especially if we're going to
be trying on clothes."

Daemonar waited until Jhett hurried to join the other

girls before he entered the Queen's square. He found Grizande wandering the courtyard, staying away from the box of sandy earth where Liath was showing Jaalan how the kitten was supposed to use that kind of toilet.

He whistled softly to catch her attention, then jumped from the second-floor balcony, spreading his wings for a controlled drop.

"We're going to the village this morning," he said. "My father's orders. I'm told you need more clothes, and it would be good for you to see some of the shops and get a feel for the village."

Grizande looked away and shook her head.

Daemonar called in the leather wallet and held it out. "A welcome gift from my family."

She took the wallet, opened it—and then stared at him.

"Money is a kind of freedom, a kind of safety," he said quietly. "A shield against hunger, if nothing else. Halaway is a good place to practice using it, because no shopkeeper will try to cheat you or take advantage of you learning something new."

"A learning."

She didn't sound excited about the prospect of having new clothes or spending money. He wondered if she'd ever experienced either of those things.

"I've asked one of the girls to help us with the clothes. Jhett. Did you meet her yesterday?"

Grizande shook her head.

"She's a Sister of the Hourglass." Daemonar watched Grizande relax and was relieved that he'd made the right choice of assistant. "Once we have the clothes—we can't come back without them—we'll visit the village weapons maker to select a gift from me. I figured you could use a good knife."

That made her purr.

Yesterday Zoey had avoided seeing anyone but her circle of close friends—girls who were curious but wouldn't ask

her to talk about what happened at the Keep. Today she
had to have meals with the other Queens and their friends,
had to go to classes. Had to pretend nothing had changed.

Everything had changed.

"Zoey?" Titian said softly when they reached the open
dining room doors. "Do you want to go back to our
rooms?"

She shook her head. Couldn't act like a coward, even if
she did want to hide.

She walked into the dining room. The boys were already in line to fill their plates. They were always the first
in line—but to be fair, they always yielded their places as
soon as any of the girls approached the table that held the
serving dishes. Ladies had first choice, and Queens were
given first choice among the distaff.

Most of the boys glanced at her, then looked away and
hurriedly filled their plates. The four Warlord Princes gave
her a careful look. Raeth dipped his head in the smallest
bow before selecting the food for his breakfast.

But the other four Queens hurried up to her.

"We heard you were summoned to the Keep," Kathlene
said, sounding concerned. "Is that true? Did you see . . . *her*?"

"What's she like?" Felisha asked. Avid curiosity.

"She's . . ." *Power and mind and knowledge and storms,
and not all the dreamers who shaped her were human,
and there is no hiding that now.* "She's hard to describe."

"I'm going to insist that the rest of us have an audience
with her," Dinah said, sniffing. "We're just as important as
you."

"It wasn't an audience," Zoey snapped, aware that even
the boys had stopped focusing on food to listen to her. "I
was chastised for ignoring some court Protocol, and being
in the same room with her when she's angry is *horrible*."

It wasn't all horrible. But somehow, when Witch had
sounded human and . . . ordinary . . . it was more unnerving. And Zoey had wondered—and worried—last night if
she'd have the courage to request one of those audiences
that had been a gift from Witch.

"What . . ." Azara looked at the other Queens and lowered her voice. "What did you do that was so bad?"

"Lord Beale told me to do something, and I tried to overrule him," Zoey replied, feeling her face burn with the shame of stepping so far out of line that she'd been *summoned* for discipline because of it.

"Why shouldn't you overrule him?" Dinah said loudly. *"He's just the butler."*

"And you're the bitch-brat who is going to pack her trunks and leave right after breakfast," Lucivar said, dropping his sight shield.

The boys sucked in a collective breath. The Warlord Princes straightened to attention. The girls just stared at the Warlord Prince of Askavi.

"You can't decide that," Dinah said. "This isn't your house."

Lucivar gave Dinah that smile. "This is the SaDiablo family seat, so this is my home more than it will ever be yours, whether or not I'm in residence. But more than that, *Lady*, the Hall is working as a court works. You are all little witches in training, and I am the Master of the Guard. That gives me the right to decide that you don't belong here." He looked at the girls clustered around Dinah. "And you have until breakfast is finished to decide if you're leaving, too, or if you're going to get it through your heads that this bitch-brat shit won't be tolerated. You've had a chance to settle in and get a feel for living at the Hall and understand what is expected of you. There's a difference between making a mistake and being a bitch. Bitches will not survive in this court."

"But Prince Sadi . . . ," Kathlene began, her voice shaking.

"If you cross an unforgivable line, you'd better hope I'm the one coming for you, because if Sadi's temper goes cold, you have no chance of surviving—and your age won't make a damn bit of difference to either of us." He looked at all of them. "And I'm going to recommend that Protocol be enforced everywhere except in your private rooms. That means addressing people by their titles and recognizing the Jewels they wear and what those Jewels mean, regardless of the work those people do. That means addressing each other as you would in any other court. That means sharp discipline if you step out of line."

Lucivar turned toward the dining room door. "You have anything to say about that?"

Zoey sucked in a breath. She hadn't realized Prince Sadi had returned—and she wondered if the Green-Jeweled witch who had come in with him was a visitor.

"You've said everything that needs to be said," Daemon replied. "It does seem that the children are not mature enough to appreciate informality within a court setting, so Protocol will be enforced." He waited a beat. "Anything else I need to know?"

"Nothing that can't wait," Lucivar said.

"I'm delighted." Daemon looked around the room. "Since most of you are here, I'd like to introduce Lady Brenda from the village of Maghre on the Isle of Scelt. She'll be your new instructor."

"Sir?" Raeth raised his hand enough to draw Daemon's and Lucivar's attention. "What will Lady Brenda be teaching?"

Daemon gave them all an amused smile. "Whatever she wants to teach."

Brenda let out a hoot of laughter. "It's going to be like that, is it? Well then, best I unpack and get on with it."

"Lord Beale." Daemon looked over his shoulder.

"Prince."

"Please escort Lady Brenda to her suite and introduce her to Helene. Make sure she has everything she needs."

"And the Lady's friend?"

"He'll be arriving later today. Also make up a guest room for Lord Kieran. I expect he'll be with us overnight."

"Very good, Prince." Beale took a step back. "Lady? If you would follow me . . ."

Brenda looked at Lucivar, then at Daemon. "That's your brother, is it? Quite a whip hand you've got there. But not to worry. When he's not around, I'm a fair hand with a whip myself."

"Good to know," Daemon murmured.

"Eat or don't eat," Lucivar said, turning back to all the youngsters. "Lessons start in an hour whether your bellies are full or empty." He looked at Zoey and Titian. "And before the lessons, the three of us are going to have a chat."

Mother Night, Zoey thought, sinking into a chair. She watched Lucivar walk out of the dining room with Daemon.

Her emotions spun, her stomach churned, and all she could think was *What have I done now?*

She gasped when Raeth set a plate down in front of her and took the seat on her right.

"It's just scrambled eggs and toast," Raeth said. "You need to eat something, and I figured that would go down and stay down."

Trent put a dish in front of Titian before circling the table and taking a seat opposite the girls.

Jhett sat next to Trent and gave Zoey a worried look.

"What did Daemonar want?" Titian asked Jhett.

The young Black Widow hesitated. "I'm going to the village with him and Grizande. She needs to buy some clothes and personal items—things a man wouldn't help a female acquaintance buy."

Zoey forced herself to swallow a bite of scrambled egg. "That's good. We should help whenever we can."

She knew there were bad Queens. She did. But until Grizande showed up at the Hall, she'd never met someone whose life had been burned by a bad Queen. She'd never been hated simply because she was a Queen.

What was she supposed to do about that?

And would the other girls blame her for Dinah's being sent away?

"We have things to discuss," Daemon said quietly as he and Lucivar crossed the great hall and headed for his study.

"Yes, old son, we do. Let's start with your new instructor."

"She's . . ." How to explain Brenda?

"Oh, I got that part. Bloodlines?"

"Morghann and Khardeen if you go back far enough."

"Hell's fire. That explains some of it."

Daemon made a sound that might have been a laugh. "It does, yes. While I was discussing the trip to Scelt with Saetien, Brenda and Jillian had a chat."

Lucivar stopped walking and stared at him. "Should I be afraid?"

"'Terrified' would be closer to the truth of it, especially since they'll both be living in Dhemlan."

"Your problem, then."

"Yes, but apparently you're my whip hand."

"Take a piss in the wind."

Daemon smiled. He could always count on Lucivar being Lucivar.

The front door opened. Surreal walked into the great hall.

"Did you get any sleep last night?" Lucivar asked.

"Enough," Surreal replied. "Why?"

"As Sadi's second-in-command, you're taking Dinah back to whatever District Queen rules the girl's home village and informing that Queen that the girl is temperamentally unsuitable for training at the Hall, and she and the Province Queen will receive a full report of the girl's conduct."

"Who's going to write this report?" Daemon asked.

"I'll dictate to you and Holt. He'll write it down, and you and I will sign it."

Hell's fire. There was a lot of temper being held on a tight leash. "What happened here?"

"Let's talk about it in your study," Surreal said.

Daemon studied her. Something different about her psychic scent and physical scent. Just enough to make him aware of it.

They went into his study. Lucivar put an Ebon-gray shield around the room to make sure they wouldn't be interrupted. Then Surreal put an aural shield around the room so they wouldn't be heard.

"I wasn't away that long." Daemon looked at the two of them.

"Dinah needs to go," Lucivar said.

"I agree," Surreal said. "She'll keep stirring things up until someone is killed. And she seems to be aiming most of her venom at Zoey."

"Then she goes." Daemon focused on Surreal. "What else? I assume there's a reason why your psychic scent and physical scent are a little different."

Her eyes widened. "You can tell?"

"Of course I can tell." They might live apart most of the time, but that didn't mean he wasn't sharply aware of her—and aware of any differences—when they were in the same place.

"Hell's fire," she muttered.

Lucivar stared at her. "You tried the tea?"

"Yes, I drank a cup of the tea after Jaenelle confirmed that one cup wouldn't harm me." Surreal frowned. "I'll have to send a note to the Keep and let her know it changes a witch's psychic scent and physical scent. Although she probably already knows that."

"Did you drink it before or after I got that mental kick in the ass from Witch, telling me that Grizande was not allowed to drink another cup of that tea?"

"What tea?" Daemon asked.

Surreal ignored the question. Her frown deepened as she looked at Lucivar. "You didn't notice the difference."

He shrugged. "It's a little like how you feel when your moontime begins and a little like how you feel when you've had too much wine." He paused and asked too casually, "Did Marian drink any of that tea?"

"No," Surreal said quickly. "No, it's . . . You and Marian and Nurian need to talk to Witch about the tea."

"What tea?" Daemon asked again.

He listened while Lucivar explained about the secret tea that was made in Tigrelan and quieted a woman's response to a Warlord Prince's sexual heat. Then Surreal told them why Witch's temper had turned cold.

Lucivar paced the study, swearing under his breath. "I'd leave Marian before I'd let her do that to herself."

Surreal nodded. "That's one of the reasons why having this show up again pissed off Witch so much."

Daemon said nothing, but he noticed how carefully Surreal wasn't looking at him.

You won't need it, he thought. Since that wasn't something he wanted to discuss, he said, "Is Grizande settling in?"

"She needs more clothes," Lucivar replied. "Daemonar is taking her to the village this morning."

Daemon raised an eyebrow.

"One of the girls is going with them to help with the underwear," Lucivar said dryly.

"Of course."

"Your turn," Surreal said. "What's going to happen with Saetien?"

"If she agrees to the terms I set, I'll escort her to Scelt in three days' time. She'll stay with Lord Kieran's family while she's on what Lady Eileen called a heart quest." A beat of silence. "Brenda is Kieran's sister."

"A student?" Surreal guessed.

"Instructor."

"Teaching . . . ?"

"Whatever she tells me she's going to teach." Daemon studied the carpet. Nice carpet. Good colors and pattern. "Her kindred friend will be arriving later today. Lord Shaye. A horse." He blew out a breath. "A mountain of a horse."

Lucivar narrowed his eyes. "When did you last eat?"

"Had breakfast while I waited for Saetien and Jillian to arrive at the estate," Daemon replied.

"Sleep?"

"Is a fond memory."

"Well, Hell's fire, you'll be less than useless in another hour. Go to bed, Bastard. Surreal will take the bitch-brat back to her family, and I'll deal with the rest of the youngsters."

"And I will be the benign presence," Daemon murmured.

"Sure," Lucivar agreed. "Time for a little chat with Zoey and Titian." He dropped the Ebon-gray shield and walked out of the study.

"This tea . . . ," Daemon said softly.

Surreal shook her head. "No need to say anything about it." Then she smiled—or tried to, anyway. "Lucivar's right. You're almost asleep on your feet. Get some rest, Sadi. You're going to need it."

Might have been a warning. Might have been a threat. Either way, he didn't argue, especially after he almost ran into Holt when he left his study. His secretary took one look at him and said there was nothing that couldn't wait. When was there *nothing* that couldn't wait when he'd been gone for a couple of days?

When he reached his suite, he put a Black lock on the door and Black shields around the rooms, remembering to leave a Sceltie-sized hole in the shield on the courtyard side. He opened the glass door that led to the balcony, ignoring the brisk air. Breen was still a puppy, and while she could air walk now, she hadn't progressed to the Craft lessons about passing through a door or wall. As soon as she realized he'd returned, she would come running to greet him. And woe to the man who was in the shower when she arrived and found herself locked out of the room, because then she'd call on the rest of the Scelties for help. He'd watched tragedies in the theater that didn't have as much pathos as a chorus of Scelties standing outside a closed door that they couldn't get through.

By the time he got out of the shower and pulled on a pair of pajama bottoms, Breen was in the sitting room, wildly happy to see him.

Daemon!

Sitting in a chair, he cuddled her. "How's my girl? Have you been playing with the other Scelties and having your lessons with Mikal?"

Yes! And playing with tiger friend.

Was that safe? She was so small, and the kitten was . . . not small. He had to trust Mikal and the other Scelties to keep her safe when he wasn't there.

"Breen, I have to sleep." Daemon put her down and went into his bedroom. He was in bed and drifting toward sleep when he felt her tumble onto the mattress before cuddling against his chest.

He'd got halfway through the thought of telling her to get down and use her own bed when he dropped into sleep.

Lucivar strode toward the training room. A quick psychic probe told him the girls were in the room—minus Zoey and Titian, who were hovering in the corridor waiting for him, and that bitch-brat Dinah, who should be in her room packing. The boys were milling around looking uncertain. Well, with Morris gone and Brenda settling in, he wasn't sure where the boys were supposed to be—or if Raine was supposed to be teaching this morning. Didn't really matter. No one's brains were going to be on lessons today. At least not the kind found in books. So he might as well give them other kinds of lessons.

"Prince Raeth," he called. "Get the girls started on the warm-up with the sticks."

"Sir?" The boy sounded like he'd just been ordered to strip naked and leap onto a bed of knives.

"Girls. Warm-up. You. Go." He pointed at Zoey and Titian. "You two with me."

He led them around the corner and put an aural shield around the three of them. Then he focused on Zoey. "What's wrong?"

"Nothing," she replied in a low voice.

"You know that's shit, and I know that's shit. So let's try it again. What's wrong?"

"Papa," Titian protested. "Zoey is upset."

"I can see that, witchling. I want to know why."

"I failed!" Zoey cried. "How can I rule even a tiny village if I fail at being a Queen?"

Lucivar leaned against a wall and studied this girl who seemed to be shattering right in front of him. "If you've reached your age without ever taking any kind of misstep as a Queen, then you have been very sheltered, or very lucky that your instincts didn't get you into trouble before now. My guess? Your instincts are sound, if inexperienced, and Weston has been very good at protecting you."

Titian called in a handkerchief and handed it to Zoey.

"Grizande hates me," Zoey said, sniffling.

He didn't disagree with that, since it was probably true. "She doesn't trust you because she's learned that Queens can't be trusted. That's her burden. It has nothing to do with you personally."

"If I'd listened to Lord Beale . . ."

"Yeah, if you had it would be easier. But you didn't yield until you were pushed back. At another time, in another place, you may have to stand your ground despite what other people say. But you will have this lesson as a balance for instinct, and the next time—because you are a Queen and there will be a next time—you will make a deliberate choice of whether to yield or to fight, even if that fight is with your own court. You skinned your knee, Zoey. That's all. Now it's time to clean the wound and stand up."

He waited.

"The other girls have been mean," Titian said when it became obvious that Zoey was still having trouble standing up after what was, in the end, a small mistake.

"'Mean' as in a physical punch or a verbal one?"

"Words."

"Sometimes those hurt worse than a fist and take longer to heal." He waited a beat. "Which girls?" He didn't raise his voice, didn't demand. The alarm in his daughter's eyes told him she knew exactly what would happen if she gave him names. "Anyone besides Dinah?"

"No, Papa."

Probably true. But the other girls, the other Queens, hadn't stood up against Dinah's attack either. Something to think about when it came to the harsh kinds of lessons.

"All right," Lucivar said. He considered what to say that might help Zoey. "Witchling, just because you're offering friendship doesn't mean Grizande is obliged to accept it—or can accept it—from you or any of the other Queens who are living at the Hall. Some scars never heal. For her, being around Queens might be one of them. Or maybe, given time, Grizande will see that people she does trust also trust you and consider you a friend, and she'll take a chance that you will be different from what she's known. Do you understand?"

Zoey nodded.

He wasn't sure she did, but he said, "Go on, then. Sweating will do you both some good." He dropped the aural shield and watched the two girls hurry away.

Lessons. He thought about some of the lessons Saetan had prepared for the coven. Most were stunningly unsuccessful for their original intent because the coven either laughed themselves silly while trying to perform the scenarios or turned on Saetan with a united anger that told the future Steward of the Dark Court a great deal about the Queens who would rule Kaeleer.

After checking on the youngsters, he didn't interfere with the workout. Weston was there, and Raeth had the support of all the boys as they paired off to spar with the girls. They were being daintier with the girls than he would have been. He wondered if they would have been so dainty if Dinah had still been among them.

Leaving them to it, Lucivar headed for the places where he would most likely find Beale and Holt. He wanted to ask them about lessons.

Jhett didn't chatter, for which Daemonar was grateful, but she did point out the spring flowers she recognized and spoke their names as the three of them walked to the village. Grizande repeated the names quietly as she scanned the land around the drive in much the same way Daemonar did—a hunter who enjoyed the scenery but was always aware of other living things and of the potential danger hidden within beauty.

Suddenly Grizande stopped and focused on the trees near the bridge that was the boundary between the Hall's drive and the village's road. She growled softly.

Before Daemonar could send out a psychic probe, two minds tapped his first inner barrier. Young. Curious. Individuals who were, for him, a normal part of the estate and didn't require vigilance.

"A pack of kindred wolves lives in the north woods," Daemonar explained. "They hunt on the estate, and they will defend anyone who belongs to the Hall. You're sensing two juveniles who are out exploring. You're both new, and they're curious about meeting you if you're now part of the Hall's pack. Is that all right?"

Jhett didn't look sure about meeting wolves, but Grizande nodded. Of course she did. Her little brother was a tiger.

A short whistle was all it took to have the youngsters trotting over to meet them. Daemonar was familiar, so they acknowledged him first with licks and a quick sniff. The females were more interesting, Grizande more than Jhett because she carried Jaalan's scent on her clothes as well as her own.

Play? one of the wolves asked on a general communication thread.

Daemonar shook his head. "We have to go to the village now. Maybe later."

Grizande said, "Later is long time?"

Whining from the wolves. If they sensed that the girl would rather play with them than go to the village, they would make a fuss to get him to agree to playtime.

"Later is after the midday meal." He had no idea what Grizande was supposed to be doing this afternoon—or what he was supposed to do—but it would be good for kindred to meet kindred before kitten and wolves stumbled into one another.

Grizande sighed. The wolves sighed. Jhett sighed—but Daemonar didn't think she sighed for the same reason.

He herded the females across the bridge. The wolves stayed behind.

"Do you know how to swim?" Daemonar asked.

"Yes," Jhett said.

Grizande nodded. "Tigrelan. Deep rivers. Must swim."

"Tigers like to swim too. There's a small lake on the estate. In the summer, we go there to swim."

"Wolves swim?"

"They do."

For the rest of the walk to Halaway, he told them the story of how Prince Smoke came to the Hall looking for Jaenelle Angelline and how his pack was invited to live in the north woods and how Smoke's descendants had lived there ever since—a link to the kindred wolves who held their own Territory, which was closed to humans.

"We'll start at this shop," Jhett said when they reached Halaway's business district, which was the village's main street.

Daemonar glanced at the shop. It wasn't the one he'd have chosen. *Jhett, my father and uncle are paying for Grizande's clothes, so . . .*

That was as far as he got before Jhett turned to Grizande and said, "It's not the shop for fancy clothes and lingerie, but it has basic clothing of good quality. I came here a couple of weeks ago to fill the gaps in my own wardrobe."

Grizande braced as if preparing for battle. She looked at Daemonar.

He raised his hands in a gesture of surrender. "Jhett knows what you Ladies need. You two take care of that. I'll wait out here."

"You do not like inside?" Grizande asked.

"It's a clothing shop for females. I am not needed inside." And he'd keep insisting on that for as long as Uncle Daemon let him.

The girls went inside. Daemonar stood on the sidewalk with his back to the shop's window. If he hadn't been standing escort, he would have gone to the bookshop a few doors down the street. Or to the bakery to pick up something for Manny and Tersa. There was nothing in the bakery that wasn't made at the Hall by one group of cooks or the other, but sometimes the novelty of eating something that wasn't made at the Hall appealed to him. And bringing a box from the bakery tended to catch Tersa's interest. Persuading her to eat was often a challenge, and her health was still fragile after she almost bled out a few months ago when she'd created several tangled webs to give warning of the troubles that were coming. He could usually get a few bites of food down her if he arrived with treats from the bakery. And Mikal would consume anything that was left when he arrived home, so nothing would turn stale, let alone go to waste.

Two of the guards who served Halaway's current Queen rode up.

"Standing escort for a couple of Ladies from the Hall," he said before they asked the question. He tipped his head. "They're shopping."

The younger guard looked amused and sympathetic. The older one leaned in his saddle, and Daemonar approached.

"We heard one of them is . . . ," the guard began.

"From Tigrelan, yes," Daemonar replied. "A tiger kitten came with her. A Warlord Prince."

The guard studied him. "Been a while since we've had visitors from that Territory."

"They're receiving their training at the Hall. An instructor from Scelt has also just arrived."

"Human?"

Daemonar bit back a smile at the hope in the guard's voice. He understood the reason for that hope all too well. "Yes. A Green-Jeweled witch from Maghre."

"Well." The guard straightened in the saddle. "Well then."

He hadn't actually seen the new instructor. While he

and Grizande had waited in the great hall for Jhett, Holt had pulled him aside and told him the basics.

"Does she know Liath?" he had asked.

"They're . . . acquainted," Holt had replied.

The way Holt had said that was not reassuring.

He watched the street, nodded to people he knew, turned down invitations from young men and women to join them for a drink at the coffeehouse. Turned down a different kind of invitation from an adult woman who should have known better—and who had paled when he reminded her that he needed his father's or his uncle's consent before having sex.

There were a couple of women in the village who were attached to the Queen's court and provided a discreet service. There were a couple of men attached to the court who provided the same service. After all, needs didn't begin in the marriage bed. But the no-sex-without-consent rule applied to *all* the youngsters living at the Hall. The staff needed permission from Beale or Helene—and anyone who had met Mrs. Beale and her meat cleaver might think long and hard about approaching Beale for permission. Everyone else required permission from Uncle Daemon. Or Lucivar or Aunt Surreal, depending on who was in charge that day.

Given those choices? Better to wait and talk to Uncle Daemon. Definitely.

It was a long hour before the girls walked out of the shop. Grizande looked a little stunned, but Jhett seemed pleased.

"Why don't we walk down the street for a bit so you can see where some of the other shops are located?" Daemonar said. "Then I'd like to . . ." He trailed off when he spotted Tersa looking into a shop window.

Nothing unusual about Tersa wandering the village on her own. Nothing at all. Although "on her own" wasn't quite accurate, since Keely, the Sceltie Black Widow who lived with Tersa, accompanied her whenever she left the cottage. If Tersa was in any kind of distress, *everyone* would know about it.

"Come on." He didn't wait to see if the girls followed him. He just strode down the street toward the mad, broken Black Widow who was Uncle Daemon's mother—and the mother of Lucivar's heart.

She turned away from the window and smiled as he approached. "It's the winged boy."

He was the winged boy. "My winged boy" meant Lucivar. "The boy" or "my boy" was Uncle Daemon.

"Hello, Tersa." Daemonar kissed her cheek.

"You have brought friends?"

"Yes. This is Jhett."

"Little Sister." Tersa's gold eyes focused on the young Black Widow—and her voice held a warning that she had slipped a little ways from the border of the Twisted Kingdom.

Keely, alert but not alarmed, watched Tersa.

"And this is Grizande," Daemonar finished.

"Tiger girl."

Grizande put a hand on her chest. "I am Tigre."

Tersa nodded. "Tiger girl. Power and grace. You hear the song of the bright dark star. The one who had your name and bloodline, she heard that song too. Others will hear, and the web that connected Kaeleer before will connect it again." She stepped toward Grizande and pressed her hand over the girl's. "Your claws are sharp. You will need them. Learn from the ones whose claws are sharper than yours. They are within your reach. Learn, little tiger. Learn—and survive."

Mother Night, Daemonar thought.

Grizande barely breathed when Tersa stepped back.

Jhett looked stunned . . . and scared . . . and mesmerized.

Tersa looked at him and smiled. "It's the winged boy."

Relieved that her mind had returned to the border, he smiled. "Yes, Tersa."

"This shop sells treats. You will come back to the cottage, and we will have treats."

"All right. Should we go inside the shop and select a few?" Daemonar asked.

"Cake. And beef flakies. Tiger girls need to be strong, just like winged boys."

Daemonar glanced at the girls. "Tersa? Jhett isn't Tigre."

Tersa patted his face. "There is more than one kind of tiger." She went into the shop.

"You okay?" Daemonar asked Jhett.

She swallowed hard and nodded. He didn't believe her, but he let it go—for now—and walked into the bakery to help Tersa select the treats.

TWENTY-NINE

Surreal stared at Dinah's outraged parents—and noticed
that the District Queen didn't look surprised to find the
girl returning home.

"But . . . she was on that list. She needs protection!"
Dinah's mother.

"What do you mean, she isn't temperamentally suited
to living at the Hall?" Dinah's father.

Surreal turned toward the Warlord. Probably a doting
father. Too much? She pushed aside the thought that she—
and Sadi—had probably failed Saetien in the same way
and dealt with the problem in front of her.

"She's been verbally attacking Lady Zoela, as well as
some of the other girls. She brags about being able to meet
challenges with no understanding of the cost. And she has
the unhealthy idea that she can win a place in Prince Sadi's
bed by acting like a bitch—which is the kind of woman he
detests."

"That explains why he doesn't sleep with you anymore,"
Dinah snapped.

"Dinah!" Dinah's mother sounded appalled.

"And the only reason Zoey gets special privileges is because she's tonguing—"

"Enough!" Surreal snapped.

But Dinah had an audience she was sure would sympa-
thize with her. "Zoey got to go to the Keep and see *her*.

The rest of us should be given equal time. We're Queens. We're just as important as *Zoey*."

After a moment, Dinah's father said, "If Zoela was given—"

"You want me to take your daughter to the Keep *now* and have her face Witch and be judged for her behavior?" Surreal interrupted. "If that's what you want, you will write a letter to that effect, to be witnessed by the District Queen and her Steward and Master of the Guard, and I will do it. And I will bring whatever is left of your daughter back to you." She watched the father pale and the mother sink to the floor. "Have you learned nothing from what happened to the coven of malice? Witch has walked roads the rest of us will never see, and even when she walked among the living, she had no use for this adolescent posturing and attitude. Consider what will happen if your girl meets with a Queen powerful enough to crush the whole damn Realm and says *anything* in that bitch-brat snotty voice with that attitude. Are you so eager for Dinah to die? Or worse—because there are worse things than a clean death."

"Zoey wasn't hurt from seeing *her*," Dinah said.

Not defiance in that statement. More like the tone of a young girl looking for a reassurance Surreal couldn't give. "Sugar, your behavior is a long step beyond the small mistake Zoey made. Keep behaving this way, and you will meet Witch—and may the Darkness have mercy on you when that day comes."

"I'll see you out," the District Queen said. Her Steward stayed behind with Dinah's family. Her Master of the Guard followed the two women at a discreet distance.

"You're not surprised I brought Dinah back home," Surreal said.

The District Queen shook her head. "I had concerns about Dinah's temperament. If she's not the darling of a group, she tries to tear down anyone she believes is superior."

"That's a dangerous attitude for a Queen." It took twelve

men to form a court around a Queen. Queens who were bitches often had their courts broken when men refused to continue serving—or they ended up ruling a small village under the hand of a strict Province Queen.

Or they ended up dead when their attitude clashed with a Warlord Prince's temper—or a desperate village hired an assassin like Surreal to set them free.

"Yes," the Queen agreed, "but she was on the list of girls targeted by the coven of malice, so I thought—hoped—that she would change once she was living at the Hall. My mistake. Please convey my apologies to Prince Sadi."

"I will."

"Is the Prince going to consider other youngsters to take Dinah's place?"

Do you have a candidate in mind? The thought was there, but Surreal said, quietly and honestly, "I don't think Sadi will be the one making those choices from now on."

THIRTY

As he and Lucivar stepped onto the gravel drive to greet the guests who had just arrived in a Coach, Daemon noticed Daemonar, Grizande, and Jhett walking up from the village, accompanied by two juvenile wolves. They all looked easy in one another's company. Well, he wasn't sure that Jhett would embrace the idea of being a wolf's playmate, but she wasn't running away, which was a good sign.

The Coach's door opened. Kieran stepped out and raised a hand in greeting as he moved out of the way. Then the Coach's other occupant stepped out.

"What is that?" Lucivar asked quietly.

"It's a horse," Daemon replied blandly.

"Uh-huh. You're usually not so gullible, old son."

"It's Brenda's friend. I was told it was a horse, so it's a horse."

"Do you ride him or use him to knock down stone walls?"

"Yes."

The horse—a black mountain on four legs—bugled and reared. The front hooves hit the ground—and Daemon felt that rumble in the gravel under his feet.

"Hell's fire," Lucivar said.

People ran toward the landing web. People skidded to a halt, then ran *away* from the landing web. Daemonar and the two girls just stared, their mouths hanging open. The wolves didn't look eager to meet this newcomer.

The stable master and some of the grooms stared at the horse, then stared at Daemon.

Kieran headed toward Daemon, his smile amused and sympathetic.

So like Khardeen, Daemon thought.

The Hall's door opened. Brenda rushed out. "Shaye, darling. There you are."

"Have you nothing to say to me, your brother?" Kieran demanded. "I was in a Coach with him for the hours it took to get here, with him fretting all the way about you being on your own."

Brenda spun, planted a smacking kiss on Kieran's cheek, and said, "You're a darling too." Then she ran to greet the horse.

A moment later, Liath ran out of the Hall, heading for the landing web, with Jaalan bounding behind him. Someone had taught the kitten to air walk but hadn't gotten around to the lesson on how to stop, especially when running at full speed on a surface that provided no traction. Seeing the horse, the kitten *tried* to stop as he skidded toward those black legs. Then Jaalan hit the air equivalent of a mound of pillows, stopping a finger length away from Shaye.

"Did you do that?" Daemon asked Lucivar.

"Nope," Lucivar replied.

"Shaye is used to small things running into him," Kieran said.

Shaye's big head lowered. He snuffled. Snorted. Lipped the fur between the kitten's ears while Liath stood nearby, on air, wagging his tail in greeting.

The wolves approached. The kindred ignored the humans while getting acquainted among themselves.

Smiling indulgently, Brenda headed for Daemon, Lucivar, and Kieran at the same time Daemonar led the girls in a wide curve around the kindred.

"He'll settle in well here," Brenda said.

"What is it?" Daemonar asked.

Brenda cocked her head. "Have you not seen a horse before?"

"Horses, sure," Daemonar replied. "But . . ."

"He's a horse," Daemon said in a tone that didn't encourage discussion.

Brenda looked at Lucivar, then tipped her head toward Daemonar. "Yours?"

Lucivar nodded. "He is."

"This is Grizande, from Tigrelan," Daemon said. "And Lady Jhett."

Brenda studied Grizande's tawny striped skin. "The kitten is with you?"

"Yes," Grizande agreed. "He is . . . young."

"Shaye's used to being around small children, two legs or four."

Brenda sounded so cheerful. It was a little terrifying. Although not quite as terrifying as the way Liath wagged his tail and looked at her as if his ally had finally arrived.

"Shaye," Brenda called. "Let's get you settled. I'm due inside for the midday meal."

The horse moved a leg. The kitten, sitting on air right in front of him, was unprepared and the push set Jaalan zipping over the drive, frantically trying to find purchase on air.

Grizande grabbed the kitten as he zipped past her. To keep her upright when the kitten's weight shoved her off her feet, Daemonar grabbed her, fanning his wings to stay upright himself. Which caught the kitten's attention. Jaalan leaped for the new toy—or tried to. Daemonar staggered back into Lucivar, who had come up behind him and braced for the tumble of bodies.

Separating the youngsters, Lucivar pointed at the kitten. "You. No playing with Eyrien wings." The finger aimed at Grizande next. "You. Use Craft when you're trying to pick up or catch that much weight. After the meal, we'll work on that move until you don't have to think about it." The finger moved, stopping at Daemonar. "You. Anything to report?"

"We had an interesting morning with Tersa," Daemonar replied.

Daemon met his nephew's eyes and nodded. A private conversation, then.

Everyone scattered, leaving Daemon on the gravel drive with Lucivar and Kieran.

"You'll stay the night?" Daemon asked Kieran.

"I will, thanks. I'd like to see what you're doing here." Kieran gave them a mischievous smile. "Does this remind you of anything?"

"Oh, yeah," Lucivar said. "And since we're the adults now, may the Darkness have mercy on us."

Using Craft, Daemon moved Kieran's Coach off the landing web moments before Surreal dropped from the Winds and guided her smaller Coach to the landing web.

"It's done," she said, walking past the men.

Lucivar followed her.

"Everything is set?" Daemon asked Kieran as they walked toward the front door.

Kieran nodded. "No guarantee that your girl will get the answers she wants."

"I know. But maybe Saetien will find the answers she needs."

"Prince Sadi doesn't have rules for how we dress for breakfast or the midday meal," Jhett said. "You can't come to the table covered in mud or manure, but otherwise he doesn't comment about clothing. Hair brushed and hands and face clean. Everyone dresses for the evening meal. Girls usually wear dresses or a skirt and blouse, and the boys wear a shirt and proper jacket. It's old-fashioned, but it's a tradition of the house and the Prince holds to it."

Grizande nodded as she hung her new clothes in the wardrobe and tucked them into dresser drawers.

There is more than one kind of tiger. The Tersa Black Widow was not confused. It was a message. The Tigre Hourglass had told her she would find many teachers in the place where the Queen who was more than a Queen had dwelled.

"You like the Zoey Queen?" she asked as she closed a dresser drawer.

"Yes, I do."

"Trust her?"

"Yes, I do." Jhett shifted on the window seat, as if uneasy. "This place is more like a Queen's court than a school, so it's new to all of us, and we're just getting to know one another. I was already friends with Zoey, Titian, and a few other girls when we were at a school in Amdarh, but I hadn't met the other Queens or their friends—or most of the boys. There was one Queen I didn't like, didn't trust, and she enjoyed saying mean things to make people feel bad about themselves, but the Prince sent her away this morning." She hesitated, then reached behind her to touch her back. "I don't think there is anyone here now who would have done . . . *that*."

Grizande nodded. Words were easy—when you had them—but she didn't think this Black Widow would be fooled by words.

"We'd better wash up and go down for the meal," Jhett said.

More food. She was used to hunger, not feasts.

As Jhett walked past her, Grizande raised a hand, almost touched the other girl's arm, wanting to offer knowledge in exchange for the knowledge that had been given. "This place. Still a court. Still *her* court. Witch power still in the stone. Safe here."

"That's what Zoey said. That we're safe here."

They washed up quickly and headed for the dining room where the midday meal was served. Grizande didn't recognize most of the adults who sat at either end of the long table, but the Black and Ebon-gray were there. So was Daemonar. She wasn't alone among strangers.

Daemonar pulled out a chair next to his. "If you're full from the treats we ate this morning, just take small servings and spread them out on your plate so it looks like you're eating enough."

Sure he was teasing her, she said, "Many people eating. No one will know."

"Ooh, someone will notice and a comment will be made, and the next thing will be Mrs. Beale and her meat cleaver cornering Uncle Daemon to find out why you didn't like what she had served for this meal."

Grizande studied him. He *had* to be teasing. "No."

"Yes. I've made that mistake when I've visited. I don't make that mistake anymore."

He put a large spoonful of something on his plate— then put a smaller spoonful on hers. She hoped she would like it. She followed his example with the other foods, noticing that his dish *did* look full even though he'd taken about half as much food as the Warlord Prince who sat across from him.

The Zoey Queen sat on the other side of the table, but far enough away that Grizande didn't have to talk to her. And yet . . .

More than one kind of tiger. More than one reason to need the safety of this place. Maybe the Zoey Queen was still licking her wounds too. Maybe there could be a little trust, a little liking.

Maybe.

"Do you think it's intentional that all the women are at the other end of the table?" Lucivar asked as he heaped food on his plate.

"Do you think it's not?" Daemon countered.

Surreal, Nadene, and Brenda chatting away and getting along just fine. Sweet Darkness.

"Lord Morris is gone?" Daemon asked, looking at Raine and Weston. Beale and Holt had been less than forthcoming about the instructor's reason for resigning— and running.

Raine and Weston exchanged a look.

"Well, there was Liath telling us about biting off a man's ball," Raine said.

"Just one?" Daemon murmured, grateful there was nothing on his plate that looked similar to that part of a man.

"And then there was Lady Surreal honing some of her knives at the breakfast table while she stared at him," Weston said.

"Hmm," Daemon said.

They all looked at Kieran, who said, "Yes, Liath did. Brenda has never sharpened any knives while we were eating, but she has been known to throw a dinner fork at someone with fierce accuracy."

"Well, your meals are going to be interesting," Lucivar said, lifting his glass of ale in a salute to Daemon. "I have another boy at home, and a wife. It's time I got back to them."

"I appreciate the help."

"Whenever you need it. After all, I'm your whip hand." Lucivar glanced at the other end of the table. "One of them, anyway."

"I am so fortunate to have more than one," Daemon said dryly.

A beat of silence. Then Kieran burst out laughing.

THIRTY-ONE

Daemon finished reviewing the last piece of financial information that had been sent by Lord Marcus, his personal man of business, as well as all the reports sent by the firm that handled the investments for the SaDiablo family as a whole. Lucivar had gone home yesterday, but Surreal was still in residence, keeping an eye on things while he tackled all the urgent paperwork for the family and the Dhemlan Territory—all the business Holt had said could wait. And it had waited. For a day.

Hell's fire, he must have looked so exhausted yesterday that Holt probably thought he couldn't make *any* decision, let alone a good one.

Beale entered the study without knocking, closed the door, and swiftly approached the desk. "High Lord."

High Lord. Not Prince Sadi, which was how he was usually addressed for the youngsters' sake. High Lord.

Daemon capped his pen and set it aside. "Beale?"

"The Queen of Tigrelan is here, requesting an audience."

"Is she?" he said too softly. "Then we shouldn't disappoint her."

"Should I have refreshments brought in?"

"Wait until I know if she's going to survive this audience."

"Very good, High Lord."

While Beale left the study to escort the Queen in, Daemon moved around to the front of his blackwood desk to wait for his guest.

She walked into his study without any personal guards or escorts, and he couldn't decide if it was a brave move or a foolish one—or an arrogant one.

"Is she here?" the Tigrelan Queen asked, her tone more of a demand than of a question. "Is Grizande safe?"

"Why do you care?" he asked, his voice viciously civil.

"I care."

"Really? Did you care when she was tortured? Did you care that she's barely educated and unprepared to meet anyone from a race that's not her own?" *And maybe even the aristos from her own race.*

"Is she safe?" the Queen shouted.

"Oh, she's safe."

"She's here? Under your protection?"

He smiled a cold, cruel smile. "Under my protection, yes. And under Witch's hand."

She sank to the floor, as if all the strength had left her legs.

He watched her, and offered nothing.

"Thank the Darkness," she whispered. She didn't ask for help as she climbed into one of the visitors' chairs in front of his desk.

"Perhaps you'd like to explain your concerns to Witch." Oh, he knew how to be so helpful, so civil. So merciless.

But she looked at him with the beginnings of hope. "That would be possible?"

Not the response he'd expected. Then again, this Queen from Tigrelan didn't know what it would be like to face the Queen of Ebon Askavi in all her dark, feral glory.

"Grizande's mother was my cousin, and we were close when I was young," the Queen said. "Different branches of the same bloodline that went back to Grizande the Queen and Prince Elan." She looked thoughtful, as if struggling to find the words to explain something she wasn't sure he would understand. "There are different kinds of Queens in

Tigrelan, different kinds of courts. My branch of the family was more . . . formal. Official. For many generations we dealt with other races in Kaeleer, had the connection for trade and an exchange of knowledge in all kinds of Craft. But as each generation got further from Grizande and Elan and the Dark Court, the connection faded. The Tigre live differently from other races."

"I'm sure the Centauran race would say the same," Daemon said.

"Yes," she agreed. "Our races haven't met in a long, long time."

Beale, he said on a spear thread. *Please arrange for refreshments.*

At once, High Lord, Beale replied.

"My cousin was a different kind of Queen," the Queen continued. "Country Queen? Small village, a simpler life. A rich life. She was loved in her village. And she earned the respect of some of the tiger Queens." A warm laugh. "She and one of the tigers used to hunt together. They made a formidable team and usually brought down enough game to feed both their families. The male who was her husband and Consort loved her fiercely, and there were some women serving in strong courts throughout our land who developed a foul envy for that devotion because it was something their own mates did not feel for them.

"Then Grizande was born, the youngest of my cousin's three children. She was . . . fierce, even as a small child. Strong of heart and will. But the Black Widows who spun their tangled webs of dreams and visions were concerned about this child and advised that she be kept from the notice of other Queens and aristo witches. Unlike the children from other families with aristo bloodlines, Grizande did not attend a school where the common tongue was learned, where aristo ways were learned—where too many eyes might see too much. But that all changed at the Birthright Ceremony when the child came away with a Sapphire Jewel."

A knock on the door before Beale entered with a tray.

After setting dishes out on the low table in the social area of the study, the butler retreated and Daemon led his guest to the other chairs.

"Coffee?" he asked, raising the pot. "Or would you prefer tea?"

She gave him a sharp, wary look. "Coffee. Thank you."

He poured cups for both of them, offered her sandwiches—which she declined—then leaned back in his chair and crossed his legs at the knees. "There was trouble over the girl wearing Birthright Sapphire?"

The Queen sipped the coffee, then set her cup on the table. "Birthright Sapphire isn't the problem."

"Having the potential to wear Ebon-gray could be a problem," Daemon said quietly.

"Yes. Ebon-gray without a strong hand to hold the leash?" The Queen shook her head. "The girl instantly became a prize to be acquired and controlled—because the Black Widows were certain she would wear the Ebon-gray and would be a warrior connected to a powerful court. Any Queen who could control her could control all of Tigrelan."

The Queen reached for the cup, saw the way her hand shook, and pressed both hands into her lap. "I don't know what happened. I don't know if my cousin received any warning, or if a warning came too late. I couldn't ask her, because she and her mate were dead and gone by the time I heard about the attack and sent some of my warriors to her aid. I heard later that the enemy warriors sent to my cousin's village finished the kill, leaving nothing of my cousin and her mate behind. I also heard that when my cousin fell, some of the villagers hid her body so that she could make the transition to demon-dead and tell the High Lord about the attack. I don't know which is true."

Daemon shook his head. "If she made the transition to demon-dead and reached the Dark Realm, she never asked for an audience with me." He didn't mention that trusted demon-dead were quietly searching for anyone who arrived in Hell from Tigrelan.

"Grizande was hidden among the village children her age. The Black Widows in the village cast an illusion spell, a kind of veil, over the girl to hide her Birthright power, while her brother took her Jewel and stashed it in a hollow where he often left messages for his sisters as a game. It was a place Grizande would be able to find again in order to retrieve her Jewel once the danger had passed. Then he joined the other men who were fighting to protect the village.

"They all died. Men. Women. All those lives, all that power, snuffed out in a slaughter grown out of envy—or some equally terrible feeling." She closed her eyes for a moment, and when she opened them, they were full of grief. "The children were divided among the courts that had participated in the slaughter. They became slaves, abused and tortured. Raped and killed. It was an obscene corruption of the ways of the Blood. Grizande was among those children—that I know. But what was done to her . . ." The Queen released a shuddering breath.

"You did nothing?" Daemon asked too softly.

She growled. "I wasn't the Territory Queen then. I ruled a Province on the other side of Tigrelan. I didn't hear about the attack until it was too late to do anything but fight a war to free Tigrelan from the corruption and return my people to the Old Ways of the Blood. We fought that war, Prince. We fought it—and we won it. And I was chosen by the victorious Queens and Warlord Princes to be the Territory Queen. Since then, I've quietly searched for my cousin's children. Her son died defending his village. The older daughter had been apprenticing in a remote village that was held by the Hourglass. When I finally found her, I learned that she had rescued Grizande, recovered the girl's Jewel, and taken her younger sister to that remote village. But the Hourglass found another place even more remote—a place where the Hourglass trained Black Widows and the men trained young Warlord Princes to be deadly fighters. It took years of searching, of following every trail that might lead to my cousin's children, but by the time I found that village, the Black Widows had told Grizande she needed to go to the place where the Queen who was more than a Queen had dwelled, a place where she would be safe. A place where she would not be corrupted by those who ruled."

"And that's what brought you here now?"

"Yes. I had hoped she would be here. It will be better for Tigrelan—and the rest of Kaeleer—if a witch who will wear Ebon-gray finishes growing up here. With you. Away from the court intrigue that still vexes my people, despite the end of war."

He sensed no deceit, and he agreed with her reason for wanting Grizande to remain here. Jaenelle had also been vulnerable when she was young. What might have happened to all of them if Saetan hadn't protected her, taught her?

Agreeing with this Tigrelan Queen didn't mean he trusted her. Still, better to find out now. *Daemonar.*

Sir?

Escort Grizande to my study.

Jaalan too?

No. No reason to bring the kitten into this. To the Tigrelan Queen he said, "My nephew will escort Grizande here. It will take a few minutes. The Hall is a large place, and I don't know where she's studying right now."

It wouldn't have taken more than a heartbeat or two for him to locate the Sapphire within the Hall, but he would pretend otherwise. Why let a potential enemy know how easily he could locate someone anywhere on the SaDiablo estate?

He waited until she reached for a sandwich before saying too casually, "While we're waiting, tell me about the special tea."

She dropped the sandwich and jerked back in her seat. "What tea?"

"The secret tea that quiets the effect a Warlord Prince has on a woman." His smile had sharp edges and a bit of a chill. Not the Sadist—although he could feel that aspect of himself straining to slip the leash—but enough to make this Tigrelan Queen wary. Enough to make her realize she might never leave that room.

Instead of the fear he expected, he found fury. "Is that your price for helping her?" she snarled. "Do you even know what it does?"

"I wasn't here when Grizande told my nephew about the tea," Daemon replied coldly. "Her living here under my protection isn't something you or anyone else can buy."

She stared at him, then seemed to deflate. "That tea is a secret because it is dangerous, Prince. Something to be used only when necessary. Yes, it cocoons a woman, protects her from a Warlord Prince's sexual heat. But it also quiets desire, and if used too often, it can smother physical desire for weeks. Months. Years." A pause. "Forever."

That confirmed what Witch had told Surreal.

Daemon uncrossed his legs and leaned toward her. "It could smother desire just for Warlord Princes, or for any lover?"

"For anyone. A woman might still love a man." The Queen pressed a hand over her heart. "But if she consumes that tea too often, he could no longer excite her body. She would no longer want physical mating."

Daemon reached for the Ebon-gray to deliver a warning, then stopped before making the psychic link. Lucivar already knew the danger that came from drinking the tea and would keep Marian safe—no matter the price.

He studied the woman before him. He didn't know her, didn't know what her psychic scent and physical scent *should* be. But . . . "You drank the tea before coming here."

"Yes."

"To deal with me?"

"Yes." She tipped her head and studied him. "But perhaps a full dose wasn't needed. Your heat is quieter than I expected it to be, given that you wear the Black."

He didn't tell her Witch had taught him how to drain enough of the heat into a tangled web to minimize the effect it would have on everyone living at the Hall. It still had a wicked punch when he let it slip the leash, but he'd been able to ease it back to where it had been before the heat had entered its final phase. And he'd bet he could overwhelm the effects the tea had on the Tigrelan Queen if the Sadist wanted to make her desperate and compliant.

This Queen wasn't his concern. But the girl, and her reasons for revealing this secret, was very much his concern.

A knock on the study door. Daemonar entered, followed by Grizande. The boy took one look at the Tigrelan Queen, shoved the girl back a couple of steps, then called in his Eyrien war blade.

"We're here to talk, Prince, not fight," Daemon said quietly.

Grizande stepped around Daemonar, earning a snarl of temper from the boy. One of her hands flexed, revealing her claws. The other hand held a knife Daemon was sure she hadn't owned when she arrived at the Hall.

The Tigrelan Queen stood. "Do you remember me? Your mother and I were cousins."

Everyone in the study waited for the girl's answer. Finally, Grizande said, "Maybe remember." A sullen response.

Daemon raised an eyebrow.

Grizande looked at him, then looked away. "I remember." Another grudging response.

Using Craft, Daemon moved a straight-backed chair closer to the sofa. "Sit down." An implacable command beneath quiet courtesy.

Grizande sat in the chair. The Tigrelan Queen sat on the sofa. Daemonar stood next to the girl's chair, his eyes—and temper—focused on the Queen.

Daemon went down on one knee and put a hand on Grizande's forearm. "Why did you make the secret tea the other day? I wasn't here, and you weren't dealing directly with Lucivar. Did traveling in the Coach with him bother you that much? Daemonar shouldn't affect you. He's in the first phase of the sexual heat and wears the Green. Your

Sapphire power should have provided enough protection." He gave her arm a gentle squeeze and repeated, "Why?"

Daemonar vanished his war blade and went down on one knee on the other side of the chair. "You showed me because you wanted to help my mother. Isn't that it?"

Grizande nodded. "Marian mother is kind. Good woman. Good witch. Loves Prince Yaslana."

"You thought this might help her deal with Lucivar's sexual heat?" Daemon asked.

She nodded. Then she frowned. "Maybe help. Something Tigrelan Hourglass not say about tea. Maybe Hourglass here know more?"

So Grizande showed Daemonar this secret tea guessing, correctly, that the boy would talk to his father and uncle—and one of them would take that tea to the strongest Black Widow they knew. "Did the Black Widows who gave you this tea tell you how to use it?"

"Make tea." Grizande raised a hand and held it out, open. "Drink one cup." She moved her hand slightly and made a fist. "Next day, no drink." Another slight move as she opened her hand. "One cup. Fertile days, drink, drink, drink. Moon days, no drink."

Suppress desire during the fertile days, when desire would be at its peak. That might protect a girl from making an imprudent mating before she was safely on the other side of her Virgin Night.

"When did you start drinking the tea?"

She shrugged. "Didn't drink while traveling. Needed . . . sharp feelings?"

"But you did drink the tea while you lived with the Hourglass?"

She nodded. "Drank tea two times before Hourglass said must run and find this place or be caught."

Daemon twisted around enough to look at the Tigrelan Queen.

"I don't know," she said in answer to his unspoken question. "I've only used it a handful of times over the years, when I've had to deal with a Warlord Prince who wears

Jewels darker than mine and isn't a trusted member of my court. To use it as Grizande describes? I don't know how long it would take to smother desire forever. But if she only drank the tea a couple of times, she should be all right."

"Not safe? You sure?" Grizande sounded alarmed. She grabbed Daemonar's arm hard enough to make him wince, despite the boy's protecting himself with a tight Green shield. "Must warn Marian mother."

"Lucivar knows about the tea," Daemon said. "Marian is safe."

The girl sagged in the chair and released Daemonar's arm.

"Is the tea really needed here?" Daemonar asked. "I know the sexual heat affects some people at the Hall more than others, but it's not *that* bad anymore. Is it?"

Grizande shook her head. "Queen blanket protects."

The Tigrelan Queen shifted on the sofa until she sat on the edge of a cushion. "Queen blanket?" She looked around. Sniffed the air. "Male—and heat—here."

"This room," Grizande agreed. "Some rooms. Other rooms still feel like Queen who was more than a Queen. Blankets male heat."

"You feel Witch's presence here after all these years?" the Tigrelan Queen asked.

Grizande nodded warily.

"Under her hand," the Queen whispered. "Who else could hold that leash?"

If this girl had lived at the same time as Jaenelle, she would have served in the Dark Court's First Circle, Daemon thought. That thought was followed by another. *Do any of the other children residing here feel that presence, feel that "blanket"?*

He didn't count Daemonar since the boy had never lost the connection to his beloved auntie J. Were the girls living in the Queen's square of rooms more protected from his sexual heat because in those rooms Jaenelle's power still saturated wood and stone from the few years she had worn Ebony while she walked among the living?

Too many questions and only one answer.

"Listen to me, Grizande," Daemon said. "Listen carefully. There is a steep price attached to drinking that tea, but the choice is yours to make. However, if you feel uncomfortable being around me or Lucivar, I want to know *before* you drink another cup of that tea. You're a young woman. I don't want you to pay a heavy price if there is another way to ease your discomfort. Do you understand?"

"Yes."

He switched to a psychic communication thread. *Would you like time to talk to the Tigrelan Queen? Would you like to be alone with her?*

Talk, yes. Alone, no.

That was clear enough.

Daemon rose and looked at Daemonar. "Thank you, Prince. You're dismissed."

Hot temper and a challenge in the boy's eyes before Daemonar yielded. He gave the Tigrelan Queen a precise bow and walked out of the study.

"I'll give the two of you time to talk," Daemon said. "I'll be at my desk, working."

Chaperon. Escort. Sword and shield. Call it what you like; he knew the Tigrelan Queen understood this was all the privacy she would be allowed around Grizande. What confirmed her sincere concern about the girl was her approval of the way he balanced privacy with protection.

Queen and girl talked for an hour. Daemon listened to tone rather than words. Listened for anger or distress—and heard none.

At the end of that hour, he escorted the Tigrelan Queen to the landing web, where a full complement of escorts and guards waited around the Coach that had brought her to the Hall. They looked relieved to see her. He wasn't sure if it was because their Queen had come away from an audience with the High Lord unharmed or because they could get away from the scrutiny of Liath and Shaye, who stood at the edge of the gravel drive. Watching.

"What is that?" the Tigrelan Queen asked quietly.

"He's a horse," Daemon replied.

"Truly?"

"That's what I was told."

A little snort of laughter.

"Jaalan is here somewhere," he added.

"Jaalan?"

"A tiger Warlord Prince. A kitten. He came with Grizande."

"You accept this?"

"He's not the first tiger who has lived at the Hall." But the kitten wasn't with Liath, so . . . *Tarl? Please send someone to check on the chickens.* Despite the home farm, which supplied a good portion of the food that was needed, the Hall's staff still bought most of the meat and dairy from shops in the village, and also supplemented the kitchen garden with fruits and vegetables from beyond the estate. But Mrs. Beale had always kept a few chickens to have fresh eggs available—and to give the Scelties something to herd besides people and horses. Daemon just wasn't sure anyone had told Jaalan to keep his paws off the squawky birds, and he really didn't want to have a conversation with Mrs. Beale and her meat cleaver about chickens devoured without her permission.

"Safer for her here," the Queen said with a sigh.

"You're welcome to visit."

He watched her enter the Coach. Watched her men watch him, Liath, and Shaye as they entered the Coach and the last man finally closed the door. He suspected that the men were more relieved to get away from Liath than from him.

He understood the feeling.

The moment the Coach lifted off the landing web and caught one of the Winds, Daemon returned to his study and summoned Surreal.

"No problems with your visitor?" she asked as soon as she walked into the study.

"No, that much was fine. She also confirmed the things you were told about the secret tea. Safe to drink, but a hefty price to pay."

Surreal nodded. "Are we past this crisis?"

That was like asking someone how they were doing while they stood on a bridge that was falling apart behind them. "Why?"

Surreal gave him a big smile. "I thought we should discuss Jillian's Virgin Night."

"Fine."

"Hell's fire, Sadi. You're suddenly looking peaky." She laughed. "I heard something and was wondering if you'd ever made cock and balls soup."

He looked at her—just looked at her—and watched the color drain out of her face as she felt the change in the room, the change in him.

The Sadist said too softly, "Why do you ask?"

THIRTY-TWO

"Geoffrey searched old documents from Tigrelan and found references to three plants that had been used to make a special kind of tea," Witch said. "That brew was used to smother desire, but not always in women. And that smothering was meant to be permanent."

"Castration without a knife?" Lucivar said. He closed a hand over Marian's. It was the first time she'd been in this part of the Keep. The first time she'd seen Witch in this form. After the initial shock of seeing the Self that had lived beneath Jaenelle Angelline's physical body, Marian seemed to focus on the problem rather than the shape of the Queen she'd considered a sister.

"Yes," Witch replied. "Not a decision that was made lightly, and was always made by a Queen's tribunal."

"Until it wasn't."

"Which was when the Tigrelan Queens decided that everyone should 'forget' the region of that Territory where these plants grow. That was a few generations before the Queens in the Dark Court came to rule. Apparently, the knowledge wasn't lost, just . . . contained . . . within certain Hourglass covens. At some point, the purpose of the tea changed, became a 'protection' against a Warlord Prince's heat. Or perhaps it was still intended to smother desire, but now it was aimed at some females so that breeding would be the only reason to tolerate mating with a male." Witch paused. "It's also possible that the Black Widows who gave the tea to Grizande didn't know what it would do over time. Knowledge does get lost." She looked around. "Even here."

"Maybe if the tea was brewed weaker?" Marian suggested.

"No!" Lucivar snapped.

She turned on him with unexpected anger. "You stay away from your own home in order to protect me from the discomfort of this last phase of your heat. Do you think I don't know that you hate staying at that hunting eyrie because you *have* to stay away? If I could do this, even once in a while . . ."

"No, Marian. *No.* Didn't you hear what Jaenelle said about the danger of drinking that tea? Do you think I could sleep with you, have sex with you, if you no longer wanted me with the same passion that I want you with? Do you really think I could do that? *Would* do that? And what about other kinds of desire? If one kind of desire is smothered, would you lose the passion for your weavings?" Lucivar sprang out of the chair and began to pace. "No. I can live with having to stay away from you for however many years it will take for the heat to wane. But I won't stand by and let you accept a possible loss of something that is part of who you are. I'll fight you into the ground if I have to. We have those special webs Jaenelle and Karla made to absorb some of the sexual heat. That has to be enough. *Will* be enough."

"The heat does wane as a Warlord Prince ages," Witch said, looking at Marian. "What Lucivar and Daemon are going through, what your families deal with because of the heat . . ." Witch sighed. "There is no precedent. Andulvar and Saetan were the only other men in the entire history of the Blood to wear Ebon-gray and Black. Even the Gray is a rare Jewel. When Chaosti walked among the living, he spent time away from home when he reached the last phase of the heat in order to spare Gabrielle."

"You're talking about a few years for a man from a short-lived race," Marian argued. "We're talking about decades, maybe centuries, before this wanes for Lucivar."

"I know, Marian," Witch said. "I know. But the sexual heat will wane on its own."

Lucivar raked his fingers through his hair. "I wish Andulvar or Saetan had said something about this. Had given us some warning."

Witch hesitated. "Andulvar had lovers but he never tried to live with a woman. The heat worked to his advantage, as it does for most Warlord Princes. And Saetan? I don't know if he reached the final phase while he was still married to Hekatah. But as soon as he became a Guardian, his heat began to wane along with all the other appetites of the living. I don't think either of them experienced this in the same way you and Daemon have."

He figured that much. "So we endure."

"Yes," Witch agreed. "You endure. And you show your sons that power does not come without a price."

Nothing more to be said or done. Leaving Witch's part of the Keep, he and Marian stopped by the office where his administrative second-in-command had left a neat stack of messages for him. He vanished the messages, and he and Marian flew back to their eyrie.

Marian immediately went to the kitchen and made a pot of coffee. Lucivar stayed in the archway, watching her.

Finally, she turned to face him. "I love you, Lucivar."

He opened his arms and welcomed her into his embrace. "I love you too. I'd make this easier for you if I could."

She smiled. "I didn't want easy. I wanted you and the life we have together." She eased out of his arms and set out a plate of nutcakes along with the coffee. "It was strange seeing Jaenelle's Self and realizing what your father meant when he said not all the dreamers had been human. But then you hear her voice and listen to what she says, and it's Jaenelle. She's still Jaenelle, just in a different shape."

Lucivar stared out the window and wondered if Marian had forgotten that not everyone had felt the same way when they'd first seen Witch.

THIRTY-THREE

AMDARH

Jillian followed Surreal into the sitting room on the Sa-Diablo side of the town house. After she met the Warlord whom Surreal had selected for the Virgin Night, it became clear that this was going to be beyond terrible, because there was no way to gauge how Lucivar and Daemon were going to react when they found out . . . Well, she hadn't lied, exactly. She just hadn't been forthcoming about one or two things that pertained to sex.

"If you're having any doubts about the Warlord I chose being able to see you safely through your Virgin Night, or if he doesn't appeal to you for any reason, I can interview a couple more men who also provide this service for aristo families," Surreal said.

"He seems like a very nice man," Jillian replied, wondering if her voice sounded thin and shaky to anyone else. "And he seems to know what he's doing."

"But . . . ?"

Jillian took a deep breath and let the words out like a flood breaking through a dam. "But I have some concerns, and I'd like to talk to Brenda about them."

Surreal studied her. Jillian wasn't sure if she was being studied by Surreal the wife of Daemon Sadi, Surreal the second-in-command to the Warlord Prince of Dhemlan, or Surreal the assassin.

Sweet Darkness, please don't let it be the assassin.

"I do have some experience, sugar," Surreal said. "You *can* talk to me."

"I know I can, and about many other things I would, but I really need to talk to Brenda about this particular thing."

"She'll be coming to Amdarh for the party, but I could ask her to come to the city the morning of—"

"Before then," Jillian interrupted. "I need to talk to her as soon as I can."

"Very well."

Judging by the tone of Surreal's voice, "very well" meant "I'll sharpen my knives."

Since she couldn't change anything now, Jillian went up to the bedroom she'd been assigned and hoped Brenda, who had been bewilderingly dismissive about something so important to every Blood female, could help her.

"Do you understand the phrase 'fox in the henhouse?'" Brenda asked once the argument with the maid about who would unpack the trunk and put Brenda's clothes in the proper bureau drawers had reached its conclusion and compromise—the maid unpacked the trunk and handed the clothes to Brenda to hang up or tuck into drawers. "I have the impression that you've stirred things up good and proper."

The maid left the room, muttering about aristos who wouldn't let her do her job.

"I don't mind having someone else put cleaned clothes in the drawers once I have everything put away to my liking." Brenda raised her voice enough for the maid to hear. "But I don't want to have to open every drawer in order to find something because someone else thinks an item should be stored somewhere else." She closed the door and smiled at Jillian. "You needed to see me, and I'm here now, with everything properly tucked away. I gather there was something about the Virgin Night that concerns you? Something you didn't want to discuss with Lady SaDiablo?"

"I'm in trouble." When Brenda's eyes went to her belly, Jillian added, "Not *that* kind of trouble."

"It wouldn't be *impossible* if you were skin to skin with a man and the juice was flowing, so to speak. Not likely, but not impossible. Or so I'm told."

Jillian stared. She had already lived *centuries* compared to Brenda's twenty-some years, but she'd never met *anyone* who was this blunt. Well, Lucivar was, but even he wouldn't talk to a daughter about *this* in *that* way.

"So what kind of trouble are you in?" Brenda asked.

"I need help figuring out how to tell Daemon and Lucivar that I've already had my Virgin Night and didn't tell them."

Now it was Brenda's turn to stare. "Hell's fire, girl, you really *are* in trouble." She went to the window and looked out. "I haven't been around either of them that long, but I've taken their measure. This will be hard for them to swallow, mostly because they didn't have a chance to pound the male into pulp if anything had gone the least little bit wrong. I'm assuming nothing went wrong?"

"Everything went just fine, but Lucivar's and Daemon's probable reaction was exactly why I did it that way. I didn't want a man torn into pieces and pulped because I broke a nail or got a paper cut while I was in the room with him! And do you really think 'the juice is going to flow' if either of them is in the same city, let alone the same building, as the man who is expected to perform?"

"Good points, and I don't disagree with you. On the other hand, they're going to be here in Amdarh and so are you, and you didn't voice any objections."

"Because the man Surreal selected wasn't going to have to do anything! But they've all decided that I need to go through a Virgin Night because . . ." Jillian faltered.

Brenda glanced at Jillian before returning her gaze to whatever was outside the window. "Because you've met someone you want as a lover, and you don't want him . . ."

"Stomped on and pulped and tossed in a vat to be cooked with the grapes for his wine. But if Stefan and I . . . before Lucivar knows about . . ."

Brenda nodded. "How long has it been since you had this secret Virgin Night?"

Jillian cringed. "A few months." A beat of silence. "Or more. And it wasn't so much a secret as it was private."

Brenda turned away from the window. "Do you have any proof you can show them that doesn't require a Healer?"

"A letter signed by the current Queen of Little Weeble and the former Queen, who serves as a consultant." Jillian swallowed hard. Did Brenda know anything about Little Weeble and what it meant to have a letter from the current and former Queens?

"I can work with that." Brenda walked out of the bedroom, her voice as brisk as her stride. "Come along now. We'll request the men's presence. The sooner this is done, the better. You show them that letter at the end of this. That might soothe them a bit."

Hurrying after Brenda, Jillian said, "End of what?"

Daemon stood on the sidewalk outside the SaDiablo town house. First Surreal sent a message to the Hall saying Brenda's presence was required at the town house *now.* Brenda was packed and gone within the hour, even though it was a couple of days ahead of when everyone was gathering for Jillian's Virgin Night.

By the clock on his desk, less than an hour after Brenda arrived in Amdarh, Surreal sent a message to *him* on a Gray psychic thread saying *he* was required in Amdarh as soon as he could get there.

Maybe one request had nothing to do with the other. Maybe Brenda, being closer to Jillian's equivalent age, was holding a friend's hand—although Jillian never struck him as a nervous sort of girl. Still, her life as a strong witch *was* at risk, and something *could* go wrong. And Surreal thought he should be here because . . .

Daemon turned in a slow circle, letting the Black flow through the square where the town house was located.

Nothing unusual. Nothing anyone would summon *him* to deal with. The only turmoil he could sense was in Surreal's side of their town house, but the one thing that would have confirmed that this was something about Jillian . . .

Daemon felt the Ebon-gray's presence in the city moments before Lucivar dropped from the Winds and almost landed on top of him.

"You were summoned?" Lucivar asked.

"I was. You too?"

"Yeah. Any idea why?"

Daemon stared at the town house. "Surreal indicated there was something Jillian needed to discuss with us. My second-in-command sounded . . . odd."

"Jillian's still young. Maybe she's not ready for this." Lucivar sounded hopeful.

He sighed. "She's ready, Prick. She's feeling passionate about a vintner who works on your Dhemlan estate."

"Shit." Lucivar narrowed his eyes. "Has he . . . ?"

"He knows enough about you—about us—not to be that foolish."

"Lust makes foolish things sound reasonable."

He'd seen the truth of that too many times to disagree. "Well, let's go in and find out. One way or the other, we'll take care of it."

"We will." Lucivar started up the steps. "Good thing I honed my skinning knife this morning."

Daemon didn't bother to reply. If it came to that, Lucivar could work out some anger by skinning the fool. The Sadist, on the other hand, would seduce their enemy to the point that the fool's cock would explode from the ecstasy.

Daemon considered himself flexible when it came to women's attire, and he couldn't fault anyone who chose to wear what amounted to a signature outfit. After all, he'd worn black jackets with black trousers and a white silk shirt for centuries and saw no reason to change his wardrobe. He just wasn't sure what Brenda's wardrobe said about her. Not the clothes she wore when she rode Shaye or worked around the stables or played some rough-and-tumble game

with the Scelties. And not the dresses she wore for the evening meals. But her working outfit seemed to consist of
brown or black or dark gray trousers with a matching—or
contrasting—vest and a soft white shirt. Not *that* dissimi-
lar to what Surreal as his second-in-command considered
her working outfits, except Brenda's vests were always
decorated with embroidery, and she always had a gold
pocket watch and chain. She seemed to consult the watch
often, even when she was between lessons and had no particular place to go—and she often found something amusing about whatever the watch revealed.

He had no idea what to think about that—or why, when
Brenda walked into the sitting room and consulted her
watch, he felt uncharacteristically nervous.

Brenda smiled at him. He smiled at her. She smiled at
Lucivar, who bared his teeth.

Jillian and Surreal walked into the sitting room. Jillian
took the chair positioned next to the sofa, while Surreal
and Brenda sat on opposite ends of the sofa, Brenda being
closer to Jillian.

Daemon eyed Surreal, who shrugged.

No idea, sugar, she said on a psychic thread.

He turned to Jillian, aware of Lucivar standing behind
him and to the side. Fighting position. "You wanted to talk
to us?" Nothing challenging in the question, and he kept
his voice pitched to sound encouraging.

Jillian sent a pleading look to Brenda.

Brenda's smile brightened. "Here's the way of it, then.
Jillian, being a bright young woman and knowing how
protective the men in her family can be when it comes
to . . . everything . . . realized her Virgin Night would
cause some excitement within the male breasts."

"Is that where male excitement is lodged?" Daemon
asked dryly.

Brenda ignored him, but her smile got a wee bit
brighter—and sharper. "When she felt it was time for her
to take that step toward protecting her power, Jillian consulted with the Queens in Little Weeble, who assisted in

making the arrangements for Jillian to have a private Virgin Night with as little fuss as possible."

"What?" Lucivar roared.

"It was all done right and proper," Brenda said as if she were soothing Lucivar after he'd skinned his knee. Then she added with some heat, "And what's wrong with wanting an important ceremony to be private the first time? When Prince Sadi married Jaenelle Angelline, their first wedding was so private, no one knew about it except the unicorns in Sceval who stood as witness, the unicorn priestess who officiated, and, if the stories are accurate, the Sceltie who helped make the arrangements and convinced my ancestors to provide the wedding meal with no questions asked. Later on, Prince Sadi and Lady Angelline had an official wedding so that everyone who needed to know about their marriage knew about it. So what's wrong with Jillian doing the same, especially when the whole thing, if done properly, shouldn't be much fuss or bother?"

Daemon couldn't tell if Surreal was appalled, delighted, or just stunned by Brenda's reasoning. And he couldn't reconcile Brenda's calling the Virgin Night an important ceremony and then saying that it shouldn't be much fuss or bother. But if this conversation continued, he was going to have to peel Lucivar off the ceiling.

"A wedding and a Virgin Night aren't the same thing," Lucivar snarled.

"And thank the Darkness for that," Brenda replied. "But here's what I'm wondering."

Go away. Daemon saw the mischievous look in Brenda's eyes and felt the solid ground of this discussion crumbling beneath him. *Stop wondering about whatever you're wondering about and go away.*

"Why are we the only ones who have a Virgin Night?" Brenda asked. "Why don't you?"

Daemon stared at her. "What?"

"Why don't males have a Virgin Night? After all, you're a virgin and then not a virgin, same as us."

"We don't have a hymen," Daemon said too sweetly.

Surreal pressed her head to her knees. Her shoulders shook.

Ignoring his comment—and the warning tone of his voice—Brenda raised her hands. The fingers of one hand made a circle. Two fingers of the other hand were straight—and heading for the circle as she said, "After all, your part goes into—" She paused as if thinking. "Well, not *your* part, because everyone knows you're very exclusive about where it goes."

Surreal made a choking sound.

"But the boy part goes into the girl part, and if all goes well, the power she was born with and the power that will be hers when she makes the Offering to the Darkness are safe. But why doesn't the boy have to worry about where he puts himself for that twenty minutes?" Brenda paused. "Maybe ten minutes." Another pause. "Might be less. Especially the first time."

Surreal rolled off the sofa and began crawling toward the door.

"Surreal?" Daemon's voice might have held a hint of hysteria. Not that anyone would dare point that out.

"I have to pee." Her voice came out high and breathy.

Swearing, Lucivar used Craft to open the sitting room door before grabbing the back of Surreal's trousers and the back of her shirt and striding into the entryway.

"Get her to the nearest toilet," Lucivar told Helton as he set her down. "And get a bucket in case she can't make it that far."

As he returned to the sitting room and swung the door shut, they all heard Surreal say, "Prick."

"So, why is that?" Brenda said, as if there hadn't been any interruption.

Sweet Darkness, did she never let go once she latched onto something? She was as bad as a Sceltie! Maybe worse.

It provoked him into giving her a reckless answer. "I don't know. According to the ancient stories, when the last Queen of the Dragons shed her scales and bestowed the power that made the Blood who and what they are, only females were gifted with that power. It took several generations of strong, intelligent males mating with those females before the first male had any power that could be recognized as the Blood. Maybe that disparity of power in our creation is the reason for the disparity of who is at risk now. If you'd really like to know, you could always go to Ebon Askavi and ask the Seneschal. After all, Draca *was* the Queen of the Dragons who created the Blood."

Brenda blinked. The smile that followed was filled with delight—and completely terrifying. "Really? We could go there and ask her?"

"No."

"Then why would you be offering it and getting our hopes up? And why is it only the *human* females who are troubled by needing a ceremony for what amounts to a poke and a pop?"

"*Stop.*" Daemon raised a hand. "Just . . . stop."

He had to put an end to this before she backed him into a corner and wore him down to the point that he *would* take her to the Keep so that someone else would have to answer the question. Questions.

Hell's fire, Mother Night, and may the Darkness be merciful, it was like being around Jaenelle and the coven again. And having Brenda go to the Keep and meet Jaenelle and Karla? No, no, no. He had enough trouble dealing with those two.

"If Lucivar and I agree that there was merit in Jillian having her Virgin Night in private, will you agree to drop the subject?"

"Jillian will still need to show up at the establishment and stay in the room for twenty minutes—"

"An hour," Lucivar snarled. "If you want anyone to believe she had an actual Virgin Night, she stays in the room with that cock and balls for an hour. Every aristo in the city knows if he took less time than that *with my daughter*, I'd skin him alive."

"An hour, then," Brenda agreed. "Maybe Lady Surreal could arrange to have drinks and nibbles slipped into the room so they'll have something to do that won't involve an activity that will require Lucivar skinning someone afterward?"

"I'll talk to Surreal," Daemon said.

"And we'll still have the party? Really, that's the best part of it all."

The Hall was a big place. Among all the wings and rooms there had to be a secret hidey-hole where he could escape from females with questions and opinions.

"We'll have the party." Daemon used Craft to open the sitting room door. "Now go away."

Jillian had been sitting through all this in open-mouthed shock. Now Brenda tapped her hand and said, "You have something for Prince Sadi?"

Jillian stood. She called in a letter and held it out for Daemon.

Not seeing a good choice, he took the letter.

Brenda sprang to her feet and looked at Jillian. "Come along, then. There are still things to be done." She strode out of the sitting room with Jillian trailing behind.

Daemon put a Black lock on the door and closed his eyes. "Not. One. Word."

Lucivar paced, swearing under his breath. He prowled, his wings opening and closing as a sign of agitation. "Someone must have asked the question at some point."

"I mean it, Prick. Not. One. Word."

"And now that it *has* been asked, it will spread through the Hall and beyond. . . ."

"Shut up, Lucivar. One more word and I will pull out your tongue and tie it around your cock!"

Lucivar stared at him before smiling that smile that always meant trouble. But he didn't say anything. He just nodded.

Remembering the letter in his hand, Daemon looked at the seal and groaned—a weeble pressed into bright blue wax. He swallowed a whimper as he opened the letter.

"Lady Perzha's written assurance that Jillian's Virgin Night was performed discreetly and safely and properly."

He held out the letter. "It's signed by Perzha and the current Queen of Little Weeble." Which amounted to a Sceltie paw print on the paper.

Lucivar sighed. "It could have been worse."

Daemon just looked at him and said, "How?"

Jillian stood outside the sitting room door, unable to move. Then she noticed the way Brenda calmly pulled out the pocket watch and studied the hands.

"That went well," Brenda said cheerfully. "And I have to give them credit. They held out twice as long as my father and brothers when I asked *them* that question before my own Virgin Night."

"You asked *your father*?"

"Well, sure, I did." She tucked the watch into the pocket in her vest. "None of you have wondered about this before now? Really?"

"Really."

"Then you'll have something to ponder while you're having your official Virgin Night without the sex."

THIRTY-FOUR

As her father drove the Coach to the Isle of Scelt, Saetien tried not to fidget, tried even harder—and with less success—not to feel a sharp regret that because Helene was traveling with them she hadn't been invited to sit in the driver's compartment and she had to make do with sitting in the passenger area. She didn't know why the Hall's housekeeper was going with them to Scelt, and Helene's precise and chilly nod of greeting made it clear questions, or any conversation, wouldn't be welcome.

Fine. Just fine. She didn't need to converse with the *staff*—a thought that made her unhappy because there was a time when she could have chatted about all kinds of things with Helene. Just another thing that had changed because of that awful house party and the unwitting part she'd played in almost getting Zoey and Titian killed.

Saetien wanted to ask her father about this family she'd be living with. She wanted to know who had the answers about Wilhelmina Benedict that she needed in order to untangle her life. But even if she had been sitting in the driver's compartment with him, her father wouldn't have engaged in weighty discussion when he was driving a Coach that was running on the Black Winds. Shelby, who was excited about returning to Scelt, couldn't tell her much beyond that Scelt had good smells and lots of other Scelties. Well, he'd been a just-weaned puppy when he'd come to Dhemlan, so human activities that didn't involve Scelties had held no interest for him. Still didn't hold much interest unless he could herd or help a human.

Saetien closed her eyes. She wanted to be done with this part of her life. Wanted to close the door on it and turn the key in the lock—and then throw away the key so there was no turning back.

Trouble was, she didn't know what, if anything, might be ahead.

Daemon guided the Coach along the Black Winds, grateful for the speed that would shorten the journey.

A part of him wished Helene had chosen another time to go to Scelt, although he understood the practicality of coming with him to personally interview the youngsters who wanted to work in service and were interested in receiving some seasoning and polish at the Hall. He would have liked to spend these last few hours with Saetien before she walked away, maybe forever. Before he let her walk away, maybe forever.

A part of him wished Helene had chosen another time because those interviews would delay his return to SaDiablo Hall, and he didn't want to be within reach when Saetien had her first collision with Butler. And there was going to be a collision because Saetien and the Green-Jeweled Prince stood on opposite sides of a line called Jaenelle Angelline.

He'd keep to the house in Maghre and to the Sceltie school. Eileen would understand if he turned down an invitation to dinner—assuming she issued one. More likely, she wanted him gone as soon as possible so that Saetien couldn't run to him if she didn't like the rules—and also so the girl couldn't give up and return to the sanctuary before she'd even tried to find the answers she claimed she needed to find.

Leaving Saetien to stand on her own without his protection grated against every instinct he had as a Warlord Prince and a father. But what he'd told Kieran was true. He knew too much, had seen too many witches destroyed. Had failed to protect strong young witches in his own Territory. Now, for her sake, he was walking away from his daughter, leaving her well-being in someone else's hands.

In Kieran's hands—and in Butler's.

"Lady Eileen, this is Lady Saetien SaDiablo. Saetien, Lady Eileen is the head of this household, and her rules are *the* rules."

"I thought Lord Kieran was in charge of things," Saetien said. The look in this woman's blue eyes made her uneasy, and being uneasy made her say things in ways adults found annoying.

Eileen had a trim figure, but the gray streaks in her brown hair and the strong lines fanning out from her eyes said "motherly" and "old." Saetien didn't want mothering, and she didn't need a *mother*.

"Kieran is the Warlord of Maghre and runs the village. This side of the house is the family home, and it's under my hand," Eileen replied. "As you are now. If you're thinking you can disregard my rules the moment your father walks out the door, think again, young lass. My house, my rules, my way. If you can't agree to that, there's no point in you unpacking your bags."

Saetien turned to her father. "I can stay somewhere else."

"No," Daemon said. "If you want to stay in Scelt, you will be staying here. Or I can take you back to the sanctuary in Dhemlan. Your choice."

How was she supposed to find the answers she needed if she was hemmed in by rules?

Then three adult Scelties joined them, looked at her— and growled.

Who were they to growl at *her*?

Shelby's distressed whining pierced her annoyance as

he sat beside her and leaned against her leg. He was failing his special friend by letting her be a bad human.

She *wasn't* being bad, and Shelby wasn't *letting* her do anything. He was still a puppy. They had no right to judge him!

But the Scelties who lived in this house protected the humans in the household, and Shelby would be miserable if he was ostracized because of her behavior. She suddenly wondered if his distress was partly due to some of those Scelties being related to him. If his *family* turned him away because of her . . .

She took a deep breath and made an effort to keep her voice civil. "I'll stay."

"Then I'll show you to your room," Eileen said. She looked at Daemon. "I'm sure you have business to attend to."

Saetien blinked. Did this woman just *dismiss* her father? Her *father*?

Daemon hesitated, then dipped his head in a slight bow. He turned to Saetien. "I hope you find the answers you seek."

"First I have to find the person who might have the answers," she replied.

He let out a pained huff of laughter. "Oh, he isn't difficult to find, but getting answers will be a different kind of challenge."

Daemon walked out of the room and out of the house before Saetien gathered her wits. Her father *knew* who she needed to see and didn't tell her?

She turned to Eileen. "Do you know who has the answers?"

Eileen gave her a long look. "Since you're asking about Wilhelmina Benedict, there's only one person who has more than surface knowledge. Kieran can take you to the cottage this evening before supper. Come along and I'll show you to your room."

"Why can't I see this person now?" Since Eileen walked briskly through the house, with the Scelties now moving into herding position, Saetien hurried to follow.

Eileen opened a door and walked into a large, airy bedroom. Obviously a guest room, since its decor didn't lean toward feminine or masculine. "There's a bathroom just behind that door. It's small but adequate. We do have a couple of maids and a cook. Kieran has a butler because his side of the house is an official residence. However, I expect you to keep your room tidy and not give the maids extra work. Any clothes that aren't placed in the hamper won't get washed unless you do them yourself. Any questions?"

"Why can't I see this person now?"

"His day begins when the sun goes down. Given who your father is, I'd think you would understand what it means when a person is only available between sunset and sunrise."

For a moment Saetien couldn't breathe. "He's . . . ?"

"Demon-dead. Yes." Eileen gave her an odd smile. "Who else would know about things and people long past?"

Did she want to talk to someone who was demon-dead? "You said other people have surface knowledge."

Eileen sighed. "I can tell you what anyone else can tell you. Wilhelmina Benedict lived in Maghre for a while. Then she moved to Tuathal, the capital of Scelt. She married, had children, and lived on this island for the rest of her life. If you need more than that, you'll have to talk to Prince Butler. He knows more about Wilhelmina Benedict than anyone else can know."

"Did he love her?"

"There was no love or liking between them. But Butler always made a point of keeping an eye on an enemy."

"Was she dangerous?"

Eileen shrugged. "You'd have to ask him. Now, I'll let you and Shelby get settled in." She walked out of the room and closed the door.

Saetien went over to the window and looked out.

Undercurrents. Secrets. And for some reason . . . shame? Eileen knew more about Wilhelmina Benedict than she'd said, but she'd revealed all she intended to reveal.

Was it telling that Eileen *didn't* mention that Wilhelmina Benedict was Jaenelle Angelline's sister?

How did one dress when meeting the demon-dead? Did it matter? The person was *dead*. Sort of dead. Had her father or Uncle Lucivar told her about the demon-dead? Or, when they told stories about *her*, had they talked about people who had died the physical death but not the final death?

"Maghre is a small village but a good one, mostly," Kieran said as they walked along the lane leading to the cottage. "We had some trouble with a man a while back who tried to force himself on a girl. He no longer lives in the village and is no longer a threat, but you'll oblige me and my mother by letting someone know where you're going. Shelby isn't old enough to be much help if you run into trouble."

"I know how to protect myself," Saetien muttered.

"Good. You'll still let someone know. If my sister Brenda could give her mother that courtesy, then so can you."

"Do you?" Since males were supposed to serve—well, serve Queens, anyway—why were the females the ones who couldn't have any privacy?

"I did when I was your age," Kieran replied. "So did my brother."

The restrictions chafed, despite being no different from the rules she'd had to follow at the Hall, at Uncle Lucivar's eyrie, and even at the sanctuary. "I'm older than I look."

"You have years over everyone else here—that much is true. But you're nowhere near as mature as you seem to think."

That stung. And who was he to judge her?

"A word of advice," Kieran said as a man opened the door of the cottage, stepped out, and walked toward the gate in the white picket fence that surrounded the cottage gardens. "Butler doesn't tolerate bitches. He never did. You should brush off your manners before you reach that gate, or he'll shut you out before you begin."

The light was fading, so it wasn't easy to see the man who waited for them. The man who studied them. Studied *her*. Fair skin but not pasty pale. Gray hair cut short in a style that probably was a fashion decades ago—or never. Hard to tell until she reached the gate, but his eyes looked gray with flecks of green. And he wore a Green Jewel.

"Prince Butler, may I present Lady Saetien SaDiablo? Lady, this is Prince Butler. He manages the literary works of Lady Fiona. She wrote the Tracker and Shadow stories."

Saetien looked past the man and studied the cottage with interest. The stories were *ancient*, but she loved the tales about Tracker and Shadow. If she asked—politely—would Butler show her the room where Lady Fiona wrote the stories?

"Lady Saetien," Butler said.

She looked into his eyes, heard his voice, and thought, *There you are.*

What in the name of Hell did *that* mean?

Something about this man called to something inside her—and it scared her.

"I want to know about Wilhelmina Benedict." A moment ago, she'd been thinking about seeing inside Lady Fiona's cottage. Now the words—the demand—just fell out of her mouth. Because something about Butler scared her, and it had nothing to do with his being demon-dead.

Kieran made a sound like a swallowed protest. Butler just stared at her.

"You are the supplicant," Butler finally said. "You're the one seeking answers. You make no demands of me."

"You have to answer my questions." He would spend time with her if he answered her questions.

"No, I do not."

"Saetien." Kieran made her name into a warning.

Ignoring Kieran, she focused on Butler and aimed her best weapon—and knew a moment too late that her best weapon would turn on her. "Do you know who my father is?"

The air around them turned bitter cold. Butler said, "I am demon-dead, child. I know who your father is and what he is far better than you do. I also know that when he asked me for this favor on your behalf, he agreed that I would do this my way, on my terms. If you think to use him as a club against me, then he's well rid of you as a daughter."

She stepped back, stunned by the verbal attack despite recognizing that she had provoked it. Her lower lip trembled and her eyes filled with tears.

"What?" Butler snarled. "You want to be the only one who can fling harsh words at people? Your father may forgive such disrespect because he loves you. But I don't know you, I don't love you, and I will not tolerate disrespect for anyone who matters to me. And that includes Daemon Sadi and Jaenelle Angelline."

Her thoughts spun and collided.

"You want to know about Wilhelmina Benedict? First tell me what you know about Jaenelle Angelline."

"I don't want to know about *her*," Saetien shouted. "I just want to know about Wilhelmina Benedict."

"Fine. Wilhelmina Benedict was born in Chaillot, an island in the Realm of Terreille. She came to Kaeleer during the last service fair. She lived at SaDiablo Hall for a little while before coming to Scelt. She lived here the rest of her life. Now you know all that anyone needs to know about Wilhelmina Benedict. In order to know more, you have to know about Jaenelle Angelline." Butler walked back to the door of his cottage. "Write down what you know about both of them. Bring it with you tomorrow. Then I'll decide if I'm going to answer your first question."

He walked into the cottage and closed the door.

"That went well," Kieran said dryly. "If those are your best manners, may the Darkness have mercy on you if you try to deal with him again."

"Isn't there someone else I can talk to?" *Someone who doesn't pull at me to be . . . something?*

Kieran didn't say anything until they were well down the lane. "If there had been anyone else, your father never would have asked Butler for this favor."

✦ ✦ ✦

Butler leaned against the cottage's door and thought, *There you are.*

Something about this girl called to something inside him, produced a feeling full of sharp edges as well as joy. He'd never felt anything like this on an assignment. Never.

Had Saetan felt this way the first time he'd met Jaenelle Angelline? Had he realized in some way that his life would never be the same?

There you are.

What in the name of Hell did *that* mean?

"Half of the individuals I spoke to aren't interested in learning to serve in an aristo house, let alone a dark house," Helene said. "They see it as an adventure away from home, with free room and board and a requirement to do a token amount of work."

Daemon swirled his brandy and said nothing, since he heard outrage in Helene's voice when she said that last bit. It didn't matter if a person was dusting the furniture or preparing a meal for visiting Queens; shoddy work was not tolerated, let alone rewarded.

"There are seven I think would benefit from working at the Hall," Helene continued. "Different positions, including a young witch who likes working with horses and is acquainted with Lord Shaye."

"Can we accommodate seven more people?" he asked. When there had been three residents at the Hall, with Lucivar and his family occasional visitors, the staff had tripped over one another as they tried to find things to do in order to earn their pay—and were put in a rotation so that they would have *some* opportunity to serve a member of the family. With the youngsters and instructors now in residence, there was more for the staff to do. Still, the Hall needed only so many people taking care of it and the people who lived there.

"We can, yes. A couple of these people are amenable to living in a city, so Beale and I thought they might get their seasoning at the town house in Amdarh, if Lady Surreal is agreeable to having them there. But they can start at the Hall, and we'll go from there."

"How long . . . ?"

"They'll be here after breakfast, packed and ready to go."

Daemon blinked. Then he wondered why he should be at all surprised. "They've all reached their majority?"

Helene hesitated. "Not all of them."

Daemon swore silently. More vulnerable youngsters, male and female.

"At least they're all human."

They both understood that, as consolation, the words were significant.

Feeling the approach of Red power, Daemon set the brandy aside and rose. "If you're comfortable with the arrangements, we'll leave after breakfast tomorrow."

Helene also rose. "Unless you need more time?"

"No." The word came out quick and sharp. He took a breath and tried to soften it. "No, there's no need to stay."

"Prince." Helene left the room as Kieran walked in.

"Brandy?" Daemon asked.

"Yes, thanks." The Warlord of Maghre took a seat.

After pouring a brandy for Kieran, Daemon resumed his seat and picked up his own snifter. "How did it go?"

"Your girl seems to think she's entitled to this information and attempted to play grand lady of the manor," Kieran replied. "A lot of girls try on that attitude like they're trying on an outfit to see how it fits. Some are born to wear it, whether they're aristo or not. And most realize they aren't suited to the work that goes with the title."

"That was Saetien's opening gambit with Butler?"

"It was."

"Hell's fire."

"Aye, it went as well as you think." Kieran stared at the brandy. "But your girl also tried to use you as a club to force him to yield."

Daemon felt his temper chill. "Did she?"

"You may be the Queen's weapon, but you are not a club for Saetien SaDiablo. Butler will handle it his own way, but you should know, here and now, that if she tries that with anyone else, she will deal with me—and I will not be kind."

"I understand." It was one thing to use him and what he was as a shield if she felt threatened; after all, it was a man's duty and privilege to protect his child. But it was quite another thing to use a man to force someone into complying with a demand when the initial answer was no.

"I wanted that to be clear between us before you left." Kieran drank the brandy and set the snifter aside.

"Kieran?" Daemon asked softly. "Do you think there's any point to this . . . quest?"

"I guess we'll all find out." Kieran sighed. "Go home, Daemon. Your being here won't help your girl."

He saw Kieran to the door and watched the Warlord of Maghre walk away.

THIRTY-FIVE

Jaenelle Angelline

- *Queen of Ebon Askavi, which made her the most important Queen in Kaeleer.*

"And didn't she know it," Saetien muttered as she made out the list Butler required before he'd talk to her about Wilhelmina Benedict.

- *Wore Black Jewels, which is how she became the Queen of Ebon Askavi, then wore a Jewel called Twilight's Dawn.*
- *Was the ruling Queen when Kaeleer fought a war with Terreille. Kaeleer won.*

Saetien paused. Had her father and Uncle Lucivar fought in that war? Was that one of those subjects that came under the "when you're old enough" rule? If they *had* fought in the war, they would have been the most important Warlord Princes in the fight, because they were the strongest.

Did Daemonar know about how their fathers fought in that war? Not that she could ask him until he stopped being angry with her about that stupid house party.

Sighing, she went back to making the list.

- *Originally lived in Chaillot, a Territory in the Realm of Terreille.*
- *Had yellow hair and blue eyes.*

She should say "blond" but saying the Queen had yellow hair sounded . . . dismissive, diminishing.

Was that being childish? Maybe. But so was this stupid requirement to make a list of things she knew about someone who wasn't the person she wanted information about.

- *Spent a lot of time in a place called Briarwood when she was a child.*

Saetien shuddered, remembering her journey through the Briarwood that Witch had created in order to determine the price each girl in the coven of malice had to pay for the lives she had ruined.

Remembering the blond-haired, blue-eyed girl who had been tied to a bed and the blood that had been spilled in that small room. So much blood.

- *Was Daemon Sadi's first wife. She was also his Queen.*

Was still his Queen. Witch snapped her fingers, and Daemon Sadi obeyed.

- *She was called Witch, the living myth, dreams made flesh.*

Saetien reviewed her list. What else did she need to know about someone she would rather forget existed? Nothing on her list that Prince Butler wouldn't know, but maybe she *did* know something about Witch that he didn't.

- *Not all the dreamers were human, so her Self is a weird mix of human and animal. She looks unnatural.*

Looked monstrous.

"And she's cruel," Saetien whispered. Best not to put that in, even if it was true.

Setting that sheet of paper aside, she focused on the information she had about the person she *wanted* to know about.
Wilhelmina Benedict

- *Originally lived in Chaillot, an island in the Realm of Terreille.*
- *Came to Kaeleer during the last service fair.*
- *Lived at SaDiablo Hall for a while, then moved to the Isle of Scelt.*
- *Was Jaenelle Angelline's sister.*

So little. And nothing helpful.

Saetien capped her pen and put the papers to one side of the small rectangular table that doubled as a dining table and desk. She called in the journal Jillian had given her the morning she left the sanctuary. Not a cheap thing for scribbling little-girl thoughts—although, to be fair, she didn't think she'd ever been given a cheap thing that would send a message that little-girl thoughts weren't worth much.

She opened the journal's leather cover. It would be a good place to record any notes and any facts she managed to squeeze out of people. She hadn't expected people to refuse to tell her what they knew about Wilhelmina Benedict, but nobody seemed to know much of anything. Eileen knew *something*, but Wilhelmina wasn't a subject the woman would discuss. Why was that? And why was there always a hint of shame when Saetien brought up the name? Maybe not shame. Sadness?

No answers there, and she couldn't talk to Butler until sunset. What was she supposed to do until then?

Walkies, Saeti? Walkies?

She looked at Shelby as the urgent tone registered. Scooping up the puppy, she hurried through the house and got him outside before his control of his bladder failed both of them.

Once the puppy did his business, Saetien cast a look at the house. She didn't know where Eileen was, even if it was easy to guess that the woman probably would be in the morning room reviewing household accounts and writing letters and doing whatever else she did. But since she didn't *know*, not specifically, she decided she didn't have to tell anyone that she had left, especially since she and Shelby were just walking over to the stables.

Maybe she could go riding, maybe even ride to the village, or over to the house that her father leased here, or even over to the Sceltie school. If she was riding, it wouldn't take that long to get to any of those places.

The stables were barely in sight of the house and much larger than the stables at the Hall. Which made sense, since her father didn't breed or train regular horses—and kindred horses made their own decisions when it came to breeding. Just like humans.

Did they make mating mistakes like humans did?

She heard a male voice and thought it was that of Lord Ryder, who was Lord Kieran's brother, but he hadn't said much at dinner last night, so she wasn't sure. The tone was encouraging. Training a horse, a rider, or both?

Lord Kildare, Kieran's father, walked out of the stables. His hard expression and the stern look in his eyes stopped her. Then he looked past her and said mildly, "Well, at least one of you remembers the rules."

Saetien looked over her shoulder at the two Scelties trotting toward them.

Did you tell the Scelties we were going to the stables? she asked Shelby.

Yes! the puppy replied. *It's a rule.* Wagging his tail, he went to greet the Sceltie witch and Warlord.

"I wasn't leaving your place," Saetien protested.

"You don't hold much to courtesy or simple kindness, do you, girl?" Kildare asked. His words stung, but before she could say anything in her defense, he added, "You get three chances to mess about. You're down to two now. After the third, you're on your way home."

"You can't decide that."

"That was my lady wife's condition for having you here,

and Kieran and Prince Sadi agreed. Best you remember it." He paused. "Did you come down to the stables for a reason, or were you looking to find out where the lines are drawn?"

They were treating her like a *child*. Well, she'd show them she wasn't a child. "I would like to go riding, if you have a horse available."

Considering the size of the stables, how could he *not* have a horse available? Which made the remark close to being bitchy.

"You know how to ride?" Kildare asked.

"Yes, I do." Politely spoken, although she wasn't sure if her expression sent a very different message.

Kildare nodded. "All right. I'll see who's willing. You can ride in the paddock over there." He pointed.

"I was thinking—"

"You ride in the paddock, where I can keep an eye on you, or not at all."

Lord Kildare's way of drawing a line reminded her more of Uncle Lucivar than of her father. Oh, her father drew lines, too, but he never sounded so . . . physical . . . about it.

"Fine," she said.

"There are a couple of low jumps, if you both have a mind to try them." Kildare walked back into the stables.

Saetien waited and watched Shelby and the Sceltie Warlord play tug with a rag one of them had found somewhere. More accurate to say the adult Sceltie was holding one end of the rag and Shelby was happily doing all the tugging and growling.

She resented that he'd told the Scelties where they were going, especially since they weren't actually going anywhere. Then it hit her, and hit hard, that though she might be his special friend and he would learn about human things from her, the Scelties who lived here were the adults, the rule makers, that he would obey.

Kildare walked out of the stables with a chestnut mare. A Rose-Jeweled witch. "This is Lady Foxx. She was going to take herself out for a gallop, but she's willing to ride in the paddock with you since you're new here and need to stay close to home." The look in his eyes dared Saetien to contradict him.

If she did, would that be another mark against her?

"It's a pleasure to meet you, Lady Foxx," Saetien said. "I appreciate you giving up your gallop."

We will gallop with Kieran or Ryder on another day, Foxx replied.

"Caitie and Stormchaser are walking around in that paddock," Kildare said. "Leave them be."

She nodded and didn't ask questions, since she wanted a chance to ride. After she'd mounted and Kildare had checked the length of the stirrups, she looked at Shelby. "You stay here, okay?"

Saeti? Puzzlement, maybe hurt, at being left behind.

"I won't be far away."

We will stay here and visit the horses, the Sceltie Warlord said.

"That's good."

"The pup will be fine," Kildare said quietly. "And it's good for him to meet the horses—and for them to meet him. Go on, now. No point frittering away the day."

As she and Foxx walked toward the paddock, Saetien wondered how different riding a regular horse was from riding with one of the kindred. She'd never ridden a regular horse.

She could pose the question at the midday meal. It would be something she could talk about with her hosts.

As they reached the paddock, the gate opened before Saetien could decide if she should dismount to open it or try to use Craft. Foxx must have opened it, and that was a relief. Saetien still wasn't always successful in using Craft now that her power was strictly Purple Dusk instead of the range of power she'd once had in her Twilight's Dawn Jewel.

Reminded of what she had lost, Saetien tightened her grip on the reins that were attached to a halter, causing Foxx to snort. No bits when riding kindred, but that didn't mean the horse didn't pick up a rider's mood by the tension in the human's body.

Best not to think about why she no longer wore Twilight's Dawn.

A horse grazed at the far end of the paddock. Probably a mare, since there was a foal gamboling nearby, his antics making the girl who was with them laugh and clap her hands. The mare was a solid black. The foal was also black, but had a white mark in the shape of a bolt of lightning running down his face.

Saetien pressed her legs against Foxx's sides to indicate she wanted to go faster than a walk.

Foxx laid her ears back in warning—and Saetien didn't doubt for a moment that the mare would toss her if this turned into a battle of wills.

"Can't we go faster?" she asked.

Caitie and Stormchaser need to see us, Foxx replied.

They weren't sight shielded. But girl and foal weren't paying attention to them. The other mare lifted her head, considered them, then went back to grazing.

Foxx continued her easy approach until the foal noticed them. He squealed a warning as he placed himself in front of the girl, ready to do battle.

Saetien sighed as his psychic scent hit her. A Warlord Prince.

The girl's psychic scent hit her too. It carried a fear so sharp, Saetien felt its jagged edge.

Foxx continued to approach until she reached some understood distance that allowed the foal to stand his ground but didn't goad him into an attack that might end with him injuring himself.

"Hello," Saetien said. "I'm Saetien, but my friends call me Saeti. Are you Caitie?"

Something very wrong with this girl. More than fear.

Caitie put a hand to her chest. "Caitie." She smiled. "Saeti. Foxx." Her other hand rested on the foal's back. "Storm." She looked at the black mare. "Mother."

Having made his point, Stormchaser returned to his dam to nurse. Caitie wandered the paddock, never going far from the two horses.

Foxx turned away from them and lifted into a canter. She and Saetien circled the paddock a few times before Foxx said, *Jump?*

"Yes!"

Small jumps, nothing challenging, but fun all the same. They took the jumps from both directions before Foxx slowed to a walk. Saetien looked over her shoulder. The mare and foal, along with Caitie, were also walking. Well, the mare and Caitie were walking while the foal dashed, hopped, and circled the two females.

Saetien looked away before Caitie noticed her observing them. *If* Caitie noticed such things. More than fear made the girl's psychic scent odd.

Caitie is lame, Foxx said. *Lame leg, lame . . . brain. Hurt bad when she was a foal.*

When they walked past the open paddock gate, Saetien said, "Should we close the gate?"

No. It is time for Caitie to rest.

Saetien dismounted at the stable door, then walked in with Foxx. Ryder was there, grooming a bay Warlord while coaching a young witch who was standing on the other side of the horse. Spotting Saetien and Foxx, he stepped away and said, "I'll show you where to put Foxx's tack."

She put the tack away and gave Foxx a quick grooming before the mare headed back out to gallop and graze and spend time with the other horses. The Warlord followed her out, and the young witch quickly said her goodbyes, leaving Saetien with Ryder—and Shelby, who came running from somewhere to greet her.

Before she could ask Ryder about the girl, Caitie walked into the stables with Stormchaser.

The puppy looked at the foal and said, *My Saeti!*

The foal looked at the puppy and said, *My Caitie!*

"Now that we all know where we stand, Caitie girl, you

should take a bit of a rest before heading for school," Ryder said.

Girl and foal walked into one of the box stalls.

Ryder closed the lower half of the door, then tipped his head to indicate that Saetien should leave the stables with him.

"She was a bright girl before some visiting aristo prick raced through the village in a pony cart he didn't have the skill to drive, not with a regular horse in the traces. If it had been a kindred horse . . ." Ryder shook his head. "The aristo lost control and the pony cart tipped over on Caitie. Snapped her leg in several places and cracked her skull, damaging her brain. The best Healers in Scelt were summoned and did their best for her, but they couldn't give her back all that she'd lost. Or maybe her mind and Self found other roads to walk while her body healed." He seemed about to say something else, then decided against it.

She could guess what he didn't say—there had been a Healer who lived long ago who could have repaired the damage to Caitie's brain, but no one had known that some part of her still existed. Besides, could a Self without flesh really do a healing?

Or had someone who was no longer flesh shown the girl the other roads she could walk?

"What happened to the aristo?" she asked, hurrying to keep up with Ryder as he headed for the house.

"Some said he was drunk when it happened and didn't shield properly to protect himself when he was thrown from the cart, and that's why his neck broke and killed him. Others said the way his neck broke didn't fit being thrown from the pony cart—and some swore that aristo was alive for a minute after he landed."

Saetien swallowed hard. "You think someone killed him?"

"Well now, some said that aristo had aimed for a group of girls standing on the side of the road, and some saw Caitie, who had just acquired her Birthright Yellow Jewel the week before, use Craft to shove her friends out of harm's way, which is why she was the only one who was caught when the cart tipped." Ryder stopped and looked at her. "It was dusk, you see. After sundown."

"Maybe the aristo didn't see the girls in the fading light?"

"Maybe the person who snapped that neck had a lot of experience with killing," Ryder said quietly. "And maybe he didn't bother the High Lord when it came to calling in the rest of the debt after that aristo made the transition to demon-dead."

Saetien couldn't seem to draw in a breath.

Butler. Ryder was talking about Butler.

"People who make the mistake of thinking he's tame because he's old don't often have the chance to make a second mistake."

"Thank you for telling me." She looked back at the stables. "Caitie stays there?"

Ryder smiled. "After the third time her parents found Stormchaser tucked into bed with her without any idea of how he managed to get into the house and up the stairs to her room, we turned a box stall into a bit of a room for her so the two of them can spend time together. For Stormchaser it was love at first sight, and there's no keeping them apart, so this suits everyone. Besides, it's easier to muck out a stall than a bedroom."

"Oh."

"Aye."

Bits of information suddenly came together. "Kieran said a man had caused trouble in the village. Did he try to harm Caitie?"

"He did. But Prince Liath took one of his balls, stopping him from doing her harm. As for the rest of him . . . He disappeared without a trace, and Kieran says it's best to let it be."

"Who killed him? Butler? Or my father?" Saetien asked.

Ryder gave her a long look. "Leave it be, Saetien. No one in Maghre wants the answer to that question."

She went to her room to wash up and braid her hair before joining Kieran's family for the midday meal.

As Kieran turned away from his brother and those blue

eyes fixed on her, predator to prey, it occurred to her that there was a third possibility regarding what happened to the man who had tried to harm Caitie—and that was the reason Kieran had told Maghre's residents not to ask questions and to leave it be.

Kieran stopped the pony cart within sight of Butler's cottage. "We'll wait for you here."

"This might take a while," Saetien said, "and you shouldn't have to miss supper with your family."

"We'll all be back in time for supper."

She didn't waste time arguing with him. She walked up to the cottage, and reached the gate at the same time Butler opened the door and walked down the flagstone path. He didn't invite her to come inside. Didn't even open the gate and invite her to stand in his front yard that was bordered by deep flower beds.

He used Craft to create a ball of witchlight that illuminated the area around them. "You have the list?"

Saetien called in the two sheets of paper and thrust them over the gate.

Butler took them, read them. Finally, he said, "Half of what you've written down is inaccurate."

"I know everything I need to know about *her*."

The look in Butler's eyes made her want to step away from the gate. He'd warned her about being disrespectful, but it was so *hard* when you resented someone so much.

"You want to know nothing about Jaenelle Angelline, so I will tell you nothing about her or anything connected to her," he said, handing the papers back. "Wilhelmina Benedict."

Yes!

"She was twenty-seven when she came to Kaeleer during the last service fair. She signed a contract with Lucivar Yaslana, which allowed her to stay in the Shadow Realm. Signing a contract to serve in a Queen's court or signing a contract with someone like Yaslana, who ruled his own territory on behalf of his Queen, was the only way someone from Terreille could stay in Kaeleer. She had very fair skin, raven hair, and eyes that were a smoky blue rather than a clear blue. She was considered beautiful, although there were times when she looked emaciated. The Purple Dusk was her Birthright, and she wore Sapphire after she made the Offering to the Darkness."

"Why did she come to Kaeleer?" Saetien asked.

Butler said nothing.

"Why did she move to Scelt?"

He said nothing.

"Maybe I should ask Uncle Lucivar about her instead of troubling you."

Butler smiled. It wasn't a kind or an amused smile. "After she left SaDiablo Hall, Lucivar saw her just once. He came to Scelt and informed Wilhelmina that in order to fulfill her contract with him, her sole duty was never to set foot in Dhemlan or Askavi again. If she did, he would rip her to pieces and then escort what was left of her to Hell."

Saetien took a step back. "Why did he say that? What did she do?"

He said nothing.

"Who were her parents? Did she ever see them again after she left Chaillot?"

Silence. Finally, "You ask questions but have already declared that you don't want the answers."

"Of course I want the answers! That's why I'm here!"

"You said you know everything you need to know about *her*. All the answers to your questions are connected to *her*. Therefore, you do not want the answers."

"Isn't there *anything* else you can tell me about Wilhelmina Benedict?"

He stared at something in the distance. Something only he could see. "My opinion? Everything has a price. She made choices that eventually made her hollow of heart. But they were her choices."

He started to walk back to the cottage.

"Anything else? Anything?"

He stopped. After a moment, he turned to look at her as the witchlight faded. "Saetan never forgave her for some of those choices."

"You had a chat with Prince Butler today," Eileen said as she added mounds of whipped potatoes to plates that held thick slices of beef.

"I'm not sure he knows anything useful," Saetien grumbled as she added a spoonful of peas to her plate. "He told me what she looked like and what Jewels she wore. That's nice, but it doesn't tell me who she was. Oh, and Uncle Lucivar threatened to kill her if she returned to Dhemlan or Askavi, and the previous High Lord never forgave her for something she'd done. But Butler didn't know what she'd done!"

Everyone focused on filling their plates, and silence was a stern presence in the room.

"He *does* know?" She stared at her plate and fumed.

"Did you set any requirements or conditions that might hobble his answers?" Kieran finally asked. "Because you're right; he does know."

"I just want to know about Wilhelmina Benedict."

"I'm guessing that's Butler's point. Jaenelle and Wilhelmina were sisters. There's no way to know about the one without knowing about the other. No way to understand about the one without having some understanding about the other."

They ate in silence. After the maid cleared the table and brought in coffee, tea, and the sweet, Kildare said, "What are the important things you need to know when you cross paths with one of the Blood? You need to know what Jewels the person wears, their caste, and their bloodlines— their family connections. Someone might try to take advantage of a witch who wears Tiger Eye because there's nothing *she* can do to you, but if she has a cousin who is an

Opal-Jeweled Warlord Prince, *he's* the one you'll be meeting on a killing field for whatever pain you caused her, and make no mistake about that. So maybe that should be the place to start when you next see Butler. Jewels, caste, and bloodlines."

She already knew about the Jewels. Didn't she?

"I don't see why everyone is being so difficult about telling me about a person who lived years and years ago," Saetien complained.

Eileen slammed her teacup down so hard she cracked the cup and saucer. Tea ran onto the tablecloth, and none of the men moved as she turned on Saetien.

"Maybe nobody but you feels the need to rake up the past," Eileen said in a voice that held a crackling fury. "Maybe nobody wants to be reminded that Wilhelmina Benedict lived in Maghre, even if it was only a short time. As for a person living years and years ago, as if that erases who and what that person was? Shall I go to the village tomorrow and tell all and sundry that you're the great-granddaughter of Dorothea SaDiablo? She who is still hated throughout the length and breadth of Kaeleer despite her being dead and gone for centuries? How many doors would be closed to you, regardless of people's fondness for your father? How many people would wonder if you being part of the coven of malice was a sign that her bloodline runs true in you? You want to remind people of the past? You'd best be sure you're willing to have your own history exposed."

Eileen pushed back from the table, knocking over her chair, and ran out of the dining room.

Silence.

Saetien sat in her chair, trembling. Soon after her arrival at the sanctuary, Surreal had paid her a visit, had handed her a sheet of paper that listed her bloodlines.

"You need to be careful, Saetien," Surreal had said. "Because of who your father is and who your grandfather was, no one asks questions about the SaDiablo family. But the information is all there in the registers at the Keep, and anyone can find your connection to Dorothea."

"They don't hold that connection against you," she'd said.

Surreal gave her a sharp smile. "I am Titian's daughter. When I helped her skin Kartane SaDiablo alive and feed him to the hounds of Hell, I proved I was Dea al Mon. But you embraced Dorothea's kind of evil. It will take a long time for people to forget that, especially among the long-lived races."

Kildare cleared his throat. "Well. I guess that's the second mark. You've only got one left, Saetien." He rose from the table. "I'd best see to Eileen."

A fierce look filled Kieran's eyes once his father left the room. "Ask your questions when you see Butler or don't ask him. But you won't bring up that woman's name in this house again. Having you here is hard enough on my mother. You will not cause her more grief."

I didn't ask to stay here! Saetien clenched her teeth to keep the words from spilling out.

"We should give the maids a chance to clean up the room," Kieran said, pushing back from the table.

Ryder stood as well.

Trembling, Saetien finally rose. "If you'll excuse me, I think I'll retire for the evening."

The men gave her a small nod.

Probably relieved to be rid of her.

As she climbed the stairs to her room, she thought about calling to Shelby. She wanted someone who loved her, who didn't think she was an awful person for wanting to know about someone a Black Widow said she needed to find in order to understand the truth about herself. But the puppy was probably playing with the adult Scelties or out for walkies. Since she didn't want to run into anyone, it was better that he go out with the other dogs.

What would the people here do if they did know she was Dorothea SaDiablo's great-granddaughter? Would they shun her? Hate her? Try to hurt her? Her father wouldn't have left her here if he thought for a moment she would come to any harm.

But as she sat by the window, looking out at the night sky, she wondered if Wilhelmina Benedict's descendants had felt the same concerns.

And she wondered what Wilhelmina had done that made people want to forget her so much.

THIRTY-SIX

The next morning, Saetien did her best to be respectful, letting Eileen know that she was walking down to the stables and maybe going out for a ride. The woman's chilly response made it clear that trespasses weren't quickly forgiven.

Her reception at the stables was cautious, but warmed as she helped feed and groom horses. Kildare and Ryder warmed even more when the kindred foals—except for Stormchaser—acted like she was one of them and expected her to go out to the paddock and play with them. Which she did.

She lost every race.

Laughing, she returned to the stables breathless and sweaty, only to discover the Scelties had decided it was her turn to brush them. By the time she had brushed them to *their* satisfaction, she was covered with fur that had stuck to her sweaty skin.

"Here." Ryder set a large bucket of water next to her. "You should wash up a bit before going to the house for the midday meal."

Saetien looked down at herself. "Just dump the water over me."

A moment's pause before Ryder grabbed the bucket and dumped the water over her head.

She gasped. She would have shrieked but . . . "Hell's fire! That's *cold*."

"Didn't hear you say anything about warming it up."

She glared at Ryder. He grinned and took the bucket into the stables. When he came back out, he said, "You might want to put a warming spell on those clothes to help them dry out a bit before you try to go inside. We'll use the back door. There's a small room near the laundry where you can strip down."

She wasn't sure if Ryder had told Eileen they were going to use the back door or if the woman just had an instinct about such things, but the lady of the house was waiting for them when they arrived.

Eileen looked her over from head to toe—and sighed. "At least it's not mud. Come in, then. Anya! Fetch a robe for Lady Saetien."

Ryder smiled at his mother and eased out of the room, as if he'd had nothing to do with Saetien's bedraggled appearance.

"Best if you take a hot shower so you won't catch a chill," Eileen said. She started to turn away, then stopped and added, "Next time, be fast enough to put a warming spell around yourself or on the water."

"Yes, ma'am."

Anya returned with the robe and held it up as a shield while Saetien stripped out of the wet clothes.

"I'll do what I can with the shoes," Anya said. "You've others you can wear for the rest of today, but you'll be wanting these for the stables tomorrow."

"I will. Thank you."

Saetien hurried to her room and took a quick hot shower. She used Craft to dry her hair well enough to avoid any comment about catching a chill and was downstairs before Eileen started to dish out the midday meal.

"I'm going up to the village," Eileen said after they'd eaten and the men had left the table to resume their work. "Would you like to come with me?"

"Shall I go to the village tomorrow and tell all and sundry that you're the great-granddaughter of Dorothea SaDiablo?"

Eileen's words rang in Saetien's head.

"I spoke in anger last night, and I'm sorry for that," Eileen said. "No one in the village will learn about your great-grandmother from me."

"I know," Saetien replied. Looking into this woman's eyes, she did know. "I just have a lot of things to think about before I see Butler tonight. Next time?"

"Next time," Eileen agreed.

Saetien went up to her room and sat near the window, letting her thoughts drift as she watched the world beyond the glass. Shelby joined her, curling up for a nap.

Jewels. Caste. Bloodlines. The Blood's place in their society was also measured by social standing, but that wasn't as important as Jewels and caste.

"Half of what you've written down is inaccurate."

She thought and thought and thought, but in the end, she didn't see any other way to find out what she wanted to know.

In order to ask about Wilhelmina Benedict, she would have to ask about Jaenelle Angelline.

Butler woke before sundown, feeling battered by troubling dreams of trying to build a sturdy wall to protect a dear friend. But no matter how fast he put up that wall or how thick he made it, parts of it crumbled, leaving her exposed. Leaving her vulnerable.

Butler, it's time.

Jaenelle Angelline had been a lovely woman, generous and compassionate, brilliant in Craft and interested in other people. A talented Healer and a beloved Queen.

She had also been terrifying, but most people didn't fully appreciate that, didn't know the choices she'd made— or what those choices had cost her. What those choices still cost her.

Butler, it's time.

Was it really time to tell some hard truths just because some child wanted answers about another woman? Did the Queen really owe this girl anything? Did he?

The people who matter already know who I am—and what I am. What I always was. I'm beyond caring what anyone thinks of me.

"No, you're not," Butler muttered as he pushed aside the covers and got out of bed. "Even when you walked among the living, you tried to convince yourself that it didn't matter what people thought of you, but it mattered. When your sister delivered that heart wound, it mattered."

He warmed a glass of yarbarah and drank it before taking a shower and getting ready for this meeting.

He would reveal some hard truths because his Queen commanded. But only the truths he had to tell in order to answer the questions the girl would ask.

"You don't have to stay," Saetien told Kieran as she stepped down from the pony cart.

"I'll stay," he said.

This pony cart had a foldable roof and sides that could be put up to protect passengers from the wind and the wet. With warming spells, it could be quite cozy. Or maybe romantic, since it would afford some privacy if a couple wanted to share a kiss or two without everyone in the village knowing about it before lips left lips.

It was also convenient for a man who wanted to do some paperwork while he waited for a girl to ask questions—and hopefully get some answers from a surly Prince.

The wind had a sharp edge this evening, a reminder that winter hadn't completely surrendered to spring. It took Saetien three tries to add a warming spell to the hooded cape she wore. By the time she succeeded, she'd started to wonder if Butler was going to come out or if she was supposed to go up and knock on the cottage door. She had her hand on the gate's latch when the cottage door opened and he walked out.

There you are.

Her heart thumped in her chest. It wasn't romantic. Not at all. But something about Butler made her want to yield, made her want to be someone he would be proud to know—and that feeling scared her and kicked in the need to fight.

He wasn't pleased to see her, but he walked to the gate and stood there, waiting.

Saetien took a deep breath and let it out slowly. "Jewels. Caste. Bloodlines. That's what I would like to talk about. Wilhelmina Benedict and . . . Jaenelle Angelline . . . were sisters. That means they had the same parents."

"The same father," Butler said. "And it wasn't Robert Benedict, the man who was registered as their father in the records kept on Chaillot."

"Then who was their father?"

"Philip Alexander, who was Robert Benedict's half brother."

"Benedict was married twice. His first wife was a journeymaid Black Widow named Adria. I don't know why she married him before she'd safely had her Virgin Night, but she did—and he broke her. A broken witch can only conceive once, and Adria, who still had enough power to wield some of the Hourglass's Craft, was determined not to give Robert a child of his loins. During the first cycle of fertile days after her wedding, she wove a dream web around Philip Alexander, making him believe he was pleasuring someone else—someone he desired. Because of the dreamlike feel of his coupling with Adria, it's fairly certain that Philip never knew he had sired Wilhelmina. At least, not while she was growing up.

"A few months after Wilhelmina was born, Adria died under mysterious circumstances and Robert Benedict settled in Beldon Mor—and focused his amorous attention on Leland, who was Alexandra Angelline's daughter. Hard to say if Robert's interest in Leland was due to her being the daughter of Chaillot's Territory Queen or due to Philip, who served as one of Alexandra's escorts, being in love with Leland. Either way, among Robert's close circle of male friends was a Hayllian named Kartane SaDiablo, who was in Beldon Mor to encourage select aristo males to form an exclusive club where certain sexual tastes could be indulged."

Saetien sucked in a breath. "Wait. Wilhelmina's father *knew* Kartane SaDiablo?"

"He knew him," Butler agreed. "Since Dorothea SaDiablo, the High Priestess of Hayll, was toppling the courts in other Territories and destroying any Queens and Warlord Princes who tried to stand against her, when Robert expressed interest in marrying Leland—and reminded Alexandra of who would look favorably on such a union—the Queen of Chaillot convinced her daughter to marry Robert, even though Leland and Philip were already lovers and were in love. But Dorothea was an encroaching threat, and Alexandra didn't hesitate to do what she could to keep Hayll's influence out of Chaillot."

"But it was already there, in that exclusive . . ." Saetien stared at Butler, horrified. "Briarwood. You're talking about Briarwood."

"The pretty poison." Butler's voice sounded rough, as if centuries hadn't purged all the rage he felt about that place.

"But Jaenelle Angelline . . . Robert had to know . . ."

"He knew. Jaenelle was a troublesome child who told the truth about the things she could see—including the things no one else could see. But that's getting ahead of the story. Leland married Robert and had one child, a daughter Robert claimed as his own. During the Birthright Ceremony for each girl, he was granted paternity."

"Did Philip know he was Jaenelle Angelline's father?"

"Possibly. But Robert quickly entrenched himself in Alexandra's home and controlled Leland. The only way Philip could stay and serve in Alexandra's court—and stay near Leland and the two girls—was not to challenge Robert."

Saetien swallowed hard. "Was Wilhelmina sent to Briarwood?"

"No. Wilhelmina was shy and easily overlooked, de-

spite being beautiful even as a child. Maybe Robert realized that having one child constantly being put in and
taken out of Briarwood wouldn't cause too much talk—she
was, after all, a difficult child. But both of his daughters?
No, there would be too much talk if both girls were deemed
unstable. And Alexandra might stop looking the other way
if the girl who caused no problems was sent to a place that
specialized in treating emotionally disturbed girls." Butler
paused a moment before adding, "I think Jaenelle did
something to make sure Wilhelmina was overlooked by
Robert Benedict's friends—or she was until that last awful
night that changed so many things and left so many scars."

Her head ached and she felt a little sick. This wasn't
what she'd expected. Not at all what she'd expected.

"Let's talk about Jewels," she said. That should be safe
enough.

It felt like time slowed until she would have been able to
see each grain of sand fall in an hourglass if one had been
present. Then Butler opened the gate in the picket fence
and said, "Come in and wait."

He went into the cottage. Saetien stepped past the gate.
Just one step, but it felt like she'd crossed some threshold
that would change everything.

Butler returned a minute later carrying a cloth bag. A
table appeared in front of Saetien, a ball of witchlight
hanging above it. He called in a purple gemstone and
placed it on the table. Might be a piece of amethyst. Then
again, it might be colored glass.

"Wilhelmina's Birthright Jewel was Purple Dusk," Butler said.

"You mentioned that before," she replied when it seemed
like he was waiting for her to acknowledge . . . something.

He opened the cloth bag and poured out pieces of colored glass, then arranged the pieces in the order of the
Jewels: White, Yellow, Tiger Eye, Rose, Summer-sky, Purple Dusk, Opal, Green, Sapphire, Red, Gray, Ebon-gray—
and thirteen Black.

"Jaenelle's Birthright."

Saetien looked at the colored glass. "Which one?" Had to be Red, if Jaenelle Angelline had worn the Black.

"All of them," Butler said quietly.

She stared at him. "All of . . . ? *How?*"

"When Jaenelle was seven years old, Lorn, the last Prince of the Dragons, gifted her with a full set of Jewels, from White to Ebon-gray, and thirteen Black Jewels to hold her reservoir of power. Seven years old and she already eclipsed the High Lord of Hell's power, already stood deeper in the abyss than he could hope to reach. So powerful. So very powerful, and able to do things no one had ever done before or will ever do again. But she was still a child, still dependent on the adults around her, still vulnerable to the demands of the adults who controlled her. A truth that pertains to all children."

Had Jaenelle Angelline realized she was so different from the rest of the Blood? Or had she simply accepted the way things were because that was the way things were and kept tripping every time she did something no one else could do, only to have people tell her she was fibbing, that she couldn't *possibly* do that?

Butler pushed the piece of dark blue glass out of the line until it was between Jaenelle's Jewels and Wilhelmina's.

"On that last night when everything changed, there was a children's party. The purpose of the party was for men like Robert and Kartane to select a couple of girls who would be drugged and raped. Broken of their power. Then the girls would be declared emotionally hysterical and taken to Briarwood to cure them. Wilhelmina was chosen but Jaenelle intervened, holding off the men who were going to take Wilhelmina to a room upstairs to recover from drinking too much sparkling wine. Wilhelmina was fourteen. Jaenelle was twelve."

Her eyes stung, but she wasn't going to cry. Not here. Not yet. "They put something in the wine?"

"Yes. Daemon was there that night, a pleasure slave serving in Alexandra's court. He had planned to get Jaenelle out of Chaillot, but Alexandra took Jaenelle away and left him to get Wilhelmina back to the Angelline estate. By the time he realized she'd done that in order to take Jaenelle to Briarwood and have Hayllian guards in place to capture and control him . . . Alexandra used the Ring of Obedience, poured agony into him to cripple him so that he couldn't fight the guards. But he did fight—and he did escape, did manage to break the Ring of Obedience by unleashing the full power of his Black Jewel. That power also ripped through the Blood in Beldon Mor, shattering a lot of Jewels, killing some people. When it was over, Wilhelmina was wearing a Sapphire Jewel." Butler tapped the piece of glass. "This Jewel. Jaenelle's Sapphire. Wilhelmina couldn't use it—she wasn't powerful enough to use it—but there were shields in that Jewel that kept her protected from men like Robert. When she made the Offering to the Darkness and acquired her own Sapphire Jewel, Jaenelle's Sapphire disappeared."

Butler called in another piece of dark blue glass and set it next to Wilhelmina's Purple Dusk. Then he moved the other Sapphire back in line with the rest of Jaenelle's Jewels. He hesitated a moment before moving six of the black pieces just enough to separate them from the rest. "When Jaenelle made the Offering to the Darkness—something she had to do before setting up her official court—six of the Black Jewels were transformed into a Jewel called Ebony. Darker than the Black, and a much deeper reservoir of power. Power beyond imagining—until the war between Kaeleer and Terreille."

He gathered up all the pieces of glass and put them back in the bag. "That's enough for today."

"But . . . What about my father? Did he escape with her?"

Butler hesitated. "No. He and Saetan managed to keep Jaenelle connected to her body—and he got her promise that she wouldn't sever the connection between her body and her Self. But after that ordeal, he was too exhausted, too damaged, to do anything more. It was Cassandra, the previous Queen of Ebon Askavi, who took Jaenelle to the Keep. And it was Surreal who helped Daemon elude the guards who were hunting for him and found a place for him to hide until he recovered." He shuddered. "Enough."

The table vanished. Butler walked into the cottage and closed the door.

Still so much she wanted to know, but she felt battered and already had so much to think about.

As she walked away from the cottage, the witchlight that had hung above the table faded, and another witchlight appeared above the pony cart.

Kieran studied her face. "You got some answers?"

"Some."

"Not what you expected?"

"No. But it's given me a lot to think about."

Kieran didn't try to fill the silence, and she was grateful. She *did* have a lot to think about. Like, her father wore a Black Jewel. Yes, it had been made into a pendant and a ring, and there were probably smaller chips of the Jewel that he used for other things, but it was still *one* Jewel.

Jaenelle Angelline had been powerful enough to need *thirteen* Black Jewels for her reservoir of power. When she was seven years old.

How old had she been when she had started protecting her sister from men like Robert Benedict and Kartane SaDiablo?

If Jaenelle had loved Wilhelmina that much, what had gone wrong between them?

THIRTY-SEVEN

P uppy school, Saeti? We go to puppy school?*
        Saetien buttoned up the long thick sweater and eyed
Shelby's wagging tail. She'd planned to go to the stables
and work with Ryder and Kildare for a bit, maybe see if
they'd let her ride one of the regular horses so that she
could understand the difference between them and the kindred.

"I don't know if we're allowed to go to puppy school."

Why not?

"I—"

He started whining—that particular pitch of whining
that made it sound like his little heart was breaking because she wouldn't allow him to do something.

She wouldn't give in to that whine. She wouldn't. It
wouldn't be good for him if she buckled and gave in.

Hell's fire, had her father felt like this when she'd whined
about not getting something she wanted? Where did an
adult draw the line between buckling in order to stop that
sound and compromising in a way that was reasonable?

Maybe she owed her father an apology for all the times
she'd whined at him in an effort to get her own way. And
maybe it was a good thing that he'd endured the whining
and held the lines he'd drawn about proper behavior and
following his rules.

"I'll go down right now and see if I can catch Kieran

before he starts his work," she said quickly. "He'll know if it's proper for us to visit the puppy school."

Shelby stopped whining and wagged his tail.

The Scelties had their meals in the kitchen, so Shelby headed in that direction, leaving Saetien to rush to the breakfast room on her own. She breathed a sigh of relief when she saw Kieran still at the table, talking to Kildare, Ryder, and Eileen.

"If you're in that much of a rush to get to breakfast, people will think we aren't feeding you enough at supper," Eileen said, her voice filled with mild amusement.

"I wanted to catch Kieran," Saetien said.

Kieran sipped his coffee. "Oh?"

"Shelby wants to visit the puppy school, but I wasn't sure if that was permitted." She said it fast. She wasn't sure why, since Kieran didn't seem to be in any hurry to leave the table.

"Have you ever been to puppy school?" Kieran asked.

The question *sounded* innocent, but she noticed Kildare wouldn't look at her, and Ryder seemed fascinated by the crumbs that were left on his plate. "Nooo."

"Well, then, it will do you both some good to go there." Kieran smiled at her. "Since I have to be out and about this morning, I can drop you off at the school. We'll leave in half an hour." He stood, gave his mother a kiss on the cheek, and left the breakfast room, chuckling.

She was pretty sure that wasn't a good sign for what she was about to do.

"Best get some food in you while you can," Eileen said briskly, whisking Saetien's plate off the table and going to the sideboard to fill it. "You'll have a busy morning."

"I will?"

Ryder began coughing loudly, then excused himself from the room.

The coughing sounded suspiciously like laughter.

Kildare carefully buttered a sweet roll before cutting it in half.

Saetien looked at Eileen when the woman put the full

plate in front of her. She looked at Kildare, who wouldn't look at her. "Is there something I should know about puppy school?"

"Some things are best learned for yourself," Kildare said. Leaving the sweet roll, he excused himself.

"Eat up," Eileen said, "or all the neighbors will know you're late when Kieran starts hollering for you to hurry up. He takes after his father that way. When Kildare puts his mind to it, his voice can carry across all the pastures and fields when he's looking for a wandering child."

"Sometimes I used to think it would be fun to have an older brother," Saetien muttered. Having met Ryder, she figured Mikal pretty much filled that spot. And then . . .

"Well, you've got a male cousin, don't you? And him being Eyrien and a Warlord Prince, he's probably well suited to being annoying and bossy like an older brother."

She couldn't argue with that.

"I know I'm late, but it's not my fault," Saetien said as she rushed toward where Kieran waited beside the pony cart. "Anya grabbed me and wouldn't let me leave until she'd braided my hair properly."

"You'll thank me for it," Anya had said.

Squeals. Stomps. And the small thunder of a stampede that Ryder stopped by throwing a shield across the open stable doors. Blocked by the shield, the handful of foals she'd played with yesterday stared at her, then squealed their demands for attention.

"Saeti and Shelby have to go to puppy school now," Ryder said, raising his voice enough to be heard. "Saeti can play with you when they get back."

Before she could give an opinion about that, Kieran boosted her into the pony cart and picked up Shelby. The moment he was seated, he told the Warlord pulling the cart to *go*.

"They won't settle down for Ryder while you're in sight," he said, holding Shelby in his lap.

"I'm not sure . . ."

"Did you play with the foals yesterday?"

"Yes."

"Did you think they would forget?"

"I . . ." She hadn't considered that an hour of play might get her into trouble.

"As a human adult, or close enough when compared to their age, you have to help Ryder maintain the rules. Otherwise, we'll have an unruly bunch of youngsters who will be bigger and stronger than a lot of humans can handle by the time they're old enough to receive their Birthright Jewels."

"I don't have to play with them if it will cause trouble." More trouble.

Kieran just looked at her.

Saetien sighed. There had been foals born at the Hall. Hadn't there? Maybe she hadn't paid much attention since she couldn't ride them? Or maybe she'd just admired them and petted them but somehow hadn't become a playmate?

"Is there anything I should know about puppy school?" she asked.

"It's an experience," Kieran replied.

After an hour of puppy school, Saetien decided that Kieran could have been a little more forthcoming about the "experience" of having that many kindred Scelties in one place. There were human teachers, and adult Scelties who were also teachers. And then there were the other helping hands who were supposed to corral and occupy the fuzz balls who were waiting their turn at a lesson or had finished a lesson.

If she stayed on her feet, the puppies, who had not yet absorbed the necessity of basic manners, scratched at her legs, clamoring to be petted or held or brushed or some combination of those things. If she sat on the floor to accommodate a pile of puppies in her lap, the ones standing behind her grabbed her braid and began an invigorating game of tug. When she'd finally rescued her hair, she stuffed it under her sweater—which, of course, was the hiding game, and the puppies who had learned to air walk clung to her shoulders while they grabbed the part of the braid they could see in order to pull the prize out of its hiding place.

Shelby was delighted with the lessons, delighted with the games, delighted to be around other puppies.

The teachers were delighted to have another human to help with the teaching games—although the female teachers suggested that she put her hair up tomorrow so that it wouldn't be mistaken for a toy.

Was she really coming back tomorrow?

The pony cart, minus Kieran, waited for her when she walked out of the school.

"Home," she told the Warlord. "Please."

Since there were no reins on a vehicle pulled by one of the kindred, she let the Warlord take care of getting them home and closed her eyes. Just for a minute. Surely only a minute. Except the next thing she knew, Kildare was giving her a little shake.

Saetien opened her eyes.

Squeal. Stomp. Small thunder up to the paddock fence.

A handful of foals stared at her.

Kildare helped her down and smiled. "You'll build up stamina. But if you're seeing Butler this evening, you might want to have a little sleep after the midday meal."

"That's a good idea."

Remembering that Ryder had promised the foals that she would play with them on her return, Saetien removed her sweater and vanished it as she walked to the paddock, where she would be the only two-legged contestant in the races.

"You said Surreal helped my father escape the guards who were hunting for him," Saetien said. "What happened to him after that?"

"You'll have to ask him," Butler replied.

"Why? I'm asking you."

They were standing on either side of the gate in the

picket fence. She wondered why he didn't invite her inside. She wondered if, unlike the outside, which looked well maintained— if you didn't look too closely at the flower beds—the inside of the cottage was a decaying mess. After all, he'd been living there for a long time.

Then again, her family had been living at SaDiablo Hall for a very long time, and no one could say any room in that huge place was untidy, let alone a mess.

No one would dare—at least not in Helene's hearing.

"I don't know your father's story," Butler said. "I don't know what happened to him between the last night that he saw Jaenelle and when he arrived in Kaeleer thirteen years later. Besides, we're not here to talk about your father."

How much of her father's past—and Uncle Lucivar's— would she know if she'd listened to the stories they'd shared during family gatherings?

"Why did Wilhelmina come to Kaeleer?" Maybe it wasn't the right question to ask next, since, like Daemon Sadi, Wilhelmina didn't arrive in Kaeleer until thirteen years after the night her sister was taken away for the last time.

"Whenever she was afraid, whenever she felt threatened, she would hold on to that Sapphire Jewel and hear Jaenelle's voice telling her to come to Kaeleer, telling her she would be safe in Kaeleer. There weren't many in Terreille who knew how to open the Gates between the Realms, so she might not have known how to reach the Shadow Realm. She could have gone to Ebon Askavi and asked for sanctuary. The ones who look after the Keep in Terreille would have opened the Gate there and escorted her to the Keep in Kaeleer. For whatever reason, she didn't attempt to reach the Shadow Realm until the last service fair."

"Did she feel threatened living with her family?"

"Yes." Butler stared at something in the distance. A physical distance, or the distance of time and memory? "One of Jaenelle's friends in Briarwood urged her to create a trap for the uncles—the men who used that place for sex and other gratifications they couldn't afford to indulge in elsewhere—a trap that would be sprung if Jaenelle's blood was spilled."

A room and a bed. And blood. So much blood.

"And that's what Jaenelle did. She wove a tangled web that took in Briarwood, *was* Briarwood. She included her friends—both the ghosts and the demon-dead—and she created the pretty poison. To each was given what he gave. That became the price of Briarwood.

"The last time Jaenelle was taken to that place, she was raped by a man named Greer, who was Dorothea SaDiablo's favorite assassin—until Surreal found him in Briarwood and slit his throat."

The first time she had walked through Briarwood, she'd seen the moment when Surreal killed that man.

"I bet Rose was the one who talked Jaenelle into making that trap," she muttered. Rose had been her sharp-tongued, unsympathetic guide when she'd seen Briarwood.

"Yes," Butler snapped, "she was."

She didn't know how, but she'd just stepped onto dangerous ground.

After a moment, Butler said, "There was some justice to Surreal being Greer's executioner, since Greer had killed her mother when Surreal was twelve. Slit Titian's throat." Butler's eyes held a strange glitter. "Titian made the transition to demon-dead and became the Queen of the Harpies. She had no use for men except as prey, but she did respect Daemon because he was Tersa's son and he had helped her and Surreal, and she allied herself with Saetan to protect Jaenelle. If you were a man, even someone who served in the Dark Court, you needed to be very careful if you crossed paths with Titian."

Was her cousin Titian named in honor of Surreal's mother, just as she'd been named for . . .

"What does all that have to do with Wilhelmina feeling threatened?"

"That night the trap was sprung, and Briarwood caught every man who used that place. It took a while for the uncles to understand that the relentless pain and nightmares of being tortured and raped, of feeling hands or legs being cut off, of feeling the terror and slow death caused by suffocation after someone walled them into an alcove specially made for such a punishment . . . It took a while for them to realize that they were feeling everything the children had felt—because there were a few boys there too. They wouldn't admit the truth, so all of those men from the important aristo houses sought out Healers. But the Healers couldn't find anything wrong with the men, had no explanation for the pain that was slowly consuming those men." Butler's smile had a nasty edge. "There is no cure for Briarwood. Some of those men tried to seek relief from the pain by choosing the physical death, but they couldn't succeed until they had paid the debt they owed. Then their bodies could die. But they hadn't known that the High Lord of Hell would be *very* interested in them once they made the transition to demon-dead. Saetan found out a great deal about Briarwood. More than Jaenelle would ever want him to know. But she had nightmares about that place all her life, and she sometimes talked in her sleep, so Saetan wasn't the only one who learned the truth about Briarwood."

Marjane. Myrol and Rebecca. Dannie. Rose. When she'd walked through the memory of Briarwood, had she seen any of the girls who had been walled in? Or had Witch spared her that much?

"Some of the uncles believed that having sex with a virgin would cure them," Butler continued after a minute. "Being one of the afflicted, Robert Benedict—or Uncle Bobby, as Jaenelle had called him—targeted Wilhelmina to be his cure. Philip Alexander intervened when he was home, but he was often absent while escorting Leland or Alexandra, which left Wilhelmina vulnerable. When she gathered the courage to tell Alexandra that Robert was trying to force himself on her, the Queen of Chaillot refused to believe her. She was making things up, trying to cause trouble by telling tales. Like her sister had done before she disappeared.

"Wilhelmina ran away, went into hiding with the help of a stable lad named Andrew who, at some point, lost an eye while trying to protect her. There was some speculation that Philip had found her, but he denied it, finally trying to do the right thing for one of his girls. No one had any news about Wilhelmina until she showed up in Kaeleer. And the person who made that discovery and broke that news to Alexandra was Dorothea SaDiablo."

"Why would Dorothea care about Wilhelmina?" Saetien asked.

"She didn't. But shortly before that last service fair, Daemon Sadi showed the most powerful and uncorrupted witches in Chaillot the truth about Briarwood, and Alexandra was about to be unseated as the Territory Queen because many of those powerful witches had lost young relatives in that place. When Alexandra learned that Wilhelmina was in Kaeleer and being controlled by a Warlord Prince who also controlled an eccentric girl who was strangely powerful, she had to go to the Shadow Realm to find her granddaughters, didn't she? She thought, being a Queen, she was Dorothea's ally, but in truth, she was the High Priestess of Hayll's pawn—and she played her part well."

Butler took a step back. "That's enough for tonight."

Nowhere near enough, but her head was swimming with the images from this recounting of Wilhelmina's life. And while she didn't think telling her this story was easy for Butler, she had a feeling that they were coming to parts that would be . . . difficult.

"See you tomorrow night," she said.

"Yes."

It felt rude just to leave. "What do you do at night?"

He gave her an odd look. "I'm sorting out my affairs. My time here is almost done."

As she walked down the lane to where Kieran waited with the pony cart, she imagined a giant hourglass slowly turning and the sand whispering *Almost done* as it fell.

Why almost done? And where would Butler go?

THIRTY-EIGHT

I diot, Daemon thought as he shut off the water and got out of the shower. *You should have known better than to spar with Lucivar when he was agitated and looking to pound someone into the ground.*

He did know better, but sparring had given them something to do during that hour when Jillian *wasn't* doing what was normally done during a Virgin Night—which was taking place in the afternoon so that Jillian could be "rested" for the party that evening.

Rested. Ha!

A tapping on his bedroom door. Recognizing Helton's psychic scent, Daemon wrapped a towel around his waist and walked into the bedroom. "Come in."

Helton glanced at him, then focused on the floor. "Some of the guests have arrived."

"Which guests?"

"Lady Nurian and Lord Rothvar. Lady Titian and Lady Zoela. Prince Daemonar and Prince Raine."

"Raine? Why? He doesn't know Jillian."

Another quick glance at him. "Prince Raine knows Lady Brenda."

"Ooohhh? Any indication of how well Raine knows Brenda?" Raine wasn't a fool, and he knew the family's rules about sex—and the consequences of getting into anyone's bed without the High Lord's permission.

"Well enough that, from what Beale conveyed as information—*not* gossip—Raine and Brenda intend to talk to you about their interest in being intimate. Beale thought you might want to be forewarned, with it being the celebration of Lady Jillian's Virgin Night."

Mother Night! That would mean another discussion with Brenda about sex.

"Thank you, Helton. I'll be down in a few minutes."

"Very good, Prince."

Helton was too good a butler to bolt out of a room—most of the time—but his retreat was a bit hasty. Daemon could blame his own state of undress for the haste, but he suspected Helton had spent enough time around Brenda yesterday to decide that the best way to deal with any request from the Green-Jeweled witch from Scelt was a speedy response followed by a quick retreat.

Daemon and Lucivar met Surreal in the room she'd made into her office. A practical place to meet, since the sitting room seemed to be overrun with excited youngsters and with adults waiting to corner him into a discussion about sex.

"Permission before action is a stupid rule for adults," he grumbled as Lucivar knocked on the door and walked in.

"Father held that line because it protected everyone who worked at any of the estates, and especially anyone who worked at the Hall, since that's where troublesome guests usually ended up," Lucivar replied.

"Guests aren't the only troublesome individuals who end up at the Hall." He knew when it was pointless to draw a line. After all, the Scelt contingent was already firmly entrenched at the Hall.

Lucivar stared at Surreal. "Well? How did it go?"

Surreal looked at the two of them. "When I explained his new role in this . . . activity . . . the Warlord, having heard that both of you were in the city, almost wept in relief. However, I gathered from the little Jillian said on the way back to the town house that she had enjoyed a frank conversation with the Warlord about what men like their lovers to do in order to stimulate and excite."

They *stared* at her.

Surreal stared back. "We have establishments that teach young men—especially aristo men and those training to be consorts—how to be good lovers. They're taught what generally pleases and what doesn't, along with variations. Why shouldn't knowledge also flow the other way?"

Lucivar looked at Daemon. Daemon looked at Lucivar.

Knowing what pleased a man, and thinking of a *daughter* doing that to please a man? No.

"Is the vintner here yet?" Lucivar asked, sounding much too reasonable.

"He is," Daemon replied, sounding just as reasonable.

Surreal called in her crossbow and aimed it at Lucivar. "*You* are going to pretend that you don't know that one of your children will be having sex and doing all kinds of other things with her lover, just like your children pretend they don't know you have sex with Marian and do whatever it is that's making you go pale right now when you think of them doing it too."

That was the moment when Marian walked into the room. She looked at Lucivar and froze. Then she looked at Surreal holding the crossbow.

"What happened?" Marian asked.

"Nothing," Surreal replied cheerfully. "We're establishing boundaries about what Lucivar isn't going to notice when Jillian and Stefan have sex."

Marian choked on a laugh. "Mother Night."

Then Surreal aimed the crossbow at Daemon. "And *you*, being marginally more rational right now, are going to give Jillian and Stefan official permission to be lovers and have sex. You're also going to give Brenda and Raine permission to be lovers and have sex."

"They haven't . . . ," Daemon began.

"Just find them together and tell them they have your permission. Then run." Surreal raised her eyebrows. "Do you *really* want to have another discussion with Brenda about sex?"

Not in several lifetimes. "Very well."

Daemon and Lucivar headed for the door, a strategic retreat.

"While you're at it, you might talk to Zoey and Titian about expanding their permissions for romantic—"

Lucivar didn't mean to rip the door off the hinges, but it made his position on Zoey and Titian quite clear.

"Maybe not today," Surreal said.

Daemon looked back at Surreal, who seemed amused, and Marian, who seemed confused.

"Two more times," he muttered. "We'll have to go through this Virgin Night with our girls two more times." Or more, depending on which girls were living at the Hall when they reached the proper age.

"Could have been worse," Lucivar said. "Karla could be here offering advice."

"Karla already talked to Jillian and offered advice. Remember?"

"Oh, yeah." Lucivar scrubbed his hands over his face. "What were you thinking?"

Daemonar watched his father and uncle circulate among the guests. Together. As a pair of predators ready to take on whatever needed to get squashed flatter than dead.

"Somebody upset them," he said quietly.

"Might have been me," Brenda said cheerfully. "There was a bit of a discussion about why females have a Virgin Night and males don't."

He looked at Raine, who just looked back at him without offering an opinion—or even making a grunting noise that might be mistaken for an opinion.

"We do have a Virgin Night of sorts," Daemonar said.

"Do you, now?" Brenda's eyes brightened with interest.

Brenda had green eyes and Auntie J.'s eyes were sapphire, but that bright interest was a familiar look—a harbinger of trouble that always began with innocent curiosity and often ended with something blowing up. Which meant Brenda would have settled into the Dark Court's First Circle without a second thought.

Had Uncle Daemon realized that yet?

"Male Virgin Night?" Brenda said.

Right. He'd been foolish enough to say that to her. "Sure. You Ladies need to have the first sexual encounter done properly to preserve your power. Males need to do it properly to preserve their reputations." Daemonar swallowed some wine to wet a suddenly dry throat as he imagined trying to explain this to Auntie J. or Karla. "A male getting careless about his choice of lover that first time could spiral into Ladies thinking he's going to accommodate anyone who has an itch and wants him to scratch it. Men who didn't train to be consorts have been denied being able to serve in courts because of a reputation for providing sex at the snap of a woman's fingers. They might be considered too unreliable to be a potential husband and father. It might take more than one bad choice for a man to damage his reputation and life beyond repair, but if he lets himself be used once, he can count on someone trying to use him again."

"Did you learn that from your father and uncle?" Raine asked.

Daemonar shook his head. "I figured that out from Jillian's first romantic entanglement. He was a Rihlander who made a bad choice about his first time and things soured for him after that, until he ended up in Ebon Rih and latched onto Jillian—and then had to deal with Lucivar."

Brenda and Raine looked across the room at Daemon and Lucivar. "I'm thinking those two got a wee bit excited about it all," she said.

"You could say that. It ended with the discovery of the 'if you loved me' spell and how it was being used—and it ended with my father taking the title of Demon Prince and ruling all of Askavi."

"What happened to the boy?" Raine asked.

Daemonar smiled. "They gave him a second chance

and sent him to Dharo to serve in a Queen's court." He lowered his voice. "One of his descendants works for Mrs. Beale now. The Dharo Boy?"

Brenda hooted. Daemonar and Raine shushed her when Daemon and Lucivar looked over—then pointedly ignored the three of them.

"Does Jillian know?" Brenda asked.

"No," Daemonar replied. "And unless the Dharo Boy is the one to tell her, she never will."

"What do you think those three are talking about?" Stefan asked as he watched Brenda, Daemonar, and Raine laughing about something.

"I don't want to know," Jillian replied. She slipped her arms around his waist and rested her head on his shoulder. "Well, it's done, and we have Prince Sadi's permission to bounce the bed."

Stefan choked. "He did not say that."

"No, Brenda said it. I'm not sure if she intended for Lucivar to hear her, but it certainly got a reaction."

"Is that why he snapped the legs off that little table?"

Jillian nodded. "He gets exercised about some things." She sighed. "You're going to make us wait until we're home, aren't you?"

"Since I'd like to keep my balls behind my zipper and not in a jar on the mantel, yes, we're going to wait."

She stifled a laugh. It was funny, but knowing Lucivar and Daemon, it was also true.

"Besides," Stefan added. "We have time."

Jillian leaned back to look at him. Loving Stefan was a quiet excitement with plenty of sparks. Rather like Lucivar and Marian's love, although she didn't think Lucivar would understand the comparison—yet.

The party was winding down and nobody had died. Lucivar figured he and Daemon had done well, and Surreal was right—as long as he didn't think too much about Jillian having a lover for a decade or two, he'd adjust to her being with Stefan.

He watched Jillian cross the room. Alone.

"If he ever hurts you . . . ," Lucivar said softly.

"I will call in my Eyrien war blade and slice him into pieces," Jillian replied. "And then I will call you to deal with whatever part of him is left. Although I guess Daemon would be the one who would deal with what's left after the transition to demon-dead."

"He'd let me help."

A beat of silence before she said, "Stefan won't hurt me."

No, Stefan wouldn't. Not because of the men in Jillian's family who would be there to protect her, but because Lucivar had seen the way the vintner looked at Jillian. Had seen love and desire rather than lust.

"If you two decide to handfast, you'll give me a little more warning?"

Jillian nodded. "We're not thinking of that just yet, but I will tell you if we do. And Stefan is drinking the contraceptive brew, so we'll give you plenty of warning before you become a grandfather."

He hadn't realized he was swaying until someone grabbed his arm to steady him.

Jillian smiled. "If you'll excuse me . . ."

Rothvar shook his head as Jillian joined Stefan, Brenda, Raine, and Daemonar. "Did she just say . . . ?"

"Yeah."

"Hell's fire." Rothvar released his hold on Lucivar's arm. "You okay?"

"Living in Terreille, I never thought I would survive long enough to have children, let alone be a grandfather," Lucivar said. "But here I am." He looked at his second-in-command. "Here we are."

Rothvar scanned the room until he located Nurian. The heat of love filled every aspect of the man. "Yeah. Here we are."

THIRTY-NINE

There, now," Anya said as she tucked the final pin into the coil she'd made of Saetien's long black hair. "Now let me cover it with this netting, and you'll be all set."

Saetien stared at her reflection. With her hair put up this way, she looked older. Looked . . . mature, which would be fine. Would be good, in fact. But if this made her look matronly . . . "Isn't netting old-fashioned?" Meaning suitable for old ladies rather than young women.

"It's black, so it matches your hair," Anya replied as she placed the netting around the coiled hair. "I've added a little shielding to it, so even sharp little puppy teeth won't be able to get a grip on your hair."

Thank the Darkness for that.

"Besides," Anya continued, "just because something is practical and traditional doesn't make it old-fashioned." She blew out a breath. "Had a guest here not long ago who thought like you. She said the same about netting being old-fashioned. Only she made the mistake of actually teasing some of the puppies with her braid, even though Kieran *and* Ryder warned her not to do that. Well, she wore herself out with the playing and fell asleep with two of the pups still with her. Don't know if they liked the smell of her hair or just weren't ready to stop playing, but there she was, sound asleep, and there they were, chewing on that braid and having a good time being quiet.

"Well, she woke up by herself and started having a fair fit because she had half the hair she'd had before she fell asleep, and there were chunks of hair all over the yard because the pups didn't know about using Craft to seal the ends to hold the braid together."

Saetien turned around so she could look Anya right in the eyes. "You're making that up."

"Hand on heart." Anya put her hand on her chest.

Saetien started to reach up to make sure she still *had* hair. Then she lowered her hand. "It's practical. And traditional."

Anya smiled. "Exactly. If you and Shelby are going to puppy school, best you go down and get some breakfast in you."

Obediently, Saetien headed downstairs. Anya wasn't *quite* as bossy as the servants who worked for her father at the Hall, but she'd give them a fair race for the trophy.

Everyone was in the breakfast room when Saetien arrived. She stopped herself from calling attention to her hair, but Kieran noticed the aborted move when she started to reach up.

"Anya found some netting for your hair?" he asked.

"Looks good," Kildare said with a nod.

"Indeed it does," Eileen agreed with a smile.

"Anya told me a silly story about a guest who had her braid chewed off." Saetien rolled her eyes to indicate that she wasn't about to be fooled, just in case Anya *had* been teasing.

Except . . . Ryder winced, and Kieran said, "Ah. Well, we *did* warn her not to get the puppies thinking that her hair was a toy."

Saetien sat down with a thump. "You mean Anya *wasn't* teasing?"

Four people shook their heads.

"Woman upset the whole stable with her screeching." Kildare buttered his toast a bit fiercely in response to the memory.

"She had her sights set on Kieran," Ryder said. "Well,

she did," he insisted when Eileen scoffed at the suggestion. "Why did you think he asked you to put her up on this side of the house and had Brenda sleep in the guest room on his side? He figured Brenda would be as fierce a protector as any Sceltie."

The look in Eileen's eyes held steel. "Kieran?"

"She never got close to my bedroom, let alone my bed, and she packed up and was gone the next day, so my reputation remains unsullied." Kieran's lips twitched with amusement. "But even the youngest pups realized that my scolding about the hair wasn't sincere, since they had solved a problem for me, which is why some of them still think braids are toys." He pointed a finger at Saetien. "You'll have to put some effort into convincing them otherwise, for your own sake as well as other young Ladies."

She bared her teeth in a smile that had Kieran's eyebrows rising.

"How was playtime with the foals yesterday?" Kildare asked.

Saetien took her time buttering a piece of toast. "It was fine." Butter, butter, butter. "They let me win a race. It was a close call. Caitie was watching and declared that I won by a nose."

A lot of male throat clearing.

Eileen reached over and patted Saetien's hand. "That was kind of the foals to let you win."

"It was," she agreed.

The men excused themselves with more haste than manners.

"The pony cart will be out front for you when you're ready," Kieran said before he closed the breakfast room door.

"What is discussed is private, but how are things going between you and Prince Butler?" Eileen asked as she refilled their cups. "He can be a bit prickly about the past."

"It's not what I expected."

"That's a truth that can be said about a lot of things."

✦ ✦ ✦

Later that day, Saetien stood on her side of the gate and waited for Butler. Kieran had said it was a bit early to be going, and it probably was, but she'd been thinking about these people all day. Alexandra Angelline, the Chaillot Queen who had struggled to hold on to her Territory in the face of a terrible scandal, with the powerful families in Beldon Mor— the ones who weren't involved in Briarwood—asking how she had let that evil remain hidden, how she'd allowed it to take root, how she could claim she didn't know about it when *one of the men who had helped make that place* lived in her own house. When one of her granddaughters had been committed to that place.

Had those powerful families begun to wonder if Jaenelle Angelline really had been an eccentric, troubled child or if she had been a child who had tried to tell them the truth about the dangers and corruption hidden by people like Robert Benedict?

And Dorothea SaDiablo. Powerful High Priestess of Hayll, who had wanted to control the Realm of Terreille. Had wanted to control more than that?

Jaenelle Angelline had ruled almost the whole of Kaeleer. Dorothea had wanted to rule Terreille. One was beloved while the other was hated for wanting the same thing. Why?

Impatient to hear the next part of the story, Saetien had started walking to Butler's cottage with only Shelby for company. It wasn't that far, and it wasn't dark yet. Besides, having Kieran and whoever was pulling the pony cart just sitting out there in the dark while she talked to Butler was foolish for both man and horse.

She was halfway to the cottage before Kieran and the pony cart caught up to her.

He said nothing. She picked up Shelby and climbed in.

"He won't open the door before he's ready," Kieran finally said.

"I know," she replied, "but the answers he gives me fill my head with more questions."

"That's not surprising. Families can be complicated."

That was certainly true of hers. It had begun to sink in, *really* sink in, that her father, whom she loved, had *hated* the woman who was her great-grandmother. And yet he'd married Surreal, Dorothea's granddaughter.

The horse stopped, then snorted when she didn't climb down.

"Shelby can wait here with us," Kieran said.

She climbed down and walked the rest of the way to the cottage, where she stood by the gate and waited. And waited.

The light was fading, but there was still enough for her to see the flower beds that created a wide border all along the fence and should have provided color along the front of the cottage, especially now that the spring flowers were starting to bloom.

"Can't the man tell the difference between a flower and a weed?" she muttered as she studied the beds. They were overgrown, unkempt, and full of weeds. They could be lovely with a little care.

Every year, her father had helped her plant flowers in a small space that was hers and hers alone. Tarl wouldn't let his gardeners touch a thing between the stakes that marked her part of the flower beds in the courtyard that was surrounded by the family's private rooms. Tarl would fill the watering can for her, and when she was very little he or her father would help her with the watering because the full can was heavy, but caring for the plants and pulling the weeds was up to her.

She'd been a fierce weeder.

She missed taking care of something that was just her own. She didn't count Shelby because she and Shelby took care of each other. Not the same thing as filling her hands with good earth.

The door opened. Butler walked down the flagstone path and stood on his side of the gate.

"You said Alexandra Angelline was Dorothea SaDiablo's pawn," Saetien said, trying not to sound like she was bursting with questions. "What did she do?"

"Alexandra arrived in Kaeleer with her daughter, Leland, and Philip Alexander, along with guards, escorts, and several Ladies who served in her court—and at least one man who was there to carry out Dorothea's orders," Butler replied. "She showed up at SaDiablo Hall with the intention of confronting the Warlord Prince of Dhemlan, the man she'd been told controlled Jaenelle and now also had Wilhelmina as his unwilling 'guest.' Whatever story Dorothea had spun about the man, Alexandra wasn't prepared to face the Black-Jeweled Warlord Prince who was the High Lord of Hell—and she wasn't prepared to see Daemon Sadi again. She wasn't prepared for the number of Warlord Princes in residence or the number of Queens who had gathered to take a look at someone they had considered an enemy since childhood.

"Wilhelmina was never without an escort, was never left unprotected. She didn't want to go back to Chaillot, didn't want to go back to any place in Terreille. Ordinary methods of persuasion weren't going to work to extract the girl from the High Lord's care and 'protection.' So Alexandra agreed to methods that required the skills of Dorothea's man. Hayll's High Priestess had provided her man with compulsion spells to use on Wilhelmina in order to get her away from the Hall and get her back to Hayll."

"You mean Chaillot," Saetien interrupted. "He would have taken her to Chaillot."

"Wilhelmina would have been Dorothea's 'guest' to make sure Alexandra continued to assist her efforts to get Jaenelle Angelline away from Saetan. Jaenelle was the real goal because whoever controlled the Queen of Ebon Askavi could control the Realms. A witch powerful enough to crush Saetan's and Daemon's power and bring those men to their knees? Factions of the Blood had been trying to get control of Jaenelle ever since Saetan became her legal guardian. What Dorothea and Alexandra didn't understand was that Saetan recognized the truth about his daughter's nature, and he didn't stand in front of Jaenelle in order to protect her from the rest of the Blood. He stood in front in order to protect the Blood from *her*."

"What could she do?"

Butler studied her as if the question puzzled him. "When Jaenelle was fifteen, the Dark Council insisted that Saetan wasn't a suitable guardian for a living girl and that they, the Council, would appoint someone else. Saetan descended to the full strength of his Black Jewel and prepared to destroy the Council. Before he could strike, Jaenelle said they could appoint another guardian when the sun next rose. Saetan was devastated by that pronouncement, since he loved her and he'd waited thousands of years for the Queen he was supposed to serve. The coven and the boyos, however, viewed her statement differently. Correctly, as it happened."

"What did happen?" Saetien asked when Butler didn't say anything else.

"The sun didn't rise. Not the next day or the one after that."

Saetien's jaw dropped. How awful, how *terrifying*, to wait for a sunrise that never came. Waiting in a forever-dark world. Did the Blood outside of this Dark Council know why the night didn't end? "But the sun did rise. It had to."

Butler nodded. "Eventually, it did. The Council sent one of its members, a man who got along well with the High Lord, and requested—begged, if you want the truth of it—that Saetan remain Jaenelle's guardian and that he ask his daughter to restore the sun. Which he did when the Seneschal finally granted him admittance to the Keep.

"Love was the only leash that could hold Jaenelle Angelline, but it was a leash that had a knife edge honed for war and had to be handled carefully."

Butler hadn't created a ball of witchlight, so he was little more than a dark shape backlit by the lights shining from the cottage windows. Somehow, that felt right for the telling—and hearing—of this part of the story.

"Dorothea's man, Osvald, used the compulsion spells and got Wilhelmina away from her rooms," Butler continued. "But he didn't take into account that kindred would react the same way as a human protector, and Wilhelmina had become friends with a young tiger Warlord Prince named Dejaal, who was the son of Jaal, a Green-Jeweled Warlord Prince who served in Jaenelle's First Circle. Wilhelmina was frightened and struggled, despite the spells Osvald had used, and Dejaal responded the same way any other Warlord Prince would respond—he attacked the man who was hurting his friend. A call to battle spread through the Hall, and kindred and humans converged on the area. An Eyrien Warlord Prince who was Lucivar's second-in-command at the time wounded Osvald, but Dejaal had been killed before the others joined the fight."

Saetien shook her head. "The residential areas of the Hall are made up of blocks of rooms that surround open-air courtyards. Unless you can fly, there's no quick way to leave."

"No, there's not," Butler agreed. "And in a place where one male sounding the alarm has *all* males responding as if they're standing on a battleground—or a killing field—a man has no chance of removing a woman who doesn't want to go with him. But Osvald tried, and a young Warlord Prince died because of it."

"What happened to Osvald?"

Silence. Another of those moments when Butler looked away. "The son of a Brother in the Court was killed by an enemy on home ground. When something like that happens, the males in the First Circle have the right to decide on the form of execution. They gave Osvald to Jaal and Kaelas, who was a Red-Jeweled Arcerian Warlord Prince. I don't know what those two cats did to that man, but having seen what two cats the size of Jaal and Kaelas can do to a human, it would have been a terrible way to die."

"But Wilhelmina was saved."

"Yes."

When he didn't say anything else, Saetien realized he

was waiting for her next question. What was she supposed to ask?

Think. Think. When it's a court, it's never just the person who commits the act who is held accountable. A debt is owed by the person who gave the order.

After a minute, Butler said, "When a Queen comes to another Queen's territory to visit or for business reasons and brings members of her court to serve her—or protect her—it is expected that she will hold the leash on everyone who came with her, that she will make sure they behave properly and not cause trouble for the hosting Queen or her court. For allowing Osvald to try to abduct Wilhelmina, Alexandra was held accountable for the death of Dejaal."

"But she wasn't executed," Saetien said quickly. "She didn't actually kill the tiger."

"She wasn't executed. She was stripped of her power, broken back to basic Craft. Still a Queen but no longer able to wear any Jewels."

Saetien stood there with her mouth open. A Queen without any power? How . . . ? "The High Lord *broke* her?"

"No," Butler said quietly. "The Queen of Ebon Askavi broke the Queen whose actions led to the death of a member of the Dark Court. Witch broke Alexandra."

"But . . . Alexandra was Jaenelle's grandmother. Witch *broke her own grandmother*?"

"What would you have had her do?" Butler's voice turned sharp. "Oohhh, I see. Alexandra should have been reprimanded for violating her responsibilities as a Queen and a guest, should have had her wrist slapped and been told she was naughty, but should not have suffered any real consequences? After all, it wasn't a *human* that was killed, was it? A Warlord Prince, yes, but just a tiger. Just an animal. Nothing important enough to defend."

"I didn't say that," Saetien snapped. But the thought had been there, quickly followed by anger that anyone would think that Shelby might be expendable because he was a dog. "But she did it to her grandmother."

"Witch called in the debt owed to her by another Queen.

Alexandra being a relative had nothing to do with Jaenelle's decision. It couldn't. That is the price of being a Queen. Every personal decision, every private choice, has consequences, since *every* choice affects your court. You've seen Witch, seen the Self that lived beneath the human skin. Living myth, dreams made flesh. But not all the dreamers were human, Saetien. Generations of kindred dreamed of a Queen who would help them, who would protect them from humans who saw them as less. Centuries of Blood with one desire. Centuries during which three strong men yearned for the Queen they wanted, *needed*, to serve. It took a long time for all those dreams to come together to shape the Queen Kaeleer needed. To shape the Queen that Saetan needed. And Lucivar needed. And Daemon needed.

"Not all the dreamers were human. *That* is why Jaenelle Angelline was beloved as a Queen and could rule the Realm of Kaeleer. Every race in the Shadow Realm had a little part of the making of this Queen, and Jaenelle saw no difference between a Warlord Prince who was a tiger and a Warlord Prince who was a human. If he was under her hand, he was hers to protect—and she did protect her own."

"Then why was Jaenelle born in Chaillot? Why wasn't she born someplace in Kaeleer? Why did she end up being Alexandra's granddaughter?"

"Because Alexandra was also one of the dreamers," Butler said quietly. "But unlike Saetan and Lucivar and Daemon, she didn't recognize the dream—and so many terrible things happened because of that. Those terrible things also became part of the living myth, just as Saetan's love—and Daemon's and Lucivar's love—also helped shape who Witch became."

"What happened to Alexandra?" Saetien asked.

"Alexandra, Leland, Philip, and the rest of the people Alexandra brought with her were escorted through the Gate nearest to Chaillot. As far as I know, they returned to Beldon Mor."

"But Wilhelmina stayed."

"Yes, Wilhelmina stayed."

"And she forgave Jaenelle for breaking their grand-mother?"

"In the discussion between Wilhelmina and Jaenelle that followed Alexandra's return to Chaillot, Wilhelmina conveniently forgot that Jaenelle had been protecting her for most of their lives. She said things that caused a heart wound that never fully healed—and that was the last time the two of them were together."

Butler's voice sounded bitter, and Saetien heard an anger that *still* burned for a woman who died centuries ago.

"What happened between Wilhelmina and Jaenelle?" Saetien asked.

Butler shook his head. "That's enough for tonight."

"Will you tell me?"

"Yes. But not tonight." Butler started to walk away; then he returned to the gate. "Who decides which races are human enough to be important, Saetien? What are the requirements? That a being have two arms and two legs? That they have hair and not fur? Skin that is all one color?" He paused. "What about wings? Is that not a sign that a race might be less than human?"

"How dare you!" The Eyrien race not considered human just because they had wings? Her *cousins* not considered human? What a filthy thing to say.

"If Jaenelle hadn't stopped the Dark Council and the Terreilleans who coveted kindred lands by refusing to see *any* race as less, do you really think it wouldn't have come to that eventually?"

Butler returned to his cottage and closed the door, leaving Saetien shrouded in dark thoughts about things she had never considered because she'd never had to.

FORTY

Daemon didn't know why Lucivar felt Holt, Beale, Helene, Nadene, Raine, Weston, and Brenda were needed for this discussion, but if Lucivar wanted reinforcements, Daemon was certain he wasn't going to like whatever his brother wanted to discuss. The only positive he could see was that Lucivar hadn't asked Liath to attend this meeting.

Maybe Yaslana was saving the Sceltie Warlord Prince in case Daemon was foolish enough not to cooperate with the humans.

He stared at his brother. "I'm listening."

"The Warlord Princes have formed their own pack, with Daemonar as the dominant and Raeth as his second-in-command," Lucivar said. "It looks like Raeth and Trent have a preference for working with Zoey and her friends, but that could be because Titian is one of those friends, which means Daemonar takes a sharp interest in those girls. Also, Grizande is now in the mix, and my first-born feels protective of her."

"Grizande wears a Sapphire Jewel and is well able to take care of herself," Brenda said, waggling her fingers to remind everyone that the Tigre witch had claws.

"Maybe in a physical fight," Daemon replied, "but there are other ways to wound someone. And there are the three days in every woman's moontime when she is vulnerable."

He waited for an argument and felt relieved when he didn't get one.

No one in the room who knew about Grizande's past mentioned the scars she carried from being tortured—a testimony that even the powerful, when young, couldn't always defend themselves. That was something he and Lucivar knew well.

"The two Princes and the Warlords are still sorting themselves out as far as which Queen they prefer to follow and who is a friend and who is just tolerated, but there's not much squabbling among themselves," Lucivar said.

Could be because they're too exhausted to squabble, Daemon thought. Eyrien stamina was not to be underestimated, and with Daemonar leading, the boys were either studying, sweating through weapons practice, playing physically active games with the kindred or among themselves, or falling asleep on their feet if they didn't manage to fall on a mattress first.

"The problem I'm seeing is the pissing contests that have boiled up between the Queens," Lucivar continued. "Zoey wears Birthright Opal, which is the darkest Jewel among the Queens and should make her dominant, but she's backing away from every disagreement instead of drawing a line and setting her heels down. And the reason for that is that the other Queens, led by Dinah, piled on her in a verbal dogfight."

"Not exactly," Raine corrected. "It's more that the other three Queens stood back and did nothing, waiting to see who won the fight for dominance, although I think Kathlene would have stepped up to the line and stood with Zoey before much longer."

Daemon studied the Dharo Prince. "Now that Dinah is gone, what is your assessment of the young Queens?"

Raine thought for a moment. "Zoey is sparkle and energy. She wants to be helpful—maybe too helpful at times. She might need firmer boundaries and more protection for a while. Kathlene is . . . solid. She's a quiet girl who watches and listens and is more intent on absorbing the lessons than any of the other girls—including Zoey. With proper nurturing, she'll grow up into a strong Queen. Felisha?" He shrugged. "She might settle into being a solid Queen. But Azara holds on to an opinion as well as a colander holds on to water. She just wants to back whoever is dominant, regardless of right or wrong. That makes me uneasy."

"Who is dominant among them will change a dozen times before any of those girls are old enough to form an official court," Daemon said. "Hell's fire, who is dominant changes every time someone enters or leaves a room."

"But the caliber of the Queen will not change in any significant way," Beale replied quietly. "They have reached an age where they are what they will be. What you teach them will help them discover their potential and refine what is inside them, but it won't change them."

"It might change them in some ways, especially if one of them is floundering because another among them keeps cutting the ground out from under her," Lucivar countered. "Protect and defend, whether the weapon being used is a whip or a word. But before we decide who we defend, we need to know what kind of Queens we're dealing with. We need to confirm Raine's assessment."

"Lucivar, they're still children," Daemon said. Was he arguing because he disagreed or because he needed to believe a girl could change if given a chance?

Maybe not change, he thought. *Maybe rediscover who she is?*

Putting thoughts of Saetien aside, he focused on the people in his study and the current discussion.

"You know better than that, Bastard," Lucivar said. "We saw plenty of Queens this age when we lived in Terreille, saw which ones already had a taste for cruelty and which ones wouldn't stand up for their people if there was any risk or inconvenience to themselves."

"What are you proposing?" he asked.

"We—"

"Meaning me, since you won't be here most of the time."

"Fine. You"—Lucivar circled with a finger to indicate all the adults in the room—"will conduct some scenarios that will give the children a challenge similar to something they might face as a ruling Queen or a member of a court. When Father did this kind of exercise one season, he assigned one of the coven to be the ruling Queen for that day and the other Queens were Province Queens or District Queens under her hand. That way they each experienced what it was like to have to answer to someone else or be a Territory's last voice in any conflict. The boyos were assigned to a Queen, and Father, along with Beale and Helene, assigned servants to assist in whatever task the Queen was given."

Beale, Helene, and Holt were working at the Hall when Jaenelle and the coven were adolescents. They all looked suspiciously stoic.

"What went wrong?" Daemon asked—because it was clear to him that *something* had gone wrong.

"It was Jaenelle and the coven," Lucivar replied. "They had no problem with following whoever was supposed to lead that day as long as an assignment went smoothly, but as soon as there was trouble, they reverted to their natural order of dominance. And when one of them was assigned to be a bad Queen and do something . . . hurtful . . . in some way—and defend her position—there was a lot of yelling. Usually at Father, because he'd made up the scenario."

"Hurtful?" Daemon asked too softly.

"As in being a guest in another Queen's court and being discourteous to members of the court or the servants working at the residence, or trying to persuade a servant to let the guest into a room that was private—or into Beale's pantry to snitch a bottle of wine. Or being a Queen who allowed someone in her court to steal from a merchant. Problem was, they all rebelled at being a bad Queen, even in an exercise."

"The time they were told someone in a visiting Queen's court kicked a puppy," Holt murmured.

Daemon's temper went cold. The men—and Helene and Nadene—shuddered as the air in the room turned frigid. Brenda just called in a heavy wool shawl and wrapped it around her shoulders.

"Well," Lucivar said, eyeing Daemon, "it's a good thing you weren't here for these scenarios. As it was, we almost had a war inside the Hall when the coven, the boyos, and the kindred exploded into a hunt for that person."

"Who was imaginary," Holt said. "And thank the Darkness for that."

Lucivar nodded. "Yeah. That was invigorating. It wasn't even an approved scenario. A servant, thinking to add some drama into the exercises—or maybe wanting a bit of malicious fun—spread the rumor."

"It sounds terrifying," Raine said.

"That's what Lucivar meant by 'invigorating,'" Daemon said dryly.

"After that, the High Lord purchased a dressmaker's dummy and a few outfits for various social functions," Helene said. "Lady Dumm became the Queen with shaky scruples whose court got up to all manner of unsavory things. A couple of the maids were assigned to be Lady Dumm's dressers, and a couple of footmen were responsible for putting her in the proper room for whatever was happening. She was even assigned a guest room to hold her wardrobe, and was sometimes seen taking a stroll through the gardens or being driven through Halaway. When the shopkeepers in Halaway understood the purpose of Lady Dumm's existence, they participated by submitting complaints about misconduct by one of Dumm's First Circle."

"The point was for the coven to experience the conflicts that can occur when the line between what is right and what is wrong starts getting smudged," Lucivar said. "It didn't work well because all the Queens in the coven were already united around Witch. But the girls who are here now aren't united. There are rivalries. Bring those out into the open. Force the girls—and the boys—to take a stand. And then we'll see what happens."

Daemon sat back. "It sounds risky, both physically and emotionally."

"I'm not saying it isn't," Lucivar replied. "And it's possible that things will happen here that will never be forgiven."

"We can't let it get that far," Brenda said. "We have to intervene before a scenario becomes too scalding, or you'll have Queens who are enemies for the rest of their lives— and that's bad enough when people live decades instead of centuries. And I'm thinking that kind of anger is some of what happened in Terreille that turned that Realm into such a mess." She looked at Daemon, then at Lucivar. "Am I wrong?"

"You're not wrong," Daemon replied. "Allowing the children to act out a scenario and then discuss it during their classes might be useful at this point. But I don't feel easy about this. Corruption begins with something small. Giving in to that small act makes it harder to refuse to do the next thing you're asked that you know is wrong, and the thing after that." He thought about where he needed to draw the lines for the children—and for himself. "No scenario will include a physical or verbal assault. Not even something as small as slapping someone's hand as discipline. And nothing that involves the kindred."

"Shuffle the deck," Raine suggested. "Four Queens in residence. Each morning, tell them who is ruling that day and what tasks need to be performed. The ruling Queen distributes the assignments. The rest of the students report to whichever Queen they're assigned to that day. Obeying someone you like and trust isn't the same experience as obeying someone you don't know as well but still need to follow in order to do the work."

Daemon nodded. "A valid point."

"Daemonar and Grizande should be excluded from this exercise," Lucivar said. "Daemonar because he won't pretend to serve another Queen and he'll simply fight anyone trying to give him orders. And Grizande has already seen enough of what bad Queens will do. I don't think she'll understand pretending, especially if anyone gets carried away and smudges a line in terms of honor."

"Agreed." Daemon pushed away from his desk. "We'll start with something simple." *And keep it simple.* "Lady Brenda, Prince Raine, your participation is appreciated."

Raine gave Daemon a small bow. "Sir." He held out a hand to Brenda, who gave Daemon a long look before allowing Raine to lead her from the room, followed by Weston and Nadene.

Daemon focused on Holt, Beale, and Helene. "A dressmaker's dummy as an adversary sounds like a good idea." *He hoped.* "I don't suppose Lady Dumm is residing in the attics somewhere?"

The three servants exchanged a look.

Beale cleared his throat. "Lady Dumm made a disparaging remark about the young Ladies within the hearing of Jaal, Kaelas, and Ladvarian. We were never sure if the cats at that age understood all the words, but Ladvarian did and . . . Well, it *was* Jaal and Kaelas."

"Ah." *The cats might have been disappointed that the bad human had no meat, but that wouldn't have stopped them from ripping the enemy to pieces.*

"I'm sure my staff and I can come up with a new Lady Dumm," Helene said, "if you'll give your consent for us to purchase a basic wardrobe from the shops in Halaway."

"That's fine. Just keep in mind, our guest doesn't need to be extravagant in her tastes."

"Of course, Prince." Helene gave Daemon a nod before walking out of the study with Beale and Holt.

"I'm in trouble," Daemon said.

Lucivar nodded. "Probably. But between the kindred who live here and the senior staff and the instructors, you should have enough observers to make sure no one crosses a line."

"This friction between the girls happened when I wasn't here. I can't always be here, Prick."

"It came to the surface because you weren't here," Lucivar countered. "You can't say that Zoey doesn't get special treatment, because she does—and some of the girls know why. Those who don't? It's none of their business. But once Surreal was through with them, I think all the children acquired some understanding of at least part of what Zoey endured." A pause. "If you're uncomfortable with this, don't do it."

"I'll think about it."

"Anything you want me to ask the Keep's residents about this?"

Daemon groaned. "Hell's fire, no. Helene looked sufficiently gleeful about bringing Lady Dumm back as a guest. I don't need suggestions from Jaenelle and Karla."

"Yeah." Lucivar rubbed the back of his neck. "The exercise didn't run that long, but Father *said* it was useful. I think it was more useful for him than the coven and boyos, although the girls did have fun with Lady Dumm."

"Something to look forward to."

When it came to meals, the Hall kept "country hours," a practical measure that allowed everyone to tuck in early. Not that all the youngsters valued sleep at that age. Still, it gave Daemon quiet evenings and time to fulfill adult social obligations.

Tonight his evening wasn't quiet or an obligation. Social? Maybe.

Daemon knocked on the door of Tersa's cottage and waited for someone to answer. He sincerely hoped it wouldn't be Keely, the Sceltie Black Widow who was learning the Hourglass's Craft from his mother. Keely had been known to slam the door in his face if on his previous visit he'd done something that she thought had upset Tersa. Most of the time he had no idea what he'd done, and the Sceltie didn't feel the need to explain—even to the High Lord of Hell.

Mikal opened the door. "Good evening, sir. You're just in time for coffee."

"Late dinner?"

"A little. Lady Jhett and Lady Grizande stopped by this

afternoon. They delivered a basket of treats to the Sisters of the Hourglass who are living in Surreal's house, and dropped off a smaller basket for Tersa and me. Plus treats for all the Scelties living in both places."

Daemon followed Mikal into the kitchen. "Jhett and Grizande?"

"It's an interesting friendship. And as far as I've heard, Jhett is the only young Black Widow living at the Hall who has gone to visit the recovering Sisters, and Grizande displays a practical sympathy and patience when the world . . . becomes veiled."

Something he would keep in mind.

Tersa set the mugs on the table with a clatter. "It's my boy." She started to smile, but the smile faded as she moved toward him and placed a hand on his chest. "Twinges. Troubles."

"Troubles," he agreed, refusing to acknowledge the other part of what she said, since the twinges were over in a moment and likely didn't mean anything. Not yet, anyway.

"Sit," Tersa ordered. "We have treats."

"Would you like me . . . ?" Mikal began.

"Please stay," Daemon replied. "I'd like your wisdom as well as Tersa's."

"I have wisdom?"

"In this case, yes."

As they drank coffee, Daemon told Tersa and Mikal about the proposed scenarios to be used as active lessons. He admitted he wasn't sure the exercises had sufficient value.

Then Mikal let out a hoot. "Are you bringing back Lady Dumm? I don't remember much because I was considered too young to participate, but I remember the times when she rode through the village in one of the Hall's open carriages. And the time she attended a play that Beron had a part in and critiqued his performance while he was onstage. Beron had been warned that she was going to do that so he wouldn't be upset, but no one had told Mother. If Uncle Saetan hadn't held on to her, she would have climbed over the seats and killed Dumm flatter than dead."

"Perhaps I can persuade Beron to give me a day or two as a guest," Daemon said.

"If you tell him he can bring a few friends, they can put on a small production for you."

"Interesting thought." At the Hall there was a room with a stage. He'd have to check with Beale and make sure it was still intact. He turned to his mother. "Tersa? What do you think?"

"Skin stripped away, revealing the truth beneath." Her gold eyes held the clarity of madness. "Shuffle the cards; roll the dice. See who stands and who falls."

"Will the children be in danger?" he asked softly.

"Sometimes pain is a necessary teacher."

Not a comforting answer.

He changed the subject and they talked about books and about the village.

Late that night, while Breen slept, Daemon spun a tangled web of dreams and visions.

See who stands and who falls. The web didn't give him an answer to that, but the web revealed the whisper that Tersa had left unsaid: *While you can.*

FORTY-ONE

Daemon stared at the object surrounded by people who worked for him—people he had mistakenly thought were sensible. And they *had* been sensible until one Green-Jeweled witch from Scelt had taken up residence at the Hall.

"What is it?" he asked. Better to know the nature of an enemy than to ignore a threat inside your own walls.

Brenda gave him a terrifyingly bright smile, but it was Helene who said with undisguised glee, "This is the new Lady Dumm."

Hell's fire.

"We used a dressmaker's dummy for the torso," Brenda said. "Then we padded it."

"I can see that," he murmured as he eyed the bust and waist and everything else.

"The girls from Scelt, as well as some of Helene's staff, are fair hands with a needle and thread, so they made up proper arms and legs," Brenda continued. "And look." She pressed on Lady Dumm's shoulder, which somehow bent the thing's hips. "Tarl and his lads came up with the idea to make bones out of lengths of wood and attach them in a way that allows her joints to bend."

Daemon stared at Tarl, who held his eyes for a moment before deciding to study the carpet.

Carpets at the Hall received a great deal of study.

Lady Dumm now sat in a chair, dressed for afternoon

visits. Maybe. "No face or hair?" he asked. The hat wouldn't have left much hair visible in any case, but wearing anything that had that many plumes was asking for trouble with a tiger in residence.

"We thought the Scelties might get confused if they saw something with an actual face," Brenda said. "This way they can see it's just a pretend human that we're using for the young humans' lessons. But we did add this."

He wasn't sure what Brenda touched, but he felt a spell engage before Dumm sneezed, then said in a stentorian voice, "I need a hanky!"

Daemon clenched his teeth.

Helene and Brenda looked at him expectantly.

He called in a handkerchief and held it out—to Brenda. The sun would shine in Hell before he willingly approached Dumm.

"When will our guest—who is an aristo from a prominent family but *not* a Queen—arrive?" He'd draw that line and hold it. This version of Dumm would be trouble enough without belonging to the caste that was the Blood's moral center.

"In a couple of days," Brenda said. "We're still working on some of her wardrobe. But we're thinking that you should start the exercises ahead of that, give the children a couple of days to get used to how this all works before we add Dumm to the mix."

"Very well. I'll explain this new set of exercises to the children, and we'll start tomorrow."

Daemon walked out of the guest room. He ignored everyone's effort to catch his attention. He simply kept going until he reached his study. Once inside, he secured all the locks on the door. Then he contacted Lucivar on an Ebongray psychic thread.

Prick?

Bastard? Something wrong?

I've just met Lady Dumm. The next time I see you I am going to kill you flatter than dead.

I thought the dummy was destroyed.

People who work for me created a new one. This one talks. Apparently, so did the previous version, but that was beside the point.

Silence filled the link between them.

Prick?

I'll check with Marian and find out if she's made any commitments for us. If we're available, we'll come to the Hall for an overnight visit. Soon.

Do that. Daemon broke the link between them, then aimed for the sofa, where he intended to stretch out for an hour—or a century.

He'd barely gotten horizontal when someone tapped on the study door.

Putting an arm over his face, he used Craft to disengage the locks and open the door to allow Beale into the room. He felt his butler walk up to the sofa, but there were no sounds, no words.

"Beale?" Daemon finally said.

"I used to find your father in here looking just like that," Beale answered.

Daemon lifted his arm enough to stare at his butler. "I am not surprised. I don't know how successful these exercises will be for the intended group of participants, but I recognize the ringleader who is encouraging the staff to engage in—"

"Fun?" Beale suggested.

He was going to say "outrageous schemes," but the amusement, mixed with a bit of sympathy, in Beale's eyes told him all he currently needed to know about life at the Hall when Jaenelle and the coven were in residence.

"Ah, Beale. I do not want to get in trouble with your wife over Lady Dumm's behavior—whatever that behavior may include."

"Understood, Prince. I will explain things to Mrs. Beale. However, if this Lady Dumm should try to enter the kitchens . . ."

Daemon jackknifed to a sitting position. "You have my permission to roast her on a spit. I'll help you."

Beale's lips twitched. "Very good." The butler turned and strode to the door—and didn't quite manage to close the door all the way before he started laughing.

Zoey listened to Prince Sadi explain the new exercise that was supposed to start tomorrow, and she didn't know what to think. Sure, District Queens had to answer to Province Queens, who had to answer to Territory Queens, and even Territory Queens took orders from *someone* before they became Territory Queens, but why did the Queens have to lose all their friends and deal with people they didn't know well? How could a court function like that? Why couldn't each of them keep at least a couple of their friends while the rest were shuffled? But how to choose? And would those who weren't chosen feel resentful?

Why were Daemonar and Grizande not included? They were students too.

Zoey? Allis nudged her calf. *Why are you smelling afraid?*

Am I? Zoey placed her hand on the Sceltie's head. Prince Sadi wouldn't take away Allis, too, would he?

"We'll do a five-day rotation," Prince Sadi said. "The other two days will be for studying, resting, and social activities of your choosing."

Five days? How . . . ?

Zoey glanced at Kathlene, Azara, and Felisha—and realized the other three Queens were looking at her.

Ask him, Kathlene said on a psychic thread.

You ask him, Zoey replied. She wasn't going to put herself forward again.

Sadi said nothing; just waited. The Queens said nothing.

Finally Raeth huffed out a breath and said, "Prince? I count four Queens here. Who takes the fifth day in the rotation?"

Sadi smiled, looking pleased that *someone* had enough spine to ask the obvious question. "On the fifth day, the Queens, with their court of the day, will be under the hand of the Warlord Prince of Dhemlan and taking orders from him."

Zoey wasn't sure what was going to happen on the other days, but even if she wasn't working with her friends, she would still be safe when Prince Sadi was in charge.

FORTY-TWO

The physical part of the new exercise seemed fairly simple. A basket of envelopes was delivered to the social room connected to the square of bedrooms where each group of youngsters resided. The Queen's envelope had her name on it and the card inside informed her of the order of dominance among the Queens.

Everyone else took a card from a blank envelope and learned which Queen they were serving that day. They would report to that Queen when they gathered for breakfast, since each court would begin the day with their Queen.

"Kathlene is the 'dominant' Queen," Zoey said, pressing a hand to her stomach. Before that disastrous house party, before she had been dosed with *safframate*, she would have seen this exercise as a challenge instead of something to fear. Now? She hated that she felt like such a coward about taking orders from someone—even someone like Kathlene, whom she liked and trusted in most ways. Titian looked at Zoey's card. "Felisha is the 'Province' Queen, and you and Azara are 'District' Queens."

"Who are you serving today?"

"Azara. I can talk to Uncle Daemon and see if he'll let me switch."

"No special treatment. The other girls resent me enough as it is."

Arlene and Laureen were part of her court that day, so

she had with her two friends whom she could trust. Three when she counted Allis. But Cara, who was also part of her court today, had been a good friend of Dinah's. The girl hadn't said anything, but the accusing looks she gave Zoey when she thought no one would notice scraped nerves that were already raw.

Jhett and Grizande approached the table with the basket. Titian handed Jhett the last envelope in the basket.

"I guess you have a different assignment," Zoey said when Grizande looked at the empty basket.

"Simple learning," Grizande replied.

Did she feel excluded? Did it sting to be left out—or was Grizande used to that?

"I'm with Kathlene today," Jhett said.

Titian put an arm around Zoey's waist—all the warmth and comfort she'd have today.

As they left their square of rooms, subdued and uncertain about what was ahead of them, Daemonar stepped into the corridor. With his longer stride, he easily caught up to Zoey and Titian.

"What's wrong?" he asked.

"Nothing," Zoey snapped. "I'm fine."

Daemonar huffed. "You're pale and sweating. You get any finer, you'll spend the day in Lady Nadene's healing room dosed with a sedative."

Zoey shuddered at the idea of being dosed with anything.

"Don't pester her," Titian said. "Uncle Daemon is being mean making us do this."

"You haven't done anything so far."

If Titian started defending her and snapped at Daemonar, they'd both be in trouble again. "Prince Yaslana, please leave us alone. I can't deal with you now."

Daemonar took a step to the side and let them continue alone.

Daemonar watched Zoey and the other girls, and was aware of Grizande coming to stand beside him.

"Zoey Queen is much—is very—afraid," Grizande said. "'Very' is right word?"

Daemonar nodded. "That is the right word. And yes, Zoey is very afraid. Too much afraid."

"Why we not part of this learning?"

She sounded a bit . . . snarly . . . that she wasn't included—and that made him smile. "I don't know. We're to report to Prince Sadi after breakfast. You can ask him then."

Daemon wasn't sure how to read Daemonar's mood, but Grizande was fairly exercised about something, and if he didn't want his blackwood desk used as a scratching post, he needed to make an effort to find out what had rubbed her the wrong way.

Daemonar nudged Grizande. "You first."

"Why we not included in learning?" she asked.

Maybe it was meant to be a polite question, but her green eyes had that predator's stare and her hands kept flexing, giving him glimpses of her claws.

"If important enough for Queens, we should learn," she continued.

"You and Daemonar aren't included because you've already experienced what these lessons are attempting to teach the other youngsters," Daemon replied. "Also, you both are already under the hand of a powerful Queen, and you answer to her. It would be difficult for you to work with another Queen in the way these lessons are intended. Besides, I would like you to focus on learning the common tongue so that you can speak it, read it, and write it. I'd also like you to learn to ride a horse. Queen Grizande and Prince Elan were excellent riders and went out riding with the Lady whenever they visited the Hall. You can be just as good."

"You should learn to ride a horse," Daemonar said.

Grizande growled. "Have feet. Can walk."

"And I can fly. It's still a good idea to learn to ride a horse—especially kindred horses."

"That . . . ?" She made a gesture that didn't need words. *Mountain.*

"The other horses are smaller," Daemon said dryly.

"Huh."

"You should report to Prince Raine. He has assignments for both of you." When neither of them moved away from his desk, he sat back. "Something else?"

"Zoey is afraid," Daemonar said.

"Of what?" Daemon asked softly.

"Not sure, but she needs watching, because something about this exercise has her by the guts."

"All right."

"Maybe not trust other Queens to give safe orders," Grizande said. "And afraid because friends are gone."

"The friends who aren't with her during the day will be around in the evenings," Daemon pointed out.

Grizande shook her head. "Allis tells Jaalan and Liath that Zoey Queen is afraid that Allis will be taken away. Allis is protector *and* friend."

So, Daemon thought. *Whatever was suppressed during Zoey's physical recovery is surfacing now.* He'd have to inform Zhara about this development.

"A court is not a static thing," he said. "People serve for a while and then leave, and new people take their place. A Queen who is always afraid of new people, who can't trust her instincts, will end up being unable to rule at all. I'll inform the instructors that Zoey may need help. You're outside of these exercises, but your own tasks will bring you in contact with the other youngsters throughout the day. If either of you notice Zoey being too afraid, tell me or any of the senior staff or instructors. They'll step in and get her out of the exercise. And Lord Weston will always be nearby when the children aren't in a classroom with an instructor."

"Yes, sir," Daemonar said. A beat of hesitation. "Zoey might not be the only one who has trouble."

"If you notice anything that pricks your instincts, let me know. Otherwise, the two of you have your own assignments, and Prince Raine is expecting you."

As soon as the two youngsters left, he requested Brenda's presence.

"Lots of pale faces at the breakfast table." She checked the time on her pocket watch before sitting in one of the chairs in front of his desk. "This lot is acting like foals spooking at shadows and laundry on the line. I saw the list of assignments for the day, and I know for a fact that juvenile Scelties are given similar assignments during their training at the school, may the Darkness have mercy on the poor humans who are on the receiving end of those queries. So I'm thinking it's the strangeness of it—or maybe Lady Surreal showed them all a little too well what could happen if they aren't smart and careful."

He hadn't considered that, and he should have since Lucivar had said something similar about Surreal's lesson.

"Still," Brenda continued, "if you don't get back up on a horse after taking a fall, you will never learn to ride, and you'll never trust yourself and your horse if you're faced with a situation where you have to take a risk."

"Speaking of horses, I'd like Grizande to learn how to ride. Is that something you could help with?"

"If she's willing to learn, I can teach her—especially since you have kindred horses here." She waited. "Anything else?"

"Zoey."

Brenda nodded. "You can't be asking Allis to step aside when her human needs her so much, but I can see how the other girls might think they're being slighted a bit by not having one of the kindred in their courts. You've plenty of Scelties here at the present. Ask them to help the young Queens."

Daemon felt a tickle in his throat. "Not Liath."

"Oh, Hell's fire, no. A Green-Jeweled Warlord Prince? You can't put him in the mix any more than you can put Daemonar—and for the same reasons. That kind of strength doesn't put up with these kinds of exercises for long. Too bossy, for one thing, and not inclined to follow orders from anyone who doesn't outrank them."

"Well, if all the Queens have a Sceltie in their courts, Zoey won't be singled out."

Brenda gave him a smile that was too knowing. "That's not the lesson, as you're well aware. Human or sheep, a Sceltie herds. And Queen or ewe, if she strays from what is deemed proper, she will get nipped one way or another."

He quietly cleared his throat. "We should both get on with our work."

"Indeed we should."

As she opened his study door, she pulled out her pocket watch and checked the time—and he wondered if he would ever have balls enough to ask her why she did that.

Each Queen had seven people in her court, plus two maids and two footmen to fetch and carry or to deliver messages.

At Kathlene's command, the Queens and their courts assembled in the Hall's main library—and stared at the books piled on the library tables and on the floor. Only one section of the library, thank the Darkness, but still!

"What happened?" Zoey asked the question before remembering she didn't want to call attention to herself.

"Prince Sadi is entertaining a guest from a prominent aristo family, and she selected a few books to read while she is recovering from her arduous journey," Kathlene replied, her stilted speech making it clear that she was repeating what she'd been told.

Raeth stared at the empty shelves. "She had to pull this many books off the shelves in order to find *a few* books? Who *is* this woman?"

Zoey, along with everyone else, turned to look at the servants standing behind them, waiting for their instructions.

The servants exchanged looks before Neala, one of the girls from Scelt, said, "We haven't seen her, but those who have say she's fearsome and tends to speak her mind, regardless of who is in the room."

"So." Kathlene's voice called their attention back to the

Queen they were supposed to be serving that day. "I've been given a list of tasks, including restoring the library to its proper order. My court will take on that task, in case Lady Dumm or one of her companions returns for more selections."

"Dumm?" Trent said. "That's her name?"

Kathlene nodded.

"I've never heard of anyone by that name," Azara said. "If she's from such a prominent family, why haven't we heard of her?"

"Maybe she's from another Territory," Jhett said.

"Well, we'll find out tomorrow," Kathlene said. "I was told Lady Dumm prefers to ride in an open carriage and will be enjoying the air around the estate as well as going to Halaway."

"If she has companions, they may prefer to ride horses," Zoey said, unable to stop herself from trying to help.

Kathlene nodded. "I wasn't informed if she has any companions with her, but that's a good point. Lady Zoela, please inquire at the stables about the availability of a carriage as well as riding horses for the guests. Felisha, we have to check with the estate's farm and find out what is available, and then consult with Mrs. Beale about what she might need from the shops in Halaway in the way of foods she will have to purchase."

"Consult?" Felisha's voice rose in pitch. *"With Mrs. Beale?"*

Kathlene hesitated.

"Ask the Dharo Boy," Titian said. "He's Mrs. Beale's primary assistant. He could check the menus for Prince Sadi's table."

Kathlene nodded. "Yes. Felisha, you can check with him instead."

"Thank the Darkness," one of the boys muttered.

Zoey wasn't sure who had said it, but she was certain they were *all* thinking it.

Kathlene continued with the assignments. "Azara, you and your people will check with the gardeners. I was told Lady Dumm requires fresh flowers in her room every day, and we need to find out what is available from the Hall's gardens. Is there a greenhouse here?"

"There is," Titian replied.

"I'll check what's available there too," Azara said.

"Then let's get started," Kathlene said.

The stable master stared at Zoey and growled, "Lady Dumm, is it? She's back?"

"Back?" Zoey hadn't considered that Lady Dumm might have visited the Hall before.

"I wasn't stable master then, but I well remember her."

Who is she? What's she like? Which family does she come from?

Not questions a Queen could ask a stable master, but if someone in her court were to show some curiosity? *Caede? Could you . . . ?*

The Warlord Prince didn't look at her, but he dipped his head in the slightest nod.

"We have a carriage the *Lady* can use, and horses who will pull it," the stable master said.

"Riding horses for her companions?" Zoey asked.

"Companions? She brought companions?"

Hell's fire, the man looked ready to chew nails—and Zoey wondered if, with an unintended bit of Craft, a person could set his own hair on fire through the sheer heat of temper. "We're not sure. I was asked to see if horses would be available."

After an excruciatingly long time, the man finally nodded. "Best to plan on her *companions* not having much experience on a horse. I'll see about having a few available who won't be inclined to toss an ill-mannered rider into the trees—or into the lake. Best to find out if Lady Dumm's companions know how to swim."

"Thank you for the information," Zoey said weakly. "I will inquire if Lady Dumm's companions are partial to swimming."

Zoey and her court, except for Caede, left the stables

and slowly headed for the Hall. He caught up a couple of minutes later.

"He wouldn't say much," Caede told them. "Just that the last time she'd been here was when Prince Sadi's father was the Warlord Prince of Dhemlan." He blew out a breath. "Something is going on. He's acting displeased about giving her access to some of the horses, but he's . . . amused."

"If she was around when Prince Sadi's father lived at the Hall, then she's from a long-lived race," Laureen said.

"Or she's demon-dead," Arlene said.

When she reached the Hall, Zoey dismissed her court except for Caede, who was standing as her escort since he was the Warlord Prince with her that day. She reported to Kathlene, who called in a pen and paper and made careful notes about the information the other Queens were bringing back with regard to Prince Sadi's mysterious guest.

Having completed her assignment, Zoey went back to her room to rest. A few minutes later, Arlene and Laureen tapped on her door.

"I received permission from Lady Nadene to make this soothing tonic anytime one of us needs it," Arlene said.

"You think I need it?" Zoey asked. Did she appear brittle? Fragile?

"Maybe you don't, but I do," Laureen said.

The pot held enough for three mugs of the soothing tonic. She wasn't being singled out as unable to cope.

"That was odd, having all of us go down to the stables to ask a question that one of us could have asked," Laureen said. "Then again, the way the stable master reacted to hearing Lady Dumm was back made me glad I wasn't on my own."

Yes, Zoey thought. *I'm not alone. And Allis wasn't concerned. I'm safe. Even if someone else has control, I'm still safe.*

After dinner that evening, Brenda summoned a select group of servants to one of the smaller libraries in the Hall.

"Here's the way of it," she said. "I'm sure you've been hearing about Lady Dumm, Prince Sadi's mysterious guest." She waited for their nods of agreement. "Well, she's meant to be an exercise for the youngsters who are training to serve in courts. Now, I chose you lot because you already had some experience serving in aristo houses before coming here, so you've had a chance to observe bad manners and bad habits and unsavory behaviors that a Queen would either have to tolerate from someone who outranked her or have to take a stand against."

Brenda called in a box with a slit in the lid. She also called in small sheets of paper, and pencils of varying lengths. "Lady Dumm needs to acquire some manners, habits, and behaviors to go along with her inclination to offer opinions about anything and everything. Write down suggestions based on what you've seen aristos do and put the suggestions in the box. I'll collect them in a couple of hours. That will give me time to put the finishing touches on Lady Dumm before she's introduced to the Hall's residents tomorrow."

Brenda left the room, then checked her pocket watch. Two hours was enough time. Guests at the Hall would be on their best behavior around the senior staff or the Prince's family, but around younger servants? She'd wager they'd seen, heard, and smelled plenty of things that aristos wouldn't dream of doing around anyone who could further their ambitions.

Tomorrow Lady Dumm would make her first appearance.

She wondered if the Hall's cellars contained any alcohol of sufficient strength to fuzz the nerves of a Black-Jeweled Warlord Prince. She had a feeling Prince Sadi would need it.

FORTY-THREE

Butler warmed a glass of yarbarah and drank it slowly as he listened for the sound of a horse and pony cart.

He didn't want to invite the girl into his home because there was something about her that tugged at him in ways no one else had, but a soft rain had been falling all day and hadn't let up. He wouldn't mind letting the wet weather shorten this session, but he knew what Jaenelle would have said about him keeping the girl outside in the wet instead of inviting her inside and offering a cup of tea. So he'd contacted Kieran and issued the invitation. The Warlord of Maghre would also appreciate not having to stay out in the weather.

Butler, it's time.

Was it? Would any of these people really understand why men like Daemon Sadi, Lucivar Yaslana—and him—had looked at the truth so long ago and embraced it? And loved *her* because of it?

"Well," Butler said quietly, "I guess we're about to find out."

"What . . . ?" Saetien said when the pony cart stopped right at the gate.

"It's a wet night, so you're invited inside to talk," Kieran replied. "I'll be back in an hour to pick you up."

"Thank you." She climbed out of the pony cart, then held up a hand to stop Shelby when the puppy gathered himself to jump down to go with her. For one thing, it was too much of a jump for a puppy. For another, she wasn't sure *she* was going to understand what was said tonight, and she didn't want the puppy to become confused by a story about humans doing strange things.

Would a Sceltie think those things were strange? Or would he see a Queen calling in a debt for a dead tiger as heroic in some way?

"You stay with Kieran," she said.

Shelby whined.

"No." She had to be firm about this.

Kieran solved the problem by snugging the puppy against his hip. "We'll be back for her soon."

Saetien opened the gate and went up the flagstone path to the cottage's front door. It opened before she reached it. Butler raised a hand in greeting to Kieran.

"Will an hour do?" Kieran asked.

"It will do," Butler replied. He stepped aside to let Saetien enter.

She wasn't sure what she'd expected. He'd been living there for centuries, and his garden was a mess. But the front room had just enough furniture to look comfortable, and it was surprisingly tidy.

"I hire a woman from the village to come in twice a week," Butler said in response to her unasked question. "Actually, I think it was her however-many-great-grandmother I hired originally, but this family has made their living by cooking and cleaning and doing laundry for those who couldn't—or didn't want to—do for themselves. When the elder among them is ready to stop working, the next one comes in with the youngest to train her."

"So they've been working in this cottage for generations?"

"They have."

And no one in that family wants to tend the garden?

She wasn't sure why that bothered her so much, but it

did. It scratched at her that Butler didn't have a tidy garden to enjoy in the evenings.

"The kettle's on. I'll make you a cup of tea, and then we'll talk."

"You don't have to do that."

Butler gave her an odd smile. "It's polite to offer it, and it's polite to drink it. Especially when you live in a small village like Maghre on the Isle of Scelt."

She hadn't gone out with Eileen for visits to the neighbors, so she didn't know if that was true, but she tucked that piece of information about social customs away in case she needed it.

When she had a mug of tea and a plate of sweet biscuits that Butler must have purchased for this visit and he had a glass of yarbarah, he said, "You want to know why, despite their feelings for each other and all the things that happened in Chaillot that bound them together, Wilhelmina and Jaenelle fell out so far, the break never healed."

Saetien hesitated. Then she nodded. "Yes, I want to know."

Silence. Then Butler said, "Very well. I don't know everything, but I'll tell you what was told to me."

FORTY-FOUR

THE PAST, SaDiablo Hall

Wilhelmina knocked on Alexandra's bedroom door and waited. Everyone from Chaillot had been confined to the guest rooms they'd been assigned and the common rooms that were connected to those guest rooms. No one had tried to reach her on a psychic thread or had asked about her. Not even Philip. Someone from the Hall would have told her if Philip had asked about her. They would have delivered a note, at the very least.

That was why she was here, standing outside Alexandra's door, with one of the footmen serving as her escort. She needed to explain that she hadn't meant to cause trouble; she just didn't want to go with Osvald. She was afraid. She'd always been afraid of doing the wrong thing or being criticized for something she'd said. Look what had happened to Jaenelle when she'd said things the adults didn't like.

There were moments here at the Hall when she didn't feel afraid, when she caught a glimpse of who she might be if the people around her hadn't smothered that girl who had her own thoughts and desires.

She was about to knock again when the door opened. Alexandra stared at her, then walked back to the bed and the trunks of clothes, leaving the door open.

Wilhelmina went in, puzzled that her grandmother hadn't used Craft to open the door. She was more puzzled that the other woman's psychic scent was . . . not different, exactly, but not the same.

Maybe her head was still muzzy. She'd been told that because so many compulsion spells had been used to try to control her, she might react erratically for a little while, until the spells faded completely. Because she might still be susceptible to suggestions or commands, the Healers and the Black Widows in residence had told her not to make any decisions or promises without consulting someone who would be impartial and would tell her if she was about to compromise herself.

"What are you doing?" Clearly, Alexandra was packing, but why? A Queen didn't pack her own trunks.

"We're leaving," Alexandra replied, her voice full of sharp bitterness. "Going back to Chaillot. You've sided with that creature who masqueraded as your sister for all these years, and there's nothing I can do now to save you from your own folly."

"I had to leave Chaillot," Wilhelmina said. She'd been so brave coming to Kaeleer. Hadn't she been brave, despite being terrified? But facing Alexandra, she felt that brave girl crumble beneath the weight of her grandmother's disapproval.

"You had to leave," Alexandra repeated, making it sound like she'd done something filthy. "First you ran away from home, leaving us to wonder what had happened to you. Then you ran here, placing yourself under the control of the High Lord of Hell. Don't you understand what he is, what he does?"

"I . . ." How could she say she felt safe here, protected here, when Alexandra thought the people who lived here were so terrible and dangerous? "Jaenelle trusts him."

Alexandra laughed. Hearing it was like listening to glass break. "Jaenelle? Have you ever really *seen* your so-called sister? She's a monster, Wilhelmina. She's not even *human*. It's no wonder she was so strange, so *different*." Alexandra straightened and faced Wilhelmina. "Haven't you noticed anything different about me?"

She looked and almost said no, she didn't see anything different. Then it struck her. "You're not wearing your Jewels."

"The Queen of Ebon Askavi, that thing that pretended to be a child living in my house, broke me back to basic Craft because *an animal* was killed when you created so much fuss and drama instead of letting Osvald escort you away from the Hall. She took me to a place full of mist and stone and *crushed* my power as if I were *nothing*."

"I—"

"You just couldn't cooperate, could you? Osvald ended up killing an animal to avoid being attacked, and the *Queen* carries on as if I'd ordered him to slaughter a human boy."

"Dejaal was trying to protect me."

"He was trying to prevent your rescue."

No. That wasn't . . . Was it?

"We're leaving this vile place. If you have any sense, you'll come with us." Alexandra closed her trunks. "But if you don't come with us now, don't come back. You've cost me enough, Wilhelmina. More than you're worth."

"I'm not supposed to decide important things right now," she said.

"You'll believe what they tell you but not what I tell you?"

"You've never believed anything *I* said!"

An awful silence filled the room.

"Believe what you like," Alexandra finally said. "But before you commit yourself to what rules this Realm, demand that Jaenelle show you her true Self. See the truth of what she is. Then you'll understand why she could do this to me—and why she might break you, too, someday."

Wilhelmina hurried back to her room, her escort hustling to keep up with her. Alexandra's words were sharp hooks sinking deep into her mind and heart.

Have you ever really seen *your so-called sister? A monster. Not even human.*

It couldn't be true. Could it?

Why would Alexandra lie?

✦ ✦ ✦

The High Lord of Hell didn't waste any time helping Alexandra return to Chaillot, along with all the people who had come with her. Philip and Leland had gone with the rest of them, without saying anything to her.

There hadn't been time to make a decision, to figure out what she really wanted for herself. She'd come to Kaeleer to find answers—or something. Instead, she'd found Jaenelle living among dangerous, frightening people. And Blood who weren't people at all. She'd found the sister she'd thought had been lost forever.

But the sharp hooks of Alexandra's words kept sinking in deeper and deeper.

Have you ever really seen *your so-called sister? A monster. Not even human.*

Alexandra was mistaken. Wilhelmina had to believe that. Otherwise, she'd just traded the rest of her family for someone she hadn't seen in thirteen years—and had never understood.

Not even human.

What did that mean?

Wilhelmina followed one of the footmen to the Craft library, where Jaenelle was working on . . . something . . . and was alone. She didn't need to be told that finding Jaenelle alone was a rare occurrence, which meant her sister had anticipated that this discussion might be difficult.

"What are you doing?" Wilhelmina asked as she looked at the open books that covered a large table. Some were printed in the common tongue. Others . . . She couldn't begin to guess the language in most of the books.

"I'm looking for an alternative to war," Jaenelle replied. She closed one book, set it aside, then stepped back from the table. "How are you feeling?"

"How should I be feeling?" Wilhelmina snapped.

Those sapphire eyes stared at her. Stared into her. Stared through her.

"All right," Jaenelle said. "How is your body feeling?"

"You're supposed to be a Healer. Can't you tell?" Where was this anger coming from? Why was she looking for a fight?

Something odd came and went in Jaenelle's eyes. The air in the room cooled until it was almost chilly.

"All right," Jaenelle said. "Let's take a look at you."

She started to move around the table. Wilhelmina stumbled back.

Jaenelle stopped. "Be careful, Wilhelmina. Right now, you're still talking to your sister. Don't draw a line that requires me to continue this as a Queen."

Was that a threat?

"Is that what you did with Alexandra? You forgot that she was your grandmother, that she was family, in order to make pronouncements as a Queen?"

"The bloodlines say she is a relative, but she is *not* family. Not to me."

Wilhelmina heard the warning, but she couldn't stop. "You *broke* her. You stripped her of her power. How is she supposed to rule Chaillot?"

"She probably won't be able to. Then again, I didn't have the impression that she had the support of Chaillot's people anymore, especially the other strong witches and Queens."

"You *broke* her!"

"Are you forgetting that she had either given the orders or given tacit consent for you to be abducted?" Jaenelle snapped. "Are you forgetting that a young Warlord Prince was killed trying to protect you? Osvald killed Dejaal, but Alexandra is responsible for allowing it to happen. I could have ordered her execution, but that wouldn't have paid the debt. Not all of it. The loss of her Jewels, the loss of her power? *That* was a debt she owed not just for Dejaal but for all the girls in Briarwood."

"But those girls are dead, and Dejaal was just—"

"Just what?" Jaenelle's eyes filled with a cold fury. "Just

an animal? Just expendable? Not worthy of holding a *human* responsible for his death? If he'd been a human boy who had been killed trying to protect you, would you be saying this? Thinking this? Maybe you would. Terreilleans are very selfish and single-minded when it comes to having what *they* want, regardless of what it costs the people already living in the lands they covet. Well, I rule Kaeleer, which means a tiger is as important to me as a human boy, and as the Queen, it is my duty to protect *everyone* in my Territory, especially those who serve in my court. Queen's price, sister. I don't get to pick and choose who is worthy of my protection based on if he has two legs or four. *Everyone* who serves in my court is under my hand—and my protection."

And that makes Alexandra expendable?

Words churned and swirled. Dug deep until there was only one way to pull free of them. "I want to see your true Self."

The person looking at her was no longer her sister. Oh, Jaenelle *looked* the same, but colder. Less . . . civilized.

"No, you don't," Jaenelle said too quietly.

"I *need* to know who you are."

"Why?"

How to explain to someone else what she couldn't explain to herself? "I need to know."

Silence. Then Jaenelle said in a midnight voice, "Very well. The truth."

One moment they were standing in a library at the Hall. The next moment there was nothing but pitch dark and biting cold. And then . . .

Mist. A stone altar. The sound of a hoof striking stone. What walked out of the mist . . .

Wilhelmina stared at the creature that was part human and part . . . many things. What horrified her the most were the sapphire eyes. No mistaking those eyes.

"The living myth," Witch said quietly. "Dreams made flesh. But not all the dreamers were human. This is who I am, Wilhelmina. This is who I've always been."

Wilhelmina shook her head. "No."

"This is the sister who protected you when we were young. Who gave you a Sapphire Jewel to protect you when it was no longer possible for me to be there."

"No."

Come to Kaeleer, the creature had said. So she had. But to come here and find this?

"You're not my sister," Wilhelmina cried. "You're not human."

"Not all of me, no," Witch replied.

"Now I understand how you could break Alexandra as if she were nothing." She felt reckless—and something pushed her to spew the words. "I wish I'd never seen you again, never seen . . . this *thing* that you are. Our lives would have been so much better if you'd just died in Briarwood!"

What she said horrified her—and filled her with a strange exultation when she saw how those words, words that had come from someplace inside her that she didn't know existed, sank in and cut deep. She'd been able to call in a debt owed to Alexandra and her family by inflicting a mortal wound on this inhuman creature.

She and Witch stood there, in that place of mist and stone. Then . . .

Pitch dark. Biting cold. And Wilhelmina stood in a library in SaDiablo Hall.

Alone.

Saetan walked into Jaenelle's sitting room and felt the Ebony shields and locks snap back into place, keeping out everyone who served in the Dark Court. The only thing keeping Daemon from exhausting himself against shields he couldn't hope to break was Ladvarian's ruthless herding. The Lady needed alone time, so they would give her alone time—and *they* included her mate.

Of course, the reason Daemon—and the rest of them—were yielding was because they all knew if the alone time went on too long, the Sceltie would find a way of getting through those shields, or raising such a commotion that Jaenelle would *have* to come out and deal with it.

One of the things she would have to deal with was that every male who wore a Ring of Honor could feel her intense emotional turmoil and was now one step away from the killing edge—without an enemy on which to focus that rage.

Then came the Queen's summons to her Steward. It bought him a little more time to keep the more volatile males—meaning his sons—under control, providing he could give them some kind of answer once he talked to the Queen.

As he walked up to her, Jaenelle continued to stare out the sitting room windows, keeping her back to him.

"Lady," he said quietly.

"High Lord."

Two words, but enough for him to recognize the huskiness that came into a woman's voice after hard crying that had gone on for too long.

He tightened the leash on his temper and swallowed rage. He didn't need rage—yet. "How may I be of service?"

"I need you to do something for me without arguing about it."

He moved until he stood beside her and could see her face. The well of pain and grief that had brought so many tears to the surface was old—and deep. And new.

"I can't promise that until I know what upset you."

"You don't need to know."

"Maybe your Steward doesn't need to know, but your father does. And I don't think you want anyone outside this room to start thinking about why you've been crying."

She looked at him, alarmed. "There is no need to issue threats, Saetan."

"That's not a threat, witch-child. That's a statement." He softened his voice. "You and Wilhelmina had words?"

A huff of laughter, bitter and cutting. "You could say that." Jaenelle's eyes filled with tears.

"Tell me." A father's command, not a Steward's request. When she hesitated, he added, "I give you my word that I will not act out of anger." Which wasn't the same as promising not to act at all, and they both knew that.

She brushed lightly against his inner barriers, a request for direct contact, mind to mind.

It would have been easier to hear the words than to receive the memory, but he opened his inner barriers and viewed this exchange between sisters.

Oh, witch-child, he thought when she withdrew. Given the steep price Jaenelle—and Daemon—had paid for that last attempt to keep Wilhelmina safe from the men who used Briarwood, the words might be forgiven, eventually, but would never be forgotten.

He, being who and what he was, would never forgive or forget.

"What do you want me to do?" he asked.

"One of the other Territories might suit Wilhelmina better than staying here," Jaenelle replied. "To be honest, it would suit me better as well. But not right now. She'll be safer at the Hall right now." She called in a slip of paper and handed it to him. "I'd like you to take money from my accounts and set up an account for Wilhelmina."

Saetan looked at the amount and swallowed a snarl. Not that Jaenelle couldn't afford it, but the amount would provide a generous lifetime income for someone from the short-lived races—provided that person spent wisely. That kind of generosity after that bitch said . . .

One way or another, she would try to take care of Wilhelmina while the woman was in Kaeleer, so she and Saetan would do this his way. "Does Lady Benedict have any experience with finances?"

She knew what his choice of formality meant, the cold temper running beneath polite words, but all she said was, "Probably less than I have, although I gathered she'd been fending for herself for a while before coming to Kaeleer."

No, she had a young man looking after her, and having worked on the Angelline estate, he would have had a keen

*appreciation of the cost of food and the need to have a
safe place to sleep.*

"Then I propose providing Lady Benedict with a quarterly income sufficient to run a modest aristo household."
And if he found her being parsimonious with her servants'
wages in order to buy things for herself, he would pay the
servants directly and take the wages out of her quarterly
income before she received it.

Nothing he needed to trouble Jaenelle about.

"All right," Jaenelle said. "Will that be enough?"

"Since I'll be investing what isn't immediately needed,
I think your gift will be more than sufficient," he said
dryly.

"Thank you, Papa."

"You're welcome, witch-child." He ran a thumb over
one of her cheeks to wipe away the last tears. "I suggest
you wash your face and drop these shields very soon."

Jaenelle looked toward the door. Then she sighed.
"They're going to want to fuss."

"Oh, yes, witch-child, they are *all* going to want to fuss.
And if you don't want any of the boyos thinking too long
or too hard about why you were upset, you will let them
fuss until they settle down. And that includes Lucivar and
Daemon. Especially Daemon."

"Maybe . . ."

"No."

"But . . ."

"No."

"I am the Queen."

"And everything has a price."

She sighed again. "Yes. It does."

Saetan walked out of the room and faced a corridor
filled with males, human and kindred. He didn't see the
cats, but you rarely saw the cats before they attacked. Still,
a quick psychic probe confirmed Jaal's and Kaelas's presence.

"She'll be all right," he said.

"What happened?" Lucivar growled.

"Easy enough to guess," Daemon said too softly.

"Perhaps," Saetan said, looking at each male in turn. "But we are all going to pretend that nothing has changed. We are not going to challenge or strike out at anyone still residing at the Hall."

"And when someone is no longer residing at the Hall?" Chaosti asked.

"You will let me handle this." Saetan made sure they heard the warning beneath the words. "Jaenelle has made her choice. I will see that it is carried out. Is that understood?"

None of them liked it, but he waited until he received agreement from each of them. Including Lucivar and Daemon. Especially Daemon.

Ladvarian's tail began to wag. A moment later, the Ebony shields and locks disappeared. The Sceltie passed through the door before any man could take the first step.

Jaenelle!

They heard the psychic shout even through the closed door.

"The rest of you can fuss later," Saetan said. He looked at Daemon. "If I were you, I'd wait a few minutes before going in."

"I'm the soother rather than the scolder?" Daemon asked.

"Exactly."

The rest of the males dispersed. Saetan walked into his suite of rooms and wasn't surprised when Lucivar followed him and closed the door.

"That's it?" Lucivar said. "You're just going to let this go?"

"You don't know—"

"I can guess, High Lord. Wilhelmina Benedict signed a contract with me, so—"

"You will do nothing." Saetan looked at this strong, volatile son. "Right now, we have other concerns, and in a place the size of the Hall, it's easy enough to keep people from being in each other's company. When the time is right, you and I will decide where and how Lady Benedict completes her contract with you."

"So I ignore the pain she's just caused my sister, my Queen?"

"You forget, Prince, that sooner or later, Wilhelmina Benedict will come to me, and as the High Lord of Hell, I will make sure that whatever debt she owes us is paid in full."

Lucivar stared at him. Then the Warlord Prince of Ebon Rih nodded. "I'll accept that, but if Wilhelmina ever hurts Jaenelle again, you should know that the Sadist will call in the debt before you do."

FORTY-FIVE

THE PAST, SaDiablo Hall

Wilhelmina added a warming spell to the wool shawl she wrapped around herself, but it didn't do anything to ease the chill inside her.

There had been fighting in the Territories throughout Kaeleer. There had been . . . war. Then the Dark Court had gone to Ebon Askavi, leaving everyone else behind. And then . . .

A terrible storm of power blasted through the Realms. A purge, the butler called it. A purge that had cleansed the Realms of Dorothea and Hekatah SaDiablo's taint.

Even with all the shields protecting the Hall, that power had ripped through everyone and . . .

Wilhelmina opened her jewelry box—good jewelry with precious gemstones, yes, but still trinkets compared to the Jewels—and removed the ring Jaenelle had commissioned for her. A ring with protection spells. A ring that would alert all the males in the First Circle if she was attacked again.

She'd been told to wear it. Each Queen in the Dark Court's coven, and Surreal as well, had been given one of these rings. But the existence of that ring said something she didn't want to think about, so she'd tossed it in her jewelry box, because if she thought too much about what the existence of that ring meant . . .

A knock on the door.

"Come in." Her voice trembled. Andrew had come to check on her after the purge had swept past the Hall, and servants had delivered meals, but no one had information about what had happened to people beyond the Hall and the village of Halaway.

The High Lord walked into the room. He looked terrible. Exhausted. In pain. And he was missing the little finger on his left hand.

He stared at her, at the Purple Dusk Jewel she wore, then seemed to gather himself to come closer.

"So," he said too softly, "you were tainted enough to forfeit your Sapphire but you retained your Birthright Purple Dusk."

She raised one hand to cover the Jewel. Would he take that from her, too, like both Jewels had been taken from Alexandra?

"The war is over," he said. "The taint of Dorothea and Hekatah will no longer threaten Kaeleer—or the survivors in Terreille."

"Survivors?"

"The purge swept through all the Realms. All the Blood who were tainted by Dorothea and Hekatah were destroyed, or forfeited some or all of their power."

Her hands tightened on the shawl. "What about Philip and Leland? What about Alexandra?"

"I don't know if they survived, Lady Benedict. Everyone who was killed by the purge . . . It was the full and final death. They are whispers in the Darkness now, beyond my reach."

"But you could find out."

The air turned cold. "My daughter sacrificed herself to save the rest of the Queens in Kaeleer. She sacrificed herself to save all the Warlord Princes who would have died fighting to save their people and the Realm. My daughter, my Queen, is gone, and I have a son who is breaking down under the weight of his grief. I don't give a damn about the Chaillot Queen or anyone connected to her. But if you need to find out, I will personally escort you to the Gate closest to Chaillot and see that you get through."

Wilhelmina shivered. "What if they're gone? What if there's no one left?"

"Then it will depend on the provisions Alexandra made for who would inherit the Angelline estate after Leland. That might be you."

She didn't know how to run an estate. "If they aren't there, can I come back?"

The room got colder. The High Lord's voice got softer. "No. If you choose to leave, you will not be welcomed back. That's not part of the promise I made to my daughter where you're concerned." He took a deep breath, then let it out slowly. "If you choose to stay in Kaeleer, I am to provide you with a quarterly income that will be sufficient for running a modest aristo household. I will not enrich *any-thing* in Terreille, so if you leave, you also forfeit the income."

"Was that Jaenelle's decision?"

"No. But she isn't here to override *my* decision."

What if she went back to Chaillot and Philip, Leland, and Alexandra were dead? What if she went back and they were still alive? Would all the reasons she'd fled in the first place still be there?

"It would be best if you removed yourself from the Hall," the High Lord said. "It's a big place, but not big enough to hold you and the grief the rest of us are feeling. Jaenelle has a house in Maghre on the Isle of Scelt. I am willing to let you have the temporary use of it while you consider what you want to do. Or you can find lodgings in Dharo or Nharkhava. Glacia is also ruled by a short-lived race, but I would not recommend crossing paths with Glacia's Queen right now."

"And the other Queens will accept me in their Territories?"

"They will tolerate you."

She wanted to be angry. She wanted to stand up for herself. But she had the feeling that she'd made a terrible mistake. An unforgivable mistake. "You're angry with me because I couldn't accept . . . But you don't know! You hadn't seen . . ."

"Everyone in the First Circle knew *exactly* who and what Witch was. We'd all seen the Self that lived beneath the human skin. She was loved *because* of who she was, Lady Benedict, not despite who she was."

They all knew—and they didn't see a monster.

Living myth. Dreams made flesh. And not all the dreamers were human.

"I . . . I'd like to go to Scelt," Wilhelmina said.

"I'll send word tonight so the house will be ready for you tomorrow. And I'll have an account set up for you in Maghre with the first quarterly payment. A Coach and driver will be available anytime you're ready to leave." The High Lord walked out of the room and closed the door.

Wilhelmina stared out the window.

Had she been tainted by those compulsion spells Osvald had used on her? Or had she been tainted by Alexandra's words—or because she hadn't heeded the advice about making decisions before the compulsion spells wore off completely? Had she said what she'd said because she truly believed it or because Alexandra believed it and, somehow, it became her truth as well?

She pictured the creature who had walked out of the mist—and shuddered. Jaenelle had always been strange, but Wilhelmina had cared about this sister who knew things— and could do things—children shouldn't know or do.

No. She loved the sister she'd held in her memory, but what she'd seen in that place of mist and stone . . . Witch was too strange and powerful, too feral in an animal way, for an ordinary person to accept. And yet . . .

Wilhelmina went back to the dresser, opened the jewelry box, and removed the ring she'd been given for protection. A ring that had been made *after* she'd seen . . .

I love you.

A last message. A last gift. She tried to picture Jaenelle as a human, but those sapphire eyes were now in a face that had a tiny spiral horn in the center of its forehead.

For the rest of her life, she would never remember her sister without seeing the creature that had lived beneath the human skin—a creature that was more than she could accept or love. And she understood that even if Jaenelle had lived through the war, Wilhelmina had lost her sister in ways no one else living at the Hall would ever lose anyone.

FORTY-SIX

Daemonar felt Grizande's arm brush his as she moved a little closer.

"What is it?" she whispered.

Good question. Too bad he didn't have an answer, except to say that he was pretty sure *that* was the reason all the students and instructors were gathered in this room.

"You know the straw-and-burlap dummies we've been using for weapons practice?" he whispered in reply. "I think it's meant to be like that, only wearing fancy clothes."

"We are learning to stab through clothes?" She sounded hopeful.

"More likely she is some kind of training for the Queens and courts."

She growled softly. "Then why we here if we can't stab it?"

He shrugged—but he watched Uncle Daemon, whose face was a mask that revealed nothing. Not thoughts, not feelings.

"This is Lady Dumm, the Hall's special guest," Daemon said. "The Queens in residence and their courts will have the pleasure of entertaining her."

Hell's fire.

Grizande growled loudly enough to draw Uncle Daemon's attention.

Daemonar nudged her in the ribs and said on a psychic thread, *Not us. We're outside of these lessons—remember?*

Still want to stab it, she replied.

Yeah. But we're not allowed to do that. Probably. Maybe.

Someone sneezed loudly. Then a stentorian voice said, "I need a hanky!"

With the exception of Uncle Daemon, who remained quiet and still, offering nothing, every male in the room froze. A few hands reached toward pockets; then the males must have remembered that the handkerchiefs weren't pristine.

Finally Felisha called in a lace-edged bit of cloth and held it out.

Brenda shook her head. "Darling, that bit of nothing is fine for dabbing away a tear or two at the theater, but it won't do if someone really needs a handkerchief." She called in a square of cloth more typical of what males carried and held it out.

Lady Dumm reached up, took the handkerchief—somehow—and brought it to her face.

Daemonar had grown up hunting with men who could put aside all pretense of being civilized, but none of them had ever made a sound so disgusting that it had his breakfast rising toward his throat.

Dumm thrust out the hand holding the handkerchief, as if she expected someone to take it. Reason told him there was nothing in or on the cloth, but unless he could use witchfire to burn it right out of her hand, he wasn't getting near it.

"Well, this is a dainty bunch," Neala said as she took the handkerchief, dropped it in a bowl, and walked out of the room.

Even the Warlord Princes scrambled to clear a path for her to avoid getting too close.

"Lady Zoela, you are the dominant Queen today," Daemon said. "Lady Dumm would like to take a carriage ride around the estate this morning and requires companions and a sufficient escort in case she wants to extend the ride into Halaway. The carriage will be at the door in twenty minutes. You have that long to give out the assignments for the day."

If Zoey collapses, Weston will call in a weapon—and only the Darkness knows what will happen after that.

Zoey paled, but she raised her chin. "It will be my pleasure to accompany Lady Dumm. If you'll excuse me, Prince, my Sisters and I will take a few minutes to discuss the assignments and who is best able to perform those duties."

Daemon gave her a small bow—his permission for Zoey and the other Queens to leave the room.

When no one else made an effort to leave, Daemon said pleasantly, "The rest of you might want to find out what you're doing today."

It was a . . . controlled . . . stampede for the door.

"Come on," Daemonar said. "You're having your first riding lesson, so let's get down to the stables. That way we'll be in position to observe."

As he followed Grizande out the door, Daemonar looked back. Uncle Daemon remained quiet and still, his face a beautiful mask that revealed nothing. Raine looked a bit stunned. Weston looked ready to bounce off the ceiling. And Brenda just pulled out her pocket watch, looked at the time—and grinned.

Because Grizande wanted to go out the front door—which meant going the long way to the stable and giving her and Daemonar some time to settle—Holt stopped them in the great hall.

"Prince Yaslana, I thought you should know that your parents will be here this afternoon and will be staying for a day or two," Holt said.

Mother Night. This was like free fall with no safe place to land.

Daemonar cleared his throat. "Does Lady Dumm join us for meals?"

"She does," Holt replied.

"She's going to sit at a table with *my mother* when *my*

father is in the same room?" If the . . . guest . . . blew her nose at the table and made *that* sound, they'd all spend a week picking bits of her out of the dining room walls after Lucivar's temper snapped the leash.

Holt smiled. "Should be interesting, don't you think?"

Daemonar walked out the door, muttering, "That's one way of putting it."

Daemon watched Raine ease away from Lady Dumm. Brenda slipped her pocket watch back into her vest pocket and gave him a bright smile.

Weston swung around to face him. "If Zoey is going out in a carriage with *that*, then I'm going with her."

"As her sword and shield, that is your privilege—and your choice," Daemon replied. Then he added quietly, "She could have assigned another Queen to accompany Dumm. She didn't."

"She used up her courage making that choice."

"I know that—and I'll make sure Dumm's handlers know it too." He looked at Brenda and smiled in warning as he raised his voice just enough to carry across the room. "But Allis will be there, and if Lady Dumm wants to keep all her stuffing, she'll take some care around Zoey."

I wonder if there is any precedent for when a Queen can toss a guest out of a moving carriage, Zoey thought. So far, Lady Dumm's family had better carriages and better horses. Obviously, no one had informed Dumm that the horses pulling *this* carriage were kindred and might express some opinions of their own. And according to Dumm, the estate's farm didn't rotate the crops properly—although how something without a face could tell was anyone's guess.

"This is the estate's lake," Zoey said. The students had arrived too late in the season for ice-skating, but they'd be able to swim and have picnics there in the summer.

"That's a puddle, not a lake," Dumm said. "On *my* family's estate, we have a *proper* lake."

"Of course you do," Zoey muttered. Hell's fire, did aristos act like this around Grandmother Zhara?

"Don't mumble, girl. It's rude."

Zoey felt movement on her right as Weston rode up beside the carriage. But the sword and shield didn't have a chance to voice his objection to Zoey's being called a *girl* instead of being addressed by her title because Allis growled. Loudly.

"Dogs should be on the floor," Dumm said.

"She's on my lap," Zoey replied. "She's not taking up space on your half of the seat." In fact, Allis had settled in Zoey's lap in such a way as to guarantee that she and Zoey had their share of the seat.

"Stupid animal."

Tough mutton, Allis replied.

Neala, who was acting as Lady Dumm's maid that day, clapped a hand over her mouth and stared beyond the carriage, her shoulders shaking. Jhett, who was Zoey's companion on this ride, closed her eyes to avoid looking at anyone. Weston, suffering from a violent coughing fit, fell back to ride beside Raeth.

"Well," Zoey said, "I think we've had enough fresh air, don't you?"

The horses must have decided her comment was a command and spun the carriage in a tight turn before heading for the stables at a speed that was just shy of reckless.

Once they reached the stables, Raeth helped Zoey and Jhett step down from the carriage, leaving Neala and the two footmen assigned to Lady Dumm to deal with their guest, who seemed to have run out of comments about the estate—and thank the Darkness for that.

Reaching the great hall, Zoey hesitated. Should she inform Prince Sadi that the kindred had shortened the carriage ride?

You are sick, said the Sceltie herding Azara into the great hall.

"I'm *not* sick!" Azara almost wailed the words, a sign that this discussion was on its second—or third—round.

You are sneezing. You are sick. You need to see the Healer, and you need blankets, and you need hot drinks. And a nap.

"Something in the greenhouse made me sneeze. That's not the same as being sick. *You* sneezed too."

There was a stinky. But that is me. That is not you.

Being the dominant Queen, Zoey took pity on Azara. "Lady Azara, go see Lady Nadene and have the Healer confirm that the sneezing is caused by a plant in the greenhouse and not by illness. Then take some quiet time. Napping is not required. Reading or writing letters are acceptable activities for quiet time."

Is dealing with them always like this? Azara asked on a psychic thread.

She's just getting started, Zoey replied.

Azara headed for the healing room with the Sceltie right behind her. Zoey, Raeth, and Jhett went into the informal reception room and collapsed.

Not looking at her friends, Jhett said, "Did you notice how Lady Dumm almost flew out of the carriage when we hit that bump in the road? If you hadn't grabbed her arm . . ." She waved a hand at Zoey.

Raeth stared at the ceiling. "Did you notice there was nothing on that smooth road to cause the carriage to bounce like that?"

Zoey and Jhett stared at him.

"There had to be something," Zoey said.

Raeth shook his head.

Allis, who had disappeared when they returned, trotted into the room. *Beale is bringing water and treats.*

Two kindred horses and one ticked-off Sceltie. Which of them had put the bounce in the road?

Deciding she didn't want the answer, Zoey nibbled on treats and waited for the rest of her court to finish their morning assignments.

✦ ✦ ✦

Daemonar watched Raeth, Caede, Trent, and Jarrod whack at straw-and-burlap dummies until the seams split. He wasn't sure if they were releasing their feelings about dealing with Lady Dumm or expressing their new understanding about dealing with Scelties when the dogs were looking at humans not as playmates but as humans who needed their help.

He waved at the other Warlord Princes. "Prince Raine is expecting me, so I'll see you at dinner."

"Daemonar?" Jarrod said. "Do you have any idea how long Lady Dumm is staying around?"

"No idea at all. But if the Scelties start digging a hole, you should let someone know."

Lucivar understood why Daemon had rearranged the seating, putting him at the other end of the table.

The battlefield was the length of the table, and the combatants were everyone seated at that table—and they were caught between the Black and the Ebon-gray.

Marian was seated next to Daemon at the head of the table, a change made because Daemon wanted to keep Grizande near him and the girl had been so pleased to see Marian. Lucivar, on the other hand, had Daemonar and Weston. Better than trying to talk to the girls, who all looked . . . Well, except for Zoey and Titian, they all looked like sheep who had seen a Sceltie for the first time—which probably wasn't far from the truth.

Lady Dumm was seated in the center across from Brenda. Everyone else, students and instructors, found their assigned seats—and Lucivar wondered who had made the seating choices.

They finished the soup course before everyone relaxed enough to start talking.

"Are you all wound up for a reason?" Lucivar asked Daemonar.

Daemonar looked at Weston, who said, "Being from an aristo family does not guarantee good manners."

Daemonar nodded. "She's . . ."

The loud smacking of lips came from the chairs at the center of the table.

Daemonar closed his eyes and muttered, "Hell's fire."

Daemon continued talking to Marian as if he couldn't hear the sound, couldn't see the way all the youngsters were staring at Dumm, then looking at Sadi as if expecting— hoping?—he would put a stop to it.

The sound stopped. The whole table—except Daemon— sighed with relief as everyone finished the second course.

The third course ended with a belch that would have earned Lucivar's boys extra chores if they'd done that at their mother's table. But the loud, protracted fart had everyone putting down their forks, leaving the desserts unfinished.

Daemon still didn't act like he'd noticed a thing—but in his gold eyes there was a glitter that warned Lucivar that they were all in trouble.

Daemon called in the red folder Saetan had left for his sons, and he flipped through the papers until he found the one he wanted. It wasn't like the spells and instructions and notes about things the coven had done. It was a simple suggestion for how to deal with a difficult guest—and where to find what was needed.

An hour later, the High Lord walked to the Dark Altar protected by the Hall. He entered the chamber and lit the black candles in the proper order to open a Gate between Kaeleer and Hell. Passing from one Realm to the other, he walked out of the Dark Altar located next to the Hall in the Dark Realm—and waited.

He didn't wait long before a couple of demon-dead Warlords approached. Cautious, yes, but not afraid.

"High Lord," they said, bowing.

"There is something I need. I know it exists in this Realm, but I don't know how easy it is to locate."

"Easy enough to locate," one said with a grin when he'd told them what he wanted. "Not so easy to procure."

"Keep it shielded and bring it to me here. In exchange, I offer a case of yarbarah from the SaDiablo vineyards and a cup of fresh blood."

"Whose blood?" the other asked.

The High Lord smiled. "Mine."

FORTY-SEVEN

Kieran pulled out his chair and sat with the rest of his family while Eileen dished out the stew and Ryder passed around the warm biscuits and butter.

"It's my quilting night," Eileen said. "Anya will heat up some stew for Saetien after you bring her back from Butler's, but you might as well have your supper with us."

"Aye," Kieran replied. He buttered a biscuit, then stared at it.

"Trouble?" Kildare asked.

Kieran sighed. "Brenda wasn't always easy to live with when she was in that stage of growing up, but you knew who you were dealing with. Saetien?"

"She came here impatient for answers, thinking the answers would be simple to obtain just because she wanted them," Eileen said. "She didn't expect to have answers doled out by someone she couldn't impress with anything but intelligence and good manners."

"Butler dealt with unruly witches as a service to Queens and courts for a lot of years," Kieran said.

Kildare drank some ale, then wagged a finger at his sons. "When I was around your age, there was a filly here who was the most fractious witch I'd ever met. Excellent bloodlines, and her dam was patient and sweet tempered, but the filly took against us almost from the moment she was born. My father tried to work with her, teach her. The sister of mine who also worked with the horses tried to connect with her. I tried. All we got were kicks and squeals and carrying on. Oh, she was smart and she paid attention when we started showing the foals basic Craft and teaching them the rest of what they needed to learn to live around humans, but she just banged around the pastures, and short of tossing her out, which would have been unforgivable in the eyes of all the kindred horses, we spent a couple of years clashing with her while we tried to figure out how to work with her.

"Then one day Lord Donal, a friend of mine, came to visit. His family had a few kindred horses, and they were open to sharing their land with a few more. Well, the filly heard his voice, and something inside her just settled. She trotted up to him, and that was that. Everything we had tried to teach her, everything she had refused to do? Donal showed her a bit of Craft or indicated by some praise or a cool look what he expected, and didn't she do it? It was like he was dealing with a different horse. And in a way, that was true. Something in him brought out the best in her. She went with him and was with him the rest of her life." Kildare shook his head and went back to eating his stew.

Kieran thought about the story while they had supper. He thought about it while he read a few letters and requests.

Even now, here in Maghre, people turned a blind eye to the fact that Daemon Sadi was the High Lord of Hell. Here he was the Warlord Prince who helped run the Sceltie school in memory of the Queen who had been his wife and the love of his life.

Here in Maghre, Saetien was a girl staying with Kieran's family while she followed a heart quest. Here she could put aside the heavy burden of being the High Lord's daughter.

Was that the reason they were seeing a fractious girl blooming into a caring young woman? Or was Saetien like the filly in Kildare's story, finally hearing a voice that could reach the core of who she was?

✦ ✦ ✦

Saetien felt relieved that Kieran didn't need to fill the silence with useless words. Not that talk about people and the village and books and all sorts of things was useless, but her head was so full of thoughts that she just didn't have room for more. Not tonight.

She appreciated the punch-in-the-gut sensation of seeing Witch for the first time. She could easily imagine Wilhelmina Benedict, who had come to Kaeleer expecting to find the sister she remembered, facing the living myth because Alexandra had prodded her to demand to see her sister's true Self.

How much anger had she felt because she'd turned away from her human family and sided with something that was so clearly not fully human? How much guilt did Wilhelmina carry because the monster she couldn't accept had still loved her enough to try to protect her one last time?

"Are there . . . ?" she began, then stopped, uncertain what to ask.

"Are there . . . ?" Kieran repeated. Kindly, not mocking.

"Are there any histories about Scelt during the time of the war or the years just after?"

A thoughtful silence before Kieran said, "Scholars wrote about those years, although they were looking at it from the outside, so to speak, because some things were not shared. If you're looking for the personal in Maghre, the family has journals left by Lady Morghann and Lord Khardeen. Khardeen wasn't much for putting down his thoughts, so most of what we know about our family history during that time comes from Morghann. Even with preservation spells, the journals have become fragile and can't leave the house. But you're welcome to read them."

"Thank you."

Saetien ate her supper alone. By the time she'd finished, Kieran had located the journals and left them on the library table for her. She turned up the lamp on the table, then hesitated to open the first journal.

Did she want to know? So far in the telling, Wilhelmina Benedict wasn't the heroine of the story, but she wasn't the villain either. She was just a woman struggling to make a new life in a place where she didn't fit in.

But Lady Morghann had been Jaenelle Angelline's good friend. What would she say about Wilhelmina? And what would Morghann say about the Queen whom Saetien had seen as some kind of rival when she wasn't trying to ignore Jaenelle's existence?

Saetien hesitated a moment longer, then opened the cover of the first journal.

FORTY-EIGHT

L ady Morghann and Lord Khardeen are here to see
you," the housekeeper announced.

Wilhelmina set aside the book she'd been trying to
read. "Show them in."

She smoothed down her dress and straightened her
shawl. The Queen of Scelt and the Warlord of Maghre had
been kind in a cool sort of way. They had invited her to
join them for an evening meal a couple of times since she'd
arrived in Maghre, but they were grieving. Everyone in
Maghre was grieving the loss of the Queen of Ebon Askavi, but no one mentioned the Queen by name or what
she'd done to save the Blood in the Shadow Realm. Not in
Wilhelmina's hearing. Not after the first few days.

*"You're staying in Lady Angelline's house? Were you
friends, then?"*

*"Never put on airs like some aristo Ladies who think
they're too important to be courteous to farmers and shopkeepers. Interested in village life, she was."*

*"Such a lovely voice she had. Lady Angelline and Lady
Morghann would sing a song or two at a harvest dance,
and it was a delight to hear them."*

Everyone in the village knew she was staying at Jaenelle's house. Everyone had a story to tell about the Black
Widow Queen who had saved a young witch from madness—
who, as a Healer, had saved a boy's leg after it had been

crushed by a wagon. They told Wilhelmina about dances and horse races and the rainbow slides the Lady had made out of Craft and air for the village children. And they all had thoughts about the school Jaenelle had created for kindred Scelties.

Jaenelle lived in that house for only a few days every season, but the remembrance of her filled the village with stories that matched the sister Wilhelmina had expected to find. These people didn't know; they hadn't seen the truth beneath the human skin.

If they had seen Witch's true Self, would they have felt as horrified as she'd felt? Or would these people have nodded and said how it made sense that all the kindred had loved the Lady so much?

Then came the awful day when she'd let something slip after *another* story about the Lady, something that made the villagers understand that not only was there a *family* connection between her and Jaenelle Angelline, but also that she held some kind of grudge against the Lady. Everyone in the village cooled toward her after that, leaving her feeling more and more isolated.

Now Morghann and Khardeen had come to call.

She knew the moment she saw Morghann's face that something had happened. Something big.

"We just received word from Uncle Saetan." Morghann smiled brilliantly as tears ran down her face. "Jaenelle survived. The kindred managed to save her. She's alive!"

Wilhelmina stared at them. "How . . . ?"

"We don't know more than that, except that she's healing in a secret place," Khardeen said. "It could be weeks, even months, before she's able to come home. But she will be coming home."

"Home?" Wilhelmina felt a sharp chill beneath her skin. "Meaning here?"

"I expect she'll be at the Hall most of the time," Morghann replied. "But yes, we're hoping she'll be returning here as well."

"Then I'd better start looking for another place to live."
She clutched the shawl.

They didn't contradict her and tell her she could stay.

"I can ask around for other cottages to let," Khardeen
offered.

She shook her head. "Not here. Not in Maghre if Jaenelle
is going to live here." Her breath came out in a pained sound.
"You think I'm cruel or cold or uncaring. The truth? I'm just
not strong enough or brave enough to live in the same village as Jaenelle, where I'll keep hearing how wonderful she
is without anyone admitting that she can be terrible and terrifying as well. I can't pretend she's the sister I remembered,
not after she broke our grandmother. Not after . . ." She
choked on a sob.

Silence. Morghann and Khardeen knew why Witch had
broken Alexandra Angelline—and they clearly approved.

Finally, Khardeen said, "Tuathal is the capital of Scelt.
We stay there on occasion because Morghann is the Territory Queen and her family has a house there. But Jaenelle
didn't spend time there except on an annual official visit.
Maghre was her place in Scelt. If you resided in Tuathal, I
doubt there would be anyone there who would connect
Wilhelmina Benedict with Jaenelle Angelline. If that's
what you want."

"Yes. That's what I want."

"I think you moving to Tuathal is for the best," Morghann
said. "I don't think the men in Jaenelle's family will react
well to anyone who causes her distress, so it would be safer
for you if you were . . . away . . . from Maghre."

"Once you figure out how much you can afford, I'll
send our man of business up to Tuathal to make inquiries,"
Khardeen said.

She told them her quarterly income and saw their eyes
widen. So. The High Lord had been more generous than
she'd realized.

"It will take him a few days, but he'll bring back a list
of possibilities," Khardeen said.

Wilhelmina thanked them, then waited for them to leave before she sank back into her chair.

Restless days. Sleepless nights while she wrestled with a single question: go back to Chaillot, where the Angelline family might still be alive but with the family name and honor in ruins, or stay here in Scelt and move to a city where no one would know Wilhelmina Benedict—where she wouldn't have to carry the burden of being related to Jaenelle Angelline?

A fresh start, then. She'd be nothing more than one of the Blood who had fled from Terreille in order to build a new life in Kaeleer. Her name would mean nothing to anyone, and that's the way she wanted it to be. Needed it to be.

After reviewing the possible residences she could lease and discussing the neighborhoods with Khardeen and Morghann—and what her potential neighbors might know about aristo families beyond Scelt—Wilhelmina chose a house in a section of Tuathal that catered to minor aristos who worked at some kind of trade or had professions. Not the kind of individuals who would serve in the top circles of courts. She didn't have a trade or profession, but she could afford to take the time to decide what she'd like to do.

What she hadn't expected was Andrew's decision not to come with her. A former stable-lad at the Angelline estate, he'd helped her when she'd run away from Robert Benedict's attentions. He'd helped her hide from her family, taking care of all the practical things she didn't know how to do. And he'd accompanied her to Kaeleer. But now . . .

"I want to work with horses, and these horses are beyond anything I could have imagined when we were in Chaillot," Andrew said. Then he added, "Dark Dancer had come close to the kindred horses. Jaenelle recognized that in him."

"We could buy a couple of horses when we get to Tuathal."

"They wouldn't be kindred," he replied gently, as if he

already knew none of the kindred would want to be around her. "I . . . We helped each other for a lot of years, but I think this is where we take different paths. I'm staying here, working for Lord Khardeen. You'll go to Tuathal and make a new life for yourself."

"Jaenelle survived. Did Khardeen tell you that? She survived, and she'll be coming back here to live."

"And I will be glad to see her." Andrew picked up a bucket that held grooming brushes.

"She *broke* Alexandra. Doesn't that matter to you?"

"It was time someone did." The black patch that covered the lost eye seemed to make the anger in Andrew's remaining eye sharper and colder. "Maybe Alexandra was a good Queen when she first began ruling Chaillot. But she wasn't a good Queen or a good grandmother the last time she sent Jaenelle to Briarwood. Have you forgotten *why* Jaenelle ended up in Briarwood that night? She was trying to protect *you*. And some of us did everything we could to help Daemon Sadi protect *her*. But we couldn't do enough. So don't ask me to feel sorry for Alexandra. Since the High Lord and the Dark Court let her live, I have to figure breaking her was what she deserved."

She'd thought of Andrew as a friend all these years. "Would you go back to Chaillot if you could?"

"Never. I'm making a home here, and I plan to stay." He made the effort to put aside his anger. "Probably best if we part now while we can still be friends. I think you'll always resent Jaenelle for breaking Alexandra—and you'll come to resent me because I will never feel that way."

She wasn't sure he was wrong, so she said nothing. Just walked out of the stables. Walked back to Jaenelle's house.

Walked away from the last connection to her old life.

FORTY-NINE

I'm asking for a favor on behalf of our Queen," the High Lord said.

Butler felt short of breath as hope filled his chest. "You've seen her?"

"Not yet, but this can't wait for the Lady to heal enough for the kindred to allow visitors."

"Do you know where she is?"

"No. But I can think of one or two places in Kaeleer where I would hide someone if I wanted to make sure that no one could survive reaching her."

Given that the kindred were the ones who had managed to save the Lady, he figured she was in a place inhospitable to humans. An assignment would keep him occupied until news came that she was someplace where she could receive visitors. "What would you like me to do?"

"Wilhelmina Benedict is moving to Tuathal and setting up her own household. She's going to need help settling in."

"Wilhelmina Benedict." Butler almost spat the name. "You want me to *help* Wilhelmina Benedict?"

"I know, Butler. I know."

Did the High Lord know why this assignment would be so difficult? Better for everyone if he refused.

Saetan slowly let out a breath. "If Wilhelmina is settled in a new life and doesn't need protection or help, then Jaenelle can let her sister go and she can focus on rebuilding her own life."

Assuming she can heal well enough to have a life. Butler didn't say it, but he figured everyone in the Dark Court was thinking it.

"How long?" he asked. He wouldn't take an open-ended assignment. He wouldn't do that. Not if it meant staying around Wilhelmina Benedict.

"Six months," Saetan replied. "A year at the most."

"I'll do what I can." *For Jaenelle's sake.*

"Thank you."

As soon as the High Lord left, Butler began packing, sorting through what he would need and what he would store at the Hall. He traveled so much on assignments for the Queens in the Dark Court that he didn't have a permanent residence beyond this suite of rooms at the Hall. Someday he would have a home. When he was ready.

He'd look at this assignment as a chance to spend time in Scelt. Jaenelle had a fondness for the village of Maghre, and he hadn't been back in years. Easy enough to ride the Winds and go to the village on his days off.

At least he could look forward to something over the next few months.

"I'm Prince Butler. I've been assigned to be your companion for a few months while you set up your household in Tuathal. I have the impression that you've had little experience in hiring staff or handling the day-to-day decisions that your butler and housekeeper will require from you."

Wilhelmina Benedict stared at him. "Who assigned you?"

"The High Lord."

"What if I don't want you with me? What if I don't want someone reporting to him about everything I do?" Her voice had taken on a hysterical edge.

Butler shrugged. "Then I don't go with you. If you don't want help, no help will be given. By anyone."

"My sister would help me."

"How long will it be before she's able to think of anything beyond her next heartbeat, her next breath?" Butler countered. "It will be months before she can think of anyone else. What will you do in the meantime? Play the part of the misunderstood woman looking for everyone else to save her while she wrings her hands and releases tears designed to elicit sympathy? Or are you going to try to put a little steel in your spine and learn how to live on your own, learn how to be someone who isn't pathetic?"

"Don't tell me I don't have any steel. I came to Kaeleer on my own!"

"So did a lot of women. They're getting on with their lives. Why aren't you?"

"You don't understand. My sister . . ."

"Living myth. Dreams made flesh. I understand more than you'll ever know." He took a moment to leash the anger. "Not everyone can accept Witch. Not everyone can serve in the Dark Court. It must be harder for someone who is related to her to realize they will never be comfortable in her presence and they need to walk away. But you need to walk away and make a life for yourself that doesn't include Jaenelle Angelline."

"And you're going to help me do that?"

"Yes. I'll stay long enough to help you put down roots. Then I'll be gone."

Wilhelmina gave him a wobbly smile. "I can tell you about Alexandra Angelline, who was a good—"

"I was born in Beldon Mor. There's *nothing* I need to know about Alexandra Angelline, but if you want to tell me about her being a good Queen, I will tell you about the families that were shattered because of her, the lives that were destroyed. I will tell you what had been happening outside your fine house."

She stared at him. He swore silently at himself for saying that much.

"You came from Chaillot?"

"I put that place behind me. It will never be mentioned

again. Not to you. Not to anyone." There would be no indulgent nostalgia for that place. Not with him.

He took a controlled breath. "Do you want my help or not?"

She hesitated. Finally, she nodded. "Yes, I want your help." She sighed. "I'm supposed to move to my new house at the end of the week."

"Give me the address. I'll go there now and start getting things prepared for your arrival."

"Wouldn't the man of business have done that?"

"No, Lady. Getting some food in the house ahead of your arrival isn't part of his job. Neither is hiring a cook—or anyone else you'll want working in your house." He held out a hand. "Did he give you any keys?"

She called in a set of house keys, handed them over, and told him the address of her residence in Tuathal.

Butler bent his head, more a courtesy than an actual bow. "I'll see you in a few days."

He left Jaenelle's house and walked to the landing web.

Helping a woman from Chaillot. Helping a woman from *that* family.

He owed Jaenelle a debt he could never fully repay, so he would do this for her—and only for her.

Everything had a price.

FIFTY

Daemon knocked on the door of Marian and Lucivar's suite and waited until Marian answered.

She smiled at him. "I was heading out to take a walk with Grizande, but if you need something . . . ?"

"A favor." He raised her hand and kissed her knuckles. "Don't come down for dinner this evening. Beale will bring you a tray."

"All right. Maybe Titian and Zoey would like . . ."

"No. All the children are required at my table tonight. So are the instructors."

She studied him. "And Lucivar?"

"Needs to be there."

"Is this going to be a repeat of last night's dinner?"

Daemon smiled. "Oh, no, darling. This will be much better."

Throughout the day, one girl after another tried to get out of showing up for dinner. Nadene examined everyone who complained of an upset stomach or a weakness in her limbs or a stubbed toe that made it impossible to walk all the way to the dining room, and why couldn't they get something to eat from the auxiliary kitchen?

Nadene made them swallow benign tonics and booted

them out of the healing room, declaring them fit to sit at the Prince's table.

The boys didn't complain, but if Daemon had offered them a choice of a week in the dungeons or sitting through another dinner with Lady Dumm, they would have run to reach the cells.

Just as well he hadn't given anyone a choice.

Just as well he'd warned Lucivar not to wear the new evening clothes Marian had insisted he buy in Amdarh during their last visit. The scent from the little surprise he'd brought back from Hell was difficult to get out of fabric.

He kept Grizande close to him—and he waited.

He waited through the first course. As he waited through the smacking of lips, he wondered how many people at the table—besides Lucivar, Daemonar, and Grizande—had knives handy that could not in any way be considered silverware.

He waited through the belching. And then came the sound he'd waited for.

The stench that rose from beneath the table immediately following that protracted fart was eye watering. Nose stinging. The people sitting next to and immediately across from Dumm covered their noses and shoved back their chairs. They eyed the dining room's closed doors with desperation, not quite daring to run past him since he sat there, calmly, as if he hadn't noticed a thing.

The stench quickly spread to both ends of the table.

Daemonar shoved away from the table. He looked at his father, who sat there staring at Daemon. Then the boy shook his head and strode for the dining room doors. As soon as the doors opened, the children and instructors hurried to follow.

Except for Brenda, who became stuck as she passed Daemon's chair.

Daemon smiled at the Scelt witch who blinked back tears and gasped for breath.

"I can appreciate, to an extent, that you intended this as

a valuable exercise in dealing with a difficult guest, but I think Lady Dumm should put aside her crude behaviors before she next sits at my table. If she doesn't, she, and her flatulence, could end up in people's bedrooms. Do we understand one another, Lady Brenda?"

"We do, Prince. We do."

"I'm delighted." Daemon released her and heard her collide with someone as she ran out of the room.

Lucivar shoved away from the table and used Craft to open all the windows in the room. "Hell's fire, Bastard. Corpses that have been bloating in the sun for days don't smell that bad."

"Funny you should say that." Daemon rose. Using Craft, he floated the glass bowl from beneath the table and put a triple Black shield around it and the object it held.

Pulpy. Fleshy. Its smell was an irresistible lure for carrion eaters—but that smell was also bait for a trap, since the plant that produced it was a carnivore.

It took nerve and a fair amount of skill to acquire this prize, and he considered it well worth the price he'd paid in bottles of yarbarah and fresh blood.

Lucivar stared at the thing in the bowl. "What is that?"

Daemon's smile was warm and wicked. "That, old son, is a corpse flower."

FIFTY-ONE

Saetien set aside the empty mug. "You went to Tuathal with Wilhelmina Benedict?"

"I did," Butler replied. "Lady Morghann and Lord Khardeen spent a few days in the city on the Queen's business and let it be known that Lady Benedict was an acquaintance, which was enough to open a few social doors. She made friends, attended gatherings, eventually began hosting literary evenings. She married a man who loved her, and they had two children. From all accounts, she was a thoughtful, caring woman who was well liked by her neighbors and loved by her family—and always carried some sadness. No one knew the cause of that sadness, but it was a burden she couldn't put aside. One of life's regrets."

"A man who loved her," Saetien repeated. "Did she love him?"

"I assume so, but I don't know. I had left Scelt and was on another assignment by the time she met him. I did what I'd promised to do and helped her put down roots. After I left Tuathal, our paths never crossed again."

"That's all you know about her?"

"I know her descendants still live in Scelt."

She frowned at the carpet. Was she supposed to feel vindicated that someone else had turned away from Jaenelle Angelline? Was she supposed to feel happy that Wilhelmina had made a life for herself and had a family of her own?

"It feels . . . incomplete." She wasn't sure what was missing from the story, but what she needed wasn't in Butler's account of Wilhelmina's life in Scelt. "I found out about Wilhelmina, which is what I came here to do, but I didn't find the answer."

Silence. Then Butler said quietly, "Maybe that's because you've been asking about the wrong sister."

FIFTY-TWO

Dinah tossed the latest letter from Cara on her desk and let out an angry sigh. At least *one* of her friends was still showing loyalty to her banished Queen.

It wasn't *fair*. The girls at the Hall were doing this interesting exercise—although that dinner ruined by an obscene stink sounded very unpleasant—while *she* was stuck with two tutors teaching her *at home* because . . . Well, her parents said it was because girls in the *important* castes of the Blood might be targeted by another coven of malice, but the real reason was because the girls who were studying at the town's private school—the aristo girls who *should have* been her friends—got bitchy when she disciplined one of them. It was just a light slap on the girl's face—not even hard enough to bring up any color on her skin. The school had no right to expel a *Queen* for one little *deserved* slap.

She wasn't a limp goody-goody like Zoey, but she wasn't *evil* like Delora. She was a *Queen*, and she deserved obedience and adoration from those in the lower castes of Blood.

So here she was, stuck with two boring tutors while the Queens who hadn't shown any spine were still at the Hall doing these interesting exercises and able to exert their rightful power over the other students.

Dinah let out another angry sigh.

"What did Lady Cara say to put you in a mood?" Ida asked as she tidied up the bedside tables.

Dinah studied her personal maid. Ida was supportive and *never* criticized. She was an adult, having made the Offering to the Darkness, but the difference in their years didn't matter. The difference in their social positions? Ida always seemed to know when to be friendly and when to treat Dinah like a ruling Queen.

"You used to work at SaDiablo Hall," Dinah said.

Ida nodded. "I did, back when . . . *she* . . . lived there."

The Queen of Ebon Askavi. Witch. *No one* said her name, even in private. She'd always been strange and un-natural. Now she was that and more. But Dinah still re-sented that *Zoey* had been granted an audience and the rest of the Queens studying at the Hall had not. Like Zoey was more important than the rest of them.

"Did they ever do exercises with something called Lady Dumm?" she asked.

"Oh, *that*." Ida made a sound that might have been a laugh with bitter undertones. "Yes, I remember Lady Dumm. A dressmaker's dummy that everyone was sup-posed to pretend was a difficult guest so that the girls and boys living at the Hall could practice their social skills. Not that all of them were capable of learning social skills, since some were more animal than human. But that all ended when a suggestion that might have been a little bit naughty was slipped into the instructions. Such an uproar about something that hadn't even happened."

Ida continued to tidy up the room, but there was a stiff-ness in her shoulders, and in the maid's psychic scent Di-nah picked up a still-burning anger over something that must have happened years and years ago.

"Was that when you were dismissed?" Dinah guessed.

Ida sniffed. "Someone had to be blamed for a *rumor*, and the housekeeper had never liked me, never thought my work was *good enough*."

Dinah looked out the window as an idea began to take shape. Her tutors had droned on and on yesterday about the responsibilities of a Queen, about how doing what was right was more important than following orders.

But what if someone gave you orders that were just a little bit naughty? Nothing *terrible*, but something that *should* be within a Queen's rights? Like ordering someone in her court to slap a person's hand? Or a person's face? Who would show some spine and follow the orders, and who would prove she didn't have the courage to rule?

And if the other Queens were expelled for breaking a rule or crossing a line?

Dinah turned away from the window and smiled. "I have an idea that could give both of us a little payback for being slighted at SaDiablo Hall."

FIFTY-THREE

Watching Kieran ride up to the cottage gate, Butler created a ball of pale witchlight, figuring this wasn't a conversation to have in the dark.

"Saetien isn't coming tonight?" he asked when Kieran dismounted.

"She says not," Kieran replied. "She spent the morning at the Sceltie school, helping out the instructors while Shelby had his lessons, and she worked with the foals in the afternoon."

"And now she's packing her trunks to go home?"

"No. She's been reading Morghann's journals, and she's thinking hard about something, but she's keeping it all to herself." Kieran studied him. "Anything I should know?" He hesitated. "Anything her father should know?"

"I fulfilled my side of the bargain," Butler replied.

"But she didn't get an answer."

"Not the one she wanted, no. But she hasn't asked the right questions." His turn to hesitate, because this was emotionally boggy ground. "Your mother might have some of the answers. Not the ones Saetien came here to find, but some answers."

A flash of temper. "That's private."

"It is."

Kieran looked away and swore softly. "Do you think it will do any good?"

"I don't know. But I would prefer to leave the girl without answers than to see Lady Eileen heartsore because of this."

"So would I, but that's not up to us."

Butler smiled. "When you're dealing with a strong-willed witch, it never is."

"Come with me," Eileen said after the evening meal.

Saetien followed the woman to the library. She'd read all of Morghann's journals—at least the ones that Kieran had provided. Since those had included a few of the years after Wilhelmina had left Maghre, she kept tripping over journal entries that included news about Jaenelle Angelline. Or Jaenelle and Daemon and how *happy* they were to be together. And how *happy* Morghann was to spend time with a woman who had been one of her closest friends since childhood.

Everyone was so *happy* to be around Jaenelle Angelline.

Except Wilhelmina Benedict.

Eileen looked at the journals carefully stacked at one end of the table. One finger drew patterns on the wood. Finally, she sighed and called in another stack of journals. "I don't know if these will help you, but you're welcome to read them—but you're not welcome to discuss them with anyone but Butler."

Saetien moved closer to the table. "Why? What are they?"

"Wilhelmina's journals."

She stared at Eileen. "Why would you have Wilhelmina Benedict's journals?"

A smile that held a hint of sorrow. Maybe even shame. "I can trace my maternal bloodline back to her. She was an old woman close to the end of her days among the living when she told one of her granddaughters that she was Jaenelle Angelline's sister, that they had been estranged for many years because she couldn't accept the truth about what Jaenelle was and what she had done. She couldn't love a monster, so she'd kept the truth of their connection a secret.

"In time, that granddaughter passed that secret on to her granddaughters—and it became a family secret passed down from one generation of girls to the next.

"My family lived in Tuathal or in towns near the capital. One day a group of friends invited me to come with them to a horse fair. Grand horses that came from the best bloodlines. And there were kindred horses as well, although 'acquiring' one of them was usually tricky since it wasn't the humans who made the final decision. I knew I was descended from Wilhelmina, but I didn't know where Wilhelmina had been before she'd arrived in Tuathal. No one remembered the name of that little village. Then I arrived in Maghre with my friends and had the strangest feeling that I had come home."

Eileen smiled, but her eyes were bright with tears. "Imagine the shock of walking around this village, seeing the Sceltie school for the first time and driving past Angelline House, which is still what it's called. Imagine the shock of rushing out of a shop and almost running into Daemon Sadi—and realizing who he was after the young Warlord he was with kept me from tumbling into the street."

"Lord Kildare?" Saetien guessed.

"Yes. Kildare. I looked into his eyes and knew I would marry him or never marry. Lucky for me, he felt the same."

"What did your family say?"

"Well, I was marrying a man who could trace his bloodline back to Morghann and Khardeen, so they couldn't say he was unsuitable. One of my uncles—may the Darkness cherish him and keep him away from the rest of us—came to Maghre to dissuade me from marrying a man who understood so little about being aristo that he mucked out stalls along with his hired help. I wouldn't yield, so my family insisted on a handfast, figuring I'd tire of country life before the year was done. Kildare's family held a dinner the night before the ceremony—and Daemon Sadi was a guest. My uncle's face turned the most peculiar shade of red and my parents didn't say a word all evening, especially after the Prince indicated he would be at the handfast." Eileen sighed, a contented sound. "Meeting Kildare and living in Maghre were the best things that could have happened to me."

"Does my father know you have a connection to Wilhelmina?"

"He knew before I said anything, and the only thing *he* said when I told him was 'Jaenelle would have liked you.'" Eileen looked at Saetien, then pressed a hand on the stack of journals. "I don't know if these will help you, but this gives you an idea of who Wilhelmina was during the years she lived in Tuathal."

"Have you ever seen Witch? Do you think you could . . . accept . . . her?"

"Accept her? I don't know."

"She's back now. At the Keep. What do you think she's like?"

Eileen gave Saetien a long look. "I think she's as terrifying as she is grand. But then, the same can be said for your father, which is why I think they were well matched."

Saetien waited until Eileen left the library before she sat at the table and opened the first journal. Would the journals tell her anything? Or was Butler right and she was looking at the wrong sister in order to find the answers?

FIFTY-FOUR

Saetien spent two evenings reading and rereading Wilhelmina's journals, but they didn't bring her any closer to figuring out who *she* was supposed to be.

Wilhelmina Benedict settled among Tuathal's minor aristos, avoiding the Queens and their courts. Butler had stayed long enough to help her put down roots; taught her how to hire staff, how to shop at the open markets in case the cook took ill; taught her how to cook a steak and make scrambled eggs so that she wasn't completely dependent on someone else for food. She had an independent income that came from an unknown source—and that was of interest to some of the men who were looking to handfast as a way to increase their social standing. But when the question of bloodlines came up, as it always did in aristo families, most of those men backed away because she had originally come from Chaillot. Being connected to someone from Terreille did *nothing* for a person's social standing—unless that Terreillean was very powerful.

According to the information supplied by the Keep, Wilhelmina Benedict's father was a Warlord named Robert Benedict and her mother was a Black Widow named Adria. There was no mention of Robert's second marriage or his connection to Alexandra through Leland, so there was no mention of the name Angelline—a name that would have meant awkward questions, since Jaenelle Angelline was known throughout the Realm.

Wilhelmina eventually married a man who loved her for herself, and if her journals were to be believed, she never felt a burning passion for her husband but she did love him, and they were content living in Tuathal and leasing a country house for a few weeks each year. They were content with raising their children.

As long as you didn't look closely, you could say Wilhelmina Benedict was content.

Her journals told a different story. She felt ashamed of her mixed feelings about her sister—a sister she didn't name even in her private journals. And she felt angry for feeling ashamed, since she was sure most of the Blood would have felt the same way upon seeing Witch's true Self.

Still, she didn't tell that one granddaughter about her sister until a month after the news that Jaenelle Angelline had died and Daemon Sadi had begun a year of mourning.

A secret that had been at the core of Wilhelmina's life. By her own choice—a choice made for her survival. Not everyone could serve in the Dark Court. Not everyone could live in the shadow of the sheer power that court represented.

Saetien understood Wilhelmina's choice. Hell's fire, she had a father and uncle who *still* served Witch. And she felt like she'd been competing with Jaenelle Angelline all her life—and losing.

She set the journals aside. She didn't *want* the answers she suspected Butler would give her, but it looked like she was going to have to ask questions about Jaenelle if there was any chance of getting the answers she needed in order to figure out her own life.

It was late, and Kieran wasn't pleased to have to ask one of the kindred to pull the pony cart so that she could go to

Butler's cottage at that hour, but he did ask and he escorted her right up to the gate.

Saetien climbed down from the cart and marched up to the cottage's front door. Then she banged on the wood until the door opened.

"I've had to compete with Jaenelle Angelline my whole life," she said. "With me always being the loser."

"A one-sided competition of your own making," Butler replied. "Do you know why this competition wouldn't have made sense to her?"

"Because she was more powerful than anyone else?"

"Nothing to do with power, Saetien. You can't compete with Jaenelle because you will never be required to pay a Queen's price." So much sadness in Butler's smile. "Wait here."

He didn't close the cottage door. She could have crossed the threshold and gone inside. It was the sadness in his smile that stopped her. The sadness and two words—"Queen's price." Was that something she should know about? Was it one of those lessons she hadn't listened to because she didn't want to know about Queens despite having had a friend who was a Queen?

What sort of price? Would Zoey be required to pay it someday? Did she know? Did Titian?

Butler returned in a few minutes, although it felt like rocks could grow in the time it took him to fetch . . .

She wasn't sure what he'd gone to fetch. A shallow wooden box, rectangular in shape, and a cloth bag. The box contained . . .

"Keep the mud moist but not soupy," Butler said. "You want it to be able to hold the sticks, and they won't stand up if the mud is too wet."

"You want me to poke sticks into mud?"

"Five hundred sticks. They're in the bag. Five hundred, Saetien. No more, no less. If the count isn't accurate, you'll have to start again."

"Then what?"

"You bring it back tomorrow at sunset."

Kieran climbed down from the pony cart and took the box, putting a tight shield around it to keep the mud from sliding out on the drive home. Saetien settled in the seat, put the bag between her feet, and held the box while she and Kieran returned to the stables.

"Leave it here," he said after arranging a couple bales of hay to form a kind of table. "If someone knocks that mud all over my mother's floor, we'll all experience Eileen's wrath."

Saetien set the bag of sticks beside the box. "Impressive wrath?"

"Not something you're likely to forget."

She took extra care wiping her feet before entering the house. Just in case.

FIFTY-FIVE

The next morning, Saetien went to the stables right after breakfast. Ryder offered to take Shelby to puppy school and fetch him when it was time for him to come home, and she took that offer, since she wasn't sure how much time this task would require.

Someone—maybe Kieran, maybe one of the stable hands—had kept the mud moist. The sticks were as long as her index finger and must have been made by hand, because they were all exactly the same length and diameter, and were perfectly smooth. She wondered if Butler had spent his nights trimming lengths of wood and sanding them to create these sticks.

"Have to start somewhere," Kildare said, using Craft to create a barrier between Saetien and the foals who would have crowded around her to see what she was doing.

There were a few stomps and squeals when they realized they couldn't reach her, but one of the Scelties looked at the foals and growled, and everyone with hooves hustled out to the paddocks, leaving her holding two sticks.

"Problem?" Eileen asked, passing through Kildare's barrier to stand beside Saetien.

Saetien started to push one of the sticks into the mud, then pulled her hand back. "If I don't do it right, I'll have to do it again. But what's the right way?"

Eileen rubbed a hand over one side of the shallow

wooden box, then another side. "Feel these holes along the top of the box? They're evenly spaced." She called in a large spool of black thread and a pincushion bristling with dressmaker pins. She fit the pins in the holes. "Do you see? You can make a grid. I'm thinking, once you set up the grid, you'll be able to place the sticks in tidy rows."

Eileen helped her get started, then went back to the house to take care of her own chores.

Saetien had finished making the grid and started setting the sticks in the mud when Caitie came by with Stormchaser. He went to his dam's stall for a meal and a nap. Caitie watched for a few minutes, then said, "Why are you doing that?"

"It's a task Prince Butler gave me." Saetien pushed another stick into the mud. "Five hundred sticks in this box, in rows. I have to bring it back to him at sunset."

"Do you have to do it alone?"

Saetien paused. Did she? "He didn't say I couldn't have help."

Caitie smiled and picked up a handful of sticks. "Then I'll help."

Since a human didn't actually drive a conveyance pulled by one of the kindred, Kieran was with her only as an escort—and to argue with the Warlord pulling the pony cart if the horse got bored going to the same cottage every evening and wanted to visit someone else.

She sat stiffly, holding the box and fretting about the one stick that must have gotten knocked so that it was leaning a bit. The mud had set before she'd noticed, so she was stuck with handing over an assignment that was less than perfect.

"It gives the whole thing a bit of character," Kieran said after she'd sighed again. "There's no point fretting over what you can't change."

No point fretting? She couldn't help fretting, since she didn't know what the box and sticks were for.

Butler didn't seem to notice the leaning stick, despite the careful way he eyed everything, as if deciding whether or not she'd used all the sticks.

Finally, he nodded. "Come back in the morning. Both of you." He looked at Kieran. "And anyone else who wants an answer to a question no one has dared to ask."

He went into the cottage and closed the door.

"What question?" Saetien asked as they headed home. "We didn't ask a question. We spent the day putting sticks in mud."

"I don't know the question either," Kieran replied. "But I think we need to prepare ourselves to face the answer."

FIFTY-SIX

T he next morning, Saetien and Eileen helped Kildare, Ryder, and Kieran with the morning chores before Ryder hitched up the pony cart while Kieran and Kildare saddled horses. They weren't the only ones who rode over to Butler's cottage. Word had spread through the village that something was going to be revealed, and aristos and shopkeepers alike were waiting for them. Except . . .

Saetien couldn't see what the people were staring at, but she recognized fear in all those pale faces as they turned toward the Warlord of Maghre.

"There are letters on the gate," a Warlord said. "One addressed to the young Lady and one for you."

"Stay here," Kieran said quietly as he dismounted to fetch the letters.

The people jostled one another until they opened a clear path to what had captured their attention.

Her box of sticks. She recognized it by the one stick that leaned a bit. But it wasn't just one box. The land beyond the cottage's fence was covered in boxes exactly like the one she'd made, snugged together so there was no space between. Box upon box, each with five hundred sticks, stretching over the land as far as she could see.

"Saetien." Kieran held out a letter. "This one is for you."

She looked at the letter, then looked at the boxes that

must have been created by an illusion spell. Then she looked at Kieran. "Could you read it?"

"Lord Kieran?" someone in the crowd asked. "What is this? What's it for?"

Kieran broke the seal, opened the letter, scanned the page—and shuddered. He took a deep breath and began to read.

> *What you see is the price of the purge that cleansed the Realms of the High Priestess of Hayll's taint. These are the Blood who were completely destroyed by the unleashing of the Queen of Ebon Askavi's power.*
>
> *Witch looked into a tangled web of dreams and visions and saw the war that was coming—a war that would have killed all of Kaeleer's Queens, all of the Warlord Princes. Everyone in the Dark Court's First Circle. Kaeleer would have won that war against Terreille, but there would have been no one left to rule the Territories, no one left to keep the human and kindred Blood united.*
>
> *But that tangled web showed another path—a path that would save all the Queens and Warlord Princes by sacrificing just one Queen.*
>
> *Witch chose that path, telling no one what the price would be. She unleashed her full power against the tainted Blood, cleansing the Realms.*
>
> *Look upon this accounting. Each stick represents one of the Blood who was sent to the final death. There was no war in the way we usually think of such things, only one Queen determined to protect everyone she loved and give them a future she didn't expect to see.*
>
> *Only one Queen shouldered the weight of all of these dead.*
>
> *Her name was Jaenelle Angelline.*

Kieran folded the letter and handed it to Saetien, but her

fingers wouldn't work right and the paper fell to the floor of the cart.

"I'll hold on to it for you," Eileen said, retrieving the letter.

Kieran opened the letter addressed to him. He cleared his throat. "'The illusion will last until tomorrow's sunrise. Anyone who wants to stand witness should do so before then.'" He folded the letter and vanished it.

"I want to see," Saetien said before anyone could suggest that she return to the house. "I want to see."

Kieran mounted his horse and led the way, Ryder and Kildare riding behind the pony cart and the other people who had assembled at the cottage scrambling into their various conveyances or mounting their horses to follow.

Over pastures and fields and crops. A sea of the dead that stretched to the horizon no matter which way she looked. Five hundred sticks per box. How many boxes? Saetien didn't know, felt too sick to try to count them.

Finally—*finally*—they reached land that had no boxes. No one else had come all the way with them.

"Mother Night," Kildare said softly.

"And may the Darkness be merciful," Kieran replied just as softly.

Eileen hugged Saetien and whispered, "How has she lived with this all these years?"

Saetien rested her head on Eileen's shoulder and wondered the same thing.

Kieran leaned against the desk in his study and waited for his father and brother. His mother would seek him out later for whatever she needed to say.

Kildare and Ryder walked into the room. Kildare closed the door and turned the lock.

"There was more to the letter Butler left for you," Kildare said. "More than you told the others."

Kieran nodded. "He didn't supply a number, but he wrote that the purge sent forty percent of the Blood in Terreille to the final death. Another thirty percent were tainted enough to be broken back to basic Craft." He scrubbed his hands over his face. "I keep thinking that none of us would be here if Jaenelle Angelline hadn't done what she did, but Mother Night!"

"We might be here," Kildare said. "Morghann and Khardeen had a child before . . . that day."

"Who would have been left to raise that child?" Kieran countered. "Assuming anyone from their bloodline would have been allowed to live?"

"There will be talk," Ryder said. "Especially since everyone knows the Lady is still at the Keep. Or has returned to the Keep."

"Do you think Daemon Sadi knows?" Kildare asked.

"Someone did a tally of the dead," Kieran replied. "If not Sadi, then the previous High Lord of Hell. So yes, I think they, and Lucivar Yaslana, understood the nature of their Queen and the choice she made. But I don't think any of them would have let her pay that price if they could have stopped her."

"Our Brenda is living at the Hall."

"I know." Sadi was powerful and lethal and everything that should be feared. But until he saw that tally of the dead, Kieran hadn't appreciated how dangerous Sadi could be. To be Consort and husband to the Queen who could do that? What other man would embrace such a Queen with so much joy?

Understanding that, he shared Kildare's concern about Brenda living at the Hall—and he had a new understanding of why Saetien couldn't live with a father she loved.

"Come in." Saetien adjusted the heavy shawl, grateful that Eileen had added a warming spell to the wool, because she kept fumbling every bit of Craft she'd tried to do since returning from that . . . accounting.

"A message from Butler," Kieran said, coming into the room but leaving the door open halfway. "He said not to come tonight."

She nodded. She wasn't sure what she could say to him after seeing . . . "When Butler said all the Warlord Princes would have died, he didn't mean *all* the Warlord Princes. Did he?"

"He did, yes. Your father and your uncle would have fought till their last breath and beyond. Would have kept fighting until they used up the last drop of reserve power in their Jewels. And maybe that would have been the difference between Kaeleer winning and losing the war. But they would have been gone. Demon-dead for a little while, maybe. But you wouldn't be here. Neither would I. Neither would so many of the people you know."

"They survived because she loved them," Saetien whispered. "Do you think she expected her spell to destroy her too?"

"I don't know. You'll have to ask Butler tomorrow."

She nodded.

"Do you want a tray in your room?"

"No, I'll come down for supper." She offered a wobbly smile and opened the shawl, revealing the puppy in her lap. "Besides, Shelby and I need to go out for walkies."

Walkies! Shelby said.

"Kieran? My father still serves her. Do you . . . Do you still like him after seeing . . . ?"

"I do, but I imagine there are many who couldn't. He is who and what he is, Saetien—and so was the Queen."

"So *is* the Queen."

"Yes."

Saetien took Shelby out for walkies, had dinner with Kieran and his family, then retreated to her room. She didn't want to talk, didn't want to read any more journals. She just sat on the window seat thinking about all those sticks and boxes—and she wondered what else Butler was going to tell her.

FIFTY-SEVEN

Titian waited with the other girls and the boyos who were serving in Felisha's court today. They'd all struggled during the first couple of weeks of these exercises, but the requirement to stand for other members in the court and stand for the people under the Queen's protection was slowly seeping past the rules and manners children learned in order to respond to adults—especially adults who were from aristo families or wore dark Jewels. Or both.

Lady Dumm's table manners had improved considerably. Whatever Uncle Daemon had done that one night to create that *smell* guaranteed there would be no more farting at the table. But the "special guest" at the Hall was still pushy and opinionated and crude and rude. Because of that, the students were all learning when to push back, when to draw a line and call in reinforcements, and when to officially report an offense to the Queen they were serving that day—and she would take it to the Queen *she* served. Unless she *was* the ruling Queen that day.

Titian had never given much thought to what the hierarchy of District Queens to Province Queens to Territory Queens meant in terms of who had to make the final decision about a wrong someone had done—and the debt owed to a family or a village for that wrong. She'd seen Queens talking to her father and seen the order of command among the men who served him directly. But she hadn't appreciated the price he must sometimes have to pay for being the person who made the final decision about someone else's life.

Was it easier for Lucivar and Daemon now that the Queen of Ebon Askavi had officially returned to the Keep? They no longer had to make that final decision if they didn't want to. But they wouldn't ask the Queen to shoulder that burden unless they weren't certain of the choice that should be made.

Maybe that was part of the price they paid for being Warlord Princes rather than being the rulers of their Territories. The Warlords and Princes who were among the students didn't seem to be changing, but the Warlord Princes . . . A look in their eyes, a slight shift in attitude that said *We are a law unto ourselves.* And they were. A lot of the Blood's laws and social rules didn't apply to them. Couldn't apply to them because they were predators born to stand on killing fields.

Had Uncle Daemon intended to nudge that predatory nature to the surface by using Lady Dumm?

Daemonar had said it was better to find out where the lines were drawn with a dressmaker's dummy than with someone who could bleed.

No one believed for a minute that Daemonar had missed the target when his arrow had pinned Lady Dumm's shoe to the ground moments after she started making comments about amateur artists—comments that had made Titian flinch. Line drawn. Warning given. The next arrow would damage more than a shoe if the subject came up again.

He'd been passing through on his way to some other lesson and had overheard Dumm's first sly comment. He'd barely checked his pace when he nocked the arrow, pivoted, and let it fly.

No one was sure what Grizande's target was supposed to be when her knife whipped past Lady Dumm and sliced off several plumes in Dumm's hat before hitting a tree. Grizande *claimed* she missed, although she became vague about what she'd intended to hit, since no one had been standing near the weapons practice area.

Defend. Protect. That was the purpose of a court.

"Any idea why Felisha is having this extra meeting with Azara?" Trent asked as he came to stand beside Titian. "If Felisha has to give Zoey and Kathlene orders for *their* courts, we won't get anything done this morning."

Azara was the Territory Queen today, Felisha the Province Queen, and Zoey and Kathlene the District Queens. Either Azara, who preferred agreeing with other people's opinions in case her own were wrong, had been given a challenging assignment for the day and needed extra time to figure out how to accomplish the task or . . .

"Something's not right," Trent said. "Raeth is with Azara today, and he says Azara and Felisha were arguing about Felisha's part of the assignment until Azara threatened to discipline her for disobedience."

Titian stared at him. "That doesn't make any sense." Especially if Azara was the one holding a line that Felisha didn't agree with.

"No, it doesn't." He studied her. "You trust your uncle?"

"Of course I do!"

"What about the instructors? Lady Dumm's table manners were an exercise pushed too far, but I didn't get the impression that Lady Brenda or Prince Raine would do anything that would *hurt* anyone. And our other instructors aren't really part of the group of adults working out these assignments."

"My uncle wouldn't put any of us at risk." Titian was sure of that. But that Trent was even wondering about that just proved he wasn't the same young Warlord Prince who had walked into the Hall a few months ago.

The door opened. Felisha walked in looking very unhappy.

Titian studied Trent, who was studying Felisha. Aunt Surreal once said there is always a moment when a Warlord Prince decides whether to obey an order or defy it, a moment when he moves a little closer to being loyal to the Queen he serves or becoming an adversary. Surreal had said with someone like Daemon or Lucivar the decision could be made in a heartbeat, but that hesitation was always there. And if it wasn't there? That meant the Prince's loyalty to his Queen went so deep, he would do anything for her without question. Anything. And that would make him the most dangerous male in the Realms.

She hadn't thought about the way Daemonar hesitated when asked to do something, even when asked by their mother or father. Hadn't considered that it was an expectation of his caste to act that way. Now, as she watched Trent, it was like seeing that aspect of a Warlord Prince's nature unfurl. Now the boy who sometimes laughingly scolded her for not eating all her vegetables was changing into a man who would draw a line and really fight with her if he believed she *needed* to eat all her vegetables.

Trent was becoming a warrior who would stand on killing fields. A dangerous man. Like her brother. Like her uncle. Like her father.

"Hold out your hands," Felisha said, gesturing to Titian, Trent, and Arlene.

Zoey frowned. Titian had said Felisha was upset after the meeting with Azara, but she didn't seem upset now. Annoyed? Uncertain? Determined?

All of those things.

Felisha slapped the hands of the three selected members of her court. Kathlene gasped, then belatedly put a hand over her mouth to hide the sound.

Felisha turned to Zoey and Kathlene. "Sometime today, before you return from your courts' assigned tasks, you will slap the hands of three people serving in your court."

"Why?" Zoey asked.

"Because that is what the Queen commands," Felisha snapped. "That was the command I was given to pass on to the two of you."

"But . . . why?"

"Because whoever is Territory Queen now has additional instructions, specific things the people under her hand are required to do."

"Like slapping someone?" Kathlene asked.

"Yes!" Maybe Felisha heard her own distress, because she stopped and took a couple of breaths before continuing. "It's . . . strange, but Azara showed me the instructions that were in the envelope she received this morning, and that is what we're required to do."

"Who wrote the instructions?" Zoey asked. "Could this be another Lady Dumm lesson?"

Felisha shook her head. "I don't know. Azara had to copy the instructions, so what I saw was in her handwriting." Another couple of breaths. "It's just a light slap. You saw how I did it."

"It's become fashionable for women to carry a fan at social events," Kathlene said, the words spoken with thoughtful slowness. "Before coming here, I attended a few social gatherings with my mother and aunt and saw quite a few Ladies use a fan to lightly slap a man's arm or hand, either to emphasize something she said or . . . something. I guess this is like that but without the fan?"

Maybe, Zoey thought. *Maybe. And a light slap on the hand isn't so bad. A little embarrassing because the rest of the court will think the people chosen had done something wrong, but no one would be harmed.*

No one would be harmed.

She wondered if Prince Sadi would agree with that. Then again, he would have been the one to make up this particular lesson.

FIFTY-EIGHT

Butler set an old door on top of two sawhorses, making a rough table for one of the hind legs of a pig that the butcher had delivered early that morning.

The first part of this lesson would be startling, more likely upsetting if Saetien understood what it meant. The second part, if she chose to participate in the second part, would be brutal.

He almost hoped she didn't have enough courage to choose the second part of the lesson.

He already knew her well enough to know her choice, and then there would be no going back—for either of them.

When Kieran dropped her off at the gate and eyed the rough table and the pig's leg, Butler said, "Go away, Lord Kieran. I'll request the return of the pony cart when we're ready, and I'll escort Saetien back to your house."

"Butler." From the Warlord of Maghre, the word was both question and warning.

"Go," he said again as Saetien climbed down from the cart.

He didn't say anything else until Kieran was far enough down the road that Butler was sure there wouldn't be anyone to interfere.

"What's that?" Saetien gestured toward the table. "Besides a big piece of meat?"

"A leg for tonight's lesson," Butler replied as he created a couple of balls of witchlight and set them above each end of the table.

"We're cooking a . . ." She suddenly went pale.

"It's pork. I bought it from the butcher this morning."

"What are we doing with it?"

"You are observing the collision of power and flesh."

"I don't understand."

"You will. Stand there and watch." He created a Green shield around the table, then looked at her. He knew why she reacted that way to a leg. He didn't need to touch her mind to supply a name and a place to go with that reaction. Dannie. In Briarwood. "Are you ready?"

Saetien nodded.

He unleashed his Green power on the meat. It exploded into tiny chunks caught in a bloody, bone-gritty mist. For several heartbeats there was nothing to see, until the chunks began to slide off his shield and the mist began to settle.

Saetien stared at the mess, then stared at him.

"Imagine getting hit with a backlash of power that exploded your body just like that. Imagine how it must have felt in the moments before the connection between your Self and your body was severed. Would you have had the courage to face that?"

"Why would I want to?" Saetien said.

"You've always thought you were competing with Jaenelle Angelline. She faced it."

"I . . ." Saetien hugged herself.

"I can use a kind of illusion," Butler said as he called in the other hind leg and used Craft to position it on the table. "Through a bit of Craft connecting you to the meat, you can feel what it would be like to have your leg explode. You'll come to no physical harm." He waited a beat, then added, "Whether or not you do this is your choice."

He watched the push-pull of conflicting wants so clearly displayed on her face. She wanted to step away from this, from the certainty of pain. And she wanted to prove she could be as strong, as special, as Jaenelle Angelline. Even now, she didn't understand that she had the freedom to choose another path—a freedom Jaenelle had never had.

Saetien lowered her arms and squared her shoulders. "I want to know. Show me."

A Black Widow would have done it differently—*could* have done it differently—but this way was simple and would work. Butler called in a spool of spider silk, wrapped one end of the thread around the pig's leg near the hock, then unwound more of the spider silk until he wrapped the other end around Saetien's leg just above her ankle.

"Stand still," he said, breaking off the thread and vanishing the spool.

She nodded, her eyes on the pig's leg.

A Green shield around the pig's leg with enough room to allow for the explosion without breaking the shield.

"Ready?" he asked.

Another nod.

The punch of Green power. This time, Butler watched Saetien at the moment the pig's leg exploded just like the first one had.

She stayed upright for a heartbeat, maybe two, her eyes wide, her mouth open in an attempt to scream. Then she collapsed.

Butler caught her as she went down. He snapped the thread connecting her with the pig's leg as he went down with her, holding her against his chest.

"You're all right, darling." He rocked her while she clutched her leg as if she needed to hold it together. "You're all right. The pain is real but your leg is intact. Breathe, Saetien. You need to breathe."

A gasping breath. Then another. And then the wailing scream—a sign that the pain was starting to fade.

Butler rubbed her leg briskly to help restore circulation. Not that it had been lacking, but the pins-and-needles sensation would be there and brisk rubbing helped.

"Let's get you inside." He picked her up and carried her into the cottage. She'd been silent after that one wailing scream, and that was a worry.

He settled her in a chair, tucked a quilt around her, and poured a generous amount of brandy into a glass. He wrapped her hands around the glass and said, "Healing tonic. Drink it down. It will help."

"It smells like brandy." Little girl voice. Hesitant to contradict an adult but certain of her facts.

"Tomorrow it will be brandy and you will be too young to drink it. Tonight it's a healing tonic."

"O-okay." She took a sip, made a face, then continued sipping until she finished.

Butler took the glass and set it aside before sitting on the hassock in front of the chair. He waited, knowing she had to come to this in her own time. That was the only way she would listen and really understand what he said.

"She felt that," Saetien finally said. "Her leg exploded and felt like that for real?"

"More than her leg," he replied quietly. "Her whole body." He gave her a moment to think about that.

"But . . . she survived."

"There was one chance to cleanse the Realms of Dorothea's and Hekatah's taint. There would never be another witch strong enough to do that if Jaenelle failed. So she needed all her power—and it took her three days to descend to her full strength. Marian and Daemonar had been taken captive and brought to Hayll. Lucivar had gone after them and was captured. Saetan went after them, intending to be captured. He hadn't known what Jaenelle was planning to do. He'd thought she was stalling because she didn't want the war they all knew was coming. He knew if he was captured, Jaenelle would go after Dorothea because he was the father of her heart and she always protected him. He didn't see in time that she was going after more than Dorothea.

"They'd sent her Saetan's little finger as a warning to surrender and become an instrument for Dorothea's rule of all the Realms. She needed those three days, so she asked Daemon to distract Dorothea and Hekatah. She asked—and he answered. But he knew what he'd have to do, and he knew the price he would pay, so he agreed to be Jaenelle's diversion only if she agreed to marry him when he returned."

"But she killed all those people," Saetien said. "Thousands and thousands of people."

"Yes. I think some part of her didn't expect to survive the unleashing of all that power. Maybe some part of her didn't want to survive and carry the burden of all those dead. But she gave Daemon her word that they would be married when he got back from Hayll, and what he wanted—what he needed—would have mattered more to her than her own peace of mind.

"She told me some things about that unleashing and what happened afterward. Not everything, but more than she'd told anyone else. Including Daemon." Butler hesitated. "Especially Daemon."

"Why didn't she tell him?"

"She had to make sure that she would succeed, so she unleashed most of her power and knew there would be some backlash. Because of her promise to Daemon, she kept some power back to form an Ebony shield around herself. She miscalculated. Or maybe in the moments when she created that shield she remembered Wilhelmina calling her a monster and wondered if everyone would see her that way. Maybe she didn't make the shield quite strong enough. Not deliberately, but in a moment when her courage failed. Maybe she expected to become a whisper in the Darkness and not have to see another person she loved look on her with horror.

"She hadn't known that the Queen of Arachna, that weaver of dreams, had seen what Jaenelle had intended and also saw a way to save her. She hadn't known that Ladvarian had rallied the rest of the kindred to use their strength and power and skills in order to tend all the healing webs and hold their Lady to the living while she was put back together, piece by piece, bone shard by bone shard. She hadn't known that Lorn, the last great Prince of the Dragon race that had created the Blood, had made it possible for Daemon, Lucivar, and Saetan to hold on to Witch's Self as she fell into the abyss.

"The backlash hit, and Jaenelle's body exploded. But the shield she created must have held her suspended in that moment just long enough for the flesh to be captured in all the webs the Arachnians had spun. And Daemon, Lucivar, and Saetan managed to stop her Self from falling into the Darkness, out of anyone's reach."

Butler let out a shuddering breath. "Would you like something to drink?"

"Not the tonic," Saetien replied.

He smiled. "Tea?" When she nodded, he went into the kitchen to put the kettle on. He gave her the illusion of privacy, but he stayed aware of her and the emotions churning inside her. He returned a few minutes later with a mug of tea and a glass of yarbarah. Handing her the mug, he resumed his seat on the hassock.

"Her whole body exploded?" Saetien asked after taking a sip of tea. "Everything?"

"Yes."

"The kindred put her back together?"

"Yes."

"So she felt that pain for a few mo—"

"Weeks," he interrupted. "She endured that pain for weeks, Saetien. Maybe not immediately afterward. Being in the healing webs would have numbed the pain, at least to some extent. But she rose before the healing was complete, and after that, there was unrelenting pain."

"Why did she rise before the healing was complete?"

"Because she loved Daemon Sadi, and he was breaking under the grief of losing her. You have to remember that he'd waited seventeen hundred years for her, and they were together for a few months. It wasn't enough time. After so many centuries of waiting, of yearning, of loving a dream he wasn't sure he would ever see, when she was finally there, it wasn't enough time. Lucivar had a few years with her, and he had a family to anchor him. Saetan had the experience of participating in the years while she grew up to become the Queen she would be. But Daemon? Given a choice, he would have died with her rather than live another day without her. He wasn't given that choice, but he'd lost the will to live. His father and brother could see him failing a little more day by day.

"Then the day came when they were told that Jaenelle had survived. And finally the day came when Daemon could bring her back to the Hall to continue healing."

"Did my father know she was in pain?"

"In pain, yes, but not the extent of the pain. She rose too soon in order to save him. She would never tell him how much his grief had cost her. She loved him with everything in her—and he loved her the same way. Still loves her. He would do anything for Jaenelle, and that was what made him so dangerous. And she would do anything for him." Butler drained his glass. "After all, she came back because he needed her to be more than an occasional dream and a song in the Darkness. She came back and made everyone aware of her return in order to help him save you."

Saetien set aside the mug of tea. "Everything has a price."

"Yes."

"I'd like to go home now."

"Home?"

"Eileen's house."

Butler touched her hand, a moment's connection. "She was dreams made flesh, Saetien. Because of the dreamers and what they needed from that dream, it was her nature to respond to people who asked for her help. Especially Daemon. Always Daemon. But I don't think she would have wanted you to choose that path in the same way. You can be so many things that she couldn't be."

"Because she was the Queen?"

"Yes. Because she was the Queen."

They didn't say anything more while they waited for the pony cart to arrive. They didn't speak on the drive back to Eileen's house.

As he walked back to his cottage, Butler wondered if he'd done too much, said too much.

He would find out when the sun set tomorrow.

FIFTY-NINE

Feelings clashed and burned through Saetien, scorching her heart, sizzling under her skin, igniting her thoughts until she had to *do* something before the fire took her and turned her into cold ash.

She tried helping out at the puppy school, but all the Scelties sensed there was something wrong with her, and with her around, the pups paid no attention to their lessons or the instructors. They were too busy trying to climb into her lap and offer comfort with licks and warm little bodies.

She tried helping Ryder with the foals, but they, too, knew something was wrong with her and crowded around her until Ryder created a shield and gently pushed them back before one—or more—of them ended up standing on her feet.

Nothing wrong with her leg. Nothing at all. Eileen had been so furious with Butler when he'd brought Saetien back last night that she'd sent Kildare to fetch the Healer to examine Saetien and tell a functioning, *feeling* adult what was wrong with the girl. The Healer confirmed there was no physical damage. A spell had created the feeling of the leg exploding, and what Saetien was experiencing now was the memory of that pain. It would fade.

But it was still there as Saetien strode to Butler's cottage. Faint, yes. Not really pain anymore, true. But it was there, and she had to *do* something with all these *feelings*.

She'd tried to leave Shelby behind, but that hadn't worked. The puppy had done his best to keep up with her at first, but by the time she realized he would struggle to follow her until he hurt himself, she couldn't send him back—and the adult Sceltie Warlord who followed both of them wasn't going to help her. Not with that. So, with the sun well into morning, there she was, carrying Shelby and striding toward the cottage of a man who hadn't seen daylight in centuries.

When she reached the cottage, she opened the gate and closed it with a crash. No movement in the cottage. No flutter of curtains to indicate someone looking out to see what the noise had been. Did Butler *sleep* during the day, or did he just have to avoid daylight? She knew so little about the demon-dead. Had never been interested. Why hadn't she been interested?

What to do? What to do?

Saetien looked at the flower beds that bordered the fence.

Okay, the cottage was probably locked and shielded, which made sense since Butler wouldn't leave himself vulnerable to attack. He might even have used an aggressive shield that would hurt anyone who tried to break through it. But the cottage wasn't the only building on the property.

"Come on, Shelby. Let's see what the man has in the shed."

The man had tools in the shed—rusty, neglected tools. Plenty of them—spade, shovel, spading fork, rakes, a variety of hoes—but each of them was in such bad condition that she suspected the business end would come away from the handle the first time she tried to use it. And the wheelbarrow had holes so big you couldn't carry *anything* in it!

It took her a couple of tries to create a Purple Dusk shield that lined the wheelbarrow and stayed in place. She found hand tools, just as rusty as the others but not as dangerous if they fell apart.

She hoped.

She put the tools in the wheelbarrow, then returned to the flower bed near the gate. It had rained last night. She'd heard the quiet patter as she lay in bed, waiting for the Healer's brew to relax her enough to sleep while nerves ping, ping, pinged with the memory of her leg exploding into pieces.

The ground was just right for weeding.

The Sceltie Warlord sat nearby, watching while Shelby did a sniff and piddle. Watching while Saetien picked up a tool and focused her scorching emotions on destroying the damn weeds.

She dug and pulled, pulled and dug, tossing weeds into the barrow. While she worked, thoughts rose and crashed.

Jaenelle Angelline had endured that pain for weeks. For *weeks*. Why? Because she loved Daemon Sadi so much, and she needed to endure it in order to return to him and stop *his* suffering and grief. Could she have told him and the kindred who had fought to keep her alive that she'd had enough, that she didn't want to remain among the living after everyone realized how many of the Blood she had killed? Daemon had been one of the dreamers responsible for creating Witch in the first place, and Butler had said that, being who and what she was, she had always answered those who had needed her.

It hadn't occurred to Saetien that the reason Daemon loved Jaenelle with such a fierce, single-minded intensity was that she was everything he needed, everything he'd wanted in a Queen and partner. He had been one of the dreamers. How could Jaenelle *not* have been perfect for him? And she loved him because . . . she was supposed to love him?

Saetien pulled out weeds, dug out weeds. Pulled and dug, dug and pulled.

Jaenelle Angelline had endured that pain for weeks, caught and trapped by a web of love. Had she returned a few months ago as a presence felt throughout the Realm because she wanted to return, or was she still trapped by the same web?

Saeti? Shelby approached when Saetien finally sat back on her heels and used her sleeve to dab the sweat from her face. *We are thirsty.*

"Me too." She'd noticed a small stable and pasture. Butler—or someone else—must have kept horses once upon a time. Maybe there was water there? Was there anything to put it in? She wasn't going to let the Scelties drink out of some rusty pan or filthy bit of crockery, and she sure wasn't going to drink out of anything like that either.

Hearing wheels and hooves, Saetien stood up and stretched her back and shoulders as Eileen drove up to the gate. She shifted her weight from one leg to the other and wondered if the leg with the phantom pain would hold her if she took a step.

"You've done a fair bit, haven't you?" Eileen said after she studied the stretch of weeded flower bed and the mound of weeds filling the wheelbarrow. "And done it well, from the look of things. But that much effort needs breathing space. You didn't come back for the midday meal, so I've brought you all something to eat and drink."

Water? The Scelties wagged their tails.

"Yes, water and food for all of you." Eileen walked into the yard, placed a heavy-bottomed bowl to one side of the flagstone walkway, and filled it with water. Then she called in a glass, filled that with water, and handed it to Saetien.

"Thanks." Saetien rubbed her hands on her trousers before taking the glass and drinking the water before taking another breath. Hell's fire, she hadn't realized she was *that* thirsty.

Eileen looked at the tools and *tsk*ed. "You can't be working with those. They're a disgrace."

"They're the best the man owns." Saetien frowned. How did Butler pay for things? *Did* he pay for things? His clothes weren't old or threadbare, so he must have to purchase *some* things. "Maybe he can't afford better tools?"

"Well now, he may not be extravagant in his spending, but the man makes a decent living. Always has. This is just him being . . . lazy . . . about parting with a few coins."

Eileen called in a basin, a bar of soap, and a towel. She filled the basin with water and used Craft to warm it. "Wash your hands so you don't end up with dirt in your food. And use your brains, girl, and put on some gloves before you get blisters."

"Yes, ma'am." Saetien washed her hands, then dug into the food Eileen had brought. The woman called in two more bowls and gave the Scelties their meal.

Eileen called in a basket and set it down near the flower bed. "You can borrow my gardening tools. The gloves in there should fit you too. Just bring them back with you when you come home."

Saetien looked into the basket and smiled. Proper, well-kept tools. "Thank you."

Eileen packed up the empty food containers, but left the second jug of water, the Scelties' water bowl, and the glass. "Are you seeing Butler this evening?"

"I don't know. I guess so." Did she want to see him? She was still angry and too full of feelings, but not as much as when she'd started weeding.

"You won't clear all this out in a day. And you don't want to collapse from the sun and the heat, so come back early enough to take a bath and rest a bit. You'll want your wits about you when you see him."

Saetien watched Eileen and the horse drive off. Then she went back to digging out and pulling out what didn't belong.

And she thought that maybe, just maybe, she was clearing out more than a flower bed.

Butler walked out of the cottage at sundown and wondered if Saetien would come that evening. Had he done too much, said too much? Eileen thought so, judging by the amount of fury she'd aimed at him last night when he'd brought Saetien back to the house.

The white flutter of paper caught his attention. What was the wheelbarrow doing there? He approached cautiously—a lifetime and more of training in the way he moved—and noticed the weeds filling the wheelbarrow. Noticed the length of flower bed cleared of debris.

When was the last time he'd noticed the flowers? Or cared about their being crowded out by weeds? He'd gotten tired. That's why it was time to go after this last assignment.

He stood at the gate as Kieran rode up.

"Saetien's not coming." Butler made it a statement, not a question.

"She was sleeping so soundly we couldn't rouse her, not even for supper," Kieran replied. "Consider it a reprieve. I expect she'll have a few things to say to you tomorrow."

Relief. Yes, this feeling was relief. "I'll look forward to hearing them."

Kieran laughed. "Oh, I doubt that, but you'll hear from her all the same." He gathered the reins. "Are you sure about this, Butler?"

"As sure as I can be."

"Good night to you, then."

"Good night, Kieran."

Butler waited until Kieran was well down the lane before creating a ball of witchlight. Only two words on the paper: *Compost bin?*

Simple words, simple question. But the shape and thickness of the letters gave him a fair idea of the level of annoyance Saetien was aiming at him. She was fighting mad, and that was just fine with him.

Smiling, Butler wheeled the barrow to the spot that used to hold the compost bins.

SIXTY

When Saetien tried to convince Shelby to go to puppy school without her, his response was to grab her shirt and hide under the bed. It took promising that he could go to Butler's cottage and help her with the digging for her to manage to retrieve the puppy and a shirt that had dust balls clinging to it. She handed the dusty shirt to Anya, who was mortified to see that the new maid wasn't taking her duties seriously. Anya suggested that Saetien be on her way before the housekeeper and Eileen were informed of this lapse, because Things Would Be Said.

Knowing how the housekeeper at SaDiablo Hall would react to such a lapse, Saetien took the hint, dressed in a hurry, gulped down her breakfast, and was out the door—which was where a speedy departure ended because Ryder and Kildare caught up to her. She had Eileen's basket of gardening tools, didn't she? And the cold box of food for her and the Scelties who would accompany her? And a couple of jugs of water? And the dishes and bowls girl and dogs required? And a hat in case she was going to be working in the sun?

She pointed out that she could use Craft to vanish all those things and call them back in when she reached the cottage.

Sure she could, but what about Shelby? Was she going to carry the pup all that way?

Somehow she ended up taking a small cart that Kildare

and Ryder had loaded with all the things she'd need that day. She and two Scelties sat on the driving seat. Not that she was driving. The Warlord hitched to the cart made that *very* clear. *He* would take care of the cart and getting her to the cottage. *She* just had to make sure she and the Scelties didn't do anything foolish and fall out of the cart.

Actually, making sure no one fell out of the cart was the job of the adult Sceltie who was standing escort since Shelby was too young for that task. Which made *her* the lone sheep being watched.

Five Warlords being helpful. Different species, sure, but still it had been five against one. She'd never stood a chance of stomping off this morning like she'd done yesterday. The Warlords were aware now and looking ahead, as males who were Blood tended to do.

No point grumbling about it. She'd save her grumbles for the damn weeds.

The wheelbarrow was where she'd left it, but it was empty.

At least the man had done that much. But . . .

Saetien unpacked the cart, thanked the Warlord, and promised to let him know when she was ready to go home. She filled a bowl with water for the Scelties, put on her hat and gloves, and, temper once again sizzling, she went after the weeds as if they were blighting *her* life instead of a flower bed.

Kieran looked at the letter in the basket where the family left mail that had to be delivered beyond the village. The letter from Eileen to Brenda was expected. His report to Prince Sadi? Also expected. But the letter from Saetien to her father? After spending her day in Butler's garden, attacking weeds while trying to deal with her reaction to that brutal lesson? She must have written it before she'd fallen asleep last evening, and dropped it in the basket on her way out the door this morning.

He took all the mail heading for SaDiablo Hall over to Angelline House and requested that one of the staff there deliver the letters personally.

Was there anything urgent? Prince Sadi wouldn't appreciate a delay in receiving news about his daughter.

Kieran assured them that there was nothing *urgent* in any of the letters.

Saetien might not agree with that, but whatever she'd said to the Warlord Prince of Dhemlan, he and Butler would deal with it—and pay the price.

Caitie and Stormchaser showed up an hour into Saetien's battle with the weeds. They entered the yard and Caitie closed the gate. Foal and Scelties immediately began a game of chase that had them circling the cottage.

"I don't think they can get into any trouble," Saetien said as the kindred rounded a corner.

Caitie nodded. "I'll help you." She selected a tool from Eileen's basket, knelt, and started weeding. A minute later, she pointed to the clump of plants Saetien was swearing at. "That's not a weed. It will claim whatever ground it can, but it's not a weed. Mother keeps it contained in large pots. The flowers are pretty."

"I don't have any pots." Saetien sat back on her heels. She was going to have to find a spade or figure out how to use Craft to dig that clump of plants out of the ground. Working around that patch, she listened to Caitie sing a Scelt folk song. She knew the next song—not the lyrics but the chorus—and joined in until a man rode up to the fence.

"Now, that's a pretty sight to warm a heart," he said.

Saetien tensed, wary of a stranger who sounded ready to take liberties, but Caitie gave the man a big smile.

"Father," Caitie said, "we need some pots. Big ones like Mother has in her garden."

"Do you, now?" he replied with a smile. "And how many will you be needing?"

Caitie looked at Saetien, who said, "Three?"

"I can fetch those for you. And you'll be needing some good soil to go in them?"

She hadn't thought that far ahead since she hadn't expected to get the pots. "Yes, sir, we will."

"Easy enough to do. You have anything to eat for the midday meal?"

"Yes, sir. Lady Eileen gave me plenty."

"That's fine, then. I'll be back in a bit." He rode away.

Saetien looked at Caitie, who gave her a sweet smile and began to sing and weed again.

It was close to midday when the foals came trotting up the lane with a Sceltie witch for escort. None of the foals knew—yet—how to work a latch on a gate, so they lined up on the other side of the fence to watch their human friends digging in the dirt. Saetien took a break to pet and praise and to drop kisses on muzzles, keeping the foals close to the cottage until she spotted Ryder and a stallion coming up the lane to retrieve the youngsters.

"Saetien and Caitie have to work now," Ryder said. "They will come to the stables in a little while to play with you."

The look in his eyes warned that there would be consequences if she made a liar out of him.

"We'll be down in a little while," she agreed.

Ryder gathered up the foals, including Stormchaser, and he and the Sceltie witch escorted the little herd back to the family stables. After being nipped for ignoring previous reminders about food, Saetien fed the Scelties and shared her own food with Caitie.

Caitie's father returned with three large pots. A couple of men drove up with a wagon filled with soil. They filled the pots, then deposited half the wagonload of soil next to the shed.

Not to worry, they all told her. They would send Butler the bill.

Hell's fire.

Caitie's father called in a spade and obligingly dug out the clumps of plants that would go into two of the pots and helped the girls with the planting by fetching a bucket of water from somewhere.

That much done, he pulled out his pocket watch and gave it a long look. "Time to be heading home, Caitie girl."

Which meant it was time for Saetien to pack up too; the Warlord with the cart came trotting up the lane and would not take kindly to being kept waiting for long.

Saetien eyed the Scelties. Shelby just wagged his tail, but the adult Sceltie who had been watching his two sheep . . . *Someone* besides Caitie's father had decided it was time for the girls to go home and play with the foals.

"Caitie can ride with me and see Stormchaser before going home," Saetien said as she wiped off Eileen's gardening tools and gathered up the rest of her supplies.

"Well then, I'll ride along with you."

They climbed into the cart and headed home, with Caitie's father riding alongside.

She'd left the wheelbarrow piled high with weeds again, and no one could miss the difference between the ground she and Caitie had cleared and all the work still to be done.

But there was a different kind of work that needed to be done once the sun set.

"Do you want to come inside?" Butler asked when Saetien arrived that evening.

"No, I want you to show me how to use Craft to remove something from the ground," she replied as she walked over to a spot in the flower beds and pointed to a clump of plants. "How do I remove that using Craft?"

"You could use a shovel or a spade."

"I could if you had tools that weren't falling apart." She took a breath. "Let's pretend there is a buried chest and I don't have any tools and I'm miles from any town, and I want to get the chest out of the ground because it might contain something important. How would I do that?"

"So we're after buried treasure—is that it?" He sounded amused—and he sounded intrigued. Willing to play along.

"Yes." Had her father tried to show her how to do this bit of Craft? Probably. But somehow, learning from him had made everything so dreadfully *important* because *he* was so important. And things had changed inside her head when Papa stopped being just Papa and was also the Warlord Prince of Dhemlan in a way that made that title more than just words.

But Butler could teach her how to extract buried treasure from the ground.

"All right, then. With a lot of practice you could stand a few feet away and pass the chest through the ground like you'd pass any object through another, or you could vanish the chest and call it back in. But if you're not sure what's in the chest, and you have to dig it out without doing any actual digging . . ." Butler knelt in front of the bed and waited for Saetien to join him. He hesitated a moment, then put his hands over hers. "You want to take care to get all of what you're after, but you don't want to spend your power on taking up more than you need. So first you release a psychic thread to give you the shape of the object." He guided her hands, let her follow the power he was using to shape the lesson. "Once you have the shape—you don't want to nip off a corner of the chest and have the treasure spilling out—you create a shield around it, like this. And then you . . . lift."

The clump of plants rose out of the ground, soil clinging to the roots.

"Since this isn't a chest, what are you going to do with the plants?" Butler asked.

"Put them back tonight," Saetien replied, lowering the clump of plants into the hole created by their removal. "I haven't decided if they will stay or go." She stood and brushed off her trousers.

Butler sat back on his heels and waited.

"Did he know?" Saetien finally asked. "Did Daemon Sadi know how much pain Jaenelle Angelline endured in order to come back to him? Was he . . . selfish . . . not letting her go?"

Butler rose and stared at the land beyond the cottage. "He knew there was pain. Everyone who saw her could sense that there was pain. He knew she was fragile for months after he was allowed to bring her back to the Hall. But she never shared what it felt like as her body exploded and was caught in all the healing webs the Arachnians had made. Daemon did not—and does not—know the extent of that pain or what it felt like when she rose from the healing webs too soon and had to endure the rest of the healing awake and aware. At that point, she was the primary Healer and was putting her own body back together. He didn't know what that felt like. Neither did Saetan or Lucivar."

"Why do you?" she asked softly.

"A few years before her body died of old age, Jaenelle and I talked about that time in her life. She shared with me the truth about what happened to her when she unleashed her power to save her friends and Kaeleer. She opened a place within herself that she'd kept well guarded for all those years, and I felt what she felt in that moment. Hideous, unimaginable pain. I wept for her, and she said, 'Everything has a price, Butler. To be with Daemon? It wasn't too high a price to pay.'"

Saetien couldn't blink back all the tears. "He meant that much to her."

"He still does," Butler said gently.

"But why did she tell you?"

"She'd spun a tangled web of dreams and visions, and it showed her that she needed to tell me about that time because I would meet someone someday who would be on a heart quest and would need to know. I guess that's you."

Her breath caught. A sob escaped. Butler gathered Saetien in his arms and held her while she cried.

Butler, it's time.

Sometimes a heart had to break in order to heal. He and Jaenelle understood that all too well.

"Her road isn't yours," he said. "You have to find the shape of your own life, Saetien. And you will find it if you allow yourself to look."

They were still standing there when Kieran drove up to take Saetien home.

SIXTY-ONE

Daemon studied the two letters, then opened Kieran's first.

A careful report about Saetien's activities. Puppy school. Playing with the foals. Making a friend her equivalent age.

Everything right and proper for an aristo girl visiting an aristo family, especially the family of the Warlord of Maghre. But not a word about Butler, which had to be a deliberate omission.

Sighing, Daemon set Kieran's letter aside before opening Saetien's letter.

He read it twice and still didn't know what to think.

A quick knock on the study door before Surreal walked in. "Sadi, I'm heading back to the sanctuary." She paused. "Is something wrong?"

"A letter from Saetien."

"Has she learned anything about Wilhelmina Benedict?"

"I don't know." Daemon checked the back of the letter in case he'd missed something. He hadn't. "She's seriously pissed off at Butler for neglecting his gardens, which could be lovely if someone cared about them, and for being so indifferent about his gardening tools that he's let them rust and rot."

"Being demon-dead, I don't imagine he spends much time in the garden," Surreal said.

"That doesn't seem to be a sufficient excuse."

Surreal blew out a breath. "Well, she always was pretty fierce about that patch of garden that you and Tarl let her claim for her own."

"And woe to any gardener in training who overlooked a weed growing anywhere near her patch." Daemon folded the letter and vanished it.

"What are you going to do?"

He gave Surreal a dry smile. "Figure out how to answer her letter without getting Butler into more trouble."

SIXTY-TWO

A town in Dhemlan

Dinah waved a letter at her maid, Ida, and laughed. "My friend Cara says those goody-goody Queens are obeying the new instructions we supplied! They're wringing their hands over giving those orders to their courts, but *they're doing it.*"

"Told you they would," Ida replied, smiling. "None of them have the gumption to challenge an order they believe is coming from Prince Sadi."

Dinah raised her chin. "I would have challenged it."

"Of course you would have. You're a proper Queen." Ida's smile changed, carried a hint of something dark and cruel. "Now that they've taken that first step in doing wrong, let's find out how many of them will take the next step."

Dinah smiled in return. "Yes, let's find out."

SIXTY-THREE

By the end of that first uncomfortable week, the Queens had adjusted to the new addition to their list of tasks. Each of them had had a turn at being the Territory Queen who gave the command for the hand slaps.

The standard assignments for the day were in Prince Sadi's handwriting. The "extra" command was in someone else's hand—and always included the instruction to write out the additional assignment in the Queen's own hand and burn the original with witchfire.

"Convenient," Zoey muttered as she wrote out the extra instruction. With the original destroyed, there was no proof that these "little disciplines" weren't the Queen's idea.

This week, the orders were that two people receive a hard slap on the hand and a third receive a light slap across the face.

What were they supposed to be learning by doing this to their own people? What were they supposed to learn by demanding the Queens who ruled under them do the same to *their* people?

And if these extras *were* part of the official lessons, why were these "disciplines" supposed to be done out of the sight of adults?

Titian and Jhett were in Zoey's court today. So was Raeth. She felt friendly toward the other four students assigned to her, but they weren't friends. Not like Jhett and Raeth. Not like Titian.

But two of those seven people would receive a hard slap on the hand today, and one would receive a slap on the face. If she didn't include at least one of her friends in that number, how would the other four feel? Favorites escaped discipline? Favorites weren't slapped in the face?

Zoey summoned one of her Warlords and asked him to go to the stable for seven pieces of straw. He nodded and hurried off without asking why.

Raeth, being a Warlord Prince, would have asked why—and that was the reason she didn't give him the assignment.

She summoned Kathlene, who was the Province Queen that day, and issued the day's tasks that the other Queens had to perform—including the extra part.

Kathlene stared at her.

"Do you want to see the instructions I was given?" Zoey asked.

Kathlene hesitated, then shook her head. "This isn't right, Zoey."

"I know. But someone has added this to the lessons."

"Who?" Kathlene didn't wait for an answer before bowing and leaving the room.

"Good question," Zoey muttered. Someone knew about these extras they were supposed to do in secret. But who, exactly, was that someone?

Zoey held seven straws. Her court drew the straws based on their Jewel rank, regardless of caste, to determine who would receive that day's discipline.

Titian drew a short straw. So did Raeth. So did the Warlord who had been sent to fetch seven pieces of straw.

Feeling sick, Zoey collected the straws and then had those three people draw again.

Raeth drew the short straw.

"Hold out your left hands," Zoey said.

She slapped Titian's hand—hard. She slapped the War-lord's hand—hard. And then she slapped Raeth in the face—and watched his hands curls into fists and his eyes glaze with temper.

"Each of you will discipline three other people in the same way you were just disciplined—by slapping a hand or slapping a face."

Titian made a wordless protest. The Warlord looked troubled.

Raeth stared at her.

Do it, she thought. *Do it.*

The instructions were clear. If *she*, the day's Territory Queen, complained to one of the instructors or, may the Darkness have mercy, to Prince Sadi, all seven of her people would be physically punished. But she'd read the instructions three times before burning the original with witchfire, and there was *nothing* in them that said another member of her court couldn't issue a complaint with the instructors or the Prince.

"We'd better get started," Zoey said. "Jhett? If you could wait a moment?"

The rest of them left the room.

"Lady Zoela?" Jhett's formality stung Zoey's feelings, but it also gave her hope. Jhett wouldn't stay in a real court with any Queen who acted like this.

"Wood and stone remember," Zoey said with the same care she'd use when crossing an ice-covered pond. "Isn't that how Black Widows can see a . . . memory . . . of something that happened in a place?"

Jhett nodded.

"Paper is made of wood." Zoey licked her lips and wished she had some water for a suddenly dry throat. "Could a Black Widow coax an image out of paper?"

"Like, an image of the sender?"

"Yes." If it was possible, that could explain why who-ever was adding these extra commands wanted the original pieces of paper burned.

"I don't know," Jhett finally said. "I'm going to Halaway this afternoon to visit the Sisters living at the Hour-glass House. I could inquire."

"Do that."

Daemonar sat at a table near the social room's sliding glass doors. Grizande had gone into the village with Jhett to visit the recovering Black Widows—and to visit Tersa, although that was implied rather than stated. Since Liath had been growling at humans all morning—and had bitten the hand of one Warlord and then refused to explain what the boy had done to earn the bite—Daemonar had offered to keep an eye on Jaalan. A Green shield around the courtyard kept the tiger confined enough to allow Daemonar to concentrate on his studies while giving the kitten room to play.

Unfortunately, most of the residential squares of rooms had a fountain somewhere in the courtyard and little tigers liked playing in water, even when the weather was chilly.

Wet tiger didn't smell any better than wet dog, but getting Jaalan to understand that he couldn't come inside until he was dry . . . He was outside with no one to play with. Bored with the available toys, he kept returning to the fountain to play in the water and pounce on anything that fell in—leaf, twig, feather of a bird that claimed this courtyard as its territory.

The birds weren't kindred, but sometimes he could swear they knew which individuals they could tease and which ones had the speed and skill to turn them into feathered mush.

Daemonar watched the kitten head back to the fountain and shook his head. When he finished reading this chapter, he'd go out and play with Jaalan long enough to get the kitten dry. Then they could both stay inside until Grizande returned.

Raeth walked into the room, then hesitated when he eyed the books Daemonar had spread out on the table.

"You got a minute?"

Daemonar marked his place and closed the book. "Sure."

Raeth pulled out a chair and slumped in it.

Anger and hurt pumped out of the younger Warlord Prince. The hurt could fester into something dangerous, and the anger was too close to the surface to dismiss.

Daemonar swallowed impatience as he waited for Raeth to say something. How many times had he interrupted his father while Lucivar was doing some work and then couldn't say the thing that had been so urgent? And each time, Lucivar had waited, letting him get to the thing in his own time.

"What if a Queen gives you an order and you can't swallow it?" Raeth finally asked.

"Then don't swallow it," Daemonar replied.

"But she's your Queen."

"Is she? Can you say that her will is your life? Or is she the Queen you're serving at this time?"

"A couple of weeks ago, I would have said the first was possible. Now?" Raeth shrugged, a move full of unhappiness.

"What's happened over the past couple of weeks to change that?" He'd noticed the boyos were all sweating out some anger during sparring practice, but none of them wanted to say what had stirred that anger. Come to think of it, the girls were all off the mark too. Not angry, just . . . off their stride. No, more than that. It was like they were skidding toward the edge of a cliff and unable to stop themselves from going over.

Instead of answering the question, Raeth said, "What would you do?"

"I would draw the line and tell her to take a piss in the wind." *Even if Witch was the one who gave the order?* Daemonar leaned closer to the other Warlord Prince. "Don't accept any order that smears your honor. Any Queen who asks that of you isn't worthy of your loyalty."

"What if she's being squeezed into giving those orders by someone more powerful?"

"Then take your concern to someone powerful enough to do something about it."

"And if that powerful someone already knows?"

Daemon Sadi would not ask any man to whore his honor. Which meant something was going on that was being carefully hidden from Sadi because it would snap the leash on his temper.

Daemonar leaned back. "Hypothetically, a Warlord Prince has been asked to . . ."

"Slap someone in the face."

"Without cause?"

"It's being called discipline, but there's no justifiable reason for it."

He nodded. "And this order is coming from . . . ?"

"Territory Queen to Province Queen to District Queens."

"The Territory Queen is deciding this is to be done?"

"No. Apparently the Territory Queen is given secret orders about this discipline, along with the other assignments for the day."

"Secret orders given to the Territory Queen by someone who outranks her? Hypothetically."

"Yes." Raeth hesitated. "Can't tell the adults or the whole court will be punished."

"Adults" meaning the instructors, senior staff, and, most of all, Sadi. "What kind of punishment?"

"That's not specified. At least, the Warlord Princes haven't been told what will happen."

"Did you slap someone?" he asked quietly.

"Was supposed to slap three of the girls, but after the first . . ." Raeth shook his head. "Couldn't."

"Will the slap leave a mark?"

"No." A flash of rage, quickly leashed. "It's not right, asking us to do that."

No, it wasn't. Did the author of this game have any understanding of the nature of Warlord Princes? The tempers of the other Warlord Princes might not be close to snapping the leash, but he'd bet his quarterly allowance that

Raeth had already sharpened his knives in preparation for a fight. "Whose court are you in today?"

"Zoela's."

Hell's fire. "Keep an eye on Jaalan. I'll be back in a bit."

Brenda stared out the window. Something was happening here. A breaking of trust. A curdling of feelings. Oh, all the youngsters were being careful to hide the reason, whatever it was, but the adults noticed. Did the young Queens and their courts think the adults *didn't* notice? She wanted to wade in and demand to know what the problem was, but she reluctantly agreed with Raine that they should give the youngsters a chance to figure out how to fix the problem on their own or come to them for help. And he agreed with her that they should keep a sharp eye on the youngsters and intervene if anyone did more than smudge a line that Prince Sadi had drawn for acceptable behavior.

She turned away from the window when someone knocked on her door. "Come in." She smiled when Neala walked into the room. "Is there something I can do for you?"

"Yes, Lady. I need some advice."

Brenda gestured to two chairs. Once they were settled, she said, "Advice about . . . ?"

"I saw something," Neala said. "Something I don't think is right, but it's hard to know with these odd lessons that have been going on."

Odd lessons? Brenda felt a prickling beneath her skin. "Something besides Lady Dumm?" She and her selected helpers had gone a bit too far there—and had learned a lesson of their own about how the Warlord Prince of Dhemlan handled some problems—but the maids had aired out the clothes that had been worn that night. Eventually.

"Not like Dumm," Neala said quietly. "These lessons . . . harm the body a little, but . . ."

But they break trust. Curdle feelings. "Tell me what you saw."

Brenda listened, saying nothing as pieces came together. When Neala finished, Brenda stood and said, "Come with me."

With the Scelt maid beside her, she strode through the Hall's corridors, heading for Prince Sadi's study.

Daemonar settled into a chair in front of Uncle Daemon's desk. He wasn't sure whom he'd be facing a minute from now, but for the moment he was dealing with his uncle.

"Hypothetical question," he began.

Daemon leaned back in his chair, steepled his fingers, and rested the forefingers against his chin. "Why do you always bring hypothetical questions?"

"I'm curious about things?"

"Uh-huh. Did anything blow up?" A mild, amused question.

"Not physically."

A chill in the air replaced amusement. "Explain. Hypothetically."

Daemonar repeated what Raeth had told him, including the part about the Queen's whole court being punished if the Queen complained to one of the adults.

"Do you think I would have added such an instruction?" Daemon asked too softly.

"Of course not. But someone added those instructions—and they were careful to make sure you wouldn't find out about it." Daemonar thought for a moment. "I doubt Brenda or Raine knows about this, although you've all probably noticed a degree of idiocy that wasn't there a couple of weeks ago."

"That's one way of putting it. I wondered if shuffling the 'courts' every day was too much of an adjustment." Daemon raised an eyebrow, turning the comment into a question.

Daemonar shrugged. "Maybe give each 'court' a week to work together before shuffling who serves which Queen. A day isn't long enough to figure out who can do what—or who will stand and fight and who will crumble in order to avoid paying a price."

"Sometimes a day is all you have to make that kind of decision," Daemon said quietly. "But your point is valid and—"

A thump of fist on wood before Brenda walked into the study, followed by Neala. When she spotted Daemonar, Brenda stopped for a moment, then approached the desk, herding the Scelt maid.

"Neala has something to tell you," Brenda said.

Daemonar started to push out of his chair. "I'll—"

"Sit," Daemon said, turning that one word into a command. He pointed to the other chair. "Neala."

Brenda stood beside the chair, one hand on Neala's shoulder. Supportive rather than restraining.

"What do you have to tell me?" Daemon asked.

Daemonar wondered if anyone else could feel the cold anger beginning to rise from the depth of the Black. He figured Brenda, wearing the Green, would notice, but she gave no indication of it.

"I was tidying the social room in the Queen's square—the square of rooms across the corridor from yours," Neala explained. "I was standing in plain sight, but it was a shadowy part of the room at that time of the morning, so I doubt Lady Cara noticed me when she slipped into the room. Her bedroom isn't in this square of rooms, and no one else was about, so she had no business being there. Except it seems she did, because she hurried over to the basket that held the envelopes with the assignments, took one out, carefully lifted the wax seal, and then added another piece of heavy paper. I think she used a bit of Craft to warm the wax enough to seal the envelope again." Neala hesitated. "Lady Cara was laughing when she left the room." Another hesitation. "She's an aristo Lady, so I wasn't sure it was my place to be telling tales about her making mischief, but after what happened this morning, with Liath biting that boy after the boy slapped one of the girls in the face . . ."

"The boy did what?" Daemon's voice was quiet and viciously polite.

"Slapped her," Brenda said. "Obeying the Queen's orders."

"Whose orders?" Still quiet. Still viciously polite. But getting colder. Getting closer to the Sadist.

"Not yours," Daemonar said. "Not Lady Brenda's or Prince Raine's or any of the other instructors. Not Beale or Holt."

Daemon's glazed gold eyes focused on him. Just him.

Daemonar swallowed hard and chose to dance on the knife's edge. "If the Queens were doing whatever this is by their own choice, you'd toss them out of the Hall before they had time to squeak. Maybe that's the intention. Maybe someone is trying to push you into expelling these Queens and the others who are here for court training and protection."

"There's sense to what Prince Yaslana is saying," Brenda said. "You've already expelled a couple of girls for crossing some lines."

"I have," Daemon agreed.

Daemonar held his breath, hoping that Brenda wouldn't point out that Cara had been one of Dinah's friends. Although he wasn't sure what difference it would make. Sadi would figure out if Cara had acted alone or if she had received those extra instructions from someone else—and he would call in the debt.

"A slap on the hand, a slap in the face," Daemon said. "Was any other kind of punishment ordered?"

"Not that Raeth mentioned," Daemonar replied. "I can see why no one growled about the hand slaps. I've had my hand slapped plenty of times, so being ordered to do that wouldn't seem important enough to report to you."

Daemon stared at him. "Having your mother slap your hand because you were trying to grab half a cake and stuff it in your mouth is significantly different from having a Queen give that order for no reason. One slap is done out of love; the other is done because a Queen wants to inflict pain and doesn't expect to pay a price."

"It wasn't *half* a cake," Daemonar muttered. "And I was *little* when I did that."

Warmth replaced cold in Daemon's psychic scent. "But it did make an impression."

The slap itself hadn't made as much of an impression as

finding his mother crying because she'd had to inflict that slap to stop him from grabbing the cake. No need to mention the crying to Uncle Daemon. Lucivar had said *plenty* about that at the time.

Daemon turned his attention back to the Scelt maid. "Thank you for reporting this, Neala. You did the right thing. If you notice anything else, please inform Lady Brenda. Or you can report to Beale, Helene, or Holt. I'll make them aware of this . . . trouble."

Daemonar pushed out of his chair. "I left Raeth watching Jaalan. I'd better rescue him."

"Which one would you be rescuing, then?" Brenda asked.

"I guess I'll find out."

Brenda and Neala left the study. Daemonar stayed a moment longer. "Is this how it begins? With something that seems so insignificant that no one challenges it?"

"Last week started with a slap on the hand," Daemon replied. "This week has added a slap in the face. How many steps between that slap and someone being ordered to use a riding crop or belt or whip on someone's back? Not that many. And once you've split someone's skin, it's easier justifying taking that next step if the choice is to inflict pain or feel the whip yourself."

"What are you going to do?"

"As long as it doesn't escalate, I'll give the youngsters a couple more days to report this to me or resolve it on their own. Either way, I will find the source of this trouble."

"Sir."

"Prince."

Daemonar hurried to return to the room where he'd left Raeth. Yes, Sadi would find the source. And may the Darkness have mercy on that person.

Daemon waited for Beale, Helene, and Holt to report to his study.

He'd been aware of emotional undercurrents. Hell's fire, there were thirty-six aristo adolescents living in the Hall—

not to mention the servants who were around the same age—so how could there not be emotional undercurrents? But this deliberate . . . corruption . . . of honor. He understood why the other girls hadn't come to him when that first command had been given, but he felt a sharp disappointment that neither Titian nor Zoey had marched into his study to ask him about it. They should have known he wouldn't allow even that much physical harm, that he wouldn't allow any mental or emotional harm to be inflicted on anyone under his protection. Instead, they had submitted to receiving and inflicting physical harm.

Well, once they got this sorted out, he knew what lessons these youngsters needed to learn for their own sakes as well as for the safety of the Realm.

Titian hurried to open the door of Zoey's bedroom just enough for Jhett to slip inside. It had been an awful day, with the instructions getting garbled as they'd been passed from Province Queen to District Queens, who gave the orders to *their* people. The result of those garbled instructions was that two of the girls had been slapped in the face hard enough to leave a bruise. Arlene and the other apprentice Healers had done what they could to reduce the pain and swelling—and the skin discoloration—instead of hauling the girls to Lady Nadene and having the resident Healer deal with the injuries. But Nadene would have reported to Uncle Daemon, and Zoey wanted a little more time before Uncle Daemon learned about the extra instructions—just enough time for the Queens to find some answers on their own.

"It's possible," Jhett said without preamble. "Paper doesn't usually hold intense emotions like a room where someone was attacked, but a skilled Black Widow could draw out some emotion or recognize a psychic scent."

"Could you . . . ?" Zoey began.

Jhett shook her head. "I don't have the skills yet to do that." She hesitated. "Prince Sadi has that skill. It's kind of

an open secret now among the Hourglass and isn't supposed to be talked about with anyone who isn't a Black
Widow, but he *is* a natural Black Widow—the only natural
male Black Widow in the history of the Blood, and the only
other male Black Widow *ever* was his father. And Witch
was one of Prince Sadi's teachers in the Hourglass's Craft."

Zoey caught her lower lip between her teeth. She trusted
Prince Sadi. She did. But she was certain *someone* was
watching the Queens to make sure they followed the secret
instructions, and she couldn't risk harm coming to her people by her breaking the rules and telling him about this.

She couldn't tell Prince Sadi, because he lived at the
Hall, *ruled* the Hall.

Her breath caught as an idea took shape. But how to get
there?

"We should tell Uncle Daemon about this," Titian said.
"He wouldn't approve of these disciplines. I know he
wouldn't."

"We have no proof that we're being given these orders
and not making them up on our own," Zoey protested.

"We could have proof tomorrow or the next day." Titian
took Zoey's hand. "It's possible, even likely, that Jhett, Arlene, Laureen, or I will be in the Territory Queen's court
tomorrow. Whoever is in the Territory Queen's court should
offer to burn the instructions. Kathlene, Felisha, and Azara
don't want to do this any more than you do. If a Queen tells
someone to burn the original instructions and that person
doesn't do it, then she's not risking her whole court being
punished—because she wasn't the one who disobeyed."

"That risks the person who didn't follow orders."

"Not if the person takes those instructions to Uncle
Daemon before anyone else finds out. And if I'm not the
one who is in position to take that paper, I'll go with whoever has it, because he'll listen to me. He always has."

Zoey swallowed hard. She could do this. She *would* do
this. "We should get advice from someone who doesn't live
at the Hall, just in case these disciplines are intentional."

"Who?" Jhett asked.

Zoey called in a small velvet pouch and removed one gold coin. She held it up. "This mark of safe passage grants me an audience with the Queen of Ebon Askavi. I'll tell her what is going on here and ask what we should do."

Titian blinked. "How are you going to get to the Keep?"

"I'll get there. And I'll ask someone who can get there a lot faster than I can to go with me."

Grizande opened her bedroom door and stared at Zoela Queen.

"May I come in?" Zoela Queen asked, her voice hushed.

When Zoela Queen slipped into the room, Jaalan bounded toward her, then stopped when Grizande didn't give him the signal that this girl was a friend.

"I need a favor," Zoela Queen said. "I need your help. Can you drive a Coach on the Winds?"

"I can." Hard to read this girl-Queen. Afraid. Uncertain. But also strong. "Why ask . . . ?" She made a gesture to indicate herself.

"You wear Sapphire, so you could get us there faster than I could travel on my own. And you're a strong warrior. An honorable witch."

Grizande studied Zoela Queen. A trap? She didn't think the girl-Queen knew anyone in Tigrelan. "Where we go?"

"Ebon Askavi." Zoela Queen held out a gold coin. "I can use this to request an audience."

"You go to ask wisdom of the Queen who is more than a Queen?"

"Yes."

A need strong enough to approach Witch? Fear and strength. That made sense now.

"When?"

"Tonight during the quiet hours, after everyone retires and before the first servants report for their duties."

She'd need help getting a Coach they could use. Which made her wonder . . . "You friend of Daemonar's sister. Why not ask him?"

Zoela Queen swallowed hard. "He's a Green-Jeweled Warlord Prince. When someone finds out we're gone, there might be trouble that could end with someone getting hurt. Daemonar might be needed here to help protect . . ."

To protect his sister, among others. That made sense too. If Daemonar sounded the battle cry, not only would Green step onto the killing field; the Black would join him.

Grizande turned to the pendulum clock and pointed at the number three. "Come to landing web. We go then."

"I'll be there." Zoela Queen hesitated. "Thank you."

Using the excuse that Jaalan needed garden time, Grizande escorted Zoela Queen out of the glass doors that opened to the inner courtyard. While Jaalan took care of his business, she watched the girl-Queen hurry back to her own room—and the friends waiting for her.

There would be trouble over this. She just wasn't sure where the trouble would fall.

Daemonar paused for a moment before opening his bedroom door. Only one Sapphire in the Hall, so this wasn't one of the girls—or one of the boys—who might be looking for a little romance.

"Grizande." He spread his wings enough to block the doorway.

"Need help." Quietly spoken words filled with fierce determination. "Need a Coach. Small."

"Why?" When she hesitated, he gave her a lazy, arrogant smile. "Darling, if you want my help to leave the Hall, you'll have to tell me why."

"Zoela Queen needs wisdom from Queen who is more than a Queen. I can drive Coach. I take her to Ebon Askavi."

Hell's fire. Uncle Daemon was going to bounce off the ceiling when he heard *that*. And yet . . . Not a solution most people would consider, but requesting wisdom from the most powerful Queen in the Realms was certainly an active effort to deal with the additional instructions the Queens had been given.

"I'll get the Coach and bring it to the landing web," he said. "When?"

"Tonight at . . ." Grizande held up three fingers.

"Okay."

"You look after Jaalan?"

"You'll be back by the evening meal. I'll look after him until then."

She looked doubtful about getting back that day. He had no doubts at all since he figured Lucivar would be the one driving the Coach back to the Hall.

And once the Demon Prince and the High Lord teamed their skills and tempers to deal with this problem . . . Wouldn't that be fun?

"Get some sleep," he said. "If you're going to be driving a Coach on the Sapphire Winds, you need to be awake and sharp."

He dozed more than slept. Judging the time, he dressed in warm clothes, went to the building that held the Coaches, and roused one of the men who was on night duty in the stables that held the mares and a couple of foals. He could have taken the small Coach without help, but *telling* someone he was taking it would cause less trouble in the morning.

There was going to be enough trouble without adding more.

At three o'clock, Daemonar stood outside the Coach he'd positioned on the landing web and waited for Zoey and Grizande. He didn't wait long. Grizande looked like a warrior prepared for battle. Zoey looked like she was running ahead of an avalanche and wasn't sure she'd get away.

"A Coach this size is meant for short distances, so it doesn't have a toilet," he said, watching Zoey. "I did borrow a bucket from the stables in case one of you needs a container."

Grizande shot him a look. Yeah, they both knew who might need it.

"There's also a jug of coffee, a jug of juice, and some food I took from the auxiliary kitchen." He focused on Grizande. "Eat something if you can."

"Thank you, Daemonar," Zoey whispered before she entered the Coach.

"I take care of her," Grizande said.

He smiled. "I know you will . . . sister."

She looked startled. Then she gave him a fierce smile, entered the Coach, and closed the door.

He moved away from the landing web but stayed nearby until Grizande used Craft to lift the Coach off the ground and catch the Sapphire Wind.

He'd give the girls a head start before he woke up Uncle Daemon and told him Zoey and Grizande were scampering off to the Keep to have a chat with Witch.

SIXTY-FOUR

It wasn't reasonable to expect a return letter so soon—Saetien wasn't even sure *her* letter had reached SaDiablo Hall yet—but she still felt disappointed that there wasn't anything for her in the morning delivery of letters and messages. Then again, she'd been tired and angry when she'd written the letter, and she didn't quite remember what she'd said, remembered only that she'd been angry with Butler about neglecting his garden. So maybe her father didn't think it was worth a reply.

No. She knew him better than that. He would reply.

Same routine as yesterday, only this time she wasn't acting like the foolish sheep trying to bolt from the pasture before she was rounded up.

The Warlord hitched to the cart would take her to the cottage? Yes.

The adult Sceltie Warlord would keep an eye on his lone human sheep unless Caitie joined her again to double his flock? Yes.

Shelby coming with her without the drama of the dusty shirt? Yes.

Food, water, hat, gloves, and everything else that someone else deemed vital to her spending a few hours in a garden away from home and could be packed into the cart? Yes.

Was it like this because she was in Scelt, or had it always been like this whenever a female went anywhere or did anything—this bringing along a hill of essentials—and she hadn't noticed because whoever was standing escort was the one who carried everything?

And if this fussing was considered necessary for a witch who wore Purple Dusk, how much more did a Queen—*any* Queen—have to put up with? Were men who served in a First Circle trained to be subtle about packing up supplies for a simple visit, as if the Lady were a witless puppy who couldn't take some responsibility for herself?

She used to get so annoyed with her father when the two of them were going somewhere and he'd ask her if she had everything she needed and she'd brush off the question, impatient to get started, only to later discover that *he* hadn't brought something she considered vital. She got even more annoyed when he quietly reminded her that packing personal items had been her responsibility, even if he would have been the one who carried them for her.

He'd been teaching her to take responsibility for herself, something she hadn't appreciated at the time. Had he extended that same courtesy to his Queen? Or were the rules different and a Queen wasn't expected to have enough sense to bring her own handkerchief because there would be a dozen men ready to hand one over if she sneezed?

And yet a Queen was expected to have the training and wisdom to rule over people's lives. Hundreds and thousands of lives in villages and towns and cities and Territories. In a whole Realm.

As the Warlord trotted toward Butler's cottage and Saetien kept an arm around each Sceltie, she wondered if Jaenelle Angelline's life had felt constricted by so many powerful men waiting to take care of the least little thing for her. And she wondered how Zoey was doing now that the young Queen was living at the Hall.

Saetien figured that Kieran and his family realized she and Butler were no longer talking about Wilhelmina Benedict, but no one hinted that she should end her visit. She was still on her heart quest. It had just taken a different direction.

How long would she be allowed to stay? The garden still needed a fierce amount of work. Would her father allow her to stay long enough to complete it?

Waiting for Butler to step out of the cottage, she looked over the beds she'd cleaned up and she felt proud of the work. Felt pleased that she'd made a friend who also enjoyed working in a garden. Whatever had been damaged inside Caitie's brain might make her vulnerable at times, but she was smart in many ways, simple in some ways, and always sweet natured. And she was kind.

The coven of malice would have torn Caitie apart.

Would she have let Delora do that to Caitie or someone like her? Or would she have drawn a line to protect someone else if the price had been Delora's friendship?

Jaenelle Angelline would have had the courage to draw the line and hold it, regardless of whose friendship was lost or any other personal cost.

"The garden is looking much better, but you don't have to do this," Butler said when he walked up to her a few minutes later.

"Someone has to." The words had more snap than she'd intended, but her thoughts had left her unsettled. Again.

He didn't respond immediately.

"If you don't want to talk this evening . . . ," he began.

"I remember being told that I was dreams made flesh." The words came out in a rush. "When I was little, I remember someone telling me that. It made me different. Special."

"Different? Maybe. Special? Certainly." Butler looked away, something he often did when the subject at hand became difficult. "A woman feels the first signs of a child in her womb and cries with joy. A man lays a hand on his lover's belly and feels a fierce love along with the first flutter of life from the child they created. Isn't every wanted child special, Saetien? Isn't every wanted child the parents' dreams made flesh?"

Pain. The words were spoken calmly enough, but underneath them Saetien heard pain. "Were you a wanted child, Butler?"

Even in the failing light, she saw his face harden with bitterness and regret.

"No," he said too softly. "We weren't wanted."

He turned and walked back to the cottage. Closed the door.

Saetien rushed to the door, but it was locked—and Butler didn't answer when she pounded on the wood.

"Butler? Butler! Who is 'we'? Butler?"

No answer. Her question had reopened an old wound, and she didn't know how to fix it.

She waited awhile, then contacted Kieran to come pick her up.

As they drove home, a thought circled: who was the other unwanted child? And why, even after so many years, did the knowledge that *they* had been unwanted hurt Butler?

SIXTY-FIVE

Daemon rose to the killing edge moments before he snapped awake and sat up in bed.

Had something—someone—entered the Hall?

No. Not someone extra. Someone *missing*.

He sent a pulse of power into the psychic web he maintained throughout the Hall. After confirming that the Sapphire wasn't within the Hall itself, he expanded the search to cover the entire estate, in case Grizande felt too confined by walls and needed to move across open land.

Nothing.

Rolling out of bed, he pulled on trousers and shrugged into a shirt. He strode out of his bedroom and yanked on the door of his sitting room, intending to search Grizande's room for some clue to the girl's whereabouts, and almost plowed into Daemonar, who stood in the corridor holding two large mugs of coffee.

"Grizande is missing," Daemon growled, expecting the boy to step aside.

"Not exactly," Daemonar replied. He held up a mug. "Coffee?"

The boy's expression was somewhere between Lucivar's lazy arrogance and Jaenelle's unsure-but-game smile. That made him hesitate enough to step back and allow the boy to enter the sitting room.

Daemon accepted a mug of coffee. "Then what, exactly?"

"Zoey and Grizande have gone to the Keep to seek wisdom from the Queen. They took a small Coach."

"They had help getting that Coach?"

"Some help," Daemonar agreed.

Well, that explained why the boy was awake at this hour. "How long ago?"

Daemonar looked toward the glass doors that led out to a balcony and the stairs down to the courtyard. "I barely had time to get back up here and make some coffee before I felt you getting . . . exercised . . . about the absence of the Sapphire."

Riding the Black, he could easily reach the Keep ahead of them. But . . . Zoey and Grizande working together?

"You *were* giving the girls a little time to figure out what to do about those bad instructions," Daemonar said. "And Auntie J. does give good advice, even if she sometimes adds a whack upside the head to make sure the advice sticks."

Daemon sipped his coffee and studied the boy. It hadn't been a flippant decision to help the girls. The choice of leaving in the middle of the night was also not a flippant decision. It would be hours before most of the people in the Hall knew Zoey was missing and might guess a young Queen was seeking help beyond the rules of the game.

But once someone knew and might start to worry about being discovered . . .

Daemon raised his right hand and released a ripple of power from the Black Jewel in his ring. That ripple engaged all the Black shields in the Hall's exterior walls, trapping everyone inside. Then he released more Black power to create a Black shield around part of the estate, starting at the bridge and creek that formed a boundary between the estate and Halaway and extending to the north woods, where the wolf pack would keep watch for anyone attempting to enter or leave. It was by no means the whole of the estate, but he hadn't sensed any humans anywhere they shouldn't be, so shielding that much would do for now.

"Uncle Daemon?" The boy sounded worried.

The High Lord smiled. "We don't want anyone else scampering off, do we?"

Daemonar looked wary but said, "No, sir, we don't. With your permission, I'll pull the Warlord Princes out of the court exercises to patrol as a group."

"Under your hand?"

"Under my command, but under your hand. We'll report to you, Beale, or Holt—and receive information from the three of you so that we can assist in . . . suppressing . . . trouble before it goes too far."

Pulling the Warlord Princes out of the exercises and keeping them under control would reduce the possibility of someone like Raeth snapping the leash and hurting another boy because a cruel command had pushed a Warlord Prince too far.

"Very well." Daemon thought for a moment. "Where is the tiger?"

"Still in Grizande's room. I'm going to ask Allis to keep him company. That will keep both of them from fretting while the girls are gone."

Oh, he doubted it would keep the Sceltie from fretting, since Zoey had broken the rules by not taking Allis with her, but it would delay Allis's announcing to everyone that Zoey wasn't where she was supposed to be.

And once Zoey returned and Allis got done explaining things, he doubted the girl would break that particular rule again.

Brenda sat up in bed, shivering and unsure as she hesitantly sent out a psychic probe. *Something* had roused her from sleep.

Her probe hit an unyielding Black shield.

"What?" Raine said, resting a hand on her arm.

"Something's wrong," she whispered.

He propped himself up on one elbow. After a minute he said, "Black shield?"

"Around the whole of the Hall."

"That's not good." Raine scrubbed a hand over his hair. "I wasn't at the Hall during that disastrous house party, but I saw some of what Sadi—what the Sadist—could and would do in response to someone putting children at risk."

"What should we do?"

"Nothing. The Black is awake and aware—and may already be hunting." Raine paused. "And Daemonar is already awake and aware—and declining to answer any questions right now. But he suggests we remain alert for any behavior that comes close to crossing a line."

Brenda didn't resist when Raine nudged her back under the covers. Resting her head on his shoulder, she said, "Maybe the servants and I were a bit too enthusiastic creating Lady Dumm's faults. Maybe crude manners and bad behavior gave someone the idea for going further and doing actual harm."

"Maybe," Raine agreed. "But if they did, the tendency to do harm was already there, and the person suggesting a Queen do that harm puts a whole court at risk, to say nothing of the damage done to the people under that Queen's hand."

"But what happened in the middle of the night to have Prince Sadi locking the Hall?"

Raine kissed her. "We'll find out in a few hours."

SIXTY-SIX

Lucivar stood on the flagstones outside his eyrie and watched the sun rise. There were mornings when he enjoyed standing here watching the lights go on in the village of Riada—and watching the sky fill with light. There were other mornings—like this one—when he was damn well going to kick someone's ass for dragging him out of bed at this hour for what amounted to a pissing contest instead of a real threat to his home or the people under his hand.

His only satisfaction, for the moment, was knowing that Daemon had been awake long before a chilly psychic tap on an Ebon-gray thread had rousted Lucivar out of bed. Two witchlings had scampered off in the wee hours of the morning, heading for Ebon Askavi to have a chat with Witch, and should reach the Keep anytime now.

Lucky for the girls that Witch no longer had a physical body. When Jaenelle had been alive, she had *not* been friendly first thing in the morning.

The eyrie's front door opened. Marian came out holding mugs of coffee.

"Is someone in trouble?" she asked, handing him a mug.

"Probably," he replied.

"Our children?"

"Oh, I'm sure at least one of them had a hand in whatever has Daemon stirred up so early in the day."

"It would be smarter to let him get enough sleep before dumping trouble on him."

Lucivar laughed softly. "It would have been smarter if they hadn't started the trouble in the first place, but since they did start it, I guess this is another day we start early."

"Do you want breakfast?"

Lucivar drew her to him and gave her a warm kiss. "I'll get something at the Keep once the witchlings . . ." He didn't see a Coach arriving at the Keep, but he knew the moment the Sapphire set foot on Ebon Askavi. He handed the mug back to Marian. "Looks like I'm heading there now."

"Bring them here after their audience with Witch. You won't want to be in a Coach very long with girls that age until they have time to settle."

"Yeah." At least there were only two of them. Of course two, full of girl drama, could make a man feel like he was dealing with two dozen.

Before he stuffed them into a Coach for the return journey, maybe he should find out if Daemon really wanted them back.

Blowing out a breath, Lucivar stepped away from Marian, spread his wings, and flew to Ebon Askavi.

Keeping one hand around Zoela Queen's arm to prevent her from bolting back to the Coach, Grizande pounded on the door. Big door. She wondered if there were still beings in the Realms that needed a door that size. Best not to think of that right now, since she didn't know what actually lived in this mountain.

She banged her fist against the door a second time before it opened silently.

She stared at the Seneschal. Human, but in a way that had Grizande's hackles rising, had her claws flexing.

The Seneschal stared back and said, "Yesss?"

When Zoela Queen remained mute, Grizande growled, "Zoela Queen needs wisdom from Queen who is more than a Queen." She shook Zoela Queen's arm. "Show coin."

Zoela Queen held out the coin she'd been clutching all the way to the Keep.

The coin vanished. The Seneschal turned and said, "Follow me."

Given how long it took them to reach the part of the Keep that she remembered from the last visit, Grizande figured she must have chosen the wrong landing web. But she'd guided the Coach to the only landing web that had a beacon she could detect, so maybe the landing web near the Queen's part of the Keep was only for Warlord Princes like Yaslana and shielded against everyone else.

It didn't matter. They were here, and Zoela Queen could ask for wisdom.

As they approached that ornate metal gate, a door opened. Grizande sniffed the air. Food. There had been food in that room the last time she was here.

"Wait in there for the Queen," the Seneschal said. She looked at Zoela Queen. "With me."

Grizande watched them until they'd walked past the metal gate and Zoela Queen's Opal power and the strange feel of the Seneschal's power vanished.

She hurried into the room, hoping for food.

The door closed behind her. Ebon-gray power filled the room, eclipsing Grizande's sharp interest in the serving dishes that covered the table.

A sight shield faded. Lucivar Yaslana gave her a lazy, arrogant smile. "Hello, witchling. You and I are going to have a chat."

Now that she was there, facing Witch, Zoey didn't know what to say. It had seemed so important to ask someone outside the Hall for advice. Maybe she should have walked down to Halaway and asked the Queen who lived there. But what if that was where these bad instructions were coming from? *Someone* was adding them, and she couldn't see how it could be anyone who wasn't close enough to know what was going on at the Hall.

It had seemed so important, but the closer she and Grizande had gotten to the Keep, the more doubts had formed, chewing away at the certainty that this was what she needed to do for herself and the other Queens. But it had been only a slap on the hand. All right, the slap on the face had not been good, but it seemed so trivial now, when she would have to explain it to *the Queen*.

"Does Daemon know you're here?" Witch asked.

"Maybe?"

"'Maybe' as in you left a note on his desk explaining that you and Grizande were going to the Keep? Or 'maybe' as in someone saw you leave, and you hoped the person would make a comment at breakfast about you going off in a Coach to some unknown destination? Or 'maybe' as in you did tell someone where you were going and asked them to convey the message after you had enough time to reach the Keep but before Daemon summoned all the Warlord Princes in Dhemlan to search for you?"

Zoey blinked. "He would do that?"

Witch stared at her. "You have a Sceltie who is your special friend."

"Yes. Allis."

"Does Allis know where you are?"

"She was still asleep when I left."

"Uh-huh. Well, my darling, there is good and there is bad. The good is that it won't be Daemon who bites you for not informing him of where you were going. The bad is that you have interfered with a Sceltie's ability to look after you, and you will have to grovel for several days before she stops being offended by this lack of understanding on your part. And until she stops being offended, you will not go *anywhere* without her knowing about it."

"Anywhere as in . . . ?"

"Anywhere." Witch took a seat on the sofa opposite Zoey's chair. "Now that we have settled that much, why are you here?"

"You'll think it's foolish."

"Anything that drives a Queen to come here and request an audience isn't foolish."

Zoey started with the students' first meeting with Lady Dumm and continued up to the meal where the stench drove everyone out of the dining room but improved Dumm's manners—once she'd been aired out sufficiently to be allowed back indoors. A few days after that, the first additional instruction was added to the Territory Queen's tasks. A punishment that was supposed to be done out of sight of the instructors or senior staff—and definitely out of Prince Sadi's sight.

"If the Queen doesn't follow the instructions, doesn't do this other thing, her whole court will be punished," Zoey said. "Ordering your people to lightly slap three people's hands seemed a small thing compared to having everyone punished."

"And then?" Witch asked quietly.

"And then the instructions changed. Two people would slap hands, and one person would slap three people on the face. A light slap, but still."

"Did you give the order?"

Tears filled Zoey's eyes. She nodded. "I gave that order to Prince Raeth. I—I'm not sure if he did it. He was so angry."

"Did you think he wouldn't be?"

"If I revealed these extra instructions, everyone in my court would be punished, but nothing in the instructions said my people were at risk if someone else reported these unjust disciplines. I'd hoped Raeth . . ."

"None of those boys have worked with you long enough to hear an unspoken command," Witch said. "You did Raeth a disservice by not making it clear to him that you wanted him to report this because your hands were tied. That said, I would be very surprised if Daemonar wasn't told about this and hasn't, in turn, told Prince Sadi." A pause. "What is the Queen's purpose?"

"To be the moral center of her court and, by extension, all the people in her territory," Zoey replied.

"What is the Queen's duty?"

"To rule with honor, strength, and compassion because her will is the law. To protect her court so that they, in turn, can protect the rest of her people."

"What is the Queen's price?"

Zoey hesitated, unable to recall anything in the lessons about a price. And yet, didn't everything have a price?

"You stand for the land and the people you rule," Witch said quietly. "You stand against what you know is wrong, no matter who gives the command. You stand and fight, no matter the cost to your court or to you. Especially to you. There is no such thing as a small wrong, Zoela. Not when you're a Queen. That's how the taint begins."

"But we don't know who is giving those orders."

"If you don't understand by now who *isn't* giving those orders, you have no business being at the Hall or dealing with Daemon Sadi." The words came out icy and sharp.

"We're supposed to copy out the orders and burn the original paper. We're trying to acquire an original to give to Prince Sadi because Jhett thinks he might be able to draw some information out of the paper and that's why the Queens were told to burn the original instructions."

Witch nodded. "Wood and stone remember. Daemon would be able to pull enough information from the paper to have a sense of who wrote the orders."

Zoey stared at her hands. "We thought it was a test for the Queens."

"Not one that Daemon devised, but yes, it was a test."

"And we failed. The Queens failed."

Witch smiled. "You haven't failed yet."

SIXTY-SEVEN

Titian breathed a sigh of relief when she found out Kathlene was the Territory Queen that day and that she was assigned to Kathlene's court. That would make this part of the plan easier. Not that Felisha or Azara wouldn't have gone along with it eventually, but Kathlene was quiet and thoughtful and had as intense a dislike for these extra assignments as Zoey did. Hopefully, Kathlene would agree to this bending of the rules without needing too much explanation.

As for the rest of what was going on in the Hall . . .

Lady Brenda not asking any questions when Titian told her that Zoey would be staying in her room that day. Tummy—and intestinal—trouble. Not serious but rather messy. Being an apprentice Healer, Arlene was staying with Zoey to look after her.

Daemonar walking into the dining room and informing Kathlene, as the Territory Queen, that the Warlord Princes had been pulled from the courts that day for a different assignment. Titian looked at the leather guards protecting her brother's wrists and forearms, looked at the sheathed fighting knife that took the place of the knife he usually wore on his belt, and figured all the Warlord Princes needed to be approached with care today.

Finally, there was one of the boys, looking baffled, returning to report that he couldn't get to the stables to request a carriage to take Lady Azara to Halaway because a shield prevented him from leaving the Hall.

Kathlene barely swallowed a bite of scrambled eggs and toast before leaving the breakfast table and returning to her room to complete the first part of the extra assignment. If it was that distressing, it had to be worse than yesterday's face slap.

Titian didn't bother making an excuse. She just hurried after Kathlene, then gave the Queen's door a quick knock before entering.

Kathlene twisted in her desk chair, her face stamped with anger and pain.

Much worse than yesterday's face slap.

Titian approached the girl who was her Queen for that day. "If you've copied out the extra assignment, I can burn the original for you."

A beat of silence as Kathlene studied her. "You can?"

"I can." Which wasn't the same as saying she would.

Kathlene hesitated, then held out the square of heavy paper, turned over so Titian couldn't see what was written on it.

Most of the rooms in the Hall were heated with warming spells, but some had fireplaces. All the rooms that had been assigned to the Queens had fireplaces. No fresh wood ready to light, which was better since no one would be in Kathlene's room for most of the day.

Keeping her back to Kathlene, Titian vanished the paper, then called in a square of paper equal in weight to the ones being used for the extra assignments. Using a tongue of witchfire, she ignited a corner of that paper, then leaned in and dropped it on the grate. She watched until it burned to ash.

When she turned around, she saw the way Kathlene studied her.

"Zoey wasn't at breakfast," Kathlene said.

"Tummy troubles," Titian replied.

Kathlene stiffened. "Not . . . ?" She mouthed the word "poison."

"No, no. I think yesterday upset her more than she realized until things . . ." She waved a hand in the vicinity of her abdomen.

"Ah. Well, she's not the only one who has felt that way." Kathlene sounded bitter.

"Maybe if you wait until after the midday meal to issue orders for the extra assignments, you won't have to issue those orders at all."

Dancing on the knife's edge. Not saying anything outright. Not putting Kathlene in the position of *knowing* anything that might be considered breaking the rules.

Kathlene rose. "I'm going to tidy up and then see what can be done today. And you will run that errand for me?"

"I will."

As Titian hurried through the corridors, dodging questions from the other students, she wondered which one had been betraying the rest of them—and why.

Daemon blocked the doorway before Weston had a chance to charge out of the Queen's square of rooms and say anything.

"Inside." Daemon took a step forward, forcing Weston to take a step back.

"Zoey—"

"Is fine. So is Grizande. Lucivar is looking after them." Daemon took another step, forcing Weston back farther. It was a big space, but it was essentially a supply room for towels and sheets and the other things the staff needed to take care of the bedrooms in this square. On this floor it was also the only room from which one could access the interior courtyard without going through someone's bedroom.

Before Weston could ask another question, Nadene walked in with Brenda, followed by Holt and Beale.

"Lord Beale," Daemon said. "Close the door. Shield the room."

When that was done, Daemon looked at them. "Zoey

and Grizande have gone to Ebon Askavi to see Witch. They left in the early hours this morning and have arrived safely."

"Zoey left without informing her sword and shield?" Weston's voice was rough with the effort of keeping his anger leashed.

Daemon smiled. "Worse than not informing you, Zoey didn't inform Allis."

Holt snorted a laugh and tried to cover it with a cough.

"Exactly," Daemon said dryly.

"I was told that Zoey is dealing with tummy and intestinal troubles," Brenda said. "Arlene is staying with her to make soothing tonics and make sure Zoey's discomfort doesn't get worse."

"You're supporting this trip to the Keep, even if that support is after the fact?" Nadene asked.

"I am," Daemon replied.

"Then I should stop by a few times today to check up on my apprentice Healer and make sure she's doing all that should be done for the young Queen."

"Broths and other easy foods should be brought in for Lady Zoey, along with something more substantial for Lady Arlene," Beale said. "The Dharo Boy can be trusted with that assignment."

Daemon turned to Holt and Beale. "Has correspondence that was delivered last evening been distributed yet?"

"I was going to sort it this morning," Holt said.

"I have collected the letters that were being sent out, but of course, those letters cannot leave the Hall until you lower the shields," Beale said.

Daemon nodded. "I want to see everything coming in for the children and everything they're sending out."

"Be canny about this and do the same for the instructors," Brenda said. "It might not be a child making this mischief."

"Point taken."

She called in two letters and handed them to Holt. "I didn't get them into the basket of outgoing letters, but you can add them to whatever else you collect. And if you're looking to give someone a hard jolt, add a slip of paper to a few incoming letters saying that the letter was read and the envelope resealed."

Assuming he let the letter go on to the recipient.

"I should put a shield around this square of rooms," Weston said. "No one should be able to reach Zoey—or find out she isn't here—by entering through one of the bedrooms."

"No, I'll put a shield around this square of rooms," Daemon said. "However, I'll leave this room open, and you can set the shield here. That way, you can approve or deny anyone who wants to enter, including the other girls who occupy these rooms."

"What should we tell anyone who asks why the Hall is locked with Black shields?" Brenda asked.

Daemon smiled—and watched Brenda shiver. "Tell them the High Lord of Hell is hunting."

"Do you think he'll be there?" Jhett asked.

Titian nodded. "Uncle Daemon is usually in his study at this time of day."

"But there's nothing usual about today, is there?"

True, but she hoped he'd be easy to find. She wanted to hand over that paper and be done with that part of the task.

She'd picked up Jhett on her way to Uncle Daemon's study, in case she needed help explaining what Jhett and Zoey thought a skilled Black Widow could extract from the paper.

She wasn't sure what to think about crossing paths with Raeth, Caede, and Liath, who were obviously patrolling the areas of the Hall where most of the students should be. She *knew* what to think when she and Jhett crossed paths with Daemonar, Trent, and Jarrod. The Warlord Princes with Liath were patrolling; Daemonar and his men were hunting.

As soon as the study door opened in response to her knock, Titian rushed inside, with Jhett a step behind her.

The man sitting behind the blackwood desk wasn't Uncle Daemon. This was the man who had returned to the Hall during that awful house party. Cold. Dangerous. Deadly. She met his glazed gold eyes for a moment before calling in the square of paper and holding it out to him.

"Sir, we believe someone is trying to cause trouble for the Queens who are receiving court training at the Hall. These extra assignments have been added to the tasks you've listed for each day."

"Why didn't you come to me before now?" he asked too softly.

"It would have sounded whiny." Not an excuse he was going to accept. Well, her father wouldn't have accepted it either—which was something she should have remembered, and mentioned to Zoey, before they'd devised this elaborate plan. "But now it's become serious enough to bring to your attention. We—I acquired the original instructions. We thought you might be able to use them to find out who is doing this."

A humming silence before the man behind the desk finally took the paper. He turned it over, read it, then looked at her and Jhett—and held up the paper for them to read.

Titian swallowed hard. This was unforgivable cruelty.

"Riding crop?" Jhett's voice rose in outrage. "Whipping people with a riding crop?"

"Is reporting this being whiny?" Uncle Daemon asked quietly.

"No, sir," Titian replied. She didn't want to think about what Lucivar would do if someone laid a strap on her—assuming there was anything left of the person after Daemonar and Uncle Daemon were through with the fool.

"I'm disappointed that you didn't come to me sooner."

Tears stung her eyes. "I'm sorry."

"So am I."

The quiet reprimand felt worse than a roaring scold. She'd hurt him. The other girls hadn't; they weren't family. But she, who'd known him all her life, had hurt him by not trusting him and telling him sooner, and she didn't know how to make it up to him.

"Zoey . . . ," she began.

"By now Zoey is having a very interesting discussion with Witch." Warm amusement appeared in Uncle Daemon's eyes. "But I understand the story being told here is that she has tummy troubles, which is why she's staying in her room today."

"Yes, sir."

He looked at her, then at Jhett. "Shield. Now."

The command surprised Titian, but she immediately formed a protective shield around herself. After a moment, she formed a second shield—and saw Uncle Daemon's lips twitch.

Jhett sucked in a breath as they both felt the lightest touch of Red power brush against their shields. Testing.

"You've been practicing," Uncle Daemon said. "Good. Now remember this: there are very few people you can trust today. There is an enemy inside these walls. Don't make the assumption that the person coming toward you is a friend. Arlene is safe. Lord Weston will make sure of that. The rest of you are vulnerable until I find the person who is helping someone play this game. Do you understand me?"

"Yes, sir," she and Jhett said.

"Very well. Titian, you may go. Jhett, you're going to stay awhile longer and learn how to weave a summoning web that can draw like to like."

Jhett beamed at him.

The study door opened. Uncle Daemon looked at Titian, then made a shooing motion. Taking the hint, she hurried to report to Kathlene and find out what she was supposed to do this morning.

Uncle Daemon said there was an enemy within the walls of SaDiablo Hall. She'd stay alert. She'd check in with Daemonar so that he'd know where she was and who she was with. Just in case.

✦ ✦ ✦

Jhett didn't ask questions or make any unnecessary remarks. She just watched as Daemon called in a small wooden frame and a spool of heavier spider silk and proceeded to weave a simple web.

"Remember when I needed to collect all those notebooks from wherever they had been stashed in bookcases and on shelves?" Daemon asked.

"I remember." Jhett sounded regretful.

He was sure the darlings sometimes regretted that they hadn't been able to hold on to any of those notebooks, but after reading a couple of the notebooks and seeing some of the things the coven had been exploring when they'd lived at the Hall, he'd quietly checked to make sure no notebooks had been left behind in the libraries the children could access easily.

Hell's fire, Jaenelle and her friends had been brilliant. And terrifying.

"We're going to use the paper that Titian acquired, together with this summoning spell, to find the source of the instructions," Daemon continued. "Like calls to like."

"It looks like you've practiced that web a lot."

Daemon considered what to say, then decided on the truth. "It works for cloth as well as paper. My little friend is a hoarder and hides her stash in some unlikely places."

"Are you running out of handkerchiefs?" Jhett asked.

"Not since my valet set up a standing order for new ones to be delivered every week," he replied dryly. "But Breen is a puppy and doesn't understand that some of her hiding places are potentially dangerous when stuffed with handkerchiefs, which is why I've become proficient at making this particular web."

Daemon and Jhett were spared further discussion of a hoarding Sceltie puppy by Holt and Beale entering the study. Beale carried a tray that held letters being sent out. Holt held a shallow rectangular basket that held the letters coming into the Hall.

"Is that everything?" Daemon asked.

"Not the correspondence addressed to you or Lady Surreal, but everything else," Holt replied. "Students, instructors, and staff. Everything from yesterday evening's delivery."

"Thank you." Daemon waited for the men to leave before putting a Black lock on the door. "Now we begin."

A simple spell, really. He held the paper with the extra instructions in one hand and the frame with the web in the other. Then he sang the four notes that completed this summoning. The same four notes, over and over.

Nothing stirred on the tray with the outgoing letters. But in the basket of letters that had arrived yesterday . . .

An envelope wiggled its way to the top of the correspondence, then shot toward him like an arrow released from a bow. Daemon formed a Red shield in front of himself and the girl a heartbeat before the envelope hit with enough force to crumple the corner.

"Hell's fire," Jhett said.

He stopped singing the notes and put a shield around the frame and web, effectively ending the spell. More cautious than he would have been otherwise, because he wanted to impress on this girl the need for caution, Daemon used Craft to turn the envelope so that they could read the name of the intended recipient.

Jhett sighed. "Cara is one of Dinah's friends. She smiles while she makes hurtful 'I'm just teasing' remarks about the other Queens, and that's unkind, but I hadn't thought she would participate in this kind of meanness. Maybe Dinah resents the rest of us because we're still here for training, so I can see her wanting to cause trouble. But Cara? What does she gain from doing this?"

"The satisfaction of witnessing the mischief and reporting back to her Queen," Daemon said quietly.

"Are you going to let her stay?"

"No. Yesterday I might have considered issuing a reprimand and a warning and giving her a second chance." He held up the paper with that day's instructions. "This changes everything. Now I have to consider what debt she owes for her part in this and how she'll be required to pay it."

He contained the instructions and the letter in a Black shield and put them aside. Then he called in another wooden frame and set it and the spool of spider silk in front of Jhett. "Now you. Do you write to anyone?"

"My parents. My aunt because she's also a Black Widow and is interested in what I'm learning here. A couple of friends."

"Are you expecting a letter from any of them?"

"All of them."

He smiled. "Pick one. Call in the last letter you received from that person."

After Jhett called in the last letter she'd received from her aunt, Daemon talked her through making the summoning web, strand by strand. When everything was placed correctly, he taught her the four-note sequence that went with the spell.

She gave him a look that was equal parts nerves and excitement, then activated the spell.

A letter leaped out of the basket of incoming correspondence, hit the edge of the table, and slid halfway across like an eager puppy on ice. Startled, Jhett stopped singing, which ended the spell.

"Well done, especially for your first try," Daemon said. "Now, put a shield around that web and take it to your room. Once you've made a sketch of the web in your notebook, along with the sequence of notes that need to be sung with the spell, break the threads."

"Notebook?" Jhett attempted to sound innocent.

Daemon just looked at her. He didn't know about the other girls, but he knew—because Allis had told him—that soon after Lady Karla's visit, all of Zoey's friends had gone to the stationery store in Halaway and purchased blank notebooks.

"Notebook." This time her voice confirmed she had one.

"Go away, witchling. I have work to do."

Jhett gathered up her things, including the newly arrived letter from her aunt, and hurried to her room.

Daemon took a moment to inform Weston that Jhett would be requesting entrance to the Queen's square of rooms in order to reach her bedroom. Then he broke the seal of the letter Dinah had sent to Cara—and learned who else was involved in mischief that had taken on the kind of edge that Lucivar used to blunt with slaughter.

SIXTY-EIGHT

The Winds looked like shining webs of power in the Darkness, with radial lines and tether lines. They began at Ebon Askavi and ran to the farthest reaches of each Realm. But they weren't all equal. Winds that corresponded to the darker Jewels had more radial and tether lines—and more speed, which required more strength and control. A White Web ran the slowest and had the fewest radial and tether lines. On the Ebon-gray the distance between Ebon Rih and the Hall still took time, but Lucivar could reach a destination in a quarter of the time—or less—that it would take someone riding the lightest Winds.

After Zoey had her audience with Witch, Lucivar had brought the girls back to the eyrie. Marian had fussed over the young Queen until the girl settled enough to eat a bowl of soup and a slice of toast. She didn't fuss over Grizande, knowing that warriors didn't respond to fussing in the same way as Queens. Instead, she had taught the Tigre girl how to make scrambled eggs—a simple thing, but Grizande almost glowed with the pleasure of having those few minutes of Marian's undivided attention.

Thinking about that, Lucivar now rose to a Red Web when it lined up with the Ebon-gray. Then he rose to the Green. When he rose to the Opal, the Coach was still far enough away from Halaway and the Hall for a lesson, so he said, "Grizande, come up here."

Wary but not afraid, she took the second driver's seat.

"We're running on the Opal Winds. Can you feel it?" he asked.

"Yes."

"You're going to take over driving the Coach. Ready?"

"Ready."

It was like rolling a large ball of yarn in front of a kitten. She almost pounced on the opportunity the moment he released his control of the Coach.

He didn't have an hourglass to mark the time, but he figured it took her only about a minute to start a familiar grumble.

"Why we use Opal?" Grizande asked. "I can fly on Sapphire. Or Green."

"You're flying on Opal because that's what I want you to do," he replied.

"Why?"

He gave her the same look he'd given Daemonar when his boy had given him the same argument while being taught to drive a Coach. Grizande met his look for a few seconds before refocusing on the Coach and grumbling under her breath. She could grumble all the way to Halaway, but if she wanted to be trusted to drive a Coach, she would follow his orders. Very few people survived making a mistake while riding the Winds unless they were lucky enough to catch another Wind when they fell through the Darkness.

One day soon he would do the same thing he'd done with Daemonar—take her in a Coach and toss it off the Wind they were riding, giving her a taste of what it felt like to fall, out of control. There were places where he could do that and then catch the Red or Ebon-gray after a few heart-pounding seconds of blind fear. He'd chosen those places because Daemonar, wearing the Green, would not have been able to save himself in that way. Grizande would learn the same lesson.

A warrior's lesson.

She settled a lot more quickly than his boy had to the

task of driving the Coach at the speed he wanted. Then again, Daemonar had taken for granted that he could have his father's and uncle's time and attention. Lucivar suspected that Grizande, not having had that, would never take for granted what he and Daemon offered.

What is the Queen's purpose? What is the Queen's duty? What is the Queen's price?

Zoey had spent the journey back to SaDiablo Hall thinking about that, about how a Queen protects her people, no matter the price to herself.

Not necessarily a physical price, although the Queen who had stood before her had certainly paid that. It could be as simple as taking a stand that wouldn't please some of the people under her hand, might even make enemies for the Queen who drew that line. A Queen who did that might lose her court, or the Queen who ruled above her might strip her of her territory, even if it was only one small village.

Everything had a price—and the Queen's price was doing what was right, regardless of the cost.

By the time the Coach landed in Halaway, Zoey knew what she needed to do.

"Why we land here?" Grizande asked. "Hall has landing web. We can go there."

"Can we?" Lucivar countered. "Do you know how to send out a psychic probe to test what's around you?"

She nodded.

"Do it. And be careful."

Not a dismissal of what she knew or could do. This was a warning, because he knew what she would find—and it could hurt her.

She released some of her Sapphire power, letting it flow quietly through the village. Nothing immediately dangerous here. No reason—

Before she realized it was there, the Black shield sucked out half of the power she'd put into the probe.

Grizande pulled back, startled. Frightened.

Lucivar just watched her. "You and I? When we fight, we leave carnage behind in a way that leaves no one in doubt of our intention. That is the nature of our races and how we fight. But Sadi? He's quiet when he kills. Clean. And devastating. Something he has in common with his father. The Hall is locked down. So is part of the estate. So is the landing web. Maybe we could land there safely, but we'd be trapped within the shields until Sadi decided whether he's dealing with friends or enemies. Maybe if we try landing there it would be like trying to survive being hit by lightning multiple times. Some of us in this Coach might survive, but not all of us."

"He angry because we took Coach to see Queen who is more than a Queen?"

"No, witchling. There is an enemy inside the walls of SaDiablo Hall. An enemy who is now trapped inside— with him."

"Ah." She was still learning, like a young cat learns by watching the adults. But . . . "We could help hunt."

Lucivar smiled. Then he looked behind him and Grizande when Zoela Queen stood up.

"I need to reach the Hall," Zoela Queen said. "There are things the other Queens and I need to discuss."

Grizande studied the other girl. Zoela Queen had been afraid when they'd gone to the Keep. Now she was ready for the fight to come.

Lucivar used Craft to glide the Coach above the road as if it were a wheeled carriage. When he reached the bridge that indicated the boundary between Halaway's land and the SaDiablo estate, he set the Coach down on the road—a barricade to keep the unwary, or the foolish, from slamming into Daemon's Black shield. Not an aggressive shield as such, but not passive either. Since it consumed a person's power so swiftly, the reservoir in a Jewel could be drained and the Jewel broken before its owner realized the danger.

The Black had gone cold, but Lucivar couldn't tell from just the feeling of cold if he would be dealing with the High Lord or the Sadist.

So we dance on the knife's edge.

Bastard? he called on a spear thread.

Prick? Where are you?

At the bridge. The girls are with me. Zoey would like to talk to the other Queens.

Zoey is in her room because of tummy troubles, came the dry reply. *I'll open the shield above the Queen's square of rooms. You better bring the girls in that way for discretion's sake.*

We'll be there in a few minutes. Lucivar ended the link, then nudged the girls out of the Coach.

"How do we reach the Hall?" Zoey asked.

Lucivar took firm hold of an arm and wrapped a shield around Zoey. After doing the same with Grizande, he said, "We fly."

That was all the warning they had before he spread his wings and launched them skyward. He needed Craft and power to hold that much weight in each hand during flight—especially because he was flying close to the shields above the Hall and didn't want a collision between the shields around the girls and the shields around the Hall. Even an Ebon-gray shield wouldn't protect them against the Black.

When they reached the Queen's square of rooms, Lucivar used Craft to create a platform of air that they could stand on while waiting for the shield to open. Zoey looked pale but still determined. Grizande quivered with . . .

"I learn to do this?"

. . . excitement. "We'll teach you."

She purred with satisfaction.

He swallowed a sigh and accepted that he would also be teaching the little tiger. Maybe not. Liath seemed to be in charge of Jaalan's education. May the Darkness have mercy on all of them.

The shield opened. Lucivar vanished the air platform and spread his wings enough to control the fall to the inner courtyard, landing lightly before he set the girls on their feet and released the shields around them.

Weston stepped onto the second-story balcony and stared at them.

"You in trouble, Zoela Queen," Grizande said, sounding amused but sympathetic.

Arlene and Jhett ran out of the social room, and skidded to a stop when they realized the Eyrien with Zoey wasn't Daemonar.

Lucivar put a hand around the back of Grizande's neck. The girl hissed a warning, which he ignored. "You are going to find the other Queens. Do it quietly. Say these words exactly: 'Lady Zoela requires your presence in the Queen's square.' Don't answer any questions. Don't tell anyone else the message you're giving the Queens."

"Not even brother Daemonar?"

Brother? Well, well, well. "You may tell your brother when you can't be overheard." He didn't point out that she could use a psychic thread to talk to Daemonar. If she didn't realize that, it would be another lesson.

He released her. "Go."

Grizande looked around. Lucivar noted with approval that she carefully probed the rooms before she said, "How?"

"Up here." Weston waved a hand. "This room is the only way in or out."

The girl moved fast, racing up the stairs with a feline grace that would make her exquisitely lethal with a few years of training.

When she disappeared with Weston, Lucivar looked at the other girls but didn't ask any questions. He walked up the stairs.

"Zoey," Weston said when Lucivar walked into the room. "Did she get the answers she needed?"

"She's asked to see the other Queens, so I guess we'll find out."

Grizande found Kathlene Queen first, but she wasn't alone.

As Grizande wondered how to separate Queen from court without being obvious that she had a message meant for Queen alone, Titian noticed her and moved toward her, leaving Kathlene Queen to deal with a screeching girl.

"I have to get out! I can't breathe!"

"We can go into one of the courtyards for fresh air," Kathlene Queen said soothingly.

"But we're still locked in! Why are we locked in?"

"Cara, I'm sure the Hall being locked is temporary and has nothing to do with us. Come on, now. We have lessons to finish."

"I can't!"

"Grizande," Titian said, looking worried but trying to smile.

"Screeching do no good," Grizande said. "Outside land also shielded. Can't get in; can't get out."

Titian looked at the other people around Cara and Kathlene Queen. "You got back in."

"Prince Lucivar got back in. Brought us with him."

"Father's here?" Titian blinked. Then she sighed. "Yes, of course he's here."

"Have message for Kathlene Queen from Zoela Queen."

"Maybe you can tell me?"

Grizande shook her head. "Only for Queens. Lucivar said."

Titian nodded. "Wait here. I'll tell Kathlene you need to speak to her."

Whatever Titian said had Kathlene Queen moving away from her court—including the screeching girl who tried to follow.

"What does *she* have to say that the rest of us can't hear?" Cara wailed, trying to shake off Titian's hold of her arm.

"Is Zoey feeling better?" Kathlene Queen asked. "Her tummy was upset this morning."

That was the untruth to explain Zoela Queen's absence from the assignments. "Better," Grizande agreed. "Zoela Queen *requires* your presence in the Queen's square."

"If my presence is required, then this must be important."

"Yes."

"Just me, or Felisha and Azara too?"

"You and them."

"We don't want everyone to notice that you're delivering a message to all the Queens. Why don't you tell Azara and I'll tell Felisha?" Kathlene Queen thought for a moment. "Better not to bring our courts to this meeting?"

"No courts. Just Queens."

"Then if you would oblige me by finding Prince Daemonar and telling him the Queens will be heading for the Queen's square without an escort? He'll know what to do."

She knew what to do. "I find Daemonar. I escort Azara Queen. He find escorts for you and Felisha Queen."

"Very well. We'll be there as soon as we can. Azara and her court are working in the main library today. Do you know where that is?"

Grizande nodded and walked away.

As she headed for the part of the Hall where she would find Azara Queen, it occurred to her that Kathlene Queen had made requests, not given orders—just like she would have done if she'd been talking to Daemonar.

Daemonar felt the presence of the Sapphire—and the presence of the Ebon-gray. Sadi's Black was a smothering presence that made it impossible for someone to know the man's exact location. Well, *Daemonar* couldn't tell. He was certain the Demon Prince would be able to locate the High Lord.

Sapphire, then. He would track down Grizande and see what she had to say about her and Zoey's adventure.

He and his men strode through the corridors until they reached the main library. As they approached, a door opened, and Daemonar heard Azara say, "The rest of you stay here and continue working. I'll be back shortly."

Azara and Grizande stepped out of the library. Azara looked uncertain about finding three Warlord Princes standing in her way. Grizande looked pleased.

"Found you," Grizande said.

He didn't point out that he'd tracked *her* down. "Trouble?" When she moved away from the others, he did too.

"Kathlene Queen needs escort to Queen's square. Felisha Queen too. I escort Azara Queen."

Daemonar tapped her shoulder. "If you're going to be Azara's sword and shield, you'd better shield as if you're going into a fight. If you don't, Lucivar will have some things to say to you about protecting yourself so that you're prepared to protect someone else."

"He would growl at me?"

"Ooooh, yeah. You could call it that."

He watched her form a Sapphire shield as snug as a second skin, then form another one a finger length away from her body. He nodded approval. Then he leaned as close as he could without hitting her shields and said quietly, "Stay alert. You can trust the Warlord Princes here. Also Holt, Beale, Raine, Mikal, and Weston. Whatever is going on, they aren't part of it."

She frowned. "No females?"

He wondered if she would have asked that question a short time ago, or if she would have assumed no females could be trusted—except Black Widows. "You can trust Titian and Jhett. Brenda, Helene, Nadene, among the adult females, although I don't think they would be much help in a fight. Afterward, sure, but not during an attack. Mrs. Beale?" He shuddered. "Let's hope Mrs. Beale doesn't need to enter the fight. And you can trust all the kindred living at the Hall."

Grizande nodded.

"Come on. Let's get this done."

It didn't take long to fetch Kathlene, telling the overly curious that she was helping Daemonar with an assignment for escorts. He and Kathlene headed for the part of the Hall where Felisha was supposed to be working, but they met up with Raeth, Trent, and Liath, who were already herding the other Queen toward the meeting.

Raeth looked at Daemonar. *I tried to tell Liath that we were supposed to wait for you because we weren't the assigned escorts, and he *growled* at me. I wasn't going to argue with him after that.*

Smart choice, since he wears the Green.

I was thinking more about his teeth.

They moved quickly, Liath in the lead, with Warlord Princes on either side of Kathlene and Felisha, while Daemonar covered their backs.

They turned into the last corridor before reaching the square and found an obstacle that stopped all of them—even Liath—in their tracks. Lucivar Yaslana, holding an Eyrien war blade.

The Demon Prince studied their formation around the Queens, nodded his approval, and stepped aside.

"Grizande?" Daemonar asked as he passed his father.

Lucivar's lips twitched. "Already here. But considering the way the young Queen was panting by the time she and Grizande reached the square, I think Azara needs more time exercising if she's going to keep up with your Tigre sister."

He didn't disagree with his father's use of the word "sister." In his own mind, Grizande had become family.

"Place your men, one on each side of the square," Lucivar said. "You should stay in motion, checking on them. I'll go downstairs and patrol those corridors with Liath."

"You're really expecting trouble?"

"Not serious trouble. But as a training exercise, you all need to learn that no entry means no entry—even when the person asking is a pretty girl."

Daemonar snorted. "I already know that."

"Yes, you do. Do those boys?" Lucivar turned away,

then hesitated. "Keep it sharp, boyo. No matter how this turns out, not everyone is going to survive."

Lucivar walked away, followed by Liath moments later.

Not everyone was going to survive. What had Uncle Daemon discovered that meant it was going to come to that?

SIXTY-NINE

Bracketed by Jhett and Arlene, Zoey waited for the other Queens to arrive.

Azara arrived first, red faced and sweaty. Grizande looked invigorated.

Not being a Sceltie, at least Grizande didn't nip to encourage her sheep to hurry up.

Kathlene and Felisha entered the social room together.

"I thought this meeting was only for the Queens," Felisha said, looking a bit put out.

"Jhett and Arlene are part of this," Zoey replied.

"Then Titian should be here too," Kathlene said. "I'm sure she's part of this—whatever this is."

Before Zoey could think of a reply, Titian hurried into the social room, then stopped when she saw the other girls.

"Holt escorted me here," Titian explained. "Said my presence was required. I expected to get a scold from my father."

Kathlene looked at Zoey. "You weren't sick, so where were you that everyone covered for you?"

Zoey swallowed hard. "Grizande drove the Coach, and we went to the Keep so that I could talk to Witch and ask her advice."

The other Queens stared at her.

"What did she say?" Kathlene finally asked.

Zoey breathed in, breathed out. "What is the Queen's purpose?" She waited.

"To be the moral center of her court and, by extension, all the people in her territory," Kathlene replied.

"What is the Queen's duty?"

"To rule with honor, strength, and compassion because her will is the law. To protect her court so that they, in turn, can protect the rest of her people," Felisha replied.

Zoey asked the last question. "What is the Queen's price?"

They stared at her just as she had stared at Witch, so she answered the question. "To stand against what you know is wrong, no matter who gives the command. To stand and fight, no matter the cost to your court or to you. Especially to you."

"Prince Sadi is disappointed in us," Titian said quietly. "We're here so that he can protect us the same way his father protected Witch and her friends, but we didn't go to him when that first extra order was added to the assignments."

"Giving that order was wrong, but it seemed so . . . trivial," Azara protested.

Zoey shivered, remembering the disappointment in Witch's eyes. "Witch said there are no small wrongs when you're a Queen, because that's how the taint begins."

"What do we do?" Felisha asked.

Kathlene looked at Zoey, then at Titian. "I didn't burn today's assignment. I believe Titian took it to Prince Sadi."

Titian nodded.

"Why did you do that? We'll be punished!" Azara cried.

"Then we'll pay that price," Kathlene replied, sounding firm. "And we'll offer to help him find out who was slipping those extra orders into the envelope meant for whichever of us was the Territory Queen that day."

"He already knows," Jhett said. "Cara is the one who was slipping the paper into the envelopes, but I think the orders were coming from Dinah or one of her other friends. The Prince used a summoning spell to connect the extra orders with a letter that had arrived for Cara." She looked at Kathlene, then at the rest of the girls. "Today the Queens were supposed to order three of their people to whip three people in a lesser Queen's court—using a riding crop."

Zoey gasped. How had it gone from a hand slap to a whipping so fast?

Kathlene brushed the sleeve of her shirt. "I'm Territory Queen today, so I'll request a meeting with Prince Sadi and tell him what we know. Yes, I'm aware he already knows this—and probably knows more than we do—but I think it's important that I report to him." She hesitated, then pulled her shoulders back. "And I will request that Cara be expelled for her part in this . . . treachery . . . for the well-being of everyone else residing at the Hall."

"You don't have to go alone," Zoey said. "We all had a chance to report this when it was our turn to be Territory Queen, and none of us did. Now we'll go to him united and make this request."

"Yes," Felisha said.

Azara hesitated but finally nodded.

Kathlene sighed. "I guess we'll pay a price for failing."

Zoey smiled. "I told Witch everything that I knew, and she said we hadn't failed yet."

They moved through the corridors of the Hall the same way they would move through enemy territory. Liath, properly shielded, scouted ahead, reporting back to Daemonar through psychic communication about any humans he encountered. Most were servants who stepped aside—and probably reported to Beale that the Queens were heading for the High Lord's study.

Daemonar had taken point. Lord Weston walked on one side of Zoey and Titian; Allis walked on the other side. Grizande had chosen Jhett and Arlene as the people she would defend—and Jaalan trotted with her. The other Warlord Princes studying at the Hall walked beside the Queens. And the Demon Prince guarded their backs.

By the time they reached the great hall, Beale stood at the door of the High Lord's study. Holt, Brenda, and Raine stood between the front door and the students and other instructors gathering to find out what had happened.

Daemonar wasn't sure what to do next. Hustle all the girls into the study and hold position? What about Zoey and Titian's friends who were gathered with the rest of the students? Were they vulnerable?

"Queens only," Lucivar said. "He's waiting for you."

Beale opened the study door and announced the Ladies Azara, Felisha, Kathlene, and Zoela.

Daemonar wasn't sure who held Allis back, but the Sceltie's sharp whine told everyone she was not a happy herder.

A light tap on his inner barriers before his father used a psychic link to show him the next step. Titian, Jhett, and Arlene to remain near the study door. Beale moving to help defend the great hall. He, along with the other human Warlord Princes and Weston, to form a half circle to prevent anyone from approaching the study until the meeting was done.

Once they had taken their positions, Daemonar watched Liath and Grizande—and the kitten—neatly extract the rest of Zoey's friends from among the other students and deliver them to Brenda. Watched them separate the youngsters who were friends with Kathlene, then Felisha's friends, then Azara's, and bring them to Beale, to Holt, to Raine. Separating the herds—or the flocks.

And the Demon Prince, holding his war blade, stood in the great hall and watched them all.

Daemon listened to four young Queens stumble through an explanation of why they hadn't challenged orders that they knew no Queen should ask of anyone in her court without good reason. Was there a reason? Were they told to punish someone who had done something wrong? To slap the hand of someone who was trying to take food from someone else's dish? Who tried to take something that belonged to someone else? Who was abusing a servant? No?

Zoey looked exhausted and close to tears. Considering what she'd already done to find answers, that didn't surprise him. Felisha and Azara? Shaken—and not as sure of the responsibilities that came with being a Queen. Kathlene. That girl already had steel in her spine. She acknowledged making a mistake by not coming to him sooner and . . .

"We talked it over, Prince," Kathlene said, "and we respectfully ask that you expel Cara from the Hall. We feel she no longer deserves the privilege of being trained by you and the other people here."

"That's all you want?" he asked quietly. "To see her banished from the Hall?"

Kathlene hesitated. "I don't think we're entitled to ask for more than that. As the Warlord Prince of Dhemlan and the owner of the Hall, you may feel differently."

"You are correct. In the current hierarchy, the four of you are not entitled to ask for more than that." Daemon rose—and watched four girls flinch. Had Jaenelle ever flinched when Saetan was about to call in a debt? He doubted it. "You are also correct that I feel differently about this. Because of the order Lady Kathlene was given this morning, I feel very differently about this."

He walked out of his study, trailed by the four Queens. Daemonar and Raeth stepped aside to let him pass, then closed ranks to protect the Queens.

Daemon walked up to Lucivar, called in the paper with that day's orders, and held it out.

After reading it, the Demon Prince looked at the High Lord. *What do you want done?*

A debt is owed to us and to everyone living at the Hall, but I think we should give this witch a choice of how to pay the debt.

What choice? Lucivar asked.

Daemon smiled a cold, cruel smile. *The kind you and I do so well.*

✦ ✦ ✦

Daemonar watched his father vanish the war blade, watched the way Lucivar and Daemon casually moved to the center of the great hall and began circling, maintaining a distance from each other that made Daemonar think they were performing the moves of a dance.

Then he considered what kind of dance the Demon Prince and High Lord might perform right now and thought, *Mother Night.*

Still circling, Lucivar called in a whip that wasn't any longer than a man's arm. Supple, like a thin branch of a young tree, and made of leather.

"There aren't any riding crops here at the Hall, so this will have to do," Lucivar said. He brushed one hand over the leather, calling attention to its length. "The bitches in Askavi Terreille used this kind of whip to punish those who wouldn't obey orders that inflicted pain and suffering on other people. Even a light touch with this would produce welts. A man driven by the fear of having it used on him would wield it with enough force to tear through skin and muscle. I've used it a few times since coming to Kaeleer. The men deserved this form of execution, but it was brutal to perform and brutal to witness. Still . . ."

Daemonar guessed what was coming, but he still wasn't prepared when Cara suddenly skidded across the floor and ended up in the center of that circle made of Black and Ebon-gray power and temper. Ice and fire—and no way to escape either.

Cara kept turning around, and the two men continued to circle, circle, circle as they watched her. Just watched her with an intensity that made Daemonar shiver.

Daemon said in that viciously civil voice, "Today's orders were to give three people in each of the lesser courts ten strokes with a riding crop. Hard strokes. That was specified. But you already know that because you're the one who slipped those orders into the Territory Queen's envelope. So you will be the person who receives that punishment. I've seen Yaslana wield that whip, so I know what your back will look like when he's done. That's why we're willing to give you a choice of how you will pay this debt to me, to him, and to all the people here at the Hall who were harmed by what you did. Your first choice: you can take the ten strokes of the whip. I'm sure Lady Nadene will be able to heal the wounds well enough that you won't have any physical problems with your back—at least while you're young—but the marks will show on your skin for the rest of your life, testimony that you crossed a line and betrayed the people around you. Your second choice: I can shatter your Birthright Jewel and break you back to basic Craft here and now. That will put an end to your ability to use power to further your ambitions. Your final choice: you can tell all of us why you participated in acts that were meant to harm other students, that were meant to inflict pain. Tell us who else was part of the game. Tell us why, and then I'll decide on an appropriate reprimand that will not include a whip or a shattered Jewel."

Daemon and Lucivar circled, circled, circled.

Daemonar saw desperate calculation in Cara's eyes as she looked at the other students. The bitch was going to try to blame someone else—or at least claim she wasn't the only one helping Dinah.

Crack!

Cara shrieked as part of her skirt hung from a slice made by the whip.

"That's for thinking you could lie," Lucivar said. "You'll earn a stroke for every lie you tell, regardless of which punishment you choose."

Cara scrambled away from Lucivar, but that brought her closer to Daemon.

Daemonar didn't see Daemon's hand move, but Cara leaped away from him as another slice appeared in her skirt, courtesy of the High Lord's lethally sharp nails.

"Tell us why," Daemon said too softly.

"The Queens gave the orders," Cara cried, pointing at the girls standing behind Daemonar. "I didn't do anything wrong!"

"Is she saying it's not wrong to whip someone for no reason?" Lucivar asked.

"It sounds that way," Daemon replied.

Lucivar shrugged. "All right."

Crack!

The lower part of the skirt fell to the floor, exposing Cara's legs.

"Last chance to choose before we choose for you," Daemon said.

Daemonar watched the way his father and uncle circled Cara. Circled and circled. There was something wrong with them. Something very wrong. It was like they were somewhere else, had slipped into some other time in their lives when they would have killed . . .

Beale, Daemonar called on a psychic thread. *Stop them. For their sakes, stop them.*

Beale looked at him, then took a step toward the circling men. "Gentlemen. That is enough."

They stopped circling and turned toward Beale. Glazed eyes that warned of hot fury in one man and cold rage in the other. Both of them riding the killing edge.

One wrong word, one wrong move, and Cara would suffer a brutal death.

If it came to that, they would be lucky if she was the only person who died.

"Is it enough, Lord Beale?" the Sadist asked too softly.

"The Lady would not want you to do more," Beale replied. "Banish the girl for the trouble she caused. Report her conduct to the Province and District Queens so that they will think long and hard before welcoming her into one of their courts. That mark on her reputation and honor will last as long as a scar on her back—and she will receive no sympathy for it."

Daemonar held his breath. *Please,* he thought. *Please.*

Whatever happened to the two of you once because some girl played this kind of game, please listen to Beale now.

Daemon looked at Lucivar.

Lucivar released a breath. "Her will is our life."

Yes! As long as Daemon and Lucivar were thinking of what Witch would expect from them, they could step away from the scourge of memories.

"Very well." Daemon exhaled slowly and looked at Cara. "You are banished from the Hall for your part in the harm done to other students. As recommended, I will send a report of your conduct to all the District and Province Queens in Dhemlan and make it clear that I will not look favorably on any Queen who allows you to serve in her First Circle. Lord Holt, Prince Liath, please escort Lady Cara to her room. Helene will help her pack. She leaves in two hours."

"That's it," Jhett whispered, peering over Raeth's shoulder as Cara was removed from the great hall.

Not yet, Daemonar thought as he watched his uncle.

"As for the rest of you," Daemon said.

Everyone tensed.

"Every one of you should have come to me to question those orders," he continued. "The fact that you didn't makes me wonder if you're ready for training that isn't conventional. Therefore, the rest of you will leave after the midday meal. I don't want to see or hear from any of you for a week. At the end of that time, you may choose to return and resume your training—or you can choose to study elsewhere. Malice isn't always big and grand, children. Not when it begins. You all saw something wrong and accepted it without question, without challenge. And more than that, you did everything you could to keep it hidden." He paused, then added, "I expected better from all of you. You disappoint me."

Daemonar didn't know what to think or what to say when Daemon walked across the great hall, then used Craft to nudge him out of the way in order to reach the study. The door opened and closed. The locks clicked into place. And the weight of the Black's silence was hard to bear.

Lucivar vanished the whip and looked at Beale. "Tossing all of them out the door was different." He studied the butler. "Wasn't it?"

"Your father sent all the youngsters home at one point because they had done something that disappointed him," Beale replied. "Since the staff didn't have to clean up a mess or call in people to do repairs, I don't know what the coven and boyos did to provoke that decision. But that temporary banishment never happened again."

"Huh. Well, I'd better gather up my three and the kitten."

Beale's expression indicated interest. "Three?"

"Three," Lucivar confirmed as he headed out of the great hall. "And the kitten."

He didn't know why the youngsters thought he'd be sympathetic, but they all wanted to cling to him like burs in fur, hoping he could somehow convince Daemon to let them stay.

How were they supposed to explain being sent home to their parents and the District Queens?

How in the name of Hell should he know? Admit to being stupid, take the scolding, and study the lessons. Then come back and be smarter.

His three didn't have to worry about a District Queen, although he was certain that Marian would have a few things to say about this—and he figured Daemonar would want to have a chat with his auntie J.

"Why can't Zoey come and stay with us?" Titian asked tearfully when he stopped at her room to make sure she was starting to pack.

"Because she has to discuss her actions with her grandmother," Lucivar replied. "This isn't a reward, witchling. It's a reprimand. Zoey goes home."

He found Daemonar with Grizande in her room. The

girl was curled up on the floor with the kitten pushing at her hip while Daemonar knelt by her head.

"Father . . . ," Daemonar began.

Lucivar knelt beside the girl. "You sick, witchling?"

"No," she whispered. "I being punished?"

"Well, you can decide that once you find out what chores Marian assigns to you while you're staying with us in Ebon Rih."

Grizande stared at him. "Ebon Rih?"

"I *told* you nobody would make you go back to Tigrelan," Daemonar said, sounding exasperated.

Lucivar wondered how many times the boy had said it since the children left the great hall. "Yes. You're coming home with us. Jaalan is coming too."

She uncurled. Daemonar gave her a brotherly shove to a sitting position.

"Now, pack up your things, including your lesson books." He looked at her, then at Daemonar. "Both of you."

"Yes, sir." The words sounded solemn. The boy's eyes danced with amusement. Then the amusement faded because Daemonar, unlike the other youngsters, understood what could have happened if the High Lord—or the Sadist—hadn't already known the enemies' names. What would have happened if Beale hadn't reminded Daemon and Lucivar that they answered to Witch.

Daemon remained in his study while the Hall emptied of students and instructors. When he felt Lucivar leave with the horde heading for Ebon Rih, he summoned Beale and Holt.

He felt unnaturally calm, so he couldn't tell which side of his temper was dominant until he watched Beale and Holt shudder.

Ah. The Sadist had come for this dance.

He smiled at the two men and said, "Tell me about Ida."

SEVENTY

At Eileen's insistence, Saetien accompanied the other woman into the village proper to do some shopping. She'd balked at first. There was still so much work to do on the cottage's gardens. But Eileen was canny and knew her quarry. The first shop they visited was the bookseller's, where Saetien bought a new copy of the first Tracker and Shadow book. She hadn't read one of Lady Fiona's novels in years, but now that she was dealing with Shelby and the puppy school—and adult Scelties who were a lot bossier than the ones who lived at the Hall—she wanted to read the book that was an adventure, yes, but was also considered a primer for humans who had never crossed paths with a Sceltie before.

The second shop sold everything a farmer—or a cottage gardener—needed to take care of land. The temptation to buy every tool available was fiercely battled by enough practicality that Saetien purchased only a basic set of gardening tools, along with shovels, rakes, and a wheelbarrow that didn't have holes or a wobbly wheel.

She vanished the tools, but she wasn't confident enough about her skill with the Purple Dusk Jewel to tackle the wheelbarrow, so she asked if it could be delivered to the cottage.

"No need for that," Eileen said as she vanished the wheelbarrow. "We can stop by the cottage and drop off your new tools. Besides, I'd like to see how you've been getting on."

After a few more stops for items on Eileen's list, they set off for the cottage.

"It's coming along well," Eileen said as they slowly walked toward the shed that stood between the cottage and the small stable. "You've done a lot of work here, Saetien."

"Caitie helped a lot, and she's identified plants I didn't recognize, so I haven't dug out anything I wanted to keep."

"It's kind of you to let Caitie work with you. She's less . . . vague . . . these days, and not wandering on her own as much."

"She's a friend," Saetien said, wondering if Eileen thought Caitie should be pitied. There was no reason to pity Caitie. Whoever she might have been was gone because of her injuries, but she was building a life that suited who she was now. If she and Saetien were helping each other? Well, wasn't that what friends did?

"You came home early yesterday." Eileen brushed a hand over Saetien's hair. "I can listen if you want to talk."

She shook her head. "I think talking to me about the past sometimes stirs up painful memories for Butler."

"I'm not surprised at that." Eileen studied a weedy length of the garden. "Did he mention that Lady Fiona asked him to look after her cottage and her books? He took it on when Fiona started needing help around the cottage and help with managing the publishing of her books here in Scelt and in the other Territories. That was a lot of years ago." She smiled. "I noticed you bought the first Tracker and Shadow story."

"The primer for dealing with Scelties."

Eileen laughed. "That's why it's still printed and read. And that's why a business manager is still required."

"Well, I hope he manages her books better than he took care of her garden," Saetien grumbled.

"When it came to the gardens, I think he was better at the digging and hauling than the planting and tending. Everyone to their own skills, aye?"

"Aye."

What sort of skills did Butler have?

✦ ✦ ✦

"I think you were waiting for this." Kieran held out a letter closed with red wax and a distinctive seal.

Her father had replied to her letter!

"Thank you, Kieran." Taking the letter, she dashed to her room.

Then she stared at the letter. What would he say in response to her . . . grumble . . . about Butler and the cottage garden?

She breathed in. Breathed out. Poured and drank a glass of water as she tried to remember exactly what she'd said.

Finally, she opened the letter.

Dear Saetien,

Your annoyance at a potentially beautiful garden being buried under weeds is understandable. However, I feel compelled to point out that gardens are best enjoyed in daylight, when most flowers bloom—and the hours of daylight don't belong to the demon-dead. While I understand your annoyance, I also understand why Butler may no longer feel the same enthusiasm when it comes to evicting weeds, since he never has the chance to see the garden at its best.

There are some lovely night-blooming flowers that grow in Scelt. You could ask Lady Eileen if she has any of those plants. Perhaps she would share some seeds or a cutting that you could add to the cottage's garden. Then Butler would have a reason to look after the land again.

With love,
Papa

She waited until after supper, when Eileen settled into the sitting room with a book and the men had gone over to

Kieran's side of the house to discuss whatever business needed to be discussed.

"Night-blooming flowers?" Eileen smiled. "Yes, I have some in my garden. It's a little too early in the season for them to be blooming, but I can show you what they look like. I have a book of drawings of plants that grow in Scelt." She set aside her book. "I think it's in the morning room, which is where I tend to make my plans for the garden. Come along, then."

It took Eileen no time at all to find the book, but she continued to scan the bookshelves until she found a second book. She set both on a table. "This one is formal and official—pen-and-ink drawings of the plants and flowers, along with descriptions of how they grow and what they need. Very useful, but a little cold, I always thought. This other one is old, and I'm not sure many copies still exist. Drawings of plants by themselves and in a garden setting."

Eileen was right about the first book. It was formal and official. Useful in identifying plants. The other book . . .

Several different artists whose work ranged from amateurish, if one was being kind, to drawings that almost made you feel the moonlight.

The first time she went through the book, she noticed the drawings. The second time, she noticed the names of the artists—noticed the names of the two artists whose work was so infused with a love of the land that Saetien wished she could walk through the gardens these women created.

Two names. Morghann. And J.A.

Saetien pressed her fingers on the edge of one of the drawings. "Lady Angelline knew a lot of the demon-dead."

"She did, yes," Eileen replied.

"Would Angelline House have night-blooming plants?"

Eileen smiled. "A whole section of the garden there has night-blooming plants. We could go over tomorrow and have a look, if you feel inclined."

"I'd like that. Maybe Caitie could come with us?"

Eileen's smile warmed. "I'll send a note to her parents,

inviting her to join us. And I'll send a note to the staff at Angelline House so they know to expect us."

Saetien said good night and went up to her room to read while Shelby snoozed, recovering from the discovery that there were kittens in the stables. Not kindred, no, but not toys for Scelties either, as the kittens made perfectly clear with their sharp little claws.

Would Butler be pleased or upset if she planted seeds or cuttings from Angelline House?

Would he ever tell her about the other unwanted child?

SEVENTY-ONE

Saetien spent time with Shelby at the Sceltie school. The pups Shelby's age were learning to make a ball of witchlight and to air walk. It embarrassed her—and startled the instructors—when she admitted she had forgotten how to air walk and couldn't assist with the lesson. She *used* to know, but she'd chosen to forget when she'd learned that bit of Craft had been handed down from Jaenelle Angelline. *All* the Scelties who went to the school learned that bit of Craft *because* the Lady had taught Ladvarian and other Scelties how to do it. And while there were many, many humans who didn't know how to air walk, the instructors were surprised that Prince Sadi hadn't taught her, since he could do it so well, having been taught by the Lady herself.

She'd spent so much time resenting Jaenelle Angelline that only now was it beginning to dawn on her that so many spells and bits of Craft the Blood used today had been created by the Queens in the Dark Court. Only now was it beginning to dawn on her that she'd resisted learning Craft from her father because *he* had learned so much of it from Jaenelle. Not everything. He'd had centuries to learn a lot of Craft before he met the Queen, but the things that were the most fun were the things that had come from the Lady, and that was why Saetien hadn't wanted to do them.

She couldn't ask her father. Oh, he'd be happy to teach

her, but learning Craft from him would get tangled up in so many things about the family that she found difficult. She needed to find an instructor who wasn't so overwhelmingly important.

Maybe the answer was right here in Maghre.

Saetien knocked on the cottage's door, then looked over her shoulder. Kieran and the kindred Warlord pulling the pony cart would wait until Butler opened the door. She should have come over earlier and spent an hour weeding the garden. Then Kieran wouldn't be waiting to make sure she wasn't on her own after sundown.

She didn't want this discussion while Kieran could overhear it—or while the horse could hear it, since *his* hearing would be even better.

Butler opened the door. Saetien waved at Kieran, who gave her a long look—and aimed a longer look at Butler—before he and the horse returned to the family home.

"Problem?" Butler asked.

Saetien took a deep breath. "I'd like you to teach me."

"Did you have something in mind?"

"Anything. Everything."

He blinked. "That's a broad range of topics."

"Yes."

They stood on the threshold. More than one threshold. She wasn't sure what he would say, but she was sure his answer, one way or another, would change so many things.

"Do you know how to make scrambled eggs?" Butler asked.

"No."

"Then that's where we'll start." He turned and walked toward the back of the cottage. "Wipe your feet and close the door."

She wiped her feet, closed the door, and hurried after him. "I was thinking about a lesson in Craft."

"You said anything, remember?" He took eggs, milk, and butter out of the cold box. "I've been thinking about

Wilhelmina Benedict. She didn't know how to make scrambled eggs either."

"Didn't she have a cook when she lived in Tuathal?" Cooking eggs wasn't what Saetien had had in mind. Obviously, it had been on Butler's mind. Why else would he have eggs, milk, and butter in his cold box when he didn't consume anything but yarbarah?

He took a pan out of a lower cupboard. "You're on a ship with a few other aristos. Small ship, small crew, and your destination is a secret because you're looking for an island that contains buried treasure. Big storm blows up out of nowhere, and a huge wave hits the ship, breaking it in half."

"Can a wave do that?"

He gave her a look. "This is my story, so yes, it can."

"Right."

"You're swept away from the rest of the people on the ship and you land, safely, on an island. You do some exploring and find fresh water. You also find ripe fruit on trees and tubers that you recognize as edible."

"How do I recognize them?"

"You've seen the cooked version on your plate."

He paused, and she figured he was waiting for another interruption, so she kept quiet.

"After a couple of days of eating tubers and fruit, you return to the beach and discover some of the ship's cargo has washed ashore. Some of the pots and pans and cooking utensils. Small barrels of butter, salt, sugar, cooking oil. You've found some clutches of eggs on the island but haven't had a way of cooking them, and eating them raw is not appealing."

"They aren't reptile eggs, are they? I'm not cooking reptiles."

"No, they are from chickens that ended up on the island because of a shipwreck years before."

"But no other humans."

"No other humans. Since *you* know some cooking basics, you will have a much better and varied diet than the aristos who landed on a different island."

"Without the cook."

"Of course without the cook. The aristos were trying to find the island that had the buried treasure, while the cook, who wasn't looking for anything beyond a job and wages, quite sensibly caught the nearest Wind before the wave hit the ship, and he rode that Web in the direction of the coast—where he, upon arriving, told the Master of the Guard who served in the nearest court about the ship and the storm."

"So everyone will be rescued?"

"Eventually. In the meantime, do you want to eat scrambled eggs along with your tubers and fruit?"

"Have to keep up my strength if I'm going to look for that buried treasure. Besides, I already know how to dig something out of the ground even if I don't have a shovel."

"Exactly." Butler put the pan on the cooktop and gave her a long look. "Do you know how to create witchfire to heat up a pan?"

"Let's assume I don't and start from there."

What was on her plate didn't look quite like the scrambled eggs she'd had for breakfast, but they were edible—especially if her other choices were raw tubers and fruit.

"Not enough butter?" Saetien asked, forking up another bite.

"Too much witchfire," Butler replied as he warmed a glass of yarbarah. "But you didn't burn down the cottage or blow up the kitchen, so you're ahead of a few people who've attempted to learn how to cook."

Since Butler had told her a bit about teaching Wilhelmina to make a few basic dishes—and shop for the ingredients—Saetien figured Lady Benedict might have used a bit too much witchfire too. Which left . . .

"Jaenelle Angelline blew up a kitchen?"

Butler nodded. "According to the story, Jaenelle and Karla were making a casserole while Mrs. Beale was out somewhere. They were also working on a complex bit of

Craft that they needed to keep an eye on, which is why that bowl was in the kitchen. Well, they put the wrong bowl in the oven and blew up the kitchen."

Saetien dropped her fork. "They blew up the kitchen at the Hall? *Mrs. Beale's kitchen?*" She shuddered.

"Yes. That kitchen. Which Saetan rebuilt to Mrs. Beale's specifications. And he didn't argue when Mrs. Beale banned Jaenelle and Karla from entering the kitchen ever again."

"But Jaenelle learned how to make scrambled eggs."

Butler roared with laughter. "Hell's fire, girl. Jaenelle couldn't even hard-boil an egg, let alone do anything else with it." He thought for a moment. "Well, she couldn't do anything with an egg that would make it edible."

I can do something Jaenelle couldn't do. She wasn't perfect after all.

The scrambled eggs still needed improvement, but they suddenly tasted better.

At supper that night, Kieran listened to Saetien's enthusiastic recounting of making scrambled eggs. He watched the way her gold eyes lit up as she responded to Eileen's questions and comments.

Something about the way her eyes lit up made him uneasy, but it wasn't until later, when his father followed him over to his side of the house, that remembering a story made him realize *why* he was uneasy.

"You've got a problem, boyo," Kildare said.

Kieran nodded. "I know it. A fire's been lit inside Saetien." He fiddled with bits and pieces on his desk. "Like the filly in your story."

"Exactly. And that means you need to find a way to tell Prince Sadi that his daughter has finally heard the right voice—and it isn't his."

SEVENTY-TWO

The days were getting longer, which meant more time to work in the garden. It also meant Saetien had to wait longer for Butler to rise so that they could work on the next lesson.

She had lessons in Craft, in Protocol, in the history of Scelt, particularly of the village of Maghre. Besides working with the puppies each morning at the Sceltie school, she had to spend extra time there each day learning how the school was run—everything from ordering supplies to paying the instructors to hiring the humans who looked after the sheep that were used to teach the puppies how to herd properly.

She'd never truly appreciated how thankful humans should be that there were sheep.

She and Caitie played with the foals and helped Kildare and Ryder in the stables. The two girls also spent time in Butler's garden, digging and pulling weeds. Caitie's father came by with another man one afternoon and got the water pump near the stable working again. On another afternoon, a couple more men from the village showed up with a tiller and turned over the soil of what had once been the kitchen garden—and Eileen and a couple of women from Angelline House showed up with seeds and seedlings to help her plant a few vegetables in the kitchen garden. Sure, the greengrocer in the village would be happy to supply her with vegetables for her cooking lessons, but there was some extra satisfaction from cooking foods that you'd grown with your own hands.

She didn't point out that she would probably be gone before there were any vegetables to harvest, and that Butler didn't eat them anymore.

The man claimed he wasn't arranging anything or hiring anyone. People were being neighborly—just like she could give a helping hand if any of them needed it.

The cottage was tidy inside and had been well maintained over the years, but Butler had ignored the outbuildings and the land. Maybe people were happy that her being there gave them an excuse to tidy things up outside?

After Caitie went home, Saetien put the tools away in the shed, washed up a bit at the pump, then returned to the part of the garden they'd cleared of weeds that day.

Butler joined her a little while later. "It's coming along."

"It just needs someone to care about it and give it some time," Saetien said.

He nodded. "It's yours, then."

She stared at him. "What?"

"The garden. It's yours to do with as you please. Hire a couple of men to plow it under and start from scratch, or rebuild from what is here. It's up to you. I'll pay for the labor or supplies."

"You can't give me your garden!"

Butler raised his eyebrows. "I just did. You ready to start tonight's lesson?"

A moment to take a breath before she said, "I have money. I can pay for whatever the garden needs."

"Suit yourself. The offer to help pay for it stands." He headed into the cottage. "You coming?"

She rushed to follow him, then stopped and looked back. The light was going, but she could still see how much she and Caitie had done—and how much more needed to be done. But . . . Hers? All hers?

Well, if it was hers, that shed needed to go. It had broken boards, and rotten wood, and holes in the roof. No wonder all the tools had rusted! She'd have to ask who she could hire to rebuild the shed and how much it would cost.

Since she couldn't do anything about that now, she focused on the lesson Butler had prepared.

Later that night, Butler stared at the stacks of papers on the table in his study.

His time here was almost over, and a lot of work still needed to be done. Papers and instructions needed to be put in clear order for whoever would take over. Personal belongings needed to be discarded or packed up.

A lot needed to be done, but he couldn't concentrate on the tasks, so he warmed a glass of yarbarah and wandered outside the cottage.

The girl had so much potential, so much *life*. The problem, as he saw it, was that she could shine in a small village like Maghre—or Halaway. She could be happy in a cottage but would flounder in a suite at SaDiablo Hall. *Had* floundered. She needed a place to call her own—something that belonged to her and not the SaDiablo family as a whole.

Saetien wouldn't thank him for the comparison, but wasn't that exactly the reason why Jaenelle had loved Angelline House? Because it was hers? Oh, Jaenelle had thrived at the Hall, too, but that was a Queen being at the center of the family and her court. For Jaenelle, the Hall was just a kind of village in her care. Now it was Daemon's domain—and would be for a very long time.

Butler didn't believe for a moment that Daemon Sadi hadn't taught Saetien all the bits of Craft she claimed she didn't know. Much of what he was doing was reminding her of what she already knew. And yet it *was* new to her, in a way he couldn't explain.

He also couldn't explain what he was starting to see in

her eyes when she looked at him. Not a romantic crush, thank the Darkness, but there were *feelings*. Affection.

Problem was, she wasn't the only one experiencing feelings. That had never happened before on one of his assignments, and he didn't know what to do about it.

SEVENTY-THREE

Kieran walked into the morning room, sure he'd find his mother there reviewing the household accounts or the family's social obligations or taking care of some of her daily correspondence. He held up a letter. "Apparently Saetien asked to extend her stay in Maghre—again—and Prince Sadi is concerned she might be outstaying her welcome."

"Nonsense," Eileen replied, capping her pen and turning to face him. "It's delightful to have her here."

"He's also a bit concerned that she's always writing about the garden but she never mentions any structured lessons."

"Not having structured lessons doesn't mean she isn't learning a great deal. And I doubt Butler is as loose with the lessons as Saetien seems to think. Just because something doesn't *look* like a lesson doesn't mean it isn't one. And look how much Caitie has improved since she and Saetien became friends. You can't tell me that isn't worth something."

"I'm not telling you anything, Mother. I have eyes. I see them going into the butcher's shop and the greengrocer's with their list of instructions—and the bakery and the sweetshop, which I gather require no instructions except, perhaps, they can't buy more than they can carry."

"A rule your father and I tried to impose on you and

your brother, with little success until you were old enough to see the wisdom in not eating yourself sick with sweets."

"We didn't get sick that often," Kieran muttered.

"Often enough."

Kieran sighed.

Eileen rose from her desk, then kissed his cheek and smoothed his hair the way she had when he was young. "You can tell Prince Sadi that his daughter is thriving."

"Mother." Kieran took her hand in his. "You see it as well as I do. Saetien isn't just thriving; she's putting down roots."

"Yes." Eileen sobered. "Talk to Butler. The course he's laid out for the girl wasn't idly laid out."

She hesitated, even seemed a little flustered.

"Mother? Is something wrong?"

"Wrong? Oh, no. It's just that Brenda's last letter mentioned that she had helped with the preparations for Lady Jillian's Virgin Night."

Kieran felt the blood drain out of his head. "Oh, Hell's fire."

"Aye. Well, Brenda *did* have some strong and . . . individual . . . thoughts about that rite of passage."

"And Prince Sadi?"

"It's a subject that is noticeably absent from the Prince's correspondence with me."

Butler opened the door. This late-night visit from the War-lord of Maghre wasn't scheduled, but it wasn't unexpected.

"Lord Kieran." Butler stepped aside to give the man room to enter.

"Prince Butler."

Butler led Kieran to the sitting room. "Would you like a whiskey? Or some brandy?"

"Whiskey is fine, thanks."

He poured a generous amount of whiskey into a glass before warming a glass of yarbarah for himself. "You're worried about Saetien."

Kieran stared into the whiskey. "Not *worried* exactly, but concerned, yes." He looked up. "She's putting down roots. I can see it. You must see it."

"Putting down roots and thriving—and learning who she is when she has a chance to step out of the shadow of the SaDiablo family."

"This was meant to be a visit to find out about Wilhelmina Benedict."

"Are you sure? I've begun to wonder if Wilhelmina was simply the signpost that indicated a choice to take a different path. I think living with your family was meant to be temporary. Living in Maghre?" He shrugged.

"She's too young to live on her own."

"She's already lived centuries, Kieran. Yes, emotionally she's an adolescent in a great many ways, but the young woman who is emerging is sharply intelligent and ready to use that intelligence to work—and to grow up in the process."

"Sadi won't agree to this."

"You can remind him that Lady Jillian was around the same age when she went to Little Weeble for her first apprenticeship in a court."

Kieran downed the whiskey and shook his head. "Sadi won't agree to this."

"What makes you think he'll be the one to decide?" Butler asked softly.

Kieran stared at him.

"The Queen's will is his life, Kieran—as it is mine."

Kieran stood. "Thanks for the whiskey. I'll let Prince Sadi know that we'll host Saetien for as long as she wants to stay in Maghre."

"If it helps you, I'll send a report to the Prince providing more details about specific things his daughter is learning."

"Thank you."

Butler waited until Kieran had mounted the Warlord who gave both humans a disapproving look for requiring him to leave his comfy stall so late at night. Then Butler closed the door and leaned against it.

He'd have to get the stables repaired and purchase a new pony cart. And find a horse or two before he left Scelt.

It's time, Butler.

Was it time, when, quite unexpectedly, he was no longer certain he wanted to go?

SEVENTY-FOUR

Surreal read the letter from Sadi twice, admiring the exquisite way he made his expectations clear without actually *saying* what he wanted from her. Of course, the thick packet of gold marks, which just happened to match her fee as an assassin, said all that needed to be said.

Very well. She would visit a particular town in Dhemlan, take the measure of a servant named Ida, and then decide what needed to be done. Well, *how* it needed to be done.

She'd visit a few towns and villages. That wouldn't be unusual for Sadi's second-in-command. Just passing through that part of Dhemlan to see if there was anything the District Queens needed to report to the Warlord Prince of Dhemlan.

She'd also visit Jillian and see how the young lovers were doing now that they could . . . enjoy . . . each other without Lucivar bouncing off the ceiling.

By the time she circled back around to that one Dhemlan town, she'd have a plan for how to make Ida's death look accidental.

Smiling, Surreal went upstairs to pack some clothes—and sharpen her knives.

SEVENTY-FIVE

Saetien followed Butler into his study and wondered why they were going to have the lesson in that room. For the past couple of weeks, they'd been in either the kitchen or the sitting room—or outside if she was trying a bit of Craft that had the potential to blow up.

"For tonight's lesson, I thought—" she began.

"You would help me with this paperwork," Butler finished. "I've already contacted Lady Eileen and told her we'd be working for several hours and she shouldn't hold supper for you."

Saetien blinked. "I'm not getting any supper?"

"There is a casserole in the cold box, along with fruits and cheeses. When you get hungry, you can heat up a piece of the casserole, either using a warming spell or putting it in the oven."

"All right." She hadn't been invited into the study before, so she looked around, interested to discover what Butler might keep in a room seen by few visitors. The picture of a girl, set in an oval frame, caught—and held—her attention. Where had she seen . . . ?

She must have made some movement that drew Butler's gaze, had him focusing on what had caught her attention.

The picture vanished. The look in Butler's eyes warned her that whatever connection he had to the girl was painful and private—and she remembered him saying he and someone else had been unwanted children. Was the girl the someone else?

She wanted to ask, wanted to know. But her curiosity was smothered by his pain. Whatever had happened, it must have been long ago. And yet he still grieved for the girl.

She approached the table stacked with papers and said briskly, "What are those?"

Butler gave her a long look, as if trying to measure something. "When Lady Fiona's health began to fail, she needed some help around the cottage. Specifically, she needed someone to handle the business side of her writing so that she could spend her time writing her stories. Since I was looking to settle down, I was offered the assignment. When Fiona's body died and she made the transition to demon-dead, she still had a couple of Tracker and Shadow books she wanted to write. She remained in the cottage and wrote after sundown while I took care of the daylight tasks. When she'd completed the second book, she went to Hell and resided there for several more years before becoming a whisper in the Darkness. I was given use of the cottage as part of my wages for being her business manager. Fiona thought people would lose interest in the Tracker and Shadow stories, and the assignment wouldn't last more than a few years."

"Wherever Scelties live, people will keep reading the books," Saetien said.

"Exactly," he replied dryly. "Which means I'm still managing business generated by Fiona's books. But it's time to put my affairs in order, and I want to make it as easy as possible for my successor."

She felt a rush of panic. "What do you mean, it's time to put your affairs in order? Why?"

"I'm old, child." Butler smiled. "I've walked among the living long enough. I informed the Queen and the High Lord of my decision months ago. I just need to find the right person to take over the cottage and the work."

Don't leave me. She wouldn't say that. She wouldn't be that selfish, not when he'd already given her so much of his time to find answers she needed instead of doing the work that would allow him to cut his last ties with the living.

"All right," she said. "What do you want me to do?"

After a couple of late nights, Saetien stopped going back to Kieran's house to sleep. Butler opened up the large bedroom with attached bathroom that had been Fiona's private space, and Saetien settled in, carrying her laundry back and forth every day until Eileen suggested that she bring a few days' worth of clothes to the cottage.

In the mornings, she still went to puppy school with Shelby, who now had his own comfy bed in the cottage. After puppy school, she still met up with Caitie to play with the foals and receive Craft lessons from Eileen and Anya and anyone else who had Kieran's approval to teach the girls the particular bit of Craft they wanted to learn.

In the afternoons she worked in the garden, more determined than ever to get it tidied up for whoever would take over the cottage. And at night, she and Butler worked on sorting through decades of contracts and other papers connected with Fiona's books.

Her father's publishing house had bought the rights to publish and sell illustrated editions of Fiona's books in Dhemlan and Askavi. Of course the deal would be for both Territories. Daemon and Lucivar didn't allow anyone or anything to draw a line between them. Not even a book.

"There is a village dance tomorrow evening," Butler said. "You should go."

"We have work," Saetien protested.

"You also have a life."

"I'll go if you go. You have a life too." *For a while longer.*

Butler hesitated. "I'll think about it."

Butler slipped inside the community hall. He'd been firm about Saetien going home and getting some rest so that she wouldn't be too tired to enjoy the dance. He couldn't be sure she'd followed his instructions—after all, he wasn't awake during the daylight hours—but she hadn't been at the cottage when he rose.

It had felt empty. *He* had felt empty.

He hadn't been to a dance in . . . Well, the last time he'd attended a village dance he'd obliged Kieran's great-grandmother by being her partner for a couple of country dances, and that was before the woman had married. Little by little he'd pulled away from the living, like he was watching a world full of colors fade to gray.

It was full of colors again, and that hurt in some ways. And yet, watching Saetien and her partner take their places for the next dance, he wouldn't have made another choice. Bright, shining child with so much intelligence and fire. She just needed a chance, needed to pour her heart and energy into something more than formal teaching and aristo customs.

Saetien made her way over to him, her eyes sparking with mischief. "May I have this dance, Prince Butler? It's a slow one."

"Not this time." He saw disappointment replace good humor, but he didn't change his intentions. He walked over to Caitie and bowed. "Lady? May I have this dance?"

Caitie's brain might be improving, but her leg never would. She was enjoying the gathering of people, but she couldn't participate in the energetic dances. This one? He kept her on the edge of the dance area, adjusting the steps to accommodate her bad leg.

As they made a turn, he looked at Saetien. No need to say anything. She absorbed this lesson too. And seeing the pleasure and understanding in her eyes when she looked at Caitie helped him make a decision.

It took another week of afternoons to finish weeding the rest of the cottage's gardens and put in the new plants. Looking at what she'd accomplished, Saetien felt a bitter-sweet pride. She hoped whoever took over the cottage loved the gardens enough to tend them. They were hers for a little while, and having them had shown her that she needed to take care of places and people—furry and otherwise—in order to fill an empty space in her heart and in her life.

Butler's personal possessions were packed—at least the ones he hadn't given away. For a man who had lived so long, he wasn't leaving much behind.

Except her. He was leaving her behind, and it surprised her how much that hurt.

Saetien stared at the paper in her hands, then stared at Butler. "You don't mean this."

"I do," he replied.

"But I can't do this!"

"You can. Yes, you are young and still have some growing up to do. But you can do this, Saetien."

"You appointed me your successor for managing Fiona's books."

"Yes. And having the cottage is part of the deal." Butler smiled. "I've talked to the staff at Angelline House. Since they would prefer to earn their keep, the cook said she'll come up a few times a week and fix some meals that you can heat up and eat when you please, and the housekeeper said she would send a couple of maids twice a week to clean and take care of laundry. I'm assuming you wouldn't want to do those things on your own all the time."

"But . . . From Angelline House?" What would her father say about her settling in Maghre? "Does my father know?"

"I can't tell him anything until I have your answer."

Saetien read the paper again. A challenge. A responsibility. Something of her own. She wanted this, but . . . "If I do this, there's still so much I need to learn."

"Your father owns a publishing house. He can help you."

No, he can't. Not because he wouldn't but because she couldn't let him. Not yet.

Panic. And an odd feeling of setting her heels down and preparing to fight. "In order to do this, I'm going to need your help awhile longer. *Your* help, no one else's."

Butler gave her an odd look. "Why? Your father—"

"Whenever he tells me things, they feel so big, I can't hear him. But I can hear you. When *you* tell me things, they make *sense*."

Butler let out a bark of laughter. "Oh, he'll be thrilled to hear *that*."

She caught her lower lip between her teeth, uncertain what to say or do. She wanted Butler to stay, but she didn't want her father to think he was inadequate in some way. She didn't want to hurt his feelings. "Do you have to tell him?"

"He is the High Lord, child. I am demon-dead. Yes, I have to tell him."

"Oh."

"But I think I can phrase it in such a way that he can accept it." Butler sighed. "The decision to stay is no longer mine alone, but if that's what you want, I will ask the Queen and the High Lord for their permission to stay in Maghre awhile longer. However . . ." He hesitated. Looked uneasy. "Before I go to Ebon Askavi and make that request, there is one thing you need to know about me."

"What is that?"

"The connection between Jaenelle Angelline and me. The reason she helped me when I first came to Kaeleer—and continued to help me. The reason she shared some things about what happened to her during and after the purge that she never shared with anyone else, not even the man she loved—and still loves. It's the reason Jaenelle and I have been friends for all these years."

Saetien wondered if he could hear her heart pounding. "What reason?"

Butler called in an oval frame and held it out to her.

The picture of the girl, the beginning of a smile lifting her lips as if someone she loved had just walked into the room.

She hadn't seen this girl smile when they had walked through Briarwood. She'd seen the anger and the slit throat—and the blood.

Saetien looked at Butler.

He said quietly, "Rose was my sister."

SEVENTY-SIX

Saetien spent two days walking and thinking and . . .
feeling. She went to the cottage during the day and
stared at the gardens, at the cottage. She thought about the
man inside the cottage and the work—and way of life—he
was offering her.

She loved her father, but she wasn't suited for life at the
Hall. It was too big. Not just the physical Hall but that way
of life itself—and the duties that came with it.

She didn't have the heart for it.

The relief that came from recognizing that truth about
herself was painful. But with the relief and pain came
hope. Hope that she could spend time with her father eventually and not feel like she was competing with the Queen,
whose will—and love—would always be his life. Hope
that she could learn from her previous mistakes and now
shape the life she wanted, choice by choice.

Even hope that, while she couldn't mend what she'd
broken, she might be able to make peace with Surreal.

But all those hopes, all those choices, came down to
making the first choice.

Blinking back tears that were part pain, part regret, and
part joy, Saetien walked back to Kieran's house to tell the
Warlord of Maghre her decision.

✦   ✦   ✦

Butler became aware of Saetien's presence the moment she walked into the cottage, but he stayed in his room until the sun went down. Sunlight caused pain for the demon-dead and also drained the reservoir of power in the Jewels. Too much pain, too much of a drain of power, and consuming yarbarah wouldn't be enough to sustain him. A few months ago, he wouldn't have cared about sustaining himself. Now . . .

Kieran offered him a cup of blood, fresh from the vein, once a month. He didn't want to get careless in his habits and need more.

Still, he was up and dressed and warming a glass of yarbarah minutes after the sun went down.

He found Saetien in the kitchen, reading a list of instructions before she gingerly put a dish in the oven.

When she finally looked at him, all she said was "Ask them."

SEVENTY-SEVEN

Daemon looked at the letter Beale carefully placed on his desk, then at his butler.

He'd given himself two days of solitude to think—and not think—about what had happened and why. Dinah being jealous of the privileges, real or imagined, that Zoey received. Zoey responding to the verbal assault by trying to prove she was a good Queen—and taking a wrong step when Grizande arrived at the Hall. His own miscalculation in giving the children exercises that would require the Queens to define boundaries and draw lines for acceptable behavior—exercises they were not yet mature enough to handle. The appearance of Lady Dumm, which likely opened the door to the children thinking that the extra orders had come from an instructor or from him. And that stung.

A lot of things stung lately, making him wonder if having children at the Hall was in any way a good idea.

"Neala found this under the bed when she and another maid did a thorough cleaning of the room Lady Cara used," Beale said. "Neala is sure the letter wasn't there the day before Cara was removed from the Hall because she'd checked under the bed when she tidied the room."

"You think Cara left this letter from Dinah deliberately? Why?" Daemon asked.

"Perhaps as an explanation for her part in the effort to get the other Queens expelled."

"Well, it does complete a circle of correspondence. I'll add it to the other letter and the order that was sent from Dinah." Daemon waited, but Beale didn't move away from the desk. "Something else?"

"Lord Mikal would like to have a word."

"Send him in."

Beale left. Mikal walked in and stood in almost the same place.

"Would you like to sit?" Daemon asked. "Or is this a report rather than a conversation?"

Mikal hesitated, then sat. "It's a little of both. First, I want to apologize for not mentioning that some odd things were going on with the students, but I didn't witness those things firsthand, and the Scelties who did see them are young and couldn't convey what they were seeing in a way that I understood. They knew the humans were behaving strangely, but they didn't understand why. When I heard about the punishments that had been added to the Queen's tasks, I figured out what they were trying to tell me."

"Hitting puppies for no reason is a wrong thing, whether they are Scelties or humans," Daemon said.

"Yeah. That's what it came down to. If I'd mentioned it, you might have figured this out sooner."

"It wasn't your duty to inform me." Daemon studied Mikal. As a boy, Mikal had made his share of mistakes, but he'd learned and he'd grown, and now he was a strong, compassionate young man . . . who was about to dump something else on him. "What?"

"Just that when Brenda and Raine took Lady Dumm to her home in the attic, they found six rolly sheep and thought the sheep would be fun for the Scelties. And they are. And you don't have to feed them or clean up after them."

"Rolly sheep." He made it sound like a confirmation rather than a question. If it sounded like a question, Mikal would explain. He did not want anyone to explain.

"They're the sheep version of Lady Dumm," Mikal explained cheerfully. "A hollow body with fleece sewn on it that fits over a large ball. The sheep roll over the ground

and do sheep things while the Scelties practice herding.
Well, they're supposed to practice herding. My pack has
been riding the rollies and having sheep races."

"Right. We got rid of Dumm and now have rolly sheep
that are a size that can be ridden by Scelties."

"Sort of a fleecy pony for dogs."

Daemon looked at the empty basket near his desk.
"Mikal?"

"Sir?"

"Breen . . . ?"

"Oh, Liath is teaching her to ride a rolly."

Mother Night. "How delightful."

Mikal left. Beale returned.

"Beale? If there are other constructed props hiding in
the attics that represent living things, perhaps one or two
of them could find their way into a box that ends up at the
bottom of the lake."

Beale looked amused. "I believe one or two of them are
already there, Prince."

"Of course they are." He sighed. "Something else?"

Amusement faded. "A message just arrived from Lady
Surreal. You're needed in Amdarh as soon as you can get
there."

SEVENTY-EIGHT

Surreal waited for Sadi in his study on the Yaslana side of the town house. This was the second-in-command reporting to the Warlord Prince of Dhemlan. This was business, not personal.

She turned away from the window when Daemon walked in. Like his study at the Hall, this one had a social side for informal discussions, and a formal side, which held his desk and the visitors' chairs.

She walked over to the desk and sat in a visitor's chair.

He followed her and sat behind the desk. "You indicated my presence is required."

Surreal huffed out a breath. "After receiving your letter, I went to the town where Dinah's family lives and went into a couple of shops, intending to ask about the maid Ida. I didn't have to. She was all anyone was talking about—and according to everything I heard, she was a liar, a manipulator, and blamed other servants for her own shoddy work. She held grudges against anyone who dismissed her, including our family, since Beale and Helene booted her out of the Hall when Jaenelle and the coven lived there with your father. No one in that town knew why she'd been dismissed—she claimed it was because of jealousy that the Ladies preferred working with her—but they were certain she'd done something to deserve it."

"She probably started the rumor that a guest kicked a puppy."

Surreal stared at Daemon. "And she got out of the Hall alive?"

"It was a rumor, which was grounds for dismissal, not execution."

He looks tired, she thought. *Maybe more than tired.* "Anyway, Zhara needs to see you."

"I said a week, and I meant a week. If any of the children show up before then, I'll extend the time another week." He sounded irritated.

"I guess Zhara explained a few things to young Zoey, and she will be back, but not a minute before you allow the doors to open."

"Then what, Surreal?"

"Apparently Dinah hadn't expected to be caught out for initiating this game to get the other Queens expelled, and she claims Ida was the one who gave her the idea in the first place, and not only encouraged her to do it but also wrote out the extra orders and the envelopes, using a false name so that no one would know who was really sending letters to Cara.

"People saw Dinah and Ida in the back garden, arguing beneath a large tree. The witnesses didn't hear the words clearly enough to repeat what was said, but Ida's tone was mocking and derogatory. While familiar, it was not a tone they expected her to use with the daughter of their employer—especially when that daughter was a Queen."

"And?" Daemon said.

"Dinah lashed out. A flash of power striking a large branch above Ida. It shouldn't have been enough to bring the branch down, but the gardener was inside, talking to Dinah's father about that branch being weakened by the winter storms and needing to be removed. By bad luck or design, Dinah's flash of power hit the branch's weak spot, and it came down on Ida, crushing her chest. The woman didn't have time to shield or try to move. Just flash, crack, and a girl watches a woman die in front of her."

"Mother Night," Daemon muttered.

"Dinah is hysterical and swears she didn't mean to hurt Ida. They were friends, despite the difference in their social status. Ida understood her. On and on. Doesn't make Ida any less dead." Surreal shifted in the chair. "Knowing Ida's nature, the town's influential residents contacted the District Queen's court and requested that Ida be moved to Amdarh and held in a secure place until you, as the High Lord, can collect her and take her to Hell. There seems to be some concern that the townspeople won't be safe if Ida, being one to hold grudges, makes the transition to demon-dead while she's still in Dhemlan."

"I'll take care of it." The High Lord would find out what else Ida had done to make people's lives difficult. Then he would finish the kill so that she would become a whisper in the Darkness—and no longer a threat to anyone.

Surreal called in the envelope of gold marks and pushed it across the desk. "I deducted expenses, but the tree did the job, not me."

"Did it?"

"It did." She could see he didn't quite believe her. After all, she was a very good assassin.

Daemon pushed the envelope of gold marks back across the desk. "A donation for your sanctuary."

"All right." She vanished the envelope—and wondered if she should say something, if she should tell him she knew the sand was running in the glass and his time among the living . . . No. She would wait until he told her. "What are you going to do about Dinah?"

"Nothing. That decision is in the hands of the District Queen and Province Queen." He rose. "I'll probably be away from Dhemlan for a couple of days. Maybe more."

"Anything you want me to do?"

She didn't know what to think about the mischievous look in his eyes. "You could spend a day at the Hall and give out the prizes to the winners of the rolly sheep races."

"Rolly what?"

"Rolly sheep. Mikal will explain."

"Why can't you do that?"

He smiled—and that smile held mischief. "Because I'm going to deny ever knowing about them."

SEVENTY-NINE

Daemon listened. Part of him was grateful, was *relieved*, that Butler had been able to do so much for Saetien. Another part of him wondered how this man had been able to cut through all the temperamental adolescent crap so that the emerging young woman reflected the wonderful child Saetien had been before her Birthright Ceremony.

"She's young, Butler," Daemon said.

"Jillian was around the same age when she went to Little Weeble," Witch said.

"That isn't helpful right now." The words came out in a growl.

"Butler will be there to continue Saetien's education in business, and he'll be there when young men come to call." Witch smiled at both of them when they stared at her. "Well, they will come to call."

"Daylight," Daemon and Butler said.

"Kindred," she countered. "Hooves and teeth and opinions. There is a whole school of Scelties in that village more than willing to offer opinions, to say nothing about acting as self-appointed chaperons. She'll also be under Kieran's protection, which everyone in Maghre has already figured out."

Witch stared at Butler. Stared through him. Then she asked softly, "For yourself as well as for her?"

"Yes," Butler replied just as softly.

"You're welcome at the Keep whenever the time comes, Prince Butler."

"Thank you, Lady." A pause. "Prince?"

So hard to say the words. "Help her grow into the life she wants for as long as it suits you both," Daemon replied. "And thank you, Butler."

"It is my pleasure, Prince." Butler bowed and walked out of the sitting room in the Queen's part of the Keep.

Daemon waited until Butler left the Keep. Then he poured a large brandy and stared into the liquid. "How did Lucivar stand it when he realized Jillian wasn't going to come back? That the leaving he thought was temporary was actually her leaving for good?"

"Ask him," Jaenelle said. She touched his right arm where four white scars reminded him that he wasn't alone. "Come into my sitting room. I'd like to show you a couple of things."

He downed the brandy and followed her across the corridor to her private sitting room. He froze when he spotted the tangled web positioned in the center of a table.

"Take a look," Jaenelle invited.

He approached the table reluctantly. "This is about Saetien?"

"She's part of it, but this tangled web is more about Butler."

Daemon looked into the tangled web of dreams and visions. Then he looked at Jaenelle. "A daughter of the heart? Saetien is the daughter of his heart?"

She smiled. "He didn't know it, but he's waited a long time for her—and this is the right time in her life to find him. He can help her build an extraordinary ordinary life."

The kind of life you would have chosen for yourself if you hadn't been Witch, the Queen of Ebon Askavi. The kind of life we tried to have, at least some of the time, despite being who and what we are.

Knowing that made it a little easier to let his daughter go. No, not let her go; to share her and let her find a life beyond his shadow—and the shadow of Ebon Askavi.

"What's the other thing you wanted to show me?"

She hesitated. He tensed.

"It has been pointed out to me that hooves are sharp, and the demon-dead can't heal if they're injured." She wandered around the sitting room, as if putting some distance between herself and Daemon without his *thinking* she was putting distance between them.

"So . . . ?" He gave her a smile that made her tail twitch. Oh, she was nervous about something.

"So if my Self is going to be contained in a shadow that can touch and be touched, and we're going to . . ." She blushed. "Well, not that but . . ."

"We're going to cuddle in bed?"

"Yes." She sounded relieved to hear his suggestion. "If we're going to cuddle, it would be better if there wasn't a chance of your legs being damaged if I . . ." More wandering. Agitated now.

"You still have nightmares about Briarwood?" he asked softly. "Even now?"

Her smile held quiet pain. "There is no cure for Briarwood. Not even for me." A beat of silence before she added, "Especially for me."

"What does that have to do with hooves?" He had a thought and wasn't sure if he wanted to hear her say it.

She swept a hand in front of herself. "This is who I am, who I always was beneath the human flesh."

"I know."

"But a shadow that clothes the Self can take another shape." Hesitation. "I thought . . ."

"Seventy."

She frowned at him.

Daemon moved slowly toward her. "If you were about to suggest creating a shadow that looks like you did when you walked among the living, and if you were about to ask me the age that should be reflected by that shadow, then my answer is seventy." He moved closer. Closer. "You were always beautiful, but you were exquisite when you were seventy. Your hair was a mix of silver and gold that shone in sunlight, and the lines on your face spoke of a good life. You were healthy." His smile had enough heat to make her blush—something he hadn't thought a shadow could do. "And you were still quite limber at that age."

"Daemon!"

"Jaenelle?"

"Would you settle for sixty-five? Based on the paintings that were available, I didn't see much difference."

"Oh?" A drawn-out word. His heat slipped the leash a little. Not that she would notice. Or would she?

One moment he was looking at Witch, at the Self who had a gold mane that was more like fur than hair; who had a tiny spiral horn in the center of her forehead; who had sharp claws and sharp hooves. The next moment he was looking at Jaenelle as she'd been at sixty-five. A shadow that looked like the woman he had adored in every way through forty years of marriage when she had been that age.

He wanted almost beyond sanity to touch her. Then he considered what it would be like if people seeking an audience with Witch saw this lovely older woman instead of the dreams that had always existed beneath the human skin. Witch was feared now because her shape revealed the truth about her Self. In this form? Too many would come seeking an audience—and making demands—just as they had done when she had walked among the living.

Instead of reaching for her, Daemon stepped back and said, "No."

She looked startled. "Daemon . . ."

"No." He shook his head. "I've told you more than once over the years that I have never cared about the way you looked. I didn't fall in love with you because of your physical body, and that has never changed. If my legs end up sliced to ribbons, so be it. Everything has a price. But you. This . . . manifestation of your true Self reflects the feral side of your nature—and the power you stored in the Misty Place. This shadow does not invite importuning people to come to the Keep expecting you to do them favors. Standing before Witch shouldn't be a small thing. Hell's fire,

Jaenelle, you purged all the Realms of our enemies, and there are a few people—myself and Lucivar included—who understand that you could do it again. If you look human, if you look approachable, people will want what you shouldn't have to give. Not anymore."

She stared at him. Her lips twitched. "You're spending too much time with Scelties. You're sounding very bossy."

"I'm a Warlord Prince. It's my nature to be bossy."

She looked amused. Had he missed something?

"I appreciate your feelings, Prince, and I agree with your reasons."

Thank the Darkness for that.

"I was thinking that my Self could be in this human-shaped shadow here in our suites. Only here. Only with you." Jaenelle looked toward the door that opened into the corridor. "Everyone else? Let them see Witch for who and what she is."

When he saw her hesitate, he said, "Lucivar doesn't care what form you take as long as he can talk to you, spend some time with you. Same with Daemonar—although I think he might miss seeing the tail if you started looking human again. It twitches faster when you're irritated." His heated smile had her taking a step back. "Or feeling wary."

She disappeared. A moment later, she reappeared as Witch, spiral horn and hooves and all the rest.

"If you've spent time creating that other shadow, I must have miscalculated, and the horizon that marks my time among the living is much closer than I thought it would be." All the more reason to be grateful that Butler would be there to help Saetien accept that day when it came. "How much time?"

Jaenelle looked sad. "A few years."

He moved toward her, leaned toward her. Brushed her lips with his. "It's enough time," he whispered before kissing her again. "It's enough."

EIGHTY

Dear Papa,
    Thank you for sending me to Butler.
    Thank you for allowing me to stay in Scelt.

    Love,
    Saetien

EIGHTY-ONE

Daemon took his position in the great hall, prepared to welcome whichever youngsters chose to return.

He wasn't surprised when Daemonar walked in, since Lucivar had given him a psychic tap the moment the Coach had set down on the landing web.

"Father wants to know if you bought some sheep for the Scelties," Daemonar said.

"Those are rolly sheep, not real sheep. They used to live in the attic."

"Okay. So no one is going to get upset about Jaalan playing stalk and pounce with them?"

Daemon shook his head. "Not unless he pounces on a sheep a Sceltie is riding at the time."

Daemonar stepped up to him. "Uncle Daemon, we've only been gone a week."

"I know that, boyo." He smiled. "I've missed *you*."

"Good to know."

"Grizande?"

Daemonar grinned. "She's been working on reading and speaking the common tongue, she prefers baking to cooking—I think it's because she can pounce on dough and pummel it—and she had weapons practice with the men every day."

Lucivar walked in—alone. Daemonar excused himself and went over to greet Holt and Mikal.

"Zoey just arrived, so Titian is outside talking to her," Lucivar said as he walked up to Daemon.

"And our Tigre?"

"She pounced on something that looked like a sheep, which rolled down a hill with Liath running after it." Lucivar studied him. "How are you, old son?"

"I'm all right."

"Are you?" A soft question that deserved truth.

"For a while longer."

Lucivar released a breath. "Then let's make the days count."

Daemon smiled. "Yes. Let's do that."

They turned and stood shoulder to shoulder, and waited for the children to arrive.

The Warlord Princes came in first—Raeth, Trent, Caede, and Jarrod. They had a different look in their eyes when they walked in this time, a different understanding of why they were here and what they would learn.

They bowed to Daemon and Lucivar, then hurried to greet Daemonar.

Zoey and Titian came in next, smiling and holding hands, followed by Kathlene and Felisha. He'd already been told that Azara wouldn't be returning, that she wasn't emotionally ready for this unconventional training of Queens and courts. He didn't doubt the truth of that, since the reports he'd received indicated that she was swayed by any loudly spoken opinion. But more likely, after seeing how he and Lucivar had responded to Cara's part in causing trouble for the other children, she was simply too frightened to return and deal with him. She would have a better chance of growing into a good—or at least adequate—Queen if her training continued somewhere else.

Jhett and Arlene came next. Arlene gave him a quick bow, then headed for Nadene. Jhett gave him a look that bristled with energy and hope. Yes. The young Black Widow would need delicate training. He might invite Karla to spend a few days at the Hall to assist with that. Maybe in the future, Jhett would benefit from spending some time at Ebon Askavi. But for now, he would pass along the knowledge and training that he had acquired from the most brilliant Black Widows in the Realm—his father and his Queen.

None of Dinah's friends returned, which didn't surprise him. As for the rest of the children, some arrived eager to resume their lessons—and some returned because their parents wanted them there.

And some people . . .

Daemon sighed when Brenda and Raine walked into the great hall. He'd known she'd be back. After all, she'd convinced Shaye to stay here while she went away with Raine for a few days. He just wasn't sure he was ready to deal with her. "Did you enjoy Amdarh?"

"It was grand," Brenda replied. "So much to see and do!"

"We saw Lord Beron in a play and had dinner with him after," Raine said.

"You've done well by him, and he knows it," Brenda said.

He heard the message underneath her words. *You can't succeed with all of the children who come under your care, no matter how hard you try. But you do a grand job with the ones who fit your hand, no matter how they came to be family.*

When it seemed like everyone had arrived, Beale started to close the door, then jerked back when Grizande and Jaalan rushed in.

"You have practice prey!" So much delight in those green eyes when she focused first on him and then on Lucivar. "Practice with bow on running prey?"

"I'll think about it," Lucivar replied.

"Grizande!" Jhett rushed up to her, then bent and gave the kitten a quick pat.

"Your rooms are ready," Daemon said. "I will see you at dinner."

They ran off, the Black Widow and the Tigre.

The great hall emptied until Daemon and Lucivar were the only ones left.

"Let's take a walk," Daemon suggested. "If we're out on the grounds somewhere, we'll be harder to find."

Lucivar followed Daemon out the door. "You might also want to find a better hiding place than your study."

Daemon just looked at him.

Lucivar returned the look. "The day it rains and the Scelties think to bring the rolly sheep inside . . ."

Daemon groaned. Then he looked at Lucivar and smiled. "I think Lady Brenda, being so wise and so familiar with sheep and Scelties, will be in charge of that."

"You really are a bastard."

"I am," Daemon agreed.

And they laughed.

CHARACTERS IN THE STORY

THE REALM OF KAELEER

ASKAVI

EBON ASKAVI

Chaosti—Warlord Prince; Dea al Mon; demon-dead; Gray Jewel

Draca—Seneschal at the Keep

Geoffrey—historian/librarian at the Keep

Jaenelle Angelline—Witch; the living myth; Queen of Ebon Askavi

Karla—demon-dead; Black Widow Queen and Healer, former Queen of Glacia; Gray Jewel

Lorn—last great Prince of the Dragons (the race that created the Blood)

EBON RIH

Falonar—Eyrien Warlord Prince; deceased

Hallevar—Eyrien Warlord; arms master

Kohlvar—Eyrien Warlord; weapons maker

Nurian—Eyrien Healer; Jillian's sister; married to Rothvar

Rothvar—Eyrien Warlord; Lucivar's second-in-command; married to Nurian; Green Jewel

Yaslana, Andulvar—Eyrien Warlord Prince; first Demon Prince; Red/Ebon-gray Jewels

Yaslana, Andulvar—Eyrien Warlord Prince; Lucivar and Marian's son

Yaslana, Daemonar—Eyrien Warlord Prince; Lucivar and Marian's son; Green Jewel

Yaslana, Lucivar—Eyrien Warlord Prince; Warlord Prince of Ebon Rih; now the Demon Prince; Red/Ebon-gray Jewels

Yaslana, Marian—Eyrien hearth witch; Lucivar's wife; Rose/Purple Dusk Jewels

Yaslana, Prothvar—Eyrien Warlord; grandson of Andulvar (Demon Prince); demon-dead

Yaslana, Titian—Eyrien witch; Lucivar and Marian's daughter; Summer-sky Jewel

LITTLE WEEBLE

Perzha—Queen; former Queen of Little Weeble; now demon-dead

DHEMLAN

AMDARH (CAPITAL CITY)

Beron—Warlord; actor; Daemon's legal ward; Purple Dusk Jewel

Cora—witch; cook at SaDiablo town house

Garek—Prince; Zhara's Consort and husband

Helton—Warlord; butler at SaDiablo town house

Marcus—Warlord; Daemon's man of business

SaDiablo, Surreal—Daemon's partner and second-in-command; assassin; Green/Gray Jewels

Zhara—Queen of Amdarh; Sapphire Jewel

HALAWAY

Keely—Sceltie Black Widow; lives with Tersa

Manny—witch; White Jewel

Mikal—Warlord; Daemon's legal ward and Beron's younger brother; lives with Tersa; Rose Jewel

Sheela—Zoey's mother

Sylvia—former Queen of Halaway; Mikal and Beron's mother; deceased

Tersa—broken Black Widow; Daemon's mother

SADIABLO HALL

Allis—Sceltie witch; Rose Jewel

Alvita—witch; student at SaDiablo Hall; friend of Dinah's; expelled

Andrew—Warlord; originally from Chaillot; has a maimed eye and wears an eye patch; deceased

Arlene—Healer; student at SaDiablo Hall; friend of Zoey's

Beale—Warlord; butler at the Hall; Red Jewel

Mrs. Beale—witch; cook at the Hall; Yellow Jewel

Breen—Sceltie witch; puppy; Daemon's special friend

Brenda—witch; Kieran's sister; teacher at SaDiablo Hall; Green Jewel

Caede—Warlord Prince; student at SaDiablo Hall

Cara—witch; student at SaDiablo Hall; friend of Dinah's

Dejaal—tiger Warlord Prince; Jaal's son; killed protecting Wilhelmina Benedict

Dharo Boy—descendant of Lord Dillon; assistant to Mrs. Beale

Dinah—Queen; student at SaDiablo Hall; expelled

[Lady] Dumm—a dummy used for lessons

Grizande—Tigre witch; descendant of Grizande and Elan; Sapphire Jewel

Helene—hearth witch; housekeeper at the Hall

Holt—Warlord; Daemon's secretary; Opal Jewel

Jaal—tiger Warlord Prince; served in Jaenelle Angelline's Dark Court; Green Jewel

Jaalan—tiger Warlord Prince; kitten; descendant of Jaal

Jarrod—Warlord Prince; student at SaDiablo Hall

Jazen—Warlord; Daemon's valet; Purple Dusk Jewel

Jhett—Black Widow; student at SaDiablo Hall; friend of Zoey's

Kaelas—Warlord Prince; Arcerian cat; served in Jaenelle Angelline's Dark Court; Red Jewel

Ladvarian—Sceltie Warlord; Jaenelle Angelline's special friend; Red Jewel

Laureen—witch; student at SaDiablo Hall; friend of Zoey's

Liath—Sceltie Warlord Prince; Green Jewel

Morris—Warlord; teacher at SaDiablo Hall

Nadene—Healer at the Hall

Raeth—Warlord Prince; student at SaDiablo Hall

Raine—Prince; teacher at SaDiablo Hall; originally from Dharo; Summer-sky/Opal Jewels

Rainier—Warlord Prince who served in Jaenelle Angelline's Dark Court and was Daemon's secretary; Opal Jewel

Sadi, Daemon—Warlord Prince of Dhemlan and High Lord of Hell; also known as the Sadist; Red/Black Jewels

SaDiablo, Mephis—Warlord Prince; Saetan's son; Gray Jewel; deceased

SaDiablo, Saetan Daemon—first High Lord of Hell; previous Warlord Prince of Dhemlan; served in Jaenelle Angelline's Dark Court as her Steward; Red/Black Jewels

Shaye—Warlord horse from Scelt

Tarl—Warlord; head gardener at the Hall

Trent—Warlord Prince; student at SaDiablo Hall

Weston—Warlord; Zoey's sword and shield; Sapphire Jewel

Zoela/Zoey—Queen; student at SaDiablo Hall; Zhara's granddaughter; Opal Jewel

OTHER PEOPLE IN DHEMLAN

Delora—witch; was the leader of the coven of malice

Jillian—Eyrien witch; works at Surreal's sanctuary; Purple Dusk Jewel

SaDiablo, Jaenelle Saetien—witch; also known as Saeti; Daemon and Surreal's daughter; wore Twilight's Dawn (Rose to Green); now wears Purple Dusk Jewel

Shelby—Sceltie Warlord; puppy

Stefan—Prince; vintner at a SaDiablo estate

Teresa—broken Black Widow who lives at Surreal's sanctuary

OTHER PEOPLE MENTIONED IN THE STORY

Dillon—Rihlander Warlord; Jillian's first romantic love; Dharo Boy's ancestor

Elan—Tigre Warlord Prince; husband and Consort to Grizande the Queen

Gabrielle—Dea al Mon Queen; friend of Jaenelle Angelline's; married to Chaosti

Grizande—Tigre Queen; was Queen of the Tigre; friend of Jaenelle Angelline

Jenkell, Jarvis—writer

ISLE OF SCELT

MAGHRE

Butler—Prince; business manager for Lady Fiona; Purple Dusk/Green Jewels

Caitie—witch; Yellow Jewel

Eileen—witch; Kieran's mother

[Lady] Fiona—writer of the Tracker and Shadow books

Foxx—witch horse; Rose Jewel

Khardeen/Khary—former Warlord of Maghre; Kieran's ancestor; married to Morghann (Queen of Scelt); served in Jaenelle Angelline's Dark Court; Opal/Sapphire Jewels

Kieran—Warlord of Maghre; Red Jewel

Kildare—Warlord; Kieran's father

Morghann—former Queen of Scelt and Jaenelle Angelline's friend; married to Lord Khardeen; Purple Dusk/Green Jewels

Ryder—Warlord; Kieran's brother

Stormchaser—Warlord Prince colt

TUATHAL (CAPITAL OF SCELT)

Benedict, Wilhelmina—witch; Sapphire Jewel; Jaenelle Angelline's sister

Donal—Warlord; lives near Tuathal; friend of Kildare

THE REALM OF TERREILLE

ASKAVI TERREILLE

Prythian—Eyrien High Priestess; deceased

CHAILLOT

BELDON MOR

Adria—broken Black Widow; Wilhelmina Benedict's mother

Alexander, Philip—Prince; served in Alexandra Angelline's court; Gray Jewel

Angelline, Alexandra—was the Queen of Chaillot; Jaenelle Angelline's grandmother

Benedict, Leland—witch; Jaenelle Angelline's mother; was married to Robert Benedict

Benedict, Robert—Warlord; friend of Kartane SaDiablo

BRIARWOOD

Dannie—girl at Briarwood; lost her leg

Marjane—girl at Briarwood; hung from a tree

Myrol—girl at Briarwood; lost her hands

Rebecca—girl at Briarwood; lost her hands

Rose—girl at Briarwood; slit throat

HAYLL

Osvald—Warlord; worked for Dorothea SaDiablo and Alexandra Angelline

SaDiablo, Dorothea—was the High Priestess of Hayll

SaDiablo, Hekatah—self-proclaimed High Priestess of Hell

SaDiablo, Kartane—Dorothea's son; Surreal's sire

ACKNOWLEDGMENTS

My thanks to Blair Boone for continuing to be my first reader and for providing encouragement and feedback in the story's roughest stage; to Debra Dixon for being second reader; to Doranna Durgin for maintaining the website; to Adrienne Roehrich for running the official fan page; to Ashley Laxton for running the Anne Bishop Fan Group and Spoiler Fan Group pages on Facebook (and also for investigating story details when I need to confirm something in a hurry); to Jennifer Crow for all our chats about books and many other things; to Anne Sowards and Jennifer Jackson for the feedback that helps me write a better story; to all the publicity and marketing folks at PRH who help get the book into readers' hands; and to Pat Feidner for always being supportive and encouraging.

THE LADY IN GLASS AND OTHER STORIES

by Anne Bishop

A magical collection of stories new and old spanning all of Anne Bishop's most beloved fantasy worlds . . .

Here, together for the first time, the shorter works of *New York Times* bestselling fantasy author Anne Bishop are included in one dazzling volume.

Bishop is a master of bringing fantasy worlds to life, and this collection showcases her impressive range, from her earliest writing to the Realms of the Blood, from dark fairy-tale retellings to the Landscapes of Ephemera, and from standalone stories of space exploration and fantastical creatures to the contemporary fantasy terrain of the World of the Others.

Included here are previously published and unpublished tales, as well as two brand-new stories, written especially for this collection: "Friends and Corpses," a murder mystery in which the corpse has some decidedly unusual qualities, and "Home for the Howlidays," a heartwarming return to blood prophet Meg Corbyn and shape-shifting Simon Wolfgard from the Others.

PenguinRandomHouse.com
AnneBishop.com